THE DIAMOND TEARDROP ILLUSION

CRAIG DOMME

BOOK ONE

Editing by Ella Medler

Copyright © 2016 Craig Domme

ISBN-13: 978-1535372985

ISBN-10: 1535372982

DEDICATION

Everyone has seen the pink ribbon, and one hangs from the bottom of my heart. I dedicate this book to Susie Lee, who taught me how to be her husband, a father of four, and mostly because of her I'm a comfortable old fool. She taught me what it meant to be a reader, and I witnessed her read at least a thousand books in our thirty-one years together. She heroically and graciously died from the dreaded breast cancer in our living room; not an easy thing for anyone involved, but she taught us all how to die with dignity. During those long agonizing months, while she read, I wrote, and started the two volumes of the *The Bell on the Bow*. Five long years later, you now hold Vol. 1 in your hands. In part, I dedicate this book to you for your courage.

I could mention my four spectacular children and their children as proof of my comfort level, could mention my brothers and my parents and their parents, but that would only prove beyond a reasonable doubt that I'm the luckiest man in the world; after all, I'm from the class of 66 SPX. Perhaps the title of the third volume will be *"The Luckiest Man in the World,"* by me.

The Diamond Teardrop Illusion is partially about the history of an isolated Catholic church in Pfeiffer, Russia, the place where my grandfather, Aloysius John Domme the 1st, was baptized in 1888. Sixty years later I was born in Kansas, and ninety-seven years later I named my only son Aloysius John Domme the 2nd. Grandpa lived to be a hundred years and six months old and has been my background inspiration virtually all my life. All through my childhood, I watched him take care of my invalid grandma until she died, something that children can't understand nor appreciate, and save for later in life. For ten years he earned heaven as her caretaker in Topeka, and his reward was to live on as the patriarch of my huge extended family. Were it not for him and Elizabeth, and that place in Russia where it all started, none of this would be here today in my old consciousness. I absolutely love the memory of my Grandpa, and now that I am one, thinking of him turns me into a very grateful grandson.

ACKNOWLEDGEMENT

I truly believe in the term 'destiny.' After writing my two books, I needed help with the publishing phase, and somehow or another, out of all the people in the universe, I found a gentleman named Ron Dahle in the cyber world. He is a quietly successful published author who didn't know me from Adam, but confided in me the name of his editor, Ella Medler, simply because of a brotherhood we shared, widowed Green Berets.

Ella took my work and cleaned it up, made it respectable and purified it. She allowed me to cross that bridge the rookie author has to stand in front of and wonder if he should go any further. She was strict and gentle, and when I followed her advice it always read better. I could not have done this publication without her. I've always asked her what to do next, and she introduced me to Patti Roberts.

I hate to admit this, but I had little experience with a profession known as Graphic Artist. Next thing I knew, Patti had designed a cover I felt was almost perfect, formatted the manuscript and got it to this point. There I was, in print for the first time, and I just had to acknowledge these three people and thank God that they exist.

There would be others besides these three and I'd like to say thanks to them all. I realize there may be some names up in front of me that I haven't even met yet. This acknowledgement is woefully inadequate.

CONTENTS

CHAPTER 1

THE GRAND ADIEU-ADIEU

The first grandson of Catherine the Great, Prince Alexander by title, was an uncommon young man; she had made sure of that. Royally well educated at sixteen, he spoke the basics of three languages, and always seemed willing to learn more. Catherine's own mother had taken her first born, Prince Peter, and raised him a political idiot, so Catherine took her first grandson, Prince Alexander, and raised him to be a future king. He had been nurtured like no other, and had been the subject of her dreams twenty years before his birth, while she studied and plotted on how to become the queen.

The young mother was mystified by a prophecy, a fable she had been told, by which this future grandson of hers would marry into the Prussian Empire and unite the two and everything in between, creating a monarchy the likes of which the world had never yet experienced. It had all come to pass just like it had been prophesized twenty years before, and this left the Great Mother of Russia stranded between her religion, Astrology and the fulfilling prophecy.

During a brief pause in all the killing and mayhem of never-ending petty wars in Europe, her grandson traveled to the Germanic capital, was introduced to the promised Princess Marlane, the First Princess of Prussia, and the world of her father,

Kysar Frederic William II, King of Germany. Frederic was somewhat new to the throne, but would find time to oversee the marriage of his precious daughter Marlane with Catherine the Great's grandson, Prince Alexander.

A secret irony of this wedding was the fact that Catherine and Prince Frederic William had met once in Russia in 1780 before he was king, and virtually no one knew of this encounter except for the two monarchs. When Prince Frederic was only thirty-six years old, his uncle, Fred the Great, had sent him on a confidential mission to St. Petersburg. The dashingly handsome prince was to meet with the beautiful fifty-one-year-old Queen of Russia over dinner, out on a courtyard overlooking spring flowers, one romantic evening in 1780. The Empress of Russia would be introduced to new ideas concerning Germanic-Russian alliances, delivered by word of mouth, from Fred the Great's first successor, Prince Frederic. Some suggested in the quietest corners of the Court that the prince had stumbled into St. Petersburg, only to find his handsome good looks had preceded him and a queen in heat awaited him.

He managed to get his message delivered, so they say, but staggered to his carriage the next morning, having lost his favorite wig, and went back to Germany. They had talked about everything during their diplomatic moments, from children to religion, and she found out about his infant daughter Marlane and confessed with great pride that she had an infant grandson named Alex. Perhaps someday, she suggested to him, those children might meet.

It was early spring seventeen ninety-six, and the time had come for the fulfillment of the prophecy. Prince Alexander, along with hundreds of Russian emissaries and diplomats, had traveled by sea from St. Petersburg to Wieck, west through the Baltic Sea — boat loads of royal travelers for the wedding. The newlyweds would return over the land route, solely for the experience of traveling fifteen hundred miles by wagon across the wild western side of Russia.

The Kysar of Prussia accepted the congregation of Russian visitors, culminating this sixteen-year-long garden experiment that Catherine had started on that spring evening in 1780. From the very beginning, it had proved a rousing success; the delegates were mending fractured fence lines, promising each other stability and friendship in long speeches that guaranteed the future would be glorious.

Catherine was thrilled as the letters and official correspondence finally started to arrive, as it took the mail a month by sea and three months by land, and she had demanded that she be sent long rambling diaries of what was happening and what was being said. Month-old news on how the reception was going returned almost weekly, and she in turn was steadily guiding her emissaries on how to manage the opportunities for the good of the game.

From the very start, the young couple was inseparable — two children who had been promised to each other without ever having met — and after the introductions neither was the slightest bit unhappy with the end result. They had everyone's consent, and if there had been any legal or other concerns, they were quashed by the end of the second hour. The young ones were healthy and showed no signs of the curse that had plagued the two monarchies over the past one hundred years or more, the living consequences of inbreeding.

Catherine instructed her most trusted female negotiator at the wedding to tell the Kysar that she had found his wig and that he could come and get it anytime. After delivering the message in private to the king, Catherine suggested that her emissary puff up her bosoms and smile the smile. There was an evident understanding amongst all the minds who did the minding of Court affairs that someday — someday in the near future — the Court might be unimaginable in its total scope. This wedding of royals was just the first step on a long road of unification.

Those 16th birthdays were hardly a memory when, next they knew, they had been married in one of the most lavish ceremonies in the history of Europe. After the wedding, and after the Prussian honeymoon, they would make their home in St. Petersburg, Russia. Catherine was waiting. They were magically in love from the moment they'd first laid eyes on each other, and became inseparable. Both Courts tried everything to entertain the couple, but nothing pleased them more than simply sitting together on a bench at the top of a walkway looking over a never-ending buffet. The dignitaries from all the neighboring realms attending the functions often stood out on the patios and lawns, making personal mental notes on how quickly that blossom had bloomed. To all the patrons who had any formal understanding concerning European hierarchy, their traditions, the lines of succession, of kingdoms and thrones, and who fully understood who the young ones were and what they represented, this union created a universe of possibilities and worries.

The whole affair had to have been written and scripted by God himself, with Catherine the Great showing the deity where to sign, in case he didn't know. She had seen that wedding ceremony in her mind long before anyone else, even before the prince was born. She would adopt him as per her right, and in due time declare him her successor, moving him from second to first. It was simply a matter of time, and the great woman kept that concept pretty much to herself.

The time had come to leave and travel back to St. Petersburg for their immediate audience with Catherine. The vast majority of the entourage of wedding guests, senior Russian diplomats, all felt they were on the verge of something equal to her name, witnessing a historic union. The entire hullabaloo over their departure revolved around the two young royals, those tender moments everyone had seen over and over, all the goodbyes, all the tears, until they finally climbed into their carriage and followed the procession out of the castle confines. For miles and miles down the road, the constant chatter amongst the travelers was that emotional farewell for the two.

The young prince could be mellow at times but would erupt into talking about his wife's hair or her smile, or the way she struggled with the Russian words and phrases he was teaching her. Any time she became frustrated with the language, he relented to speaking German, which he spoke and understood better than she knew Russian.

He taught her to say, "He is the most handsome prince there is," which she practiced and practiced till she handled the words perfectly, with gestures and sincerity. At a spectacular dinner, a few nights after the wedding, the newlyweds' table informed the audience that the princess was learning Russian and would like to welcome and thank the Russian visitors in their own language. He had convinced her that what she was saying was, "Welcome to our lands in peace, dear friends," but that was only in her mind.

She rose and quietly cleared her throat. The room went silent and every eye and ear was on her. She took a deep breath and let her arms flow out to her side. "He is the most handsome prince there is." The Russian delegation began to "Rah! Rah!" and clap their hands, their women were smiling all over as the men puffed up, congratulating themselves on the observation as the interpreters throughout the German audience translated what she had said.

The princess was stunned and embarrassed at first by the response, as the entire dining hall erupted in commotion and cheering, all reacting to her words. The prince was sitting below her when she looked down for support, only to find him laughing with all the rest. He pulled her close and told her in German what she had said as she faked being upset, but with perfectly elegant timing she leaned forward and kissed him on the nose. They looked at each other the way young lovers do, and he left her standing there, waved his right arm out and introduced her to the thunderous applause. That audience was absolutely mesmerized by it all.

They would be older before they would be able to speak casual Russian to each other, but their educations and upbringings so far had left no doubt in their young minds exactly who they were and some of what might be in store; for the most part, nothing came as a surprise. The prince had no idea about his Grandmother Catherine's plans, neither did Kysar Frederic — no one did, for that matter — but the king had instructed his daughter in a hushed moment to tell Queen Catherine that he couldn't wait to have an audience with her someday soon. The wink in his eye told the young beauty that Daddy would be coming to visit, and made the goodbye a little less harsh.

Everyone assumed that both of the young royals would simply wait out their time, their children would wait out their time, and, for the most part, this union was a good thing for everyone concerned. In both monarchies, no one ever spoke the idea aloud that the prince would ever assume the throne before he was an old man, if ever at all. He had a father who would inherit the throne after Catherine was through, but she was still a healthy woman of only sixty-four and had many years to go. It was naturally very complicated, but Catherine the Great was a complicated woman, and she played three-dimensional chess with the Courts; a game she'd invented.

People would ask the newlyweds what they thought of the other, and their eyes would light up as if they had not a care in the world. Whatever was in store could wait. The youngsters had discovered each other, along with all the desires, all that emotion, and it was an exciting time for them both. He promised and told everyone he would love his new bride forever. She promised the same, and was often times heard humming the wedding song, "I do, I do," as the Castle and Kingdom were preparing for the Grand Adieu-Adieu.

Fifteen hundred miles away, Catherine anticipated that departure date and marked her calendars accordingly. So also did her Russian Empire citizens, all waiting and expecting their new princess and hopefully the new grand-baby. Catherine would study her situation and eventually stun her kingdom and the rest of the world in due time, at her own convenience, as to the stature of her own son and his son, which would change the stature of her soon-to-be new grandchild. The young princess was as fertile as young women can be, and the fact that she and the prince would be cooped up and confined inside their carriage for a great deal of time during the journey would almost guarantee this happy outcome. By the time they arrived, just before winter set in, the princess would hopefully be with child.

Catherine didn't mind one way or the other as to the gender of the child, didn't mind at all. That child would unite Mother Russia with the Prussian Empire and he or she would have the potential to be the King or the Queen of the World. Catherine was bothered by a rumor about a squeamish little Frenchman, and the French revolution, and felt that her people and the Germans could keep those radical ideas about democracy in check. Catherine found almost all that logic on the third level of her board, a place very few of her subjects ever even considered.

The wedding parties, dinners, concerts, and other festivities had gone on for three weeks, and all of the preparations for the journey to St. Petersburg had been completed. It was time to leave, springtime was upon them, and they had a long way to go. The wagon train would be an extreme assembly of people, along with fourteen wagons, hundreds of horses, dozens of stable hands, forty veteran Cavalry and ferocious war dogs. There were ladies in waiting, cooks, secretaries and scribes, a priest, two nurses and an assortment of servants and attendees. The convoy would be carrying some of the princess' treasures, her wardrobe, some of her favorite childhood furniture, and many gifts the couple hadn't opened just yet.

Some of the wagons contained the gifts for Catherine from the Kysar and his wife, gifts from one royal family to another on a scale that would simply make one gasp; Frederic William II appeared to have a special spot in his heart for the distant queen. Those wagons had been loaded in secret and appeared to be nothing more than regular heavy-duty supply wagons, but under the tarps lay an unimaginable fortune in long coffins of gold, artwork, praying utensils and diamonds. Other wagons were full of supplies, as would be necessary, huge cooking wagons, and, of course, the two carriages that belonged to the couple, one for her, and one for him.

After that came the living quarters, wagons for the Cavalry officers, followed by a variety of other specialty carts. It was all lining up for that majestic exit. In fact, the journey was a time-honored tradition, a difficult excursion, and for the most part had been done many times in the past. It wasn't easy by any means, and never taken lightly, but memorable to anyone who did it, and the only other way besides the wagon route was by water. All of the Cavalry soldiers were senior war veterans, archers and bowsmen, swordsmen of the highest caliber, extremely dangerous individuals, fearless and ruthless when necessary, but gentlemen of the Court.

The prince and princess were on their way to live near and with Catherine, and she was openly excited about that distant arrival date. Her grandson and his German Princess wife were traveling just under fifteen hundred arduous miles, six months on the trail, just to see Grandma, and her first great-grandchild would be born in Russia. That monarch was destined to inherit what could conceivably be all of Europe, all of Russia, and anything else he or she may have wanted. The main requirement was a reasonable plan, plenty of positioning, some good luck, great astrology, along with a little mysticism thrown in.

They were both young, well groomed, predestined, and finally everything was as it should be. It had already been a long and sometimes painful reign for the great queen, but she seemed to have intuitions and knowledge about the world, the future, her kingdom to come, which few others even contemplated. When it came to being a grandmother, she relished the title, the whole idea, and even though she hadn't done all that well with her own son in her own mind, she assumed the role of grandmother like an old Russian peasant woman whose grandsons were her specialty.

The weeks turned into the first two months, and the caravan found itself on the edge of the Great Plains of Russia, while the couriers periodically passed alongside the caravan delivering the mail and riding away in the other direction. The princess' first letters back home took two weeks, and the prince's to Catherine hadn't even gotten there yet. The couriers were heavily armed soldiers who always traveled in pairs or more, with trumpets that announced their approach, bringing a month's old news, then two months old, and they weren't even to the halfway point.

There was no turning back, and not too much to fear from the road ahead, a well-worn highway of people and traders, small villages and hamlets, never-ending prairies and savannahs, river valleys and dry wash beds. It was often times incredibly scenic, almost frightening to see the other side of an immense river valley and know it would be perilous, taking no less than two or three days just to get from one side to the other. As they watched the sunrise, they could sometimes see their distant goals out over the prairie, see fifty miles, and know it would take a week to cross to them. In places, there was nothing, no settlements, no farmers, no peasants, nothing for hundreds of miles in any direction. The campsites were places along the route that demanded the travelers stop for any of a number of different reasons: build their fires there, get fresh water, see a beautiful view, rest. Fresh water was always essential.

There were camp dogs who always congregated when the nightly food wagon passed through each campsite, but after two months there were not near so many. The war dogs were never allowed to run free; they were tied up each night out along the perimeter of the campsites, and no one but their caretakers got near their guard post. Periodically, a camp dog would be heard dying in the night after trying to steal guard dog food and thus becoming such. Generally, everyone ate in the early morning and then again at the sunset dinner. It was done with such precision that it made the trip for most of those concerned nothing more than a moving occupation. Three to four more months and they would be home, in St. Petersburg.

The prince did not know what his grandmother had in store — he was much too young — but she did, and the plans for the next fifty years were glorious in her imagination. His children would rule the civilized world, and the world according to Catherine would have a substantial Russian flavor. Nothing would stand in her way, and the Russian Royal Realm had barely begun to see its magnificent glory. Absolutely nothing could, or would, block her way once the caravan arrived at her palace steps.

It was necessary by the royal nature of this convoy that the children travel in a form of luxury, but they loved the horses and could hardly wait in the early mornings for their favorite beast to be brought up to their wagon, saddled and ready for the day. Most of the caravan would enjoy long stretches of the trip on horseback, and there were times when one could not ride another inch in a wagon. Many in the entire group would walk, in long and well-worn trails left by previous travelers. It frequently happened in the river valleys, where the wagons would go one way and the pedestrians would go another, and then join back up sometime later, high up on a ridge line. Infrequently, they would loiter a day or two, waiting for the wagons to get to where they were, sometimes all night, with few provisions, which made the waiting time very unpleasant.

When it came to the royalty, not everyone could manage the physical effort it took for a land trip across Prussia, Poland and then Russia — or wanted to, for that matter. The sea route was safer, much faster, sometimes boring, and best saved for old age. The newlyweds might not ever have the opportunity again to take such a journey, something Catherine had done a number of times in her youth and still remembered everything.

Their honeymoon trip together, supervised to an extent, and highly protected, would last for many miles, until they arrived in a very different world. The world according to Catherine the Great, Czarina of Russia. These two newlyweds would end up being the

King and the Queen of Catherine the Great's personal living chessboard.

The Deluge of 1796

It seemed as though the landscape was a never-ending series of canyons, mountain ranges, plateaus, but they knew the river's edge wherever they were. In some places, those river valleys were tight along the cliff lines and thick with forest trying to steal back the roadway. There was often a canopy of branches above, and the birds and wildlife were abundant. There were bears and wolves, but the war dogs kept them at bay, and the big animals, too, nibbled on camp dog periodically. The Cavalry's war dogs were never allowed to run loose, as they were dangerous and not one bit friendly, especially the huge red one, and most of all the black one that looked like a wolf.

Late one afternoon it started to rain as hard as it had on the entire journey so far. They hadn't stopped soon enough, and the whole party was drenched to the bone by the time they got everything to a higher area on the trail. The road had instantly dissolved into a thick brown sludge as everything came to a stop. This wasn't the first time they had been stalled by Mother Nature opening the prospect to a long night in the heavy rain, with an all too familiar recent memory of that misery. It seemed to be the one thing that caused the biggest problem for everyone and, for the most part, they were getting used to it.

In the cold morning light they discovered that the road would need a few days to dry, and they planned to spend it repairing things and gathering some of the plentiful firewood that lay in piles just off the roadway. The piles were everywhere, usually thick at the base of old massive trees or rock formations. There was a particular size of wood that was preferred by the cooks, while the campfires at night were a never-ending pleasure and consumed huge amounts. The size of the wood mattered. Firewood could completely disappear at times, but it appeared that they had driven into the firewood Mecca of all time.

In a matter of days the engineers had managed to move every wagon out of the worst rut it had fallen into, caused, or had been a part of, until the group was once again a convoy, and underway.

Thanks in great part to the fact that there was so much dead and dried timber all over the area, they left quite a mark on the roads by the time they rolled away again. The convoy continued, and there was a promise from the scouts that once they were out of this valley it would be much smoother traveling.

Meanwhile, with each passing mile, the piles continued, only they were taller and the logs in the front were much bigger — old logs that had been shattered, splintered, on their ends. Some were huge, frazzled, as if snapped by a giant under his heel. The road hardened to some degree, and they left the log piles behind as a more desolate but manageable surface allowed them fast travel. They only needed a half a dozen more miles until they would climb out of the wash and up onto the other side of this river region.

Unfortunately, it started to rain again. The roadway was hard when it was dry, but in less than an hour it had turned into a quagmire. They had to stop early, and would make the last six miles the next day. It was late May, 1796, with two months into the journey and three of four months left to go. It was raining, and like so many valleys before, they were trying to cross a vast swampland that had turned into a bog of never-ending mud holes from previous rains. A broad and deep river valley just like all the others before it, and in every one there were a limited number of places to cross each river, gorge or creek.

This particular valley was without a doubt as isolated and barren of life as any that had come before, and they found themselves bogged down in the marsh that paralleled the river. Now they were stuck, but good, with no way to turn the wagons around, every single one being an immense logistical nightmare; horses were stuck up to their chest straps, and the center points on the wheels were hidden below the surface of the sludge. It was the only area they hadn't surveyed as well as they should have, and missed a washout that stopped the first wagon. Had they done that correctly, they would not have taken this detour from the prescribed route. It was proving to have been a big mistake — their best option at the time, they thought, but a big mistake nonetheless.

The wagons in the caravan had spread out for a mile and were unable to turn around, wherever they were, sealing their fates in place for the next few days. All were embedded in the mud, and none of the horses could move, as the rains continued with no apparent care that it only made things worse. The marsh, slowly at first, became a pond, and then moving water, flowing through the sandbars, and the men found themselves standing in water and unable to see the mud. The edge of the river had been off to the right of the trail a hundred yards or more when the convoy had first stopped, and it now appeared they were standing in it knee deep.

Two of the heaviest supply wagons and both of the treasure wagons had been left on an elevated sandbar, where they had been collected, had their teams unhitched before the animals panicked, and went to the aid of the leading royal carriages. The front guards of the Cavalry attempted to rescue the carriages, brought the supply wagon horses online, hitched them to the first royal wagon and drove those dozen horses deep into the mud, dragging themselves to death. The animals panicked. It was an absolute disaster, with the royal couple even farther out of reach.

Panic set in around sundown, as everyone knew they were stuck where they were for the night, with no fires, no light, and only an occasional lightning bolt that reminded every single soul exactly how alone they actually were, and how deep. A man couldn't walk from one side of his horse to the other, and the most experienced among them knew it was going to be a long rainy night. Many of the horses had already died in the mud; still harnessed to their wagons, they had drowned when their nostrils and mouths had filled up with the mud. The ones that were still alive were making their respective mud hole deeper with every effort to climb out and escape.

The men were exhausted in no time and couldn't move themselves, had to stay back from the frantic drowning beasts, couldn't save their dogs, couldn't save their horses, and were beginning to think they wouldn't be able to save themselves. No one had made it to high ground, and in the dark they didn't even know which way to swim as the current around them increased.

It was a cold rain, powerful and constant and seemingly more intense with every passing hour. By nine P.M., in the freezing darkness, the royal couple watched as the water came in through the floor area of the single-candle carriage. They could hear the shouts in the night, the terror in the people's voices and the screaming from the horses, never stopping, until finally, they ceased. The water rose up through the floorboards until they were seated in it, and all they could do was cry in each other's arms as the water came into view through their royal carriage windows.

They drowned about an hour later, unable to push open the doors, listening to an approaching rumbling roar getting closer and louder with every second. In an instant, they disintegrated under a giant wave of flash-flood debris that swept over the entire convoy, ten feet higher than the tallest mast assembly of any wagon, at the speed of the fastest horse.

When the flood water receded, a few days later, the only thing visible were the two wooden seats of the treasure wagons sticking a foot above the sand, side by side. The four wagons were so heavy that all they did was sink into the marsh as the ground softened, and were entombed in the sand before the wave arrived. The steel arching springs that held the front benches on the wagon seemed to grow up out of the sand, and for the most part were invisible. There, in the middle of this washed-out ravine, four sets of seat brackets suck up out of the sand, waiting to be discovered.

It was well over a month before the news reached the empire castle, concerning the group's last whereabouts and the fact that they hadn't been seen by the couriers who were barely able to traverse the region. Panic set in at all levels.

The news from that entire area was overwhelmingly bad, as thousands of people were evidently missing and there was widespread disease and famine already. Five thousand Prussian horse soldiers and fast Cavalry headed out to search as best they could in the hostile region from their side, but they found nothing. The rains were relentless at that time of the year, and when they entered the flat lands, the roads became impassable. Scouts and guides helped the search parties up onto the plains, but the rains had been so profound that summer that even they were perplexed by the landscape. They found mountainous piles of the remnants of small communities by certain junctures on two rivers they crossed, but had not found a single living person past a village near Hrodna, on the border of Belarus. Perhaps the caravan had made it to the other side of the vast region and was safely headed to Moscow. There was nothing that could be done from the western side of the endless Polish lands. Search parties traveling into Belarus could only travel on horseback, and for only a few miles a day, acting at times as if they were explorers. Winter was coming, and those plains became impassable once the snows piled deep. The couriers told of river valleys that once had roads, but all the roads were gone, all the villages had been removed.

There was not a trace of the procession on the Russian side, a fact that would take months to confirm, but one thing was for sure, no wagon trains had come out of the flatlands in months. It was prayed and hoped for from both sides that the children were only trapped somewhere and would eventually be found, lost in Belarus. The prayers and hopes were wasted. There had been a cataclysmic flatland flood — nothing left on the edges, no roads had survived, and the settlements that had once been there were gone. The whole region had been destroyed, and it would be years before people got back into the most distant areas. Miles and miles of ancient roadways had been entirely erased, the landscape had been altered to the most extreme, in places leaving it unrecognizable. It had been a storm that all others would be measured by.

Everything was lost, all the human lives and all the animals. The four heavy wagons on the sand bar had utterly sunk in quicksand, while others exploded, disappearing into tiny fragments of the once proud mile-long caravan, into the islands of debris downstream for miles and miles, too small to even notice. From the rescue parties' point of view, no one was ever certain they were in the right place to begin with, they didn't know exactly where to start, only had so much time, and ran out of that, too.

Catherine's great plan, the grand scheme, the great treasure, the children, everything was lost, and the search was abandoned as the winter approached. Absolutely nothing could console the two monarchies and, even though the treasure wagons had a mighty value, only Frederic William II knew its true worth, and it was nothing compared to the loss of his Lilly Marlane.

Catherine was devastated, as she slowly dealt with the bad news, waiting to hear about search expeditions in progress, anxiously awaiting the couriers, and then crashing into anguish with the bad news. It was a horrible time for the woman, totally understandable, equally miserable for everyone else concerned. She had lost all hope and her handpicked heir to the largest empire in all the history of womankind has vanished. Her chosen one was gone, and her Queendom was hopelessly demoralized by the effects it was having on their queen; there were rumors that she had slid off her crown and started to sleep all day for weeks at a time. Her magnificent experiment, the plan, was exhausted and had evidently drowned in the rains on the plains.

On November 16, 1796, she went into her bathroom, laid down on the floor and started to die. King Frederic William II did the same thing in Berlin, and died that very same day at noon. It took her a little longer, but she took her last breath the next day.

Thirty-some years before all this, a man named Johann Adam Thomae, a German peasant, along with dozens and dozens of his in-laws, gathered up all their possessions and decided to accept an invitation from Catherine. She had extended a welcome to the Anglo-Saxon peasants of Germany and the Rhine Land, in his case a village named Lohr am Main, and encouraged them to move to Russia. They were guaranteed huge expanses of free land in what Catherine described as the fertile Volga Basin. They were also guaranteed in writing no taxation, no military service for a hundred years and freedom of religion.

Whole villages grouped together, protected each other in caravans of wagons, families and livestock. They crossed the mountains and rivers by the tens of thousands in wagons pulled by cattle and horses, headed for the promised land. Five hundred miles across the Slovakian mountain regions, five hundred miles of Ukrainian wilderness, and finally the hundreds of miles over the barren plains of western Russia, until they arrived in that promised land. There were many different religions besides his, including Mennonite, Lutheran, Jewish and many others; Johann was Catholic through and through, and he and his clan were basically escaping religious insanity.

Thomae and his friends and family carved out a community, and eventually named their village Pfeiffer. All the many different religious groups established communities from scratch, always alongside a river, where there was clean water, and they took large sections of free land, split it up amongst the families, starting new traditions based on the old.

As the years went by, the communities grew into small towns, inventing commerce, trade, practicing tolerance as best they could, with the isolated freedom having an incredible effect on all their lives, and they prospered.

In 1846, construction of the new St Francis of Assisi Catholic Church on the Ilava was started in Pfeiffer, Russia, on a high point meadow on the northern end of the community. They needed to praise their God and thank him every day for the blessings they were experiencing, and decided to name the church after Saint Francis. They were good times for the wheat and potatoes, huge orchards of fruit trees had matured, and all the other crops were plentiful. These Catholics needed a bigger church and decided to build a minor cathedral on the hill above Pfeiffer.

Ten years before, an old priest had shown up in the town one day, leaning on a tall walking cane, accompanied by his four monks and five hunting dogs. They called him The Saint. He had arrived with this treasure of altar items, candle abrades, a processional crucifix, the elevator pole, golden chalices, platters, ciboria and goblets for the Mass. The incense burner and its holding stand were ancient works of art, as was the magnificent monstrance, and there were many others besides these. They needed a place to call home, and the log cabin church would end up being the rectory for the new church.

The Saint was the one who brought the large sections of marble for the altar, up the Ilava River from the mighty Don, load after load, for a year or more. He and his monks managed the heavy duty wagons, pulled by horses to match, and brought everything needed for construction from the port city Tsaritsyn on the Volga fifty miles south or from Rostov on Don. This old priest somehow knew exactly how to build the massive church out in the middle of nowhere, a project evidently ordained by God himself, and he sold the idea to a willing populace.

He made it sound easy to build, and the building would be one the likes of which these peasants had never seen, and they would be paid for their labor to build it. When it was done, it would compliment the builders forever, and last for at least five hundred years. The Saint and his monks had acquired everything they needed to start such a project and had secretly prepared the foundation for the church, working for ten years on that northern hilltop. They made their own bells, along with lift cranes and ramparts necessary for the stone work. The Saint gave the altar items to the parish priest and explained how they had been salvaged from a river bed, and had always been destined to be in Pfeiffer, inside the new church. The value of the altar items was unknown, other than to call it priceless, and the architect had always been able to finance the project without asking much from the faithful. He traded with gold and silver coins at times, sometimes with diamonds and other gems.

The Saint and his helpers brought two other large wagon loads of living necessities, things the community always desperately needed for basic survival on the very edge of civilization, not to mention dozens of beautiful Cinderella dresses, cooking ware and lanterns, and hand tools of all sorts. Buried underneath the necessities and out of sight lay the six treasure chests he and his monks had discovered. It had taken a year for them to uncover everything they had found buried in that riverbed a thousand miles away, taking another year to get it to Pfeiffer. He told no one except the priest about the six treasure chests, and they hid them away from prying eyes inside a massive hidden fortress.

In 1782, the earliest residents of Pfeiffer discovered what they called The Diamond Teardrop, a small stream of water that poured out of granite rock, from the corner of what resembled a human eye. They created a vast covered cavity between two rock formations on the far north end of the settlement using giant wooden timbers floated down from the mountain region up the Ilava River. Massive forest timbers, placed one at a time, formed the vertical and horizontal backbone of the shelter. It took a long time — ten years — and when it was finished it was covered with twenty feet of dirt and ended up looking like a pasture.

The huge underground shelter became a memory in only a generation or two, never having been occupied except by the parish pastor. It would always be available, just in case they ever needed a place to hide a lot of people, but they never did. For the Saint, his entire destiny had been to find and then deliver this treasure to that very spot, to that first priest, with the plans for the church. He would mastermind the construction, help the people build a magnificent church on top of that underground shelter and force their eyes to always look up instead of down. That was his task in life and that's what he did.

It wasn't long after the church was finished, two years later, that they found him dead, in the last pew. He'd died one night of exhausted old age, praying from his book by candlelight, looking peaceful, like he was sleeping, when they found him. They laid him to rest and prayed for his soul from that time on. His soul ended up with two gravesites, one in the cemetery and the real one hidden, and with time he was barely a memory, and became just like all the others. The Grotto of Saint Francis he had envisioned became a reality, and the Catholic faithful began to make pilgrimages from miles around just to see the church and pray near the Grotto, especially during the Easter season, seeing miracles in the stained glass, which became the legend of The Diamond Teardrop.

Johann and his Margaretha left Germany with five children in tow, and when they got to their destination, two long years after the journey began, they had their fifth daughter. They named her Katharina Domme. She was born in 1769 and baptized in the little log church in the tiny hamlet of Pfeiffer, Russia. Her older brother, the patriarch's only son, the firstborn, a man named Johann Balthazar Thomae, worked into his adult life there in Pfeiffer and married a German girl who blessed him with eight sons and two daughters.

Every one of those children was named Domme, and for all intents and purposes the name Thomae died and a new name took its place — no one knows why. No one knows when the old couple died, but for some reason they changed the family name, and their only son did the same thing. That was when it began, and for the next hundred years they increased the numbers of the Dommes like a flood in a fertile valley. It took seventy years for them to lay those cornerstones for the church, and when they were done St Francis of Assisi on the Ilava became a legend in the world of Catholicism. The annual Easter miracle where the faithful see the Diamond Teardrop on the Blessed Mother's face during the sunrise Mass. By 1850, it was already standing room only.

Like with all good promises and guarantees, eventually the time runs out, and it did so for the inhabitants of the fertile Volga Basin. The Russian government in the 1870s had an entirely different point of view compared to the one Catherine the Great might have had. They invented new taxes and decided that the vast population of the basin was a grand resource for conscription into the army. There was always a war going on, and in the early 1870s the first of the Volga German / Russian Catholics started to leave the Volga lands and headed out to the land they'd heard about and read letters about in Kansas, America. There were so many problems there, on the Volga, and it was time to leave.

The first pioneers arrived on the banks of a small river ten miles south of where they got off a train in Hays, the heart of Kansas, and the Domme clan along with all their neighbors named their new town after their old town: Pfeifer, Kansas. It was born sometime after the great civil war ended in America, with the first of the adventurers arriving on August 20, 1876. Early explorers had come and gone back to Russia a number of times, and practically all of the Germans in Russia wanted to be Kansans after they heard the stories about the buffalo.

Things were much different in America for the Volga Catholics, and their new community was thriving, according to the letters they sent back to those who were still in Russia. Everyone was encouraged to make the 6000-mile trek, and start all over in Kansas, but not everyone could, and as eighteen ninety turned into ninety-one, that spring an unimaginable horror was sweeping the land. Historians called it the Great Famine of 1891, and it would leave everyone who hadn't left either dead or dying. It stopped raining, that spring, when it was needed most. Never rained again, and the famine set in. Then came the epidemics of cholera and smallpox, and much of the old records from that time simply stopped.

Just in the nick of time, however, one last group of Pfeiffer, Russia, residents, brothers and cousins, neighbors and friends, wives and children, bundled it all together and they left their town of Pfeiffer, headed back to Germany, retracing and following the exact same route their ancient fathers had traveled a hundred and twenty years before. They would sail across the Atlantic and land in a place called New York City on October 31, 1891, aboard the SS Furst Bismarck.

There were many names on the manifest of the Bismarck that day, with almost everyone having survived the trip so far across the desolate plains of Russia and Ukraine; those who did not survive were buried near where they died. One of the Domme men was a fellow named Peter Aloysius, and he had brought his wife and two children all that way without anyone being hurt, considering the fact that his daughter had been born in late February in Pfeiffer, Russia, and they'd arrived in New York City exactly eight months later. It was an awesome tribute to his wife; she had taken wonderful care of their infant.

His best friend back in Pfeiffer was a man named Peter Desch, and the two families acted like one as they traveled towards Hamburg. They both had brothers with families along for the ride, sixty-three men, seventy-seven women, two children for every adult, and the entire group took care of each other every step of the way. Two thousand miles by foot and by wagon, twenty miles a day with luck, and an absolute deadline at the docks in Hamburg. Peter Domme had taken charge of his three-year-old son, Aloysius John, and it appeared the little family had beaten the odds. They would have had no chance whatsoever back in Russia, and had barely made it to the mountains with the water they had rationed, as the entire caravan was only a few days from running out of water entirely on the Ukrainian plateau. His wife's name was Katherine, and they would have eight more children once they made it to Kansas. She was very good with babies. As a reward for that kind of a life, they both lived for eighty-seven years and had no idea when they died just how big their family would be.

From New York, they traveled another thousand miles by train due west, out into the Kansas heartland, and once again they started all over by Christmas that year. All except for one, that is. Peter Desch had three brothers back in the Pfeiffer village. Two couldn't leave at the time, but his youngest brother, his wife and two sons made it out just in time. As they came into Hamburg after all those miles across Russia and Europe, their two boys took sick and the family missed the boat to America. They spoke fluent German, and were rescued by distant relatives there in Hamburg, distant family they had never known. By the spring of the next year, when everyone was back to being well, that Desch boy decided to stay in Germany. He and his wife went back to being Germans without a second thought, having three more sons as the years went by. It was as good a place as any to start all over, and he benefitted from a number of early introductions that got him on the right path immediately.

By 1933, they had five sons and the family was totally engulfed in the rise of the German Third Reich. They were pure ethnic provable Germans, and their male children started off with blond hair and blue eyes. By the time they were young men, everyone in Germany was ready for change; they, like everyone else, had suffered terribly after the war. The youngest son seemed to be the perfect fit for the Third Reich from the very beginning, except for his Catholicism, but he managed to conceal it from the Army just in time as he never felt any desire to be a martyr before he knew how to be a man. He was swept up in the furor of the Fuhrer und Reichskanzzie just like everyone else, joined the army and rose like a rocket to the rank of an SS Colonel by the time he was forty years old. They thought they knew who the commandant was, thought they could see it in his eyes while he assisted in every way he could to bolster the idea that he was a loyal Nazi. None of his superiors ever suspected that he wasted even a single minute praying on his knees. That he did whenever he could, still prayed in quiet, and was loyal to his ancient vows.

CHAPTER 2

ST. MICHAEL'S SEMINARY

St Michael's Seminary had once been a castle on the border between Germany and Czechoslovakia. Built in the ancient times for protection of the eastern border of Prussia, the edge of the realm, it was seldom used. A young prince had been known to frequent the castle. His only passion for the longest time had been the art of falconry, and he trained his birds in the ancient art form all through his teens, but that discipline was replaced with other interests when his favorite bird flew away and never came back.

The prince became quite the nobleman and came and went a few times, as a prince might do, caused a bit of turmoil each and every time, and then went back to where he had come from. The staff at the castle had dwindled to only a few dozen servants and caretakers, and when the prince's father, Frederic William III, Kysar of Prussia, found out the place was in a state of disrepair, he gave it to the Catholic Church.

The monarch was always trying to keep the many religions satisfied and cooperative, and that single gesture kept the Catholics at bay for quite a while. The castle became a theological seminary that produced priests by the thousands and gradually, over time, lost the castle appearance to some extent, becoming a world renowned study hall for Catholicism. As the years passed, it grew in stature and prestige among learning institutions, while theologians and scholars from all over the realm traveled to the place to read and write, to teach, to learn, and most of all to pray to their hearts' content.

A river passed by on the downhill side of the property, intersecting with another larger river a few miles downstream. It was at that junction where they built an enormous bridge in 1911 for the railroad that crossed over, with side lanes for pedestrians, horses, and wagons. That bridge connected ancient roads and train tracks that traveled south, down into the lower Slovak regions.

The Emperor of Germany, a relatively new title for the German monarchy, two of his many sons and the Prince of Slovakia, had visited the seminary one summer for a week in 1881, but never came back. A vast army of Royal Guard and infantry accompanied the Emperor, for good reason, and their encampment along the river and nearby forest had practically decimated the foliage for a mile in every direction from the camps. The hunting parties killed just about every deer, all the fowl, the wild boars, birds and bear for ten miles in every direction. They trapped everything, and it was years before the fowl flew back and the fish returned in the river. Twelve thousand men have a tendency to ruin completely all that nature has spent centuries building, and it took years for the area to recover.

The royals were returning from a conference with the King of Slovakia, touring the borderlands, and were surprised that the ancient fortification had become so theological, so Catholic. This caused the king — and the prince, in particular — to think twice. That many priests, monks and nuns, plus all the hired help, always praying, fervently, morning, noon and night, had a profound effect on visitors, Catholic or not.

The visitors were encouraged to participate, and inevitably suffered the pain of not measuring up, a feeling that grows in the heart of laity if there are too many religious in the area. Everyone at St. Michael's was Catholic to the bone, and as far as running an empire under an individual banner is concerned, the German banner was all about Christ and the Christian way, and not necessarily Catholic.

Teaching, praying and learning were three disciplines they specialized in at the seminary, and the young prince had managed to indiscipline himself of at least one. He felt a bit guilty about his lifestyle compared to theirs, but he knew he would have a different road to walk, so he asked them for their prayers and promised to keep them in his. He vowed to them the seminary would always be a place of reverence and that many of his most favorite childhood memories were from this place. He said he would never forget all that, but when he died in the war of 1887, most of his memories of St. Michael's were never mentioned at his eulogy.

The headmaster had bid the king and his princes farewell, encouraged them to return anytime for a retreat from the trials of the kingdom and the demands it caused, but he actually hoped and prayed with vigor that they would forever be too busy to take him up on his offer.

The whole area there in the center of Europe swung like a pendulum from peace into war, and no promise ever made was understood to be forever. The histories in the logbooks showed there was always a threat. Tyrants and barbarians came and went, and they always passed by but never stayed long and didn't seem to want that area any more than the previous ill-willed visitor. The challenge was being flexible, sociable, and understand that if there was to be a tomorrow, one had to capitulate as best one could today and hope that the sunrise found the intruders down the road and across the bridge, whichever way they were going. That was perfectly fine with the residents of the valley, the management of the seminary, and all the men and women who called that corner of Earth home.

On the twentieth day of March in 1939, the German army arrived at the bridge from the north and was headed south to conquer the world from that direction. They did, in fact, want the place for an encampment that would never be abandoned. It was early in the reign and rise of the Third Reich; it had nine hundred and ninety years still to come.

There would be no need for the types of people at this or any other seminary anywhere in the whole scheme of the Third Rich, and the colonel who attended to that first gathering of soldiers and priests made it perfectly clear within the first few minutes how the residents were to behave, what was important and what wasn't. His name was Reinhard Heydrich and, in fact, the evilest man on earth had been driven up their road and was now looking down on them all.

The headmaster and spokesman for the seminary had been

shouted at, manhandled and practically dragged by his escorts to the center point of the front grounds, then thrown to the ground in front of the tree-shaded gathering area. He stood there in front of the demon as a man, as a priest, not at full attention, and seemed to be struggling with the idea of such rude and pompous behavior. Thirty minutes before, he had been planning future events with his acolytes, some of the Easter ceremonies, and was going to concelebrate the funeral Mass at sundown for one of his favorite friar monks who had passed away after 90 years, a very good and holy man.

"I don't suppose there are any Jews hiding here in your secret playground, your holiness. Could I be mistaken in that?" Heydrich was shouting the question over their heads at the distant buildings in the background.

The monster was unlike any soldier they had ever seen. The best way to describe him was he was polished with silver, all over shades and tones of black, was very loud, tall and extremely dislikable. He wore a high brimmed hat that elevated him far above six foot six. He appeared to be waiting for his subordinates to assure him that everyone on the grounds was now standing on the grass under the pine trees. There were soldiers off in the kitchen area shouting at the people cooking in there and were exceptionally violent in escorting them all out to the center grounds. Two newly ordained young men watched from a hidden tree line and disappeared towards the east.

The colonel was deep in thought and appeared to be analyzing the statue of St. Michael the Archangel, the undisputed leader of God's angels, who cast the devil into hell for all eternity. The magnificent statue and shrine dominated the far corner of the entrance to the grounds and was flanked by towering pines and a small creek that ran along the downhill side, with benches, small altars and tables in and around the area. The statue was a replica of a similar statue on the Vatican grounds in Rome and had been brought to the seminary some fifty years before as a gift from the emperor himself. It took almost a year to construct the entire statue and then surround it with a fountain that overflowed down through some boulders into a beautiful pond. The area was bordered with bushes and plants, and the pond was teeming with exotic fish. Many of the outdoor services had St. Michael as the backdrop.

The statue had arrived in four different, massive marble carvings that made up the pedestal and the 12-foot tall angel. St. Michael was carved into a landing pose in all his majesty, with his enormous wings spread out to the sides and his foot pressed down hard on the throat of the devil. His spear was deep inside the devil's chest, and it was obvious who the winner of the battle was going to be. The colonel was standing on an elevated platform directly in front of the headmaster and could see all the way to the back of the group. They in turn could see him.

He slowly turned on his platform and faced towards the statue some fifty meters off and down the road to the right. He slowly raised his right hand as if he were preparing to conduct a symphony, and lightly waved it in a swirl of his fingers. An incredible roar of gunfire exploded out of the backs of the two trucks that were near the statue, and huge bullets slammed into it. The sound of the fury took their breath away; the nuns began to scream, and everyone held their ears from the concussion. The ground all around the statue became a storm of dust and flying debris, and some of the giant pine trees directly behind the statue exploded into the air and tumbled forwards and backwards like tiny firewood logs thrown on a pile. As suddenly as it had started it was over, and as the dust drifted back down to the ground there was literally nothing left of the statue and the fountain. It was all gone, incinerated and obliterated in ten seconds.

"Listen to what I say to you! Listen very well now!"

He lowered his voice, and there was absolute dead silence. He had each and every one's undivided attention, and they could see he was drooling.

The colonel began by saying there would no longer be a need for a seminary at this location and that all of the members of the place would be transferred to other facilities in other regions and their talents would not be wasted in the future. He said they would all be leaving in the morning at sunrise and would walk to the railhead in Sebnita. They were to pack a single suitcase with their most treasured possessions, and would be given food, water, along with personal hygiene kits at the station. He apologized for the fact that he could not provide transportation for them, and he strongly advised they should consider how to assist anyone who might not be able to handle the walk on their own. He suggested that they carry a little food and water, but there would be food and drink at the station. He smiled and said he had not a clue about their future, and vehemently insisted that they stay off to the right-hand side of the road and out of the way of the army for their own wellbeing.

Once again, there was an ominous silence until the headmaster raised his arms into the air and began to demand an explanation for all of this. He seemed to think that there must be some sort of mistake and that this was a place of God. He turned to see the eyes of everyone, engulfed all of the men and women in his circle of view, and he began to explain how long the place had been there and some of the renowned names, the dignitaries, all the scholars who had spent time there. He said it would take time to prepare the place, and there was so much work to do in order to have a more smooth transition if at all. He reminded the colonel about the promise the King of Germany had made so long ago and asked if the colonel was absolutely confident this was the wish of the powers that were. Was there anyone he could visit with and plead to for the wellbeing and survival of the institution?

Heydrich jumped from the platform and took a few fast and direct steps up to the master, then turned him to face the monks, the priests, and the nuns. He had his left arm out and around the master's shoulder. With his right hand he pulled his pistol from its pitch black holster and pressed the barrel under the master's jaw.

In a fury of spit and shouting, he screamed into the master's ear that all of this kind of scum, motioning with the pistol barrel at all of them, would be leaving by foot in the morning. He finished waving the gun, repeated the passage about "scum," slid the barrel back to its spot on the master's chin and pulled the trigger. The entire left side of his head exploded off his body, which crashed in a heap at his feet. The colonel then instantly murdered the master's first disciple as he crawled along the ground to the dead man's side, and then pointed his gun at the crowd of the astonished clergy.

"Go to your rooms and be ready to leave at dawn. Now!"

All they could do was leave them laying there as they were pushed in the right direction. In a matter of twelve hours, the long and vaulted history of St. Michael's was over, as a long procession of a hundred and fifty-six dispelled clergy walked out the gate and down the road into oblivion at sunrise the next morning. There were timeworn men and women who hadn't been down the road in years and never thought they'd be leaving, especially in this fashion. Some would never even make it to the crossroads at the train station just a few miles down in the valley. If someone fell and seemed to be unable to stand, they were shot in the face where they lay. Usually, older and very dear friends standing near the dead were ordered to drag their friend's body off to the side of the roadway and then ordered at gunpoint to return to the line and continue in the procession or die with their friend on the spot. It was all very loud.

Two young nuns who were wearing the novice garb were so traumatized when their most treasured elderly sister was shot there on the road, they began to scream and wail as only young women can do, a shrieking howl. They were shouted at by angry guards to get back in the lines, but their anguish was more than they could manage, and two young German guards shot them dead for not being able to stop their grief. The three women lay there almost in the middle of the road, and a half-track troop carrier that was charging up the road from the other direction ran directly over their bodies a few moments after they died. The driver never hesitated, and the vehicle churned up and around the corner of the roadway without so much as the slightest indication that there had been something there, in its way. Their bodies were torn to shreds and seemed to explode as their clothing got tangled in the tracks of the machine as it sped up the road, around the corner, and was gone.

The nuns had been up near the front of the procession and were constantly being ordered to walk faster and faster. There was nothing to drink, and in just the first mile they were exhausted. The horror of the morning was just beginning, and the seminary was disappearing behind the group.

Many of these saintly people never had in their lives seen another human being murdered, and for most, the entire concept was so foreign, they discovered they couldn't even talk. As was always the case, Father Peter Whelans seemed to be drawing the others near to his side, causing them to stumble over each other as they walked.

As confused as he was and scared for his life and the lives of those around him, in a rare moment of quiet, he opened his hands to the heavens and said, "God is surely with us and not them!"

The shouting and screaming of orders hardly ever stopped

except for that brief moment, and there was constant crying in the ranks, screaming in death, and every so often there was a gunshot. Someone would die every few minutes, usually in the most violent and instantaneous form, and as the sun continued to climb into the morning sky, there were fewer and fewer members of St. Michael's Seminary left.

The frenzy of killing spread through the troops of guards, and as the railroad yard came into view, their terror and viciousness heightened, their shouts got louder, and they became even more ruthless. Standing there on the terminal platform was a group of a different sort of German soldiers, and they were impatiently waiting for the exhausted group to arrive. They were in flamboyant black and silver uniforms, and had top coats, high up the leg black shiny boots and a different style of hat. They were viciously calm and unmistakably in charge of the operation. The monster was back; Reinhard was in charge of this, too.

He climbed the steps of the rail yard loading dock and motioned for the soldiers to open the sliding doors on the two cattle cars standing level with the platform. The next car was not up to the platform, a flat-bed type with a dozen soldiers hidden behind green bags of sand and heavy machine guns facing over both sides of the car.

Some of the soldiers were cursing the name of Jesus and spat at the nuns as they climbed the steps up onto the platform. The soldiers were pointing at two novice girls who had lost their veils, and whose hair was hanging down their backs. They were shouting to the captain there on the platform to let the young women ride on their car. He pulled the two women out of line by their hair and asked the troops if those were the ones they wanted, and a cheer rose from their throats as they, one and all, unanimously agreed they were.

The captain called another officer up near the platform and hurled his two ladies over the edge, down five feet, onto the ground and told him to take them to a car that was much farther up the train, while another group of soldiers cheered his decision. He looked into the huddle of surviving nuns and grabbed two who were holding up an older woman, dragged them to the edge of the platform and pushed them over the side, down along the stairs, and motioned for the gunners to take them up onto their car. There were more cheers and whistles as the two virgins were pulled up over the side of the car and disappeared, screaming, behind the bags.

The engine for the train was a dozen cars down the tracks; black smoke was billowing out of its stack and drifting down to the river bank. It was as if it were clawing at the tracks, eager to leave. The whistle blew, and the guards were screaming for the group of clergy to get into the cars as fast as they could. The rolling barnyards were filled with straw and filth, animal waste, and the smell was instantly overpowering.

The surviving members of the congregation scrambled to enter the dungeons and raced to the opposite sides of the carriage to be as far from the monsters as possible. There was no over ramp, and the gap of over three feet was more than a few could manage. When they fell down along the tracks they were shot before they could clamber back up onto the platform.

Some of the stronger men stayed by the doors and grabbed those trying to make the leap. Before long, each car was packed with the human cargo, and there was hardly any room left for another soul. Perhaps fifty people per car, and there had been at least half again that many when the morning started. They all stood in terrified silence, and the doors of the cars slammed against each other. Everyone could hear the metal latches griping together on the doors, and the locks clicking shut as a tiny requiem to the morning's affairs.

The guards began to cheer and, through the slats on the boxcar, spittle occasionally splashed through onto the clothes and faces of the doomed passengers. Many of the prisoners collapsed and slowly began to sob. Once again, the whistle up on the engine screamed that infamous sound heard all throughout Europe, and the train lurched forward as only a fully loaded train can do. Most of the passengers fell backward against each other and piled up in heaps of human flesh. There was very little room to lay down, and they all ended up sitting as the train left the station. On the destination plaques of both cars, both sides, were the words, "THERESIENSTADT."

CHAPTER 3

THE KNIGHT TEMPLAR

Part of this story is about a German SS Colonel, a man named Desch. He was the Camp Commandant at a horrific place that became known as the Theresienstadt Concentration Camp on the northern edge of Czechoslovakia, not far south of the German border, at the start of the Second World War. It was he who would recognize these particular priests for who they were, where they had come from, and he would arrange for them to escape the place and find a way out of hell back into the world.

He carried another title, a secret title, 'Fourth Degree Templar.' He was able to secretly hang on to his Catholic religion in a very quiet and close way, appreciated where his father told him they had come from, and knew he might still have distant family in Pfeiffer, Russia, had uncles, aunts and cousins in Pfeiffer, Kansas, wherever that was, and had parents and brothers in Hamburg, Germany. It was a few steps back in his genealogy, and he knew full well why he would risk so much for these men; the change the monster Hitler had promised was anything but the change the vast majority of the people had wanted. It was too late, however, and the world was now along for the ride.

Perhaps his mind had experienced a Divine intervention, and the secret history of his love for his church and its priests and his vows to protect them had obviously never been disavowed. Not long after his seventh birthday, his father involved him in an ancient art and discipline. It was a very secretive Catholic back-room education, and by the time he was ten he had become totally absorbed in a process that would lead to a Knighthood in his future. No one would ever know he had become such a vigilante except for a very select few, and they guarded their secrets with a death oath. By the time he graduated from the university with two masters degrees, he was already a Fourth Degree Knight Templar in a world so secret only a few men would know this truth. They were trying to keep alive an ideal for living that made everything else almost insignificant in the whole scheme of things, and it demanded that the Knight perform on the highest level of honor. "One for all. For the only true God and His Mankind."

JUDE

His name was Jude, Father Jude. He was born in 1887, ordained in 1914, and the number tattooed into his arm was 64397C. He was born in Germany. He was ordained at the Cathedral in Mannheim, and he was arrested and sent to Theresienstadt Concentration Camp from St. Michael's Catholic Seminary in late March 1939, a mere hundred miles east from this hell hole. He had been a priest, a teacher, a student; St. Michael's was where his friends were, and where his life was. The C after his number indicated he was a Christian and not a Jew, and although there was a difference, for all intents and purposes, there was none. He was at Theresienstadt for almost two years and worked on the Potato Farm number six.

He was one of the first to arrive at its gates, and a survivor, chosen in a selection process as a laborer in the fields, but after two years he was running out of time; he was utterly and completely worn out. On only the second day, just the second day, they were tattooed on their arms, inside the walls of this unimaginable nightmare. They had been stored for a second sleepless night, deep burns to their arms, sleeping outside near some crowded buildings, with little water or food, and they woke on the third day to more terror. They were loaded chaotically on trucks and sent to Potato Farm Six; it was where they worked all day, and were then brought back to the camp each night, assuming they had lived through the day.

Theresienstadt was an ancient walled city from the medieval times and had been designed with high walls, a defensive fortification that protected the residents and was impenetrable in its day. Thousands of people could retreat from the distant countryside inside the walls and defend themselves, and most enemies found the fortress a challenge.

The German SS had recently arrived in force, taken charge of the place, and they, the former residents of St. Michael's, were some of its first occupants. Theresienstadt had become an enormous prison. All of the talented craftsmen and musicians had been taken to a separate barracks area and were told they were going to fix and entertain the whole facility. A rumor persisted for months on end that the Red Cross was coming to inspect the camp and conditions would surely improve, but they never did. The Red Cross came and inspected the facility, but they only saw what the Germans wanted them to see, and they never saw Jude.

Men like him, who had no real skills, went to the fields. By his blinded recollections, after one week, he had hardly eaten anything and drank only the sourest water imaginable. He'd actually had a few large cups of water, but not near enough, and worst of all, he had been hit on the left shoulder with a heavy whip-like baton. The pain raced through his body, and he began to cry harder than normal, having cried to himself for so long by then. He remembered someone saying there was no loud crying allowed.

His crime had been that he stepped over a dark blue line that they were never to cross, but there were so many of them, and they were running in panic for the doors to the barracks. He lost his balance and could have died right on that spot, but the baton drove him to his right, and he made it to the third floor in anguish, with no blood spilt. There were already a dozen men resting up against the walls, and there were many spots left on the bunks. Those would fill up last because of the maggots, worms, and lice. It was better to be on the floor, but that would all reverse in the winter. He could tell that these men were all Jews, and many seemed far worse off than he. They seldom talked, and he found that, for the most part, he couldn't understand a word the vast majority spoke. He didn't know where they had come from, but they seemed illiterate.

As soon as he calmed down, he would begin his Mass

preparations in his mind as if he were back at St. Michael's and about to be the 'Lead Celebrant.' Even though he'd said Mass every day of his adult life after his ordination, to be the lead was always a great pleasure. He would first make a tiny sign of the cross on his right leg. He always did that first. He began to rub his shoulder, closed his eyes and began the Mass. As he raised the body of Christ in his mind, he knew there were other priests in this place doing the same thing; at least he hoped so, anyhow. He hadn't seen anyone he'd known before in quite some time. When it was time for him to receive the Sacrament, he would take a small nibble of toast from his pocket and let it dissolve on his tongue. It was against the rules to eat in the barracks, but most people did it anyway if they had anything. Most of them even cried out loud at times.

He remembered losing track of time entirely, and being shocked at how close to death he looked as he stared at himself in a puddle of water one day. He didn't even recognize himself but knew those eyes in the water were his; he was beginning to look like a Jew, if there was such a face. They all ended up looking exactly the same, and their striped work clothes made them look even more so. He knew he would die in this place.

It's difficult to start this story, but Jude usually did by saying that one day they were free and they were all alone in a small room on the backside of an old barn, a ten-hour trudge through the forest from where they had been released. They had been in the last truck of the convoy, the accountants' truck, and were returning to the main camp at Theresienstadt after a long day in the fields at Potato Farm Six. The second terrible winter was fading in those earlier days of spring, 1941. They worked in those fields from dawn to dusk and were doing the things they had seen animals do in the fields. The farm was being built and cultivated to plant potatoes in that spring and was being carved out of virgin land on the edge of a thick pine forest. It was uncultivated land, was covered and overgrown with deep-rooted sage plants and a form of scrub oak. The land was literally plowed by human hand by the square inch; all the roots were pulled and burned, and every rock within a foot of the surface had been removed to the roadways.

The road back to the internment camp was a dozen miles of ruts and dust and cold. The winters would kill as many of the inmates as anything, almost as if it were the will and mercy of God, and there never seemed to be a day when someone didn't die. When they did die, they were hauled away like trash and heaped onto a cart that had the remains of dozens of others who had finally just died from it all or had been murdered because of the job they were doing or not doing right. They were worked to death.

There was a trio of men who spent their entire day hauling dead bodies back and forth to the burial pit. All day long, they pulled the cart from one end of the farm to the other, and they had a quota; they were accountable, and that kept them busy all day. Under the threat of death, they walked the farm in the day and hauled dead people to that grave pit, a mass grave, and a deep mass grave at that. No man should ever have to do such a thing, and there were hundreds and hundreds of people who had spent their last days doing just that, on a potato farm on the outskirts of Theresienstadt.

If they failed to reach their quota, they died at the pits. Their final tally each day was concluded at the burial site, moments after their last load, and right before they all climbed into the trucks for the trip back to the camp. Usually, one of the three would die at the pits every week from a gunshot wound to the face, would fall into the pit and be forgotten by midnight. The other two would grovel back to the trucks, climb the ladder and know that probably next week it would be their turn to stay behind, if not tomorrow.

As that winter wore on, they were shuffled from one job on the farm to another, and there was not one that anyone would want. It was unimaginable horror day in and day out, every waking hour until they died. Some of the lead trucks would head for a ridge line where they would gather topsoil into baskets, with no rocks, and would then spread this basket of dirt exactly where they were told, under penalty of death. They were marked on their arms every time they completed the trip back and forth from the ridge to the field, and they had to find every stone that was out there and haul them to a spot on the roadway where others broke the larger ones into the road gravel. Under penalty of death, they had to meet the requirement of loads, back and forth, and everyone witnessed the accounting procedures at just past sundown before returning to the camp.

There were accountings for just about everything at the farm, and this last truck carried all the accountants. Those who ended up in the accounting truck had been asked in the not so distant past by the colonel of the guard, a man named Desch, if they were Jews or not. He would come upon them as they were working, anywhere on the farm, and it seemed like he was a great deal taller than any one of the inmates and was massive across the chest. An SS Colonel who wore an impeccable uniform, slapped black gloves out of habit and had never killed a man in their presence; Jude could attest to that. The man had witnessed and watched a thousand deaths at close range and never seemed to have to tell someone to murder one of them; they just instantly did it. They instinctively knew what to do and were merciless in their judgment and execution. It was all about numbers and quotas, and people who failed to meet a quota died at sundown. Once you indicated that you were useless by being useless, they murdered you, and someone else drank your water. Long trains passed the farm all day long, back and forth, dozens of cattle cars headed towards Theresienstadt while the whistles blew day and night.

Sometimes people died by simply walking away from a prescribed walking line towards the forest. It was a form of suicide, and Jude never saw the action fail to succeed. From the backside, they all looked exactly the same, and when someone would walk that walk, they would usually be too far away to be anything other than just one of them. One minute they'd be walking, and the next they would be gone as the echo of a rifle shot faded from their ears. Jude found himself oblivious to the sounds of gunfire, and even when it was very close he discovered he hardly felt a twinge. He remembered how a few years before he had felt an almost complete heartbreak when he witnessed a hunter kill a deer just on the other side of the rock hedgerow outside the St. Michael's property line. On any given day at Number Six, he'd see at least half a dozen fellow human beings get shot in the head, beaten with the butt of a rifle or any of a dozen other horrible assaults. He knew it was how he would die, someday soon, in this God-forsaken hell on Earth. He was very close to the end, and he knew it.

The colonel would stand very close to their face and not say anything at times. He would stare into the eyes he saw and would sometimes ask, "Are you a Jew?" And when each of them said,

"No," he laughed a shallow chuckle, the exact same laugh each and every time. All the accountants would later admit and agree that it had been the same for each of them at that moment of truth. Everyone agreed in their private talks that the scenario had been exactly the same for each of them when their time had come. Not a real laugh, not even close. Not even men like him could really laugh, and real true laughter was something Jude hadn't heard in two years.

He would then say, "My hopeless friend, what that admission simply means is that you're only a non-Jew in this place. Sorry be the back of the Jew who lies to me and tries to be a non-Jew. So sorry will be that Jew."

The words seemed to be as frightening a group of words as has ever been spoken in this world, and yet, to be honest, Jude also felt like the colonel was lying to him. He said he had never failed to see the real man, and to each and every one of them he added that he could tell, he knew something about them, something from their past, something about them that made them different. He had said to each of them on that last truck, in private, looking directly into their eyes... that he knew they were more than just Christian, and then watched them react.

Jude's eyes probably gave him away, but he said nothing. He didn't know how he knew, but he did, and when he realized his predicament, Jude shivered on the spot and began to tremble. The colonel raised his hand to calm him, and just like him, said not a word, but his eyes told him not to be afraid. He turned and walked away. The man knew he was a priest, and Jude had always said to himself that he would try to speak to the Blessed Mother just before he died, just before they shot him, and maybe he would die with just a trace of dignity, her name on his lips, just before they fired.

They had all learned early on never to say a single extra word to a man like Desch, and as often as not, everyone knew this from previous experiences. They could be looking into those eyes and they'd be seeing the eyes of a fellow human being for the last time if they gave the wrong answer. Many people died the moment after they said the wrong thing to a man like him. Although, not him that Jude ever saw.

There was no accountability for anything they seemed to want to do to the prisoners, so they came, worked and died, and try as they might, they couldn't seem to keep track of them by face or number or the job they did or anything about them. They were bodies on trucks, bodies at work sites, part of a work group — and that was all. Especially when the freezing cold winter set in; they turned into frozen mannequins barely able to move. It was so cold, they had no mercy, and the winds didn't either. Those driving winds on that plain killed so many. They all looked exactly the same, so filthy, so thin, so cold, so average, and so close to death's door.

One evening, after they had arrived back at the camp, someone shouted Jude's number. It had been the first time he had heard it in many months, but he knew it well and, of course, he saw it on his arm every day. He knew he was to die soon; there was no other reason for all this. How could he possibly know such a thing about him or even care? Why now? Jude wondered if he might have been one of those German Black Devils standing on that platform at the railroad station that day, but he had to have been here, and so he ruled that out. Maybe he was there when they unloaded them and remembered Jude from that day? He didn't know, but he worked his way to the front of the files.

Jude was so cold and hungry that he could barely hear, and he could only think that God himself helped him hear it and remember the numbers. When he heard them scream at him he was sure this was his last sundown, and couldn't for the life and death of him remember what it was that he had done to cause this, other than to have been outed, if that be the word. But they had to know. No way they didn't know he had once been a priest, that he was still a priest.

He worked his way up to the front and out onto the walkway and tried to think of the Blessed Mother's face as she had watched her Son walk by with his cross. Jude asked her to watch over him, and told Her he was sorry he was such a pathetic looking human being. Probably not near as sad and pathetic as He must have looked on His last trudge to Calvary.

A young man who looked too small for the uniform he was wearing, almost too young to even be a soldier, looked up at Jude from his tally sheet and stared into his eyes for a moment.

"Are you 64397C?"

"Yes, I am," he practically squeaked back the answer.

"Last truck in the morning, for you," and he handed Jude the board and the two pencils. "Do not loose these pencils. Back into the files!"

Jude cradled the board against his chest and gripped the two pencils as if they were his forever. He found a spot near the back of the formation and shuddered the entire length of his body. A shallow gasp came out of his lips, and that feeling that he thought he was going to die a few moments before passed out of him with that sound. He made a little cross on his leg with his finger, his mind found that spot in the rosary where he had been earlier in the day, and he resumed with a fresh Hail Mary. He had survived, and for some unfathomable reason he had been chosen out of all those hundreds if not thousands of poor souls to be an accountant. He became oblivious to it all for a while and prayed with as much intensity as he had ever done before in his life. It now appeared to be his lucky day after all.

It had been an exceptionally hard day on all of them who had been down on the flat land pulling out the sage. They used broken branches from recently removed bushes to dig out the small spiny plants that grew thick on the land all around. It was a stubborn shrub and resisted the attack, so they had to dig deep for the roots and piled mounds of rock that were just under the surface. They had been given a short break around midday, but they only had a putrid tank of water for the workers. They drank it all, and some of the slower and weaker souls didn't get any.

Jude knew of a man who'd died later that afternoon. The only thing he'd asked for was a cup of water, and he could have gone on. Just as the cart was arriving with its ghostly cargo, one of the guards who had witnessed the plea watched in silence as P5866J fell to the ground and choked to death. The merciless guard nearby walked forward and pissed all over the dead man's head. He buttoned himself up as he walked back to where he had been and motioned for the cart men to do what they came to do. The rest of them simply continued to dig and grab for the roots, and in the entire day their group managed two more sage than they had them accounted for. Jude could bet he ate at least a ton of root tips, caught mice every day, and they relished the earthworms. They had been lucky that day. The size of the bush had nothing to do with their total. A bush was a bush, and the large bushes took far more work than the smaller ones. As they worked and kept their own scores of such things, they all knew there were three huge bushes there waiting for them the next day. There was no way their group would make the total count, and they all knew someone would die because of it. Jude needed to sleep.

The sun was gone when they loaded onto the trucks that fateful day, and the compound was dark when they finally arrived. Jude only wanted to sleep, and before long they were done with them and they had no idea that a wonderful, simple man had died out there that day. He had died by that bush where Jude dug.

There was the occasional talk amongst the riders as they headed for the fields each day, but it usually only had to do with the weather or food. Jude noticed him on his first day as the new accountant, something familiar about his face, someone whom he had known before. He couldn't be sure. Again, on his second day, Jude looked up from the floorboards of the truck bed, on the way back to the camp, and there he sat looking directly at him. He knew, and Jude now knew that they had both been in that procession out of St. Michael's that terrible day so long ago. Jude couldn't take his eyes off his, and he in turn stared back into Jude's. He watched his lips form the words of his name, "Andrew," and Jude in turn said his with no sound. Andrew nodded that he knew that, and Jude saw a smile crease the corners of his lips. Jude's mind was not used to really thinking anymore, and when he remembered things of substance, it always had something to do with St. Michael's. Andrew. They both knew and remembered the same things.

They'd always had good food at St. Michaels, and sometimes it had been sinful, the fact that there had been so much. Jude often thought about that. Near the end of January they were at first slightly observant of the fact that they had known each other in another life, and at best they were glad when they saw each other's eyes, and that they were still alive. It was just a guess, but Jude had a day to survive and got lost in the thoughts of the day before.

It was hard to recognize a friend from the past, and no memory of the past could do anything to relieve the anguish and despair of the present. No one mentioned the names of the dead anymore; it was hopeless, and there was not the slightest thing about any one them that distinguished them from the others. They were all dead men, and the only difference between them was the weeks between the time they died and someone else did. They would all die here, and it was the easiest thing for the new ones to understand. They had arrived in hell, and there was no way out. Once a person understood there was no way out, there was no way out except to die, and it was very hard to do, die.

First there were just the two of them, then a third, a fourth, and then five and six. They all knew what they knew, without saying too much. On the last day of February 1941, they were up to ten in that last truck. Ten former priests from St. Michael's Seminary riding in that last dirty filthy truck, heading back to the most God-forsaken place anyone could have ever imagined. Anyone there would have excellent reason to doubt that God cared at all about his people on earth, or at the very least the thousands inside the walls of Theresienstadt. They knew nothing about anything anymore. The only music in their ears was the sound of the train whistle coming and going, morning, noon, and night.

What had started out as just the two of them, in a matter of weeks, had grown to the point where there were only two other accountants on the truck they didn't know, and they all knew the truth, but said nothing of it to each other. Knowing that most all ears hear, and the fact that they had two strangers in their midst, kept their conversations guarded and somewhat coded. The ten of them rode back to the camp each night knowing this truth, and they gradually started to speak some words to each other that brought very slight traces of the past back into their thoughts. All of them went to their bed boards each night with the same thought in their minds. Knowing that the others would be thinking the same thought seemed to warm Jude's soul, and he was a little warmer in his body because of it. He was almost dead.

As the trucks spread out the distance between themselves on that trek through the last hour of sunlight, every night, the difference between the time when the first one entered their section of the enormous compound and when the last one arrived was sometimes half an hour or more. Every night, there would be murderous mayhem for a brief time when the trucks rolled in. There would be food and water and murder. Just as quickly as it raised its ugly head, the entire place would go silent as the inmates took their food. Sometimes, if the accountant truck was late and delayed at the farm, the camp would be quiet when it arrived. The driver would park the truck at the end of the rows and the accountants would hurry off to their barracks under penalty of death for being out on the walkways. There would be no food and no water, but they would be alive and see the next day if a drunken guard in those last steps to the barracks didn't murder them for the sport of it all. It had been known to happen, and sometimes the accountants lost their pencils that way.

It was the first Friday of March when two new accountants showed at the back of the truck that morning. Just like all of them, they had their paper holders and held their two pencils as if their lives depended on it, which they did. The penalty for losing both pencils was death. They both climbed the ladder and told the driver their number, and he made a note on a pad of papers they all noticed he never looked at. He always carried it, never bothered with it, and tossed it on the seat next to him when the truck left for the farm each morning, but not this morning. He wrote down their numbers and tore the page from his pad. He folded the paper in half and handed it to a guard standing nearby, and ordered the soldier to take it to the colonel. He went back up to the front of the truck, climbed in, started it, and they headed for the farm like so many mornings before.

It was barely past dawn, and there had been rain through the night. It was freezing. Without a second thought from any of them, they slid from their seats on the bench and quickly grouped together on the floorboards of the truck and pressed themselves together for warmth. It was the way they slept, and no one was too proud to get warm this way. It was the only way, and the only time they were warm in the winter. Otherwise, they died from the cold. They all had the standard work pants and shirt, and no one wore socks. They had miles to go, and the truck could barely negotiate some of the ruts in the road. The sound of the tires in the puddles told them the work on the farm would be deadly that day. The only times they got more water than they needed was when it rained, and that would be one of the only good things associated with the early spring drizzle. They simply wouldn't be so thirsty. They would be wet and very cold, and the fact that they wouldn't be thirsty seemed a very high price to pay; it was that way with everything.

They all sat there in total silence, and there was not a man who wasn't thinking the same thing. There were no strangers in their midst; they were one and all from the same place, and they were all sitting on that floorboard, trying to stay warm in hell.

There were three things they knew for sure. They knew who they were, someone else knew who they were, and now they were together. It was during that ride that they all realized it was Desch who knew everything and who and what they had once been. For Jude, it was suddenly the strangest realization he had ever had about himself. He was lost in the math.

As the two new accountants climbed into the truck that morning, Jude recognized them both as if it had only been yesterday when he had last seen them. He was getting used to thinking again and now after nine times he almost felt human, as pathetic as it sounded. Jude had had absolutely no idea these men had been here at this camp the whole time he had. The camp was a sprawling complex, feeding other work farms, and there were thousands and thousands of workers. The truth was Jude had actually only seen parts of it in the entire time he had been there.

Father James had always been an impossible figure to ignore, and Jude remembered him in an instant. He had been a priest at St. Michael's for as long as he, and they were fishing buddies. He spoke half a dozen languages and specialized in mathematics and philosophy. He seemed to have managed to withstand the rigors of the camp better than most of the rest of them, and even though he was frail and drawn, he wore it rather well.

His companion that morning was Father Peter, and he, too, seemed to climb the ladder into the truck with very little trouble. The ladders were a good test for all of them on how they would handle the day, and Jude knew he would never forget not being able to use his left arm there for a while, which had caused him problems with the ladder. He stumbled and fell off it one morning, ending up in a heap on the ground as a guard looked at him and considered shooting him. He scampered to his feet and discovered there was nothing wrong with his shoulder after all. If one could manage the strength to help someone else make it up the ladders into the back of the trucks, they often did, but as often as not, the person who was struggling with something as basic as climbing the ladder in the morning sometimes didn't get back on the truck that night. The ladders told a story one way or the other.

Father Peter had been one of the true leaders of the priests back at the seminary. He was one of the best confessor priests to the others, and his council and guidance were sought out by virtually one and all. He seemed to encourage the things that had helped many a priest stay true to their vows, and was able to theologically answer those questions they asked themselves about whether or not they were on the right path of life. He was not a man one could easily forget, nor would anyone want to. A pleasure to be around, and no matter the occasion, Jude had always been glad he was there. Jude was literally overwhelmed with joy when he realized they were now in that truck, and there was no reason they couldn't talk to each other.

He broke the silence and said, "God is surely with us and not them!" Jude's eyes welled up with tears, and someone took his hand and squeezed it the way a father might take the hand of a son at a moment like that. He was some fifty-odd years old and had teared up like a child.

Peter began to tell a story, and all the ears in the back of the truck were on his every word. He said that the colonel of the guard, a man named Desch, had come to his barracks a few nights before looking for a Jew who had stolen four extra slices of toast. He said, "Don't ever forget that name… Desch."

He continued on and said that one by one they had been ordered out to a table the guards had set up near the entrance to the building, and they stood there and listened to him ask about who may have done such a thing as steal an extra slice of toast. Almost everyone returned to his bed area after their personal interrogation, except for the four who admitted to being thieves. He continued to question every one of the workers till the clock tower rang ten. Peter said he had been pulled out of the group and ordered to be last in line. The toast thieves were standing alongside the building, and everyone else was gone except for three guards. They, too, were at a distance. It was Peter's turn to be questioned, and he said the colonel told him he had been chosen for a very special detail. He was to be the captain of the accountants, starting in the morning, and Desch gave him a clipboard and pencils.

They continued to huddle, with a very long way to go. Jude

knew the tree patterns along the side of the road, and as he watched the world go by the back of the truck, Peter continued with his story of the toast. He said the colonel had called him by his name and even prefaced it with the term "Father." He said he stood there in front of this man and thought his life was almost over. Jude knew that feeling for sure. There was no one else in line, no guard so close as to hear what he was saying.

"Bless me, Father, for I have sinned. My last confession was a long, long time ago." It was brief, and he was forgiven his sins with the nod of the head.

The colonel then began to explain how he had a plan and how it would work. In two nights, at the start of that second night, the accountant's truck would stop after passing over the small bridge a mile from the work farm on the way back to the main camp. It would be dark, it would be cold, and it would only stop for a moment or two.

He said there would be twelve priests on the truck, all of them would be set free, and they would begin a trek through the night to escape that place. The colonel said Peter would recognize all of them as fellow priests from St. Michael's, and that he knew Peter could lead them all to a safe place. He said they would be given food, water, and clothing. They would have a map and were to follow a stream till it intersected with a river thirty miles south, and the partisans, the Bakar, would be there to rescue them by that river. After the first night of hiking alongside the creek, they would come to the barn by sunrise, and their supplies would be in a small room inside the archaic abandoned grange. They were to continue along the stream for the next two nights, and they would eventually arrive at the river.

The Bakar would take them to a place where they would then say goodbye to each other, head out into the chaos, and tell the world as best we could that there were such places as this one we were leaving behind. The priests were to become the storytellers. The colonel told Peter there were hundreds of these camps, and it had to stop. Told him the Germans were on the verge of building a super bomb the likes of which the world had never known.

The colonel then stood up from the table and placed his hands on its corners and drew very close to his face.

"Can you do this?"

Peter said that all he could do was nod his head up and down, and discovered a platter full of destiny all of a sudden. He admitted to them that he had come close, thought about walking the walk, but found a prayer in the nick of time, and lived another day.

The colonel said he would tell him more the next day, ordered him to try and get some sleep and fully appreciated that the priest was undoubtedly overwhelmed. That was enough for now, and it was time to go pray. He then turned and ordered the guards to bring the toast thieves over to the table and ordered Peter to take the thieves back to the barracks. The five of them walked back inside and found their spots on the end of the rows of sleeping souls.

The next day Peter was counting the large rocks stacked along the side of the roadway near the entrance to the farm barns when the colonel walked up behind him. He was still dealing with having climbed the ladder that morning and finding eleven of his former soul mates sitting in the truck and waiting. All along, they had been waiting for him, and they didn't even know it.

"Father Peter," the colonel said in a very calm and soothing voice, "let me see your clipboard." He appeared to be reading the totals and was not in any hurry to finish the inspection.

Once again, they were somewhat alone, and the guards watched from a distance but seemed to be intentionally trying to occupy themselves with other workers and what they were doing.

He folded the tablet inside his crossed-over hands and held it to his chest as he looked out over the roadway and down towards the control tower at the entrance to the farm. Only Peter could hear his voice.

"Tomorrow night you will be set free. Tonight will be your last night in the compound, and you need to tell the others of the plan in the morning."

He looked over at the priest, and the priest seemed to have changed in only the last twelve hours. There was a glow in his eyes, and he was standing taller than before.

The colonel explained that there would be new accountants at the truck when the time came for it to leave for the farm on that next morning, and that the twelve were not to worry about being missed. They wouldn't be missed. They could only be caught and captured if they were foolish and stupid. In two days, instead of climbing onto the truck, they would be resting for the entire day out of sight inside the barn, very cautious and observant, and waiting for the night to begin another journey alongside the stream. After three nights of this, ten miles a night, they would find themselves at the river, and their saviors and guides would find them.

The colonel explained that when the truck stopped they had to immediately get out and go off the side of the road on the right side and start their journeys. They were not to look back, but spread out in pairs and walk as best they could through the night, and by sunrise they would be at the barn. Frail as they were, they would have to make it, crawl if necessary but get to the barn before sunrise.

He said to leave the tablets and pencils in the back of the truck, and when that time came there were for sure a dozen clipboards, but there were only nineteen pencils.

His directions to them had been flawless. Just like the German colonel had said, the barn was abandoned and the room in the back was full of things they would need: water jugs, a number of dried fish, beans, apples, and some baskets with loaves of bread. There was a table up against a wall, two large candles, matches, a bottle of wine, the Bible and a beautiful crucifix about eight inches long. A map of the region showed streams and rivers, and there was a mark that showed where they were. There were large piles of shoes and pants, shirts and jackets.

They had been told to be very quiet on the walk, to walk as fast as they could, and to stay as close to the edge of the stream as was reasonable; never walk on any road. They were to find clothing that fit their needs and to leave their prison shirts and pants there in the room. Jude found the perfect coat and a pair of wonderful boots.

They could only stay at the barn for one short day, and then they had to begin their journey down along the stream as far as they could go through the night. That day in the barn was spent celebrating the Mass over and over a dozen times, and they did it in their new clothes, with underclothes and even two pairs of socks.

Father Andrew and Jude were on watch in the loft and heard it a few minutes before it arrived. It was late in the afternoon when a small truck came up the road and stopped at the front doors to the barn. Their friend, the accountant truck driver, got out and walked into the building, picked up all the used prison uniforms, went out to his truck and piled them in the back. He came in again, walked into the room they were cowering in and took a head count, looking into each of their eyes. He never said a word, gathered a few other things, and went back to his wheel. The twelve of them surrounded two windows, and there, standing by the side of the truck, was Colonel Desch. He blessed them, climbed back in and drove away.

They slept and rested all day the second day along an ancient overgrown hedgerow, and waited there till an hour after sundown. All they did was rest and talk in whispers, discovering the gift together; able to hear sounds none of them had ever heard before, and being able to speak and understand any language there was, it seemed. Someone had whispered to himself, "Sancta Caca," when he, too, discovered he could still hear the accountants' truck after all that time. He said it in the dialect of his childhood, known only to himself, and all of the rest of them heard it and understood it as if they'd grown up just down the path. "Holy shit!"

They needed to put as much distance between the camp and themselves as possible, and they had ten hours of darkness to get down to the stream. In essence, they would only walk at night, thirty hours total, and traveled almost that many miles. Jude kept waiting for his body to give out, but instead he gained strength by the hour as they listened to each other refine the story they all seemed to be learning together. The story they memorized was a symphony of horror from the memories of twelve survivors, the tragedy of St. Michael's and Theresienstadt along with the guarantee about super bombs. A message to all mankind that there was only so much time, a matter of only a few years until doomsday. Stand and fight, don't be blind, and most of all try to survive.

Jude couldn't be sure but it felt like every sense he had was overwhelmed by the Holy Ghost, and he could convince anyone that Theresienstadt did in fact exist. When the other priests told their version and added their thoughts or experiences, Jude listened, and when it was his turn, he included their version in his and vice versa. Long-range hearing with the new sense of vibration secured their safety, and they all understood that sensation almost immediately. All Jude would need was fifteen minutes of your time and he would change your life forever.

They needed to be at least ten miles farther down towards the river each night. They'd been ordered to walk in pairs and stay within sight of the pair in front of them, and try to walk where they walked and stop when they stopped. An hour after sundown, they left the barn and started their second night, and enjoyed the light of the full moon; Desch had even thought of the full moon. When they came to the river, they were to wait in the shadows, no movement or noise. He'd told them it would take three hard nights of hiking down along the stream, but on the end of the third night they would be at the river. There would be a boat and some people there to help them.

He'd said he was simply trying to make a difference from the inside out, fulfill an old vow. That they should do their level best to try to tell the world about the place they had just survived. The colonel said he had seen them in a dream, and that they would be able to convince everyone they met that the story was true, and the horror of it all needed to be stopped. He said the devil himself had come to life, and the whole world could die if the demons weren't killed or arrested. He said the Germans were building a super bomb for the hard to reach.

Jude remember Desch very well — the colonel of the guard. He remember all of those horrible buildings, chock-full of thousands and thousands of starving, desperate human beings. For two years, they'd known only the inside of the place and nothing else; there was no world left. Life had become worthless. All of those inmates were in his custody on both sides of the compounds walls. There were barracks for the guards and special barracks for the officers. Construction was everywhere, and Jude realized that he ended up as a farm laborer through no fault of his own. He could have just as easily ended up somewhere else inside or outside the project. It was as if they were creating a fairytale land; it made no sense whatsoever. He must have been in the wrong place at the wrong time. First in a line, or last, this truck this way and that truck that way, and as they wondered where they were going, they would see a man standing on a platform directing the traffic out the back of their truck. It had been his choice all along.

For no reason in particular, the colonel gathered some of them around him during a water break one day, and he began to read out loud. Jude saw him look at him and he felt as if the colonel was studying him, or so it seemed, and in their social circle of the times that was quite possibly the most terrifying relationship Jude had known up to that time. They stood and listened to him read from a Nazi propaganda book that he carried in a satchel, and Jude never knew why, but he was not offended by what he read. It was hard to explain, but there was always something about the passages that suggested there were still some good and decent people in the most unlikely of places. One pamphlet talked about how the detainees were to accept their fate and sacrifice the way the German foot soldier sacrificed. Jude sometimes felt that it didn't really matter which side of the wire they were on, life for one and all was a miserable cesspool of filth, and the one and only thing they all had in common was that the war would probably kill them all one way or the other.

One and all, they had known each other back at St. Michael's. They were not the same men who had prayed in those chapels or toiled in the gardens. They were dead men walking. They had seen more death in the last twenty-four months than they should have ever been allowed, and only some sort of direct intervention on the part of God Almighty would save them from that hell on earth. That seemed to be the plan.

There was a purpose after all. The most powerful man for many miles in any direction had conceived of this idea that basically freed them and sent them off into the world. They were to head off into places that they were slightly familiar with and try to convince the world out there that there was, in fact, a hell on earth before it was too late.

Peter, their leader, was to find Pope Pius XII, a man who had become Pope at almost the exact same time as the Nazis took over St. Michael's. Rumor had it that the Pontiff was trapped inside the Vatican by a similar insanity in Italy. All the rest of them were to warn the rest of the world one set of ears at a time. Each of them would develop a story that they could tell over and over, and they understood it would be almost infallible in its nature. They would carry the power of persuasion from a distance, an ability to convince anyone that what they were saying was true, and they would have no trouble with language, any language. They were given the gift of tongues, would possess the ability to remember the intricate past, all the details, a total and complete recall of that horrible concentration camp and an ability to exclaim the details as the absolute truth. Each of them had a walking partner at the beginning, but that would change, as each had a destiny that had been predetermined, a destination, a route. Eventually, they would all end up on their own, telling their stories to anyone who would listen.

That was Jude's story, and he was sticking to it. Hard to believe, but true just the same. They vowed to meet again someday at the front entrance to St. Michael's.

Early on during his release, after only the first mile, Jude discovered that he could hear much better than he had ever heard before as he watched that rattletrap truck he had been in climb that far distant ridge line on its way back to the camp, entirely empty except for a driver and twelve accounting pads. The truth was it was far too far away for Jude to actually hear its struggle, but he did. They could hear each other whisper in the night, they would whisper back and be heard as they talked about the future, where they were and what God had in store for them all, as if they were all sitting side by side around a camp fire. They prayed together even though they were hundreds of yards apart. The six pairs of priests stumbled at times along the stream side and chattered in those whispers, remembering the past and working on their destinies. To say the least, it was the first of the most miraculous.

They made it to the river in three nights, just like they should have, and they were rescued just like they were promised. The Bakar took them to an abandoned old church fifty miles south in only two days, and they rested for almost a week, were fed, watered, and reinvigorated towards recovery.

Jude's destination was described as "East" and before long Father Steven and Jude were guided in that direction, but Steven veered off after two hundred miles and went with a guide due south towards Romania, while Jude's guide and he headed for the Ukrainian borderlands. Jude was still so weak, but gradually improving, and was allowed to sleep for long stretches.

They found themselves on the twenty-first day of June 1941 staring down into a valley that had thousands and thousands of

German war tanks all lined up and facing Russia. They had walked out of the mountains and onto a scenic overlook, and that corner of the trail was a lookout point that was reputed to be the most scenic spot of all for observing the western edge of the Ukrainian frontier. For miles and miles, the Germans had amassed the mighty 6th Army and all of their Panzer Divisions, all looking east at Russia. Jude, unfortunately, had to get in front of them, and he had to stay in front of them no matter what. They were resting, he was rested, and the race was on. No matter how fast they went, Jude had to go faster. In front of them was the battle frontier, a wavy line a few miles wide and two thousand miles long, a dead man's zone and on the other side of the no man's land was the Russian Army.

Even though he remembered it all and had watched so much of it in his rear view mind, he could only say that once those tanks began to roll forward it was a wave of terror the land had never seen before in all its history. Jude was talking about Mother Earth and how she, as Queen of the land, felt the German war machine roll through the people like they were blades of grass. Jude and his guide managed to stay just ahead of the slaughter, just ahead of the Germans and their invasion, something they called 'Operation Barbarossa,' until he found himself on the back side of the Russian Army and witnessed their resistance as they tried to stop the German onslaught. It was not a fair fight.

Jude was exhausted after so many months of hiding and running, running and hiding again, until he ended up being carried in a wagon covered with straw and nestled into a secret cavity just behind the driver's seat. They were headed east through the front when all the refugees trapped in the middle were headed back into the monster's throat, where there would be no refuge. The hay wagon passed alongside German infantry and huge armored columns with trucks pulling enormous artillery cannons, and there was always, absolutely every single solitary time, there was just enough room for the horse and wagon to pass by and continue east. Jude had a bed of straw and two little peepholes that showed him some of what was happening, had constant food and water, and quickly gained back some of his strength. There were a number of short boat trips after the hay ride, usually at night, and from the end of July and for the rest of his journey east, it appeared the world was on fire back to the west, from the north to the south, exactly where he had come from.

He and his guide had crossed through the German-Russian front as if they were invisible and bulletproof, passed through a no man's land that no man should have survived, and walked directly into the face of the Russian terrified defenders. They paid them no mind and let them pass after they answered their questions, and they told them what they had seen just over the horizon. It was wonderful when he let Jude out of his tiny travel box, and he and Jude turned into refugees just like all the others, only these were headed east towards the Volga.

When it came to looking like and being a refugee, Jude was a hard act to follow, and not a single aggressive person who ever looked at him once thought twice about wasting another minute deciding if he was worth another moment. As good as he felt, he hadn't yet filled in his cheeks, and his eye sockets were sunken, deeply hollow and dark. The Russians hardly glanced at them as they stayed out of their way, and they knew almost as well as the refugees that the German war machine was coming, just over the western horizon. That was far more important than dealing with two refugees who were simply trying to get behind it all.

Once they were east of the front, they tried to not look back and spent every waking moment trying to get closer to the Volga. They skirted just below Kursk in late September and learned that Kiev had fallen, and there was nothing left of the Russian Army. So far, this thing the Germans called 'Barbarossa' was succeeding with deadly efficiency, and much of the news a hundred miles east of the front lines turned the roads into quagmires of refugees, soldiers in retreat and total despair.

The Germans were clearly after Stalingrad, and there were hardly any Russians left to tell them otherwise, or so everyone thought. As for Jude, he was escorted to a boat on the outskirts of Voronezh and they pushed off out into the Don River and floated quietly for almost a week until they came to a river that flowed out into the Don a hundred miles from Rostov. Up that river was a town called Litzi, and there was a small cabin nestled on the point just off the beach front that Jude was given the key to and told it was where he should wait for his next guide. He waited through the Christmas season, had everything he needed, managed to stay warm, and finally the new year came and 1941 was over. It had actually been rather mild for a winter, at least in that area, but very wet, and the war would continue without fail as soon as the spring rains were over and the mud dried.

Every day that went by meant the Germans were that much closer, and Jude was sure they were probably less than a hundred miles west, slowed by the mud and the remains of a Russian Army. As for him at the time, he really had nowhere to go. He waited every day for the new guide just like he had done so many times before, and never once did they not show up, find and guide him even farther down the road.

Down near the place where the smaller river merged with the Don, Jude found a sandstone outcrop that he loved to sit on and say his daily prayers. He did it every single day, as it seemed to be the perfect place to sit, wait and pray.

CHAPTER 4

THE GROTTO

Pfeiffer, Russia

Out beyond the back east end of St. Francis of Assisi Catholic Church, a wandering soul would find themselves walking uphill and coming up on the Saint Francis of Assisi Grotto in a few hundred steps or so, depending. A beautiful walkway was lined with large flat boulders, many benches, the Stations of the Cross, and ended up encircling the grotto with a slate rock sidewalk. It was beautiful. There were many more rock benches out beyond the grotto and down the other side of the hill. You wouldn't know that from what you could see in front of you as you walked up on the rock formation, but on the other side, looking due east at those distant mountains, was the statue of St. Francis. The grotto sat out in a flat land and appeared to be the first of a series of megalithic rock formations with each one getting progressively bigger until it became a mountain chain off to the southeast, with the highest being called 'Easter Peak.' The flatland high up above the river was the perfect location for the church that overlooked the now deserted community. Someone had figured that out a hundred years before.

It hadn't always been deserted like this, but then again there were no Communists once upon a time. Once upon a time, there had been real, genuine communal life in that little abandoned town. There had been times when every soul that called it home was up there on that hilltop and all around the grotto. Big picnics and outdoor concerts where frequent, where people played, where they praised their God and fell in love with each other. There were fire pits and cooking pits, and not too far off, down near the rock cliffs, were the best toilets in the whole valley. They were very private and extremely friendly, including plumbing; one of the benefits of taking the time to meditate near the grotto.

Standing out in the field behind the church, this monolith of black granite appeared to burst out of the surrounding topsoil and was almost as tall as the tallest tree in the area; there were lots of those, or at least their stumps. For the most part, everything to the east was mountainous and suitable for hunting and finding wood. On the other side of those mountains was the mighty Volga River, thirty miles as the crows fly. Not too far distant in the direction of the mountains were the tree forests, and they had always done well and survived a number of droughts, better than everything else in the valley. To the north and west were the flatland plains of Russia and Ukraine, 'The Outback.'

From the backside, the giant monolith was barren of any vegetation and didn't appear to need any. All around its base was a pleasant garden that grew berries and other edibles, starting early and ending late. They, too, had always done well in the droughts, mainly because any rain that fell on the monolith ended up watering the plants and gardens at its base. Every living thing around the grotto had always done well, and the fact that the water well some three hundred feet out in front of the church had seldom gone dry confirmed the idea that there was a lot of water under the rocks. All that invisible water flowed down towards the river underneath the town, and it had turned out to be an excellent place for a small community of like-minded individuals. That was really all they were.

There were a number of water wells in the town, and water had seldom been a problem.

Water had always been an issue, if not the primary one, when it came to founding a settlement. Without water, especially fresh clean water, more than likely they wouldn't make it.

In Pfeiffer, not only did they have the wells, they also had their own personal river, and from their little pier and dock on the Ilava, in only ten miles, this beautiful winding tributary mingled with the mighty Don River. Fifty miles south, down the Don, through Rostov, the small fishing boats would eventually find their way into the Sea of Azov, and finally into the Black Sea. Only the most experienced river man and seaman could manage such a feat, but there were men who did it all the time back during the turn of the century.

Sailing the rivers to the sea was a perilous undertaking: twenty hairpin turns on the Ilava before they reached the Don, snaking and floating the entire distance, idling their pistons and managing their sails in the current. It was all part of the business, as money and trade made things work. The primary concern was actually getting all the way back up those rivers, as supplies of fuel could be an issue, and the ever-present snipers, but not so much in the old days. Even the rumor of a sniper could stop the traffic on any river for days at a time, and the best times for travel were often late at night or very early in the mornings with no moon. Not many men would attempt to float the rivers in the dark, but there were a few, and they were legends in their own time.

Another thing that had always helped with Pfeiffer's isolation was the fact that it bordered the edge of the Great Plains, and there were many other ways to cross into the outback. She had never been an easy place to get to in the first place, and neither were many of her neighbors who were equally of the same mind. In fact, there were hundreds of thousands of these like-minded people, living in thousands of small communities just like Pfeiffer all throughout the Volga Basin, and they didn't mind one bit being at the end of a road or a river. Left alone and in peace, they would quickly prosper, and besides that, the only other thing they insisted on was their freedom to practice their religion. It was the one thing that motivated them in the first place, the one thing that they craved the most. For the longest time, they maintained that the religious issues had always been the one thing that caused them the most grief. That was somewhat debatable, because they had another issue, concerning assimilation, and were almost inflexible concerning their rights to speak German, be German Catholics, in the heartland of Orthodox Russia.

The Volga Basin Catholics would be no exception to any rule in the realm of Communism. That new government in Moscow had somehow or another managed to make it illegal to believe in God as of 1918, and it didn't matter one bit what one might call God; it was against the law to believe in Him. He didn't exist. The punishment was death, imprisonment or re-education, and they always appeared ready, willing, and able to kill everyone they determined couldn't quit believing, and did it on a grand scale for everyone to see.

The settlers should have known from the very beginning that they would never be left alone, and even though they may not have been first on the list for the communists, they were in fact fairly close to the top. The fact that everyone had insisted on speaking the old world language — that being German — meant they never stood a chance; they were doomed from the start. Anyone who spoke German in Russia after 1915, when the enemy always seemed to be the Germans, ended up being considered the enemy. It was too late from the very start. By the end of the war to end all wars, there were no Germans left in Pfeiffer except for one.

Standing out in front of the grotto, out a dozen paces, a petitioner, an admirer, a devotee, would see this impressive solid marble statue of the saint, holding the birds, of course, and wearing his half-bald halo. Down the long walkway of the hill was the magnificent church and the tiny abandoned town of Pfeiffer, Russia.

The saint's ultimate prayer was etched in bronze on two separate tablets, and the people in this valley parish lived by most of his rules, aspirations, and guidelines. It appeared that the granite flowed over the edge of the bronze plates and embedded them forever. Not possible, but it looked that way. These epitaphs were centered in the second and fourth of five large chunks of granite that protected the front of the grotto. All five pedestals surrounded the base of the statue on the front side and turned out to be perfect platforms in front of kneelers. No one ever ventured past these and any closer — no need to. It was a grotto; stand back and beseech.

Behind the shoulders of the statue, the granite formed a cavity as if the rock had split apart and created an entrance down into the core of the rock, into its heart. It was an illusion of solid rock, but there was an opening, disguised from the curious. If one were to walk behind the statue and become invisible, there in the back corner of the saint's right rear pocket, a tall narrow notch, a groove, an opening led down into somewhere. It was dark back in the corner but that all depended on whether you were coming or going, in or out, up or down, daytime or nighttime. Mother Nature had built this doorway millions of years before so that men could walk down inside her and feel what God himself was all about. It was hidden, almost invisible, shielded, eventually protected by the saint, and out on the edge of civilization, if that's the term that best described it all. It was what it was before the men came, and only animals knew about it way back in time.

A legend from the foundation times told how a hunter saw an animal disappear into the rock and followed it all the way down. As that early settler predator followed the deer down through the crevice, he came out into a bowl clearing and discovered what could only be described as 'the eye in the rock.' Those first men hunter-gatherers, led by a fellow named Johann Thomae, were the ones who found it, blessed it, and made it sacred. They were the first settlers, way back in the mid-1770s.

Back in those days, after following the cavity all the way to the bottom, they came back out into the open light, and discovered 'the eye in the rock.' Water poured out of the granite at about a man's height, down the six feet of cliff face and across a rock plateau. The water poured out of the corner of a conception, the unmistakable image of a human eye engraved in granite, from exactly where our teardrops do, and formed into a thin stream that poured over the cheek and flowed forty feet across a huge rock platform and then disappeared back into the cracks of the granite. It became a holy spot for the men who found it, and that spot where the stream disappeared was open to the sun and the moon once upon a different time.

The settlers decided to hide it. They left it that way for a short time and then began to enclose it, designing a massive shelter that could protect them if necessary, taking fifty years from start to pasture, covering a giant cavity between two granite ledges and turning it into an invisible fortress.

The men at the time saw the grotto for what it was destined to be, had experienced a group revelation that couldn't be denied. A miracle at a campfire one night, where a dozen men and four women were inspired in unison. What had originally started off as the idea of building a giant fence between the two cliff faces, an insurmountable structure they planned to congregate and hide behind in case of barbarians. At the time, they were easily able to justify the effort, never asking themselves why they went through so much trouble. Before long, they decided to put a roof on it. After that, they covered it with boulders, timbers, and soil, with many of the final construction personnel having no idea what lay beneath.

The community went from burying the shelter to building the foundation for the new church that would have a beautiful grotto behind it. The huge statue and the ideas it offered kept their eyes on the goal, and nothing behind the statue itself mattered in the slightest. Swallows lived up high on the sides of the grotto; there were bees, ants, and spiders in all the crevices and cracks.

During those years when the walkways were always busy, starting in the 1790s and ending a hundred and twenty years later, for the most part, none of the petitioners ever walked behind the statue of St. Francis and knew nothing about a shelter. If nothing else, it was a priestly domain and it might have been sacrilegious to stand behind a saint. It was one of those places on this planet where most people would never want to go, if for no other reason than it just wouldn't be respectful nor necessary. When the vicious winter storms swept in from the west, St. Francis never felt a flake, and the backdrop behind the saint was always open.

The Statue of St. Francis was larger than life, maybe twice our size, and he stood on a marble pedestal that elevated him even more, but that beautiful rock shield behind him made him look normal. Back in the day when people came to this spot out in the wilderness, behind that magnificent church, and wondered about life, God, and themselves, this grotto was a beautiful place to practice their rituals. Most folks found it easy to pray, had a favorite spot, and each generation tried to wear out the sidewalk.

A Holy Thursday inspection, April 25th, 1928.

Colonel Sokolov had asked Hammer about the grotto during the tour; what it was and why it was there. Hammer explained that it was simply an outdoor shrine to St. Francis of Assisi and hadn't been used since the Revolution had condemned such activity, to say nothing of the fact that there weren't any people left in the town to do that in the first place.

The inspection party was standing on the front steps of the church that fateful day, when the priests were notified about the Easter Sunrise Mass. Colonel Sokolov pointed to the grotto far off in the distance, hard to see from the front steps of the church, and identified it as 'The Grotto'. It was there in his notes, an object on the property, identified as 'The Grotto, a very large rock, one hundred yards or more out behind the church on a hilltop.' Sokolov took a long look and decided it was probably the most unimportant item on his list. Besides that, it was quite a way away and all uphill, and it looked and felt like it was going to rain.

"It looks from here like an enormous black rock. You have a fifty-foot tall black rock that resembles your saint? You see that in the rock?"

'The statue of St. Francis of Assisi is on the other side, stupid,' was a clarification neither priest bothered to mention.

Hammer leaned hard on his cane, squinting at the distant monolith, and could only hope that the brilliant colonel would believe him if he said yes. "Some people see him and some people don't. I do. I have to be closer than most people because I can't see all that well anymore. I have a hard time seeing the details that I used to see when I was younger. If I stand and look very hard and I'm patient, I can still see it. I grew up here, as you know, and when I was young I could see much better. One of the first things I remembered as a boy was seeing St. Francis in the rock face for the first time."

The colonel was listening intently, for some strange reason, nodding his head in agreement for another strange reason, unsure the story was ever going to end, so before Hammer could bring up something else, the colonel shouted, "OK! Enough of that!"

Three of his subordinates who were close by all shouted back in harmony, "Yes, Sir."

From there they toured the inside of the spectacular church, empty of the faithful, beautiful in every detail and immaculate. A spectacular bell tower climbed over a hundred feet straight up above the entrance foyer, the magnificent confessional, and dozens and dozens of handmade pews. There had been times in the far distant past when there were a thousand souls inside.

On this tour, fifteen Russian soldiers, four men in suits and two priests stood along the communion rail as their guide and the pastor, Father Karl Hammer, pointed to the uppermost distant left-hand corner of the stained-glass windows. This is what they had come to see, high up above the altar: the stained-glass image of Mary. Father Karl explained that the miracle occurred in that lower corner of the Blessed Mother's eye; that was where the 'Diamond Teardrop' appeared during and only during the Easter sunrise service, assuming it wasn't raining.

At sunrise, those stained-glass windows turned into a spectacular display of colored lights as hundreds of glass panels exploded into the story of God. Eventually, the teardrop formed and attention was pulled to that spot in the corner of her eye, where the blinding diamond appeared for a brief moment, and that moment occurred traditionally during the Consecration of the Eucharist, as per Father Hammer's timing.

The old priest was emphatic about certain aspects of the event, especially the timing, and the fact that it was a religious phenomenon and dependent on the sanctity of the service. By mid-afternoon, the tour was over, for the most part, and all of the parties involved worked their way to the parking lot again. The Diamond Teardrop was all the colonel really wanted to know about, exactly what time it would appear, and he told the priest to pray that it didn't rain.

Once the assembly was out of the church, Sokolov turned to the two priests, came up close to his two subordinate clergymen, and spoke so everyone could hear, "Do not leave these premises, and we shall see you two on Saturday afternoon. You both be ready, have your church ready, and we shall witness this Diamond Teardrop together on Sunday morning. Have either of you ever seen electric lights?"

Basil admitted that he had, Hammer was a virgin on the subject but had heard of such things, so Sokolov decided to educate everyone with his technical prowess and began to explain what a light bulb actually was. They would use modern lighting while filming the Mass, having learned that it made all the difference sometimes. Just the idea of explaining to candle folk what an electric bulb did could be a challenge and took the genius a number of tries, as his elderly student couldn't seem to grasp the notion. Eventually, he ended up using the term, 'a thousand candles in a bunch times twelve,' to which the old priest imagined the church without a roof on a sunny day. He had much experience with a couple of dozen and couldn't fathom the idea of twelve thousand.

"You both will be famous. This film will become a national treasure. You should be honored, and I know you are."

With that, the old man realized that it was checkmate. He loved chess, was very good at it, and all you had to do was ask Basil about that. Down at the bottom of the steps leading into the church, dwarfed by the giant bell tower above them, the three men gazed out at the large group of attending officers and enlisted men.

Before the colonel could back away, the old man grew a half a foot or so and took center stage with a loud voice.

"We are both so honored to be a part of this. Truly, truly honored. You have no idea how honored we both are. Thank you, thank you, thank you."

And without shrinking in the slightest, he assumed the domineering position of a strong Russian manly man who is about to give very manly 'thank you kisses' on the cheeks of the thankee. What was the colonel to do? Basil was feeling an overwhelming déjà vu, and so did his pastor. This kissing of the cheeks was an ancient tradition, his bodyguards were not on guard at all by now, and besides, everyone did it; the colonel had done it to his own father, and he had set himself up. From somewhere on the back right corner of his brain, he could hear some wheezier holler "Checkmate," but it might have been a bird or something else.

It's a natural fact that old people often times prove to be much stronger than they appear, and the colonel discovered the hands that gripped his ears so tight could not be pried off his face without him looking unkissable, perhaps ungrateful, un-Russian, and any effort to escape the grasp could remove his skin.

First, there was a full lip encounter on his right cheek, and in their manly struggle, as the could-have-been-a-bishop priest was changing sides of the nose, he stumbled and their mouths were virtually wide open as their teeth touched for a moment just before the second kiss on the other cheek.

The colonel was venturing into a scream, never having touched teeth with anyone before in his life, and was positive there was a tongue involved in there somewhere. He flashed back to his childhood and could hear his mother telling him to close his mouth; she had warned him about flies and other things.

Suddenly he heard all his men cheering, and was confused as to what they had seen. Altogether, they were overcome with emotion, and must have thought they had just seen something special; they didn't know about the tongue and teeth just yet, but the film would clear that up in a few days.

They were bouncing around at the bottom of the stairs, cheering and clapping, as the colonel had no choice but to casually wipe off his mouth and smile at the cameras. He had orchestrated this entire tour, and the cameras had it all on film. By the time he made it to the car door, the priests had retreated up the steps to the open doors into the church and waited for them to leave. That day has always been an integral part of Holy Week and was best referred to as Holy Thursday. Good Friday was the next day, and the colonel promised them he wouldn't be back till Saturday.

When it was all said and done, and the doors were closed and the barbarians were gone, the two priests stood there in the vestibule, rested against the walls and thought on the past few hours.

"Reminds me of the day we met, Father. You know, he would have killed you if he had his druthers. You should be more careful."

The old man walked over to the little niche where he always hid his glasses and stood for a moment, seeing the far distant altar more clearly, and all the empty pews between him and it.

"I didn't know about the filming, and now that I do, I need to pray on that a bit. So do you. We need to have a very good plan and practice our presentation. I rather doubt they will have any need for us after that Mass, and for that reason I rather doubt I'll be careful at all from here on out. I don't trust them in the slightest. This is all too bizarre. Let's you and I go talk to God for a while. He calls us. That colonel can't wait to kill me, and he's going to kill you, too. They need us for now, but when the Mass is over, they won't."

Often times we never know when people are listening to us, and we happen to be talking about them. Sometimes the damage is irreparable and irrevocable. In the case of Father Karl Hammer and Colonel Sokolov, the former managed to hear the latter tell one of his cronies that his intention was to lock that old bastard in his own confessional and burn his church down on top of him with his cane by his side.

CHAPTER 5

HOLY THURSDAY 1928

A first-hand account.

My name is Basil, Father Edward Basil. It was one of those times when I was certain that God himself, his spirit, was engulfing me, my world, the church, and everyone around it. All of our Catholic churches had been closed years before I even got here, and as often as not, burned and looted of everything, from the most precious to the least. There would be nothing left, and even possessing something like a solid gold chalice was a death sentence. In some cases, it was hard to find the spot where the churches had been, much less what had happened to the two priests who might have been there on duty when the sickle swung through.

The Soviet State would prove to the disbelieving world their religious tolerance through a cinema made by the brilliant Colonel Sokolov, who would direct the filming of the Mass. They hailed it loud and clear from the steps, announced that St. Francis of Assisi Catholic Church on the Ilava was open to the public. That there would be a sunrise Mass on Easter Sunday morning 1928, with the first and only announcement coming three days before the event. No one except those of us at the church steps heard the hail, loud and clear as it was.

I so vividly recall that afternoon when the Red Army Colonel came to our church with his huge motorized support staff. There were men with moving picture cameras, still cameras, and two western journalists from Bulgaria who looked exactly like the ones from Russia. It was Holy Thursday of the Catholic Holy Week, and Father Hammer and I were sharing tea in the back of the church when they all pulled up. Earlier and just in passing he'd told me they were coming an hour or so before they arrived, and I could only conclude that his cane had told him about the visitors and their vibrations. I'll tell you more about the cane as I go along.

It was just Father Hammer and myself sitting in the vestibule in the back of the church that afternoon, passing the time and wondering aloud to each other, when out of nowhere he said we were going to have guests very soon. His cane stood quietly by his side, straight up and down, leaning on nothing, and waiting. We were getting good at trying our best to be honest listeners, I know I did, and he was such a wonderful man, he did, too. We were down to just him and me, and it almost seemed the epitome of absurdity. Ever since I had arrived two years before, we had evolved into routines. He would say Mass one day, and I would be his co-celebrant, play that magnificent organ, singing, whatever, and I would say Mass the next and he would assist me. I said Mass every other morning of the week in this big beautiful church, but no one ever came. We would daringly open the doors, and still we would be alone through the worship. No one ever ventured over that threshold to the Church, not even once, because there was no one left. In the old days, before my time, when the faithful would come up to the communion railing, kneel down and wait their turn, that seemed to be what the Mass was all about. That never happened anywhere anymore. It had been years since a Eucharistic recipient had graced this altar rail. I yearned for that, so much, and never saw it once. To turn there on the altar, walk down to that rail and place the body of Christ on the tongue of someone. One more time, please.

There was a heavy pounding at the door to the church, and even though we never locked it, the knocking persisted until both of us arrived to push it open. All they had to do was pull on the handle, and the door would have opened, but they didn't. Hammer set his glasses in a tiny niche in the woodwork, invisible for the most part, not too far from the entrance doors, not too far from the confessionals, nodded at me, and we pushed the main doors open.

An explosion of flashbulbs accompanied a gentle applause from a large throng of dignitaries and military policemen, all standing on the bottom landing patio in front of the church steps — that's what greeted the two of us, yet for some reason, it sounded like it came from their elbows, hollow.

It was only a matter of eight solid block steps up from that patio to where Hammer stood there next to me, holding my right arm with his left, his cane with his right, while gazing at the foggy horizon just above the treetops. He had an elegant smile on his face, rested the cane against his chest, and held out his right hand in a very Christ-like finger wave. The V sign, it meant peace to a man like him and was a universal sign for that to all other honest men, but to some it meant victory and everyone knew who the enemy was at this photo opportunity. I'm not sure that Father Hammer could have waved any other way; it was just something he had done all his adult life, and how could he have known their minds?

A distinguished gentleman in a suit followed a colonel up the stairs and to the side of Father Hammer. The colonel stood facing into the open doors of the church and seemed to wave his right hand in front of his face as he lowered his chin to his chest in a nodding gesture. It was complicated, obviously rehearsed as if one important dignitary was approaching another on an equal footing. It appeared to be his acknowledgment of something behind the priests and still inside the building. The flash bulbs were smoking once again.

The man in the suit never took his eyes off me and his smile was that of a good man, but that didn't prevent me from being extremely uncomfortable knowing he kept looking at me, and this crowd he had arrived with was anything but good.

The colonel turned to face the crowd below him and raised Father Hammer's right hand a little higher, gently, farther up into the air. I don't know what Hammer was thinking, but I knew he couldn't see what I could see. Alternatively, maybe he could, I wasn't sure, but he allowed his hand to be raised and continued with his first and second fingers forming that famous 'V'. The face on his cane was scanning the crowd below, but no one down there made eye contact with it for long. Father Hammer continued to smile into the fog he professed to see without his glasses and I in turn could see the eyes of the devil's dogs out there in that crowd of witnesses. It was all for show, and they were here to inspect the premises, the house of God, and make sure everyone was on the same page when it came to the end of Holy Week and Easter Sunday. Unfortunately, they had missed Palm Sunday's services the previous Sunday, and the early part of the week, when all Christian churches prepare for Good Friday. I rather doubted he was planning to invite them to dinner that night, but the man was a never-ending surprise.

There was a tour planned for the guests by the guests, and Hammer would be the guide, show them everything they wanted to see and tell them everything they wanted to know. It took the better part of two hours for this charade to wander through the church and the grounds until they all formed up on the patio, directly in front of the church, and waited for all the vehicles to come back.

While we stood there, waiting for them to leave, the man in a suit came back up the steps and stood on the one step just below and directly in front of my face. We were eye to eye, and Hammer could now see him plain as day. Hammer could see what I could see. He folded his hands in front of his chest and looked left and right to make sure there was no one listening to his words.

"On Easter Sunday morning, I pray that you two make it perfect. Light the church with candles, light the incense, and wear the vestments that are appropriate. This will be your only chance to show the world, and I doubt you will ever get this chance again. Just in case, I'll make sure there are two copies at least. Praise God as best you both can. Light that incense; I miss it."

We both stood there and nodded our willingness to do just that, and Father Hammer and I glanced back and forth at each other while he fumbled with a few papers and flyers he had in hand.

"I'm going to post these flyers that announce there will be a public Mass in this building on Easter Sunday morning, at or near sunrise, on the door. Isn't that your ideal time frame?"

I was nodding and yesing and wondering about it all. What else could I do? Father Hammer, just like me, was also yesing and nodding. There was a slight lapse in the conversation as the man seemed to be finding the contract and locating where I was to sign, when I reminded him that I was just the assistant pastor here at St. Francis. I made it humbly clear that I was Father Hammer's assistant, and that he was the pastor.

He looked at me with the softest eyes. "I understand all that," he said, "and Father Hammer knows all that. Don't you, Father Hammer?"

Hammer looked at me, and I could see in his eyes that there was something going on of which I had no clue. These two men knew each other, and there was so much more for me to learn, but not then. The man with the smiling eyes never quit his smiling as he escorted Hammer down to the bottom of the steps and up to the front of his waiting car and laid the papers on the fender for Hammer and I to sign. The army colonel signed for the government first, and there was a modest cheer from all the people waiting to leave. Hammer took the pen and signed where it said, and I grossly abbreviate here, "That ... he had to say Mass on Easter Sunday, and do it right."

There was a great deal more to it, but in essence, he had to say the Mass just like in the old days, no different from any time before, and hopefully the 'Diamond Teardrop' would show itself to the cameras so the whole world could see the miracle.

The Soviet State now owned the church, and this would undoubtedly give it some additional creditability, and perhaps discredit the idea concerning the silk purse and sow's ear theory.

He signaled into the air his peace sign again to all those people he couldn't really see. He could see where to sign, but he couldn't see any of the witnesses, except for the man in the suit. There was a monotonousness to the flash bulbs. It was then my turn to sign, and I stepped up and leaned over the document. There was my name and a line for my signature — what else could I do?

Someone somewhere had picked me to help Hammer in every way I could, negotiated me from some distant control center, starting when I was just a young man. The Communists had picked this church to tell the world they, in fact, didn't burn down churches, after all. I hadn't had anything to do with any of that, and neither had Hammer, yet here we both were, me recently and he for the entire duration of his life. It was impossible to explain at the time, but Hammer knew the truth, knew the past, knew the future, and as it would turn out, the man in the suit had two faces. It would be a long process knowing everything there is to know about St. Francis of Assisi Catholic Church, and I was only at the end of my sophomore year, so to speak. It was now apparent to me that I had been groomed all my life to be his assistant for that Easter sunrise Mass.

The colonel walked back up to our bumper, and then turned to face the cameras. He then invited the man in a suit to place his initials next to the colonel's and our signatures as a witness to the whole proceedings.

He introduced the man to all of us within range as Mr. Xander Aloysius Desch, First Secretary to the Premier. Suddenly, the entire assemblage erupted into a frenzy of excitement and surprise. More photos and questions burst out of the newspaper people, but for the time being all he did was look for those places on the documents where he had to put his mark, his X. No one seemed to have been sure exactly who he was or why he was there. He was quietly mysterious and apparently not the sort of person one might casually ask what the time was. He had three plain-suited assistants, and they traveled in a much finer sedan then everyone else. For everyone but Hammer and I, this seemed to be just about the biggest thing to happen to most of them lately, and to have traveled all this way, done everything we had done so far and they didn't know who he was?

It was obvious I didn't appreciate the secretary's actual importance as much as the press core, and his introduction had taken the wind out of their sails. Perhaps he existed on the invisible side of Communism. In an answer to a reporter's question, he admitted that he had a vested interest in the whole affair as he had spent his childhood on a farm not far from here. Everything considered, it would have been Hammer who poured the water over his forehead at his baptism, but he didn't mention that.

Desch had a special way of initialing documents, where he could rapidly do all three letters of his name without lifting his pen; well, almost. He started with the X, surrounded it with a small 'a' and slid off the right of the A with a baby 'd'. He only lifted his pen to put a slight hyphen on the upper right leg of the X. Often times it was hardly noticeable, and he didn't do it all the time. On this particular occasion, and especially on the copies that went to the priests, he caught himself exaggerating that hyphen. He rolled up the colonel's copy — with no hyphen — and placed a ribbon halfway down. As he handed it to the officer, the bulbs went off one last time. He turned, gave Hammer and me our copies, and took his own and rolled it into a long slim tube.

Without much fanfare, the occasion was over; the Mass was scheduled, and everyone knew their assignments. It was sometime after that when the cheek-kissing event occurred, and in no time at all the entire group left for the other side of town, where they planned to establish a headquarters area. Hammer heard everything they said much better than I did, and learned almost everything about what else was happening to this army. There were more coming, a whole lot more; half of the entire Southern Red was headed this way, on this side of the mountains and this side of the river.

A series of two-post warning signs had been spotted all across the front of the property line out to the roadways and all along the southern side of the church. It wasn't necessary on the back two. They had been first installed in the spring of 1920 by a small army of boy scouts who walked behind the wagon for twenty miles just to do that. The signs forbid any form of trespassing or vandalism, and there would be no further religious activity whatsoever, so ordered by the Commanding General himself. This church was state property and was to be considered a state historical treasure. Absolutely no trespassing.

From that corner, where the road came up to the church, there was a sign every twenty paces that warned about the danger of trespassing onto that side of the road, as ordered by the power and authority of the commanding general of the entire Southern Red Army. No further authority was needed. The punishment was death, of course. For a few hundred yards the signs were only a few hundred feet from the edge of the river. As the river curved and wound its way through that half mile, so did the road.

The signs warned that tampering with the signs was also a serious criminal offense, also ordered by the commanding general, with a note that only he could authorize the removal of one of these signs. It could create a bottleneck if the conditions were just right.

There, tacked to the inside of the front doors of the church, were these two notices informing the reader about the sunrise service planned for Sunday. This was above and beyond the lower step hails. The colonel had made a scene about it all, four or five pictures up close and personal after Desch had nailed those posters to those open doors. The cameramen did their jobs, and the colonel waited in his position for a few more photographers to see the moment and not miss their chance. The poster read the same way they had always read; the language was almost exact.

"A Mass of celebration."

The only problem was that we had to close the doors after they left. No one ever saw the posters, not only because they were on the inside, but also because there wasn't anybody left to read one. I wasn't sure the cameras had caught any of the action out on the streets of Pfeiffer. I also wasn't sure who would have the honor of opening these doors that Easter sunrise morning. Occasionally, when passersby came or went out on the roadway, most would not even glance at the front doors of the church. The government had succeeded in scaring us all half to death, and if it didn't scare you, that pretty much meant that you must be dead or dying. There were no locals left anywhere to attend Mass, and there was no such thing as Sunday services in the Red Army, north, south, east, or west, so in fact having those posters up didn't matter in the slightest.

After they had left, Hammer and I went back to the vestibule and continued with our tea. It was as if I had suddenly been through one of the most awkward and difficult afternoons of my entire life. I wasn't quite sure I had any idea what had just happened, why it had happened, or, for that matter, who all those people had been. I thought I was going to die, and I ended up having my picture taken a hundred times or more. This priest I thought I knew and had lived with for over two years was suddenly a whole lot more complicated than I expected. There was so much more to Hammer than met the eye, and now I realized that all this time he had been evaluating me in every regard there was. He now seemed to know me like a book, and all I knew about him was vague and assuming. I was trying to figure out why I was still alive and so many others were not. It was incomprehensible to me why I was still breathing on my own and working in this abandoned beautiful small cathedral. It wasn't really a cathedral like the ancient ones I knew about, but it was still remarkable.

As a young priest, I simply went where I was told, and that had proved to be Pfeiffer and their beautiful church, St. Francis of Assisi. I was too young and inexperienced to be a pastor, no matter how small the congregation, and I had heard of Hammer, and that he was a very good man. I never knew why I was picked for Pfeiffer, other than the fact that Bishop Andersoniski said to me personally that Father Hammer would need a strong, young helping assistant in the years to come, and so would the church of Pfeiffer. I hardly even knew where it was, didn't have much to pack, and it proved to take everything I had to get here from where I was.

Past Kiev, it was so chaotic when it came to dealing with the State people; they were so frightening, hateful and threatening, having a hard time believing a priest could have such gall as to travel into Russia. By the time I arrived, in '26, most police stations couldn't find a rule that said priests couldn't travel to a region where they had all been killed already.

It was as if a hunted species like myself had gone extinct and they were trying to introduce it back, with the problem being that no one had paid any attention to the bag limit in the first place. I had never anticipated being driven to the church steps in a police car, and I had to think they wanted to be absolutely sure where I was when my time came. Exactly why it had to be done that way was none of my doing; I was just along for the ride.

It wasn't long after I arrived with the policeman at the rectory door that Father Hammer and I were expressly ordered not to leave the church grounds for any reason whatsoever without permission. We were ordered to keep the church immaculately clean, but there would no longer be a parish, a diocese, or whatever else we might have had in mind. We were commanded to maintain the church, keep it in good condition and appearance, and we were told there would be inspections from time to time. That, in fact, never happened until Holy Thursday 1928. We were to eventually turn over the church records and inventory the entire contents of the holy place and not damage or lose anything within the confines, which was now considered State property.

As I thought about that time when Hammer and I were ordered to be priests again, I remember how I found myself wanting to simply stay alive, and to stay that way as long as possible. Over and over, I kept seeing Desch, the smiling man standing off in the distance by the cars the policemen had arrived in, the man with the eyes and his never-ending smile. It was Desch way back then at the police station in Kamyshin, where I ended up after my escort into the region, and here he was again, putting his initials on my new orders.

I knew I had seen him before, and after the first brief encounter had always wondered about him, and now I knew who he was. He was extremely important, one of the gifted, you might say, and an awful long way from Moscow, where the Communists ran things… but they had their people all the way down south. He seemed extraordinary, and yet I never felt that bitter twinge of fear deep in my spine when I saw him, like I often did whenever I was even remotely close to the rest of the police. I don't know how a man with what I'll call 'vibrations,' 'good vibrations,' very good vibrations, almost like peaceful, how could he possibly want to be around some of the high boots unless he was a fraud.

I will always remember how that colonel, who seemed so pleasant and respectful for the cameras, turned to the two of us priests, gently nestled his face between ours, and whispered into our ears, "Don't make me come back here and kill both of you. Neither of you has any idea how important it is that this Mass, this 'Diamond Teardrop' early morning Mass of yours, how everything about it must happen flawlessly. If it happens that way, everything will be just fine, at least for the time being."

He glanced over at Desch, as if that last little whisper needed the Secretary's approval, and I saw him nod his head, but I wasn't sure how to judge it. There was something missing in the look.

The colonel finally headed for his car after being thanked so vigorously, and then Desch was able to say a few quiet last words to both of us.

"Foolish threats and poisonous promises get us nowhere! I will be here on Sunday and am excitedly anxious about that. Not so much for the 'teardrop,' as I've seen it before, but to watch this service and relive the past."

On that Easter Sunday morning, when they pushed the main doors open and latched the foot pedals to the hard rock floor, I could see from my corner of the foyer what appeared to be thousands and thousands of Red Army soldiers out on the road. They were bringing their tanks and trucks, horses and infantry, and as far as the eye could see in any direction they were moving north.

They were everywhere, all along the side streets, and standing with their weapons in the yards of all the abandoned houses and businesses in the ruins of Pfeiffer. Everywhere I looked, I could see all these faces from all these different angles, and it was as if someone had ordered everyone to look at the church at least once.

All through the day before Good Friday and up till that Holy Saturday night, thousands and thousands of troops had been systematically working their way through the valley. This part of the army was headed northwest and made short work of some of the obstacles that had kept the lands isolated in the past. Our church was ready, and so were we; there was nothing left for us to do, but wait. After the second tour on Holy Saturday afternoon, we had been confined to the floor in the vestibule, and they would not even let us go pee. It had been a long and arduous night, but dawn was in the air, and it would soon be time to start our tribute to the Risen Savior.

CHAPTER 6

HOLY SATURDAY NIGHT

The Second Inspection

Colonel Sokolov had invited the old priest to recap some of his favorite histories of St. Francis while guiding the small group on his second personal tour of the inside of the church. That was mid-afternoon on Holy Saturday, roughly fifteen hours before the sunrise service was to begin. Basil seldom spoke, unless they spoke to him, and, for the most part, that didn't happen. He followed close behind the pastor and frequently assisted the old man with a stair or two.

He was cold, shivering, hungry and thirsty, with his lips moving a mile a minute, and appeared to be praying in silence; his fluttering lips suggested he was either praying or freezing to death. No noise, no sound, just lips. Arguably, this lowly and humble assistant to the semi-blind old man didn't appear the slightest threat. He was obviously thin, starving, and felt like vomiting over and over during the so-called tour charade. It showed all over his face that he was harmless, second only to the old pastor. It had now been almost twenty-four hours since they had had any food or water. The night was just beginning, and they were ordered to sit in a corner, which they both did in a dash.

The colonel took a long drink from a canteen while he studied the two priests sitting in their brown raggedy old priest clothes, almost like two bags of people; nothing more. He tossed the container at Basil's feet and nodded his head a few times. Both men drank feverishly, and when Hammer was through, the third time, Basil screwed on the cap and was thinking about handing it back, but the colonel and his men had all walked away. One of their guards gave each priest a potato and they split a chunk of toast. This corner would be their home for the night, and Basil began to consider the notion that it might be their last night alive.

They sat there and watched the goings-on for quite some time, until the officers all left for the night and went back to their distant compound. The church became a beehive of activity as the real work began for the camera crews as they set about their business.

"Go to sleep, my son," the old man whispered directly into Basil's ear. "Try not to worry, as this is all part of a grand plan. Trust me; I'll watch them while you sleep. We both need you to rest, for you're going to need your strength tomorrow and probably have to carry me if we plan on going anywhere. OK? OK? Ok! Sleep."

It would be easier said than done, because the barbarians were way past the front doors and had transformed the inside of the church into a movie production site. They had lighting assemblies that had been set up on the inside aisles of the church pointed at the ceiling. Their extension lines converged in the vestibule, then mingled and flowed out the back through the side door to a diesel-powered generator on a trailer fifty feet away. The only lights in the church had always been candles and lamps after dark. Very soon, the brightest lights the modern Russian military movie industry had to offer would light the way to the altar.

Once everything was in position, stable and secure, it was time to plug in their extension cords and begin their manual adjustments, an art form that was in its infancy. It would be just a test, not last too long, and the sergeant major signaled the others to turn on the generator and attach the cables. The lights were fragile and very expensive, to say nothing of being rare and difficult to replace, being new to the world.

The huge bulbs began to glow, and heat started to radiate off in visible waves. In a matter of only a few minutes, all twelve lamps were at full power, shining straight up at the ceiling that was designed to give a few well-placed candles enough reflection to light the entire place. Two or three candles here and there had always been plenty when it came to lighting the church for simple prayers, plus reflective mirrors that illuminated the shrines and mosaics, eliminating the darkness just enough. During a solemn High Mass at night, with dozens of candles on the altar, all along the side aisles and corners, the lighting was perfect for that kind of celebration.

The inside walls of the bell tower became radiant in their reflection as fine particles of dust started to swirl in a moving cloud of brilliance. It didn't fall like dust usually does, it moved in every direction at once till all the dust and lint that had ever found a spot up there seemed to be moving away from the other dust and fog, and then back again. Both priests witnessed what some might say was the kind of light God really liked in the Old Testament.

Initially, it was the most spectacular glow either priest had ever seen, and then they looked away and into the face on the end of Hammer's cane. The reflected light was so intense, shining back on all of the men, into their cameras, into their eyes, even through their closed eyelids. Everything seemed radiant, reflective — so much so, that one and all were blinded by the recherché of light and heat. This light demanded that they look at it, see through it, not look away, and forced the men to try to see more. The priests approached the event in much the same way as Lot may have done, looked into those wooden eyes, and waited it out.

Who would have thought the light would be magnified so many times over? Before they knew it, they were being damaged, assaulted in the face, injured, and couldn't look away. They had all been bathed in that intense ultra-glow for almost five minutes, before the sergeant major discovered he was being cooked and finally shouted at the top of his lungs, "TURN OFF THOSE LIGHTS, FOR CHRIST'S SAKE!"

It may have been against the law for the sergeant major to invoke such a cause, but those old habits were proving to be every bit of that and very hard to break. At his court martial, he instantly imagined his defense being that he was a victim of the moment, a circumstance, a reaction that was caused by the environment.

Maybe he could say instead of the word 'Christ,' what he'd said was 'state.' He was now dead, and he knew it.

The extension cables had to be unplugged out at the generator, and the generator operator had to be yelled at up close for him to hear anything. It was probably too late for some of the film packs, and it took thirty men, thirty minutes each, no matter where they had stood inside the place, for their eyes to begin adjusting back to the way they had been before the lights went on. They were all having trouble seeing again, there were black spots in their vision, and most were afraid to move, so they sat where they were. Those who were directly under the steeple took longer, because they had been more mesmerized when that ceiling exploded, so to speak, in white and blue light. Instead of looking away from the light, which was impossible, they stared into the reflections harder, to see deeper into them, if that makes any sense. Some of the staff worried out loud later that the entire film package might have been damaged by such brilliant light, and because the Kremlin itself had ordered it, they couldn't run the risk of failing. Everyone agreed in general that they should re-film what they could a second time just to make sure, but that would have to wait until later.

The black spot in their vision was dead center of their focus, true in every case, for every man inside the church, and they all agreed in unison that they couldn't see their parallel thumbs when they held them up in front of the face at arm's length. Most could see their knuckles, and none could see their thumbs. No matter what they looked at, they couldn't see dead center of it, couldn't see each other's eyes.

They had to wait it out, wouldn't be able to read for the time being, and couldn't find the wick on a candle if they needed to light it. The spots were shrinking to some degree as time passed, and they all agreed they needed to rest their eyes. There was one thing for sure, it would be a cold day in hell before they ever shined their lights up into a mosaic bell tower again.

Had they not turned off the power on that generator, some of the men could have been blinded for good, and besides all that, all of the soldiers agreed that their ears were also affected, and some were now partially deaf. There was no ringing or pain, just silence. Neither their sight nor their hearing was coming back very quickly. Some said it was improving slightly after an hour or so, but most impressive of all was the fact that neither Hammer nor Basil had been affected in the slightest. Both priests understood immediately that there was something seriously wrong with all the troops, but neither of them had any problems. A verifiable miracle, no doubt. Perhaps it was due to their particular location, the fact they were in the shadow of the huge confessional, or it was just a typical minor miracle people encounter off and on in daily life. The mere fact that they were both still alive proved that.

They didn't tell anyone, of course, and at one point Hammer was waving his arms out in front of himself as if he were trying to touch something, acting just shy of totally blind. He knew a number of the soldiers were standing a dozen steps away and were watching the two ragamuffins, but he didn't fully understand that they were practically blind and deaf. The soldiers were sliding into a panic.

Truth of the matter was, Hammer had eighty-two-year-old eyes, and they looked worse than they actually saw. Before Basil had arrived, he used to walk at night with his cane in hand for miles and miles, and could see in the dark, a secret he kept to himself. He had always consoled himself over his semi-nearsightedness by firmly believing that it was surely a fundamental fact of human life, that too much detail and clarity can be equal to, if not more painful than, looking at life through a slight fog. When it came to the five senses, he made up for the seeing deficiency with a thick pair of western-style glasses and a very powerful nose, exceptional taste buds, and his ears were ten times as good as ever.

Most of all, he had two specialties. One was being able to touch God in the Eucharist virtually every day, as few men ever do — and he believed that made him just shy of perfect. Second, he had been given the walking cane of all walking canes, a gift from his predecessor, to lean on, and it had gotten him to old age without him ever falling to the ground, never once. He might look like a pathetic old brown bag of human bones just piled in the corner, but there was truly a whole lot more to him. He also had a fresh pile of human curled there at his feet that was only twenty-eight and simply needed a little nourishment to pop back to normal. Besides the obvious, he could see that tiny niche not too far off to his right, where his western-style glasses were sitting safe and concealed. This was one of those occasions where being half blind was far better than being spot-on.

Basil caught on just as fast and decided that he would have a hard time hearing anything unless they yelled it at him. His hearing was almost cat-like, and he knew his eyesight was flawless, but there, too, he was not squinting for nothing. Anyone who checked on the priests saw two famished and impoverished creatures, blind and deaf, apparently getting ready to die. It was common for the soldiers to see everyone on the sidelines as either dead or preparing to die, and in this particular case, every single one of them had a number of new personal problems to deal with, and the night was still young for the enlisted.

Basil didn't know it, but he slept like a log and even snored at times, which sounded like a big sheep dog snorting after scaring off something out there in the night. Some of the soldiers were practically falling over each other, they were all so exhausted, most still couldn't see all that well, and they were practically yelling at each other to be heard. Many insisted that everyone should speak much louder for the time being. The idea of a dazzling light hurting the ears was actually never considered by any of the afflicted. It was, however, an absolute reality.

There had been a break in the action. Everything seemed ready for the morning, and all the cameras were loaded and primed. They had taken all the lights apart except for two and managed to get the extension cords wound up and back where they belonged without damaging anything. It took them a while to appreciate the truth about candles, and they had plenty burning here and there.

All of the men were told they should not talk about this to anyone just yet, that they would eventually be asked to write a report on the incident and measure their own progress once they could see the tip of a pencil. Every one of the men found himself there at the generator throughout the evening as the lighting assembly was reattached to the sides of the wagon, and each man had a new respect for the power of lights. They had unwittingly become test dummies, had actually experimented on themselves, and didn't even know they were testing anything until it was too late.

There was no telling how bad the damage was to each man, but most would have said they had good vision and good hearing when they woke up that day, and now they couldn't do either very well and may not be able to get by. They would surely know better at the break of day.

The church was empty of all their paraphernalia, except for two lights, the cameras and their bedrolls on the pew-seats. Everything was ready, everything had been tested, new fresh film, and they agreed they would only need two lights at the most if they needed them at all. They had discovered the lanterns and candles were more than enough. Gradually, the exhausted troops found their pews and backpacks, and in almost every case they were asleep before they got to the second letter of the word they couldn't read.

Each and every one had closed his eyes and hoped that when he woke in the morning he could see and hear the way he used to. As they all fell asleep, they blew out many of the candles, and the massive interior of the church fell silent. Hammer felt a peace wash over him that rivaled any he could recently recall, and he was instantaneously sitting there in the far distant past, his favorite spot in that first pew, praying his daily 'office,' his rosary, reading a book, way back before all the insanity began. Back when the people used to come, the families and all those services, all those seasons and celebrations. There had been beautiful times when he would find himself all alone, early in the mornings before Mass, sometimes late at night, all by himself, alone with his God, and it would be so quiet. Just like now.

At that very moment, Basil seemed to readjust his semi-fetal sleeping position and then belched out a four-note snore of successive pig noises, which seemed to obliterate the silence. With his nostrils staring straight into the bell tower, his mouth virtually a perfect fully open circle, he dry-throated those gasps straight into that giant echo chamber above. Instantly, all thirty Russian Red Army troops, no matter what their specialty, no matter where they were, were now on full alert and trying to pinpoint the location of the pig. The noise had echoed off the walls as one would expect in a church like this, from the baritone's distant solo, high in the choir loft, awakening the deaf.

There was no way that noise had been human, and none of the soldiers suspected either of the priests since they were both obviously sound asleep. Who would have ever guessed they were such competent fakers? Many of the men were still having trouble with their eyes, ears, and lack of sleep, but the intensely personal fact existed that each one of them had heard that noise, and that kind of sound was never intended for the inside of a church.

The wiser of the bunch decided it could have been a dog and it might be hiding somewhere inside the church, and the idea worked its way around the pews rapidly in very loud whispers. They teamed up in groups of four and five and started to search all the distant corners and behind everything that might hide such an animal. Some suggested it had to have been nothing more than a pig grunting for food near one of the open side doors, and they should track it down first thing in the morning and have ham for Easter Sunday.

The older senior sergeant major yelled out an order that they all be quiet and listen for a while; he said the last time he saw a live pig was months ago and it was rabid. A hush fell over the room again as all of the soldiers were now standing on top of the pew seats and being mute. They stayed that way for almost an hour, until they all got so tired they lay back down in the pews and fell asleep again, leaving not a single soul inside the building on guard.

The snoring began and rose in volume to a crescendo of thick ones and raspy ones, breath holders and almost indefinable gurgles, men with many nasal and throat problems trying to catch up on months of lost sleep. If ever a church had been filled with a finer all-male orchestration of snoring exhaustees, completely in tune with each other, only God knew where it was. It was not something one could compare to a concert by Mozart in E for example, or a Beethoven's 5th, because this concert was being conducted by a spirit not of this world, not of this consciousness.

Gradually, these ghastly and unearthly animalistic noises began to harmonize of a sort, to a mostly indefinable human creation of sound. It took a while for everyone to evolve into their own personal deep, dark, exhausted-soldier sleep, with each man becoming oblivious to the escalating volumes and subconscious competitions for the most audacious deep-throated, gut-wailing male sounds possible.

Hammer rustled the younger priest awake, which wasn't really necessary, and told him to listen. He wanted another human being to hear this noise, and Basil was suddenly aware that he was hearing something few men had ever heard. The only time he had ever slept in a room with a lot of other men was back at St. Michael's Seminary, where for one thing there were never more than ten men in the dorm, and seminarians didn't snore like this. This noise could wake the dead. They couldn't see a single other person in the entire church, and yet they knew they were all lying flat in the pews, probably on their backs, resting their heads on prayer books and snoring with all their might and vigor straight up at the ceiling.

High up in that fragile bell tower two small sections of mosaic tiles vibrated loose and crashed into pews and walkways, but no one screamed in pain. No one sat up, no one woke up, and the noise just continued. Once again, the church was being attacked, and she would have her revenge. Much like that unprecedented event a few hours before with the strobe lights, this unbelievable noise event was basically going unheard, except by the two clerics.

Perhaps no one would ever really know; both priests could hear it, but all the participants who were making it were one and all completely sound asleep, when suddenly there was this concussion of a commotion. This huge punctuation of noise. It was a sound the likes of which neither priest had ever heard before, the final note of the concert, off the keys, instantaneous and abrupt, incredibly loud, sharp, and then dead silence for another second.

It was as if someone had clapped gigantic hands together just behind their heads, in between their hairs and their skin, in that space that was left between those hairs on their side of the book. It's a hard place to define, but all thirty of them were there at that very same moment. They all hit that note they never thought they could, never thought they would, never knew they ever even tried. Most always did when they slept, and when they did hit that note together, the building exploded with a sound that only lasted a second, and no echo at all.

From Hammer's position in his distant corner, it appeared that all thirty soldiers were once again instantly standing on the pew-seats, one split second after that last snore note. Perfectly erect in their respective pews, scattered throughout the church, guns at the ready, and not a single one had any idea what had just happened.

One second before, or maybe three, every single one of them had been sound asleep, singing in the choir.

At first, there was a lot of eye talk, out-of-the-corner-of-the-eye talk, and then some head bobbing, until they were assuring each other that they for one were completely under control and no one else need worry about anything. The old sergeant major reminded them all of the rabid pig, and most of them managed to keep their balance pretty well, considering the time and everything they had done the day before. Around four in the morning, a private fell asleep sitting on the backrest of his pew, feet on the seat. He tumbled backward, heels over head, down into the kneeler. You could tell his head hit something solid. Everyone knows that sound; usually the neighbor's kid, slipping off the kneeler, smashing his chin into the top of the backrest and concluding the acrobatics with his head bouncing off the seat he should have been sitting in. He was sound asleep until the very end.

"FUCK ME!" he screamed. "Save me, save me, shoot that fucking pig, save me!"

In a burst of extraordinary courage, he lifted himself out from under the maze of the kneeler and onto the seat, flat on his back, exhausted but alive, and barely awake. No one was positive exactly where he was. The blood began to run down into his eyes and the corners of his mouth, and when he wiped his face with his hand all he could see was red all over everything. He shouted for the sergeant major.

"Sergeant Major, can you hear me?"

The sergeant major was standing in a pew about five pews back and told the young soldier that yes, indeed, he could hear him, and he just needed to stay calm.

"Sergeant Major, it got me, got me right between the eyes, and I wouldn't be a bit surprised if I don't die from rabies. Sergeant Major, can you hear me?"

"I hear you. I've got eyes, too, and no one capsized on Tuesday. This is the army, not the navy. What in the world are you talking about? Calm down, you idiot!"

CHAPTER 7

TIME FOR MASS

5:30 a.m. Easter Sunday Sunrise 1928

If there was one thing these two priests loved to do, it was celebrate the Mass. It had been against the law for many years now, and according to the colonel this early morning Mass would be the very last one ever said in the hallowed hall. The first one was said before the church was even finished in 1848, and that meant they were being honored like no other priests had ever been honored before.

"Father Karl Hammer. The most honored priest of them all."

Hammer was sure his plaque wouldn't say that, but that was how he felt. It had been festering in his mind since that first meeting on Thursday afternoon, and now he was only an hour or so away from the Eucharist. He and Basil had been spared up till now, first and foremost to say that sunrise Mass, exactly like it had always been celebrated in the past. It would be the last Mass, he would be the last priest, and that would end the story for now.

Not only that. It was all being filmed, recorded for all time, and since that were true, if nothing else, their faces might last as long as the film. There were still pictures of the church, of course, but no one had ever made a movie on the grounds.

Neither priest had ever seen a movie, much less one being made, but from their vantage point and lack of knowledge concerning such things, this particular operation seemed to have a number of unique problems Colonel Sokolov wasn't fully aware of. He had missed it all, as colonels often do, and would discover his film crew was half blind and deaf by five a.m., only moments away. He would also find the church was damaged to some extent, littered and perhaps infested with pig rabies.

The way Hammer figured it, the colonel would show up in the very near future, and the news would be bad, maybe even worse than he thought. The congregation might see the man lose control of himself; people might die. He might die — probably not yet, though; there was still the Mass.

Somewhere during the tour on Holy Thursday, Hammer had explained to the colonel exactly who he was, and noted the fact that he had been born just down the main road from this church; it was conceived with a cornerstone in 1846, and so was he. Sokolov already knew all that, had quite a dossier on the priest, with plenty of detailed notes, dating back to when he was born. The movie director considered the fact most interesting, and he would have loved to have known more, but time didn't permit.

Hammer had been named the pastor of St. Francis of Assisi on the first day of the new year in 1876, the thirtieth birth year for both he and the Church itself. His parents had worried about the boy coming home to preach in the town where he'd been born and raised, using the ancient gospel that talks about Jesus going back where he had come from as the example for why he should not. He took it slow, and the people ended up loving him all over again, and were glad to have him back from St. Michael's Seminary in Czechoslovakia.

Father Basil, his assistant, had been born on New Year's Day 1900, in the very first minute of the very first hour, deep in the heart of central Europe, while the entire world looked forward to a new century and perhaps a little less war and mayhem. That honeymoon time lasted about ten years, and then things seemed to slowly but surely dissolve back into chaos. By 1914, a terrible war had erupted in Europe, 'the war to end all wars,' but was nothing more than a testing ground for insanity, caused by and blamed on the Germans. All the while, The Communist Manifesto took roots in the minds of men, developed and led by Lenin, who took Russia out of the war. An idea conceived of and financed by the Germans themselves, who hoped for a different sort of outcome. Communism made sense in Russia, merely because it made more sense than what they had at the time in most cases, especially if it were shouted really loud. It found its cradle, its bosoms in the chaos of the Russian society, and very quickly took total control of the empire. In Russia, by 1920, it was against the law to believe in God because a new god had taken his place.

When Basil was 16, he disappeared into the seminary, into the piano, and into the Catholic understanding of God. In the summer after his eighteenth birthday, he began a long journey into Theology and a wide assortment of other disciplines, one of which was the Russian language. When his education was all said and done, at the age of twenty-five, his graduation assignment came out. Knowing that language appeared to be the main reason he was sent to Pfeiffer, a destination about which he and his closest friends joked in private that it might lead to his immediate martyrdom. God only knew why he had picked such an elective in the first place, when he could have just as easily picked English. There was a new God in Russia, a new understanding about the way men were to look at things, see things, and besides all that, the light bulb was just catching on. There was always so much to think about.

Basil received his first assignment: to travel to one of the last known Catholic Churches in the Soviet State of Russia. All he had in the file was a picture of this spectacular church, another of an old priest named Hammer, and a tragically sad story about an abandoned town called Pfeiffer. He also carried a personal letter from the director of the seminary to Father Hammer; they'd been classmates together back in the seventies, and he had been told stories about what those times were like. The old man needed help with a cross the Lord had shackled him with: being the caretaker of the last church. The old priest couldn't do it anymore. Basil's journey would involve traveling a little less than two thousand miles from St. Michael's Seminary in eastern Czechoslovakia, across Ukraine to the fertile Volga Basin in Southern Russia, simply to be old Father Hammer's last assistant. The word 'last' was a fact he had never even considered, hadn't seen it in the sentence the way he should have, and hadn't defined it quite right. Two of Basil's room-mates had noticed it on the first read, the word last, and their conversation evolved into a long play on words.

Edward was ordained a Catholic priest and said goodbye to all his friends and teachers at St. Michael's in 1925, headed east to Pfeiffer, Russia, and the Church of St. Francis of Assisi on the Ilava. The seminary had received the request courtesy of a letter from the First Secretary to the Premier of the Soviet State, a gentleman named Xander Aloysius Desch. Mr. Desch had guaranteed the young priest's safety once he entered Russia, would have all the necessary papers, and the seminary had no choice but to honor the request; after all, Father Hammer had received his education at St. Michael's sixty-some-odd years before. The seminary was ecstatic to discover that Hammer was still alive, as the request had pictures of the church and pictures of Hammer walking in the courtyards. Perhaps the Soviet State was coming to its senses and was turning over a new leaf, starting all over again on their attitudes about deities, one assistant pastor at a time. St. Michael's had plenty more where this first one had come from, if that indeed turned out to be the case.

The convoy of headlights heading for the church aroused the congregation, and the sleepless troops mustered themselves for an early morning formation. The sergeant major had his cripples at 'parade rest' until the colonel had exited his command car, at which time he called the troops to attention. Their reactions were directly proportional to how badly their hearing had been damaged, and their squints up and down the line confirmed who could see and who couldn't. The sergeant major was afflicted with both, and would try to hide it as best he could; more blind than deaf, and shattered in his soul that he woke up this way. No matter where he looked, no matter which eye, he saw a perfectly round black spot that took out the face of a man standing five feet away. If that man spoke in a normal voice, he couldn't hear him. He had hoped that things would be better this morning, but they were not, not for him or any of his men. He was partially blind and partially deaf, and there would be no place for him in the army by the end of the day if anyone found out, and he knew they would.

When the colonel had left the area the night before, everything had been explained in rough-cut detail; nothing out of the ordinary, except they would probably need the additional lights for the indoor filming simply because the church didn't have anything except for candles and the sun wouldn't be up yet. The Diamond Teardrop would be preserved on film for posterity. Six cameras were scattered about the church, modern lighting, professional direction — a guaranteed success.

The colonel had already explained to the priests what he expected from them, and primarily he stressed that this final Mass should and would be said to the best of their ability, exactly like normal. He'd insinuated that their lives depended on it. He had his orders and understood his assignment, and hoped they understood theirs. His people were very busy, and would be ready for the two priests when they walked out onto their stage. There was nothing about all this that should have caused the film crew any problems, and he couldn't imagine the priests having any trouble with what was expected of them.

All of that, unfortunately, was the original plan, but things had happened while he was away, and now the situation required leadership and direction with a sharp eye on the clock.

"What in the name of God is going on here?"

He tilted his head a little and looked close into the sergeant major's bloodshot eyes. Those eyes flashed forward to the court martial again, and he thought that perhaps he could float along on the coattails of the colonel for having suggested something about God at a military formation. The word was just not allowed, and the sergeant major was incapable of coming up with a prompt answer, wasn't sure he had heard the whole question, and never got a good look at the colonel, except out of the corner of his eye.

Without a moment's pause, the colonel stood on his tiptoes, and with the back pleats of his pants firmly grasped in his fists, screamed at the top of his might, "WHAT IN THE NAME OF GOD IS GOING ON HERE?"

With that, the sergeant major slumped a tad lower, now knowing that they were both dead, but instead of answering, he motioned for the colonel to follow him up the steps and into the main foyer. The colonel had no choice, as the sergeant major was already five steps away, slightly below his usual robust manner.

There was a good reason why he was a sergeant major, and most officers seem to understand by the ends of their careers that sergeant majors are often times well worth following and listening to, and they are the most in-charge when necessary. Lower ranking enlisted men, draftees and the sideline public learned that lesson on the first try with this sergeant major, but those glorious days were probably over now.

Still sitting in that same corner, the priests had what proved to be the best seat in the house for watching the colonel enter that mezzanine. They both pretended to have sight and hearing issues, and there was no order to stand, so they didn't.

The sergeant major relinquished his command to his third subordinate, a staff sergeant who was obviously much less impaired, and the man began the explanation for the mess. The whole time he was waiting for permission to speak, he kept cautiously looking at the corners of the room and the walkways with his weapon very much at the ready. He was finally allowed to begin, and so he began.

"Sir. First of all, heaven forbid, there might be a rabid pig loose in the church somewhere, sir, a big one. We were all, all of us, everyone, almost blinded last night, testing the lights. When the lights lit up the inside last night, they were facing the ceiling that we've later discovered reflects candlelight a thousand times over. It was unbelievably intense and bright, the likes of which none of us had ever seen before, and you couldn't look away, nowhere to hide. No matter where we looked, there was blinding light, through our closed eyelids and through our fingers; it was all we had. For me, it lasted a minute, for others, two minutes, and for some, I don't know. Those three men standing there by the wall are evidently blind, and those two on that bench are deaf. Our eyes, sir, they're damaged, and we see a black spot wherever we focus. Black spots and a silence in our ears.

"It was the generator outside, over there, too loud, and they couldn't hear us when we shouted for them to turn it off. I ran out there, and that's why I can see a little better, hear a little better, and I'm not as bad as many of the others. Sergeant Major is injured, and so is everyone else who stayed in the church. They were under that light for at least a few minutes — four, five, who knows? — before it shut down. Loud, bright, hot, you know? Not only that, but all of us have hearing problems. Our ears are damaged, it's bad, and you need to yell at people for them to hear. Not you, sir, but everyone else needs to yell at each other if they want to communicate. If you tell me to, I can yell at them for you. Just yell at me.

"Early this morning the pig came in. We couldn't see very well, but everyone heard it. And if we could hear it, you should hear it without any problem. We ruled out dogs because of the sound it made. You know the sound that rabid pigs make? Sir! We may have scared it off, because we haven't seen it since. It may have bitten Demburusky right on top of his head on the way out, we're not sure, but we'll sure keep an eye on him. Demburusky is a real dumb fuck, and we can't figure out why the pig picked him unless that's what pigs do.

"Something else happened, sir, but I don't know what it was. I must have been asleep, but it sure enough woke me up and everyone else besides. No one is sure of anything except the pig part."

He was through with his briefing and backed away, hoping his role was over. It wasn't even close. The close-quarter question-and-answer period had just begun.

There were at least two eyes and two ears working well, they were definitely wide open, and they belonged to the colonel. The only personal capability he had over everyone else, he thought and knew, was his innate ability to comprehend things faster than your average bear. It was an old saying for Russians, 'smarter than your average bear,' and he always prided himself in knowing that he was just that. However, that talent wasn't working very well at the moment, nor was his ability to speak. He checked his watch and wanted to know what time sunrise was.

It was time to get going, or at least headed in the direction of that altar. He could hear more about last night as they got themselves together. He had to design an entrance procession with whatever talent was available, and had no trouble with the yelling part. The colonel glanced at the two squinting priests and motioned for them to follow him as he turned and walked off a few steps alone. He turned and noticed that neither of them had moved a muscle. It wasn't enough of a motion for them to see, or so they pretended. With that, the colonel took four steps across the floor and locked his heels, towering directly over their heads and peering down at the two kneeling faces. He was just shy of boiling and had his leg pant pleats firmly in his grasp.

"CAN YOU HEAR ME?"

And even before they could nod that they could hear, he clarified his question with, "CAN YOU SEE ME?"

Hammer immediately reached out his hands to the colonel as he tried to stand, and the colonel instinctively reached down and helped the old man to his feet, firmly grasped the right hand and took hold of that wrist with his left. The cane seemed useless and almost in the way, pinched between the old man's bicep and resting against his cheek, after which the old priest took his left hand and gently covered the three gripping hands in a gesture of unity until he was standing tall. He had stumbled and teetered a tad, which caused their many grips to clamp as you would expect.

It was as if they had both dipped their hands in a bowl of water before this expression of assistance and the colonel was equally instinctively keeping his toes out of the rainfall long ahead of the rationale as to why it was even happening. The toes were spit shined and slightly dusty already, and they sure didn't need this. It takes time, at times, for the mind to flip-flop back and forth from one unexplainable phenomenon to another, one after another, but unexpected dripping wet hands is generally a personal attention getter no matter what else is going on.

Hammer began to explain that he could only hear so well in the first place, before all of this, and now it was worse, of course, but he could, in fact, hear him just a little. The colonel was totally aggravated by the fact he had touched the old man to begin with, was now dripping, for some reason, and was being flooded with all this bullshasheska, but had to concur and found himself nodding in agreement that it was, of course, worse.

The entire time he was explaining the hearing side of the issue, Hammer was wiping his hands off on the tattered bottom edge of his cassock, apparently leaning against the cane as if it were the top of a spear that was embedded three feet down in the rock.

As the colonel was comprehending all this, he tried to decide the most basic of geometric logic, the mathematical logic of exactly what he saw in that lean, a fundamental and basic impossibility. The way the old man was doing it, not holding the cane with either hand, there was absolutely no reason in the world why he shouldn't fall over immediately and completely onto his face. A mind-boggling bend, and just another something else to consider at the moment. It was not even close to how one uses a cane, and even though he had his basic education in photography, he knew a fucking thing or two about engineering. This was either the epitome of illusion, impossible, a parlor trick, or a miracle. And then it was over, with the old man standing straight up. He would have to save that question and answer for later, because the wet one just wouldn't go away.

As Basil stood up on a slippery wooden tongue-in-groove floor, he too seemed very preoccupied with his hands. Those were the same kinds of hands as on the old priest, and the colonel realized he had just moments before held them tight in his grip, and there was nothing to wipe his on, nothing without everyone noticing, that is. There they hung by his side, and he could feel the drips and the drops off every fingertip on both hands. He sometimes wore gloves, but never on the set — it was very unprofessional — but he decided it was a wonderful time to break that old habit and start something new.

It was a very sad internal revelation at that instant, when he realized the priests had been sitting in their own piss water for the past so many hours; make that fermented piss water. That was piss water all over his hands. That was piss water that had, in fact, landed on his spit-shined boots. That was piss water on his thumb and first finger that had so uncontrollably wiped the corners of his lips and then twisted his mustache when he told them not to; he had forbidden it as it was happening, tried to stop it, but they did it anyhow. He had tried to forget during those early sensations of figuring out what could be so wet that when his nose sensed and warned of the urine, he didn't want to believe it. He had tried to think quickly of other possible explanations for why there would be that particularly disgusting fermented smell of urine, but there it was, no doubt. Strong, close, very close. Unfortunately, now he knew that it would be there a while, the aroma of urine, lingering, perhaps embedded deep into the hairs just under his nose, and there was nothing he could do about that. He needed a hankie.

Without any hesitation, Hammer started another exposé on his eyesight and began to tell how he was legally blind and had lost his glasses some time ago, and that was why he needed the young assistant priest, Basil. Couldn't do this without him. Basil and the cane, that is. The cane was his indispensable crutch and Basil was his eyes, and that was before all of this. He could barely see in the first place, as the colonel was well aware, before all this, and now it was worse, of course, but he could, in fact, see him just a little. Once again, the director was nodding his agreement, and it was getting late or early, one or the other, whatever.

There was a significant deadline for this filming, and it had been understood by everyone that it was a one-take production. If the Kremlin and those monsters in charge back in Moscow had in fact ordered this production, and someone would see it in less than a month, like all the other war footage, Father Hammer, Father Basil and Colonel Sokolov would live on forever, and not necessarily in that order. No excuses, one chance only, it had to happen, and happen right. His gloves were never intended to by slid on over dripping wet hands, but he finally managed to get them on with the help of his teeth. That too was an instinct, and the deed was over before he had time to stop. His tongue told him he had not thought it through.

Having come along for the ride, evidently, the man in the tailored suit, Xander Aloysius Desch, was back and was flanked by other officers standing some distance away from the colonel and his priests. They acted like mid-level officers and were taking notes of things the gentleman was saying, and were constantly whispering into his ears on either side. They were explaining what had happened and that the investigation into the blinding and the deafening light episode was just under way.

Whispered or not, Hammer heard every word they said, and he heard the secretary tell one of his assistants that he wanted to be in the first pew, right next to the center aisle, in the very front. He hoped that someone would suggest to this production team that there would be absolutely no more yelling after those entrance bells chimed. It wasn't exactly a suggestion, wasn't exactly whispered, and within only minutes the church was back to being relatively silent.

The old man nodded a thankful nod across the foyer and closed his eyes for a moment after making the sign of the cross on himself. The gentleman was expected, and so was his intervention. The whisper may have been intended for just the pastor and his own assistants, but whispers that loud have intended consequences, and every ear in the place was struggling to hear anything from that point on.

The colonel heard that request and turned to acknowledge the whisperer, and also nodded his approval. The secretary's assistants had learned over time that any time this man had a request, said he didn't want to miss anything, suggested anything, or opened his mouth at all, it should be noted and acted on immediately. It was usually exactly what he meant or needed. He stood there being innocuous and private, not interfering, and staring into the old man's eyes from thirty feet away. Basil joined the stares and read the dignitary's lips.

"I don't want to miss a single thing this morning. This is a church, and it's their stage until their service is over. Then and only then, will the Soviet State have her way with it. We will respect that idea as best we can, and I don't want to miss a thing. I want to see the Diamond Teardrop, and so do all of you. I promise you, one and all, YOU want to see that miracle."

His assistant reminded him that the priests would be speaking in Latin, or so he had been told, and wondered if they were going to order the priests to say the Mass in Russian. No one would understand it otherwise. He was told the young priest had a book, called it a 'rocket,' and it had a Russian translation in red under every one of their prayers in Latin. Basil told him it was the only one, and if someone wanted to follow along, they could use the rocket.

Desch walked up to the rookie, reached out with a hand to shake and a hand for the book. He handed it to the secretary, and the man rifled through the thousand pages with a respectful thumb. Evidently, he wasn't the first.

"Used to have one of these myself. Ever heard from St. Michael's?"

Desch winked, not needing a response. He wasn't whispering anymore, and had managed to make eye contact with almost every set of eyes in the room as he crossed it. He raised his chin and looked at the face of the man hanging on the cross above the altar, on the other side of the enormous room, turned his vision to the dark glass behind the crucifix and pointed to an area in the upper left-hand corner, where Jesus' mother was looking down. He started to speak, louder than normal but still respectful. They could hear him all over the place, and had waited for this very moment all along. Now they would know what to do, to look for, to expect. They needed guidance; the procession had a long way to go from the back of the church to the front. It was almost time, so he said the last words and made his move.

"That's where the Diamond Teardrop will come from, up in that corner, out of that lady's right eye, sometime during the Mass. Latin is the language of this church; I thought everyone understood that when they entered a place like this. Why wouldn't a person want to understand and speak Latin if one wanted to be a Catholic in this place? If you understand Latin, you know Spanish, French, Italian, and many others. If you don't know Latin, then none of this matters and all everyone here needs to do is watch this celebration, wait for the miracle, PROFESSIONALLY. Film the entire service and try to be fair and balanced, respectful like the fox, from a distance.

"One of the reasons this place is empty is because the ancient ones insisted on listening to the sermons in German and not Russian. Even though the message is exactly the same in either language, they insisted, they insisted, they insisted until push came to shove. For those of you who have never seen this Catholic Mass before, I encourage you to memorize it, for you may never ever see it again. This is historic, very historic, and we should try hard not to fuck this up. Excuse my vulgar word, Father Hammer, it won't happen again. Quiet, please, so that they can project their message to the cameras. We sure wouldn't want their message obscured with some irrational outburst, and I hope what I just now said was captured on film, as the one and only warning anyone will get on the subject. They must use the language of their church, and use it as loud as they wish. Louder, if they wish. The louder, the better, one last time. We are about to watch an extinction of sorts, the end of the amount of time for things, the last time for something very special."

With that, he managed to make eye contact again throughout the seating area and along the two sides, and there was no such thing as rank, it was his eyes and their eyes, comrade to comrade. He politely bowed to the colonel and the rest of his cast.

"Father Hammer, I will make sure this Mass is immortalized in the annals of Soviet history. Father Basil, you are young, and perhaps there's more to your destiny then just getting here. My condolences to you both for your choices, and may this memory live on. Try not to be too angry. Colonel Sokolov, the stage is yours."

Desch walked up the center aisle to that first pew on the left side in the very front and wasn't quite sure how he had gotten there. He had spent his entire life trying to be sophisticated and flawless, dignified and respected. There he stood, before God's altar, an avowed Communist, Secretary to the Premier. His entire youth and upbringing were now an enigma, and what they thought they knew about him was anything but what he really was. If he continued with what he was doing, he could accomplish a great deal someday, from the inside out. He wasn't sure what that would be, but for now it had all come down to this center-aisle walkway. He had walked this very same walk in other similar places thousands of times before, and then it was over. He hadn't done it since.

Before this time, before all this change, this promised change, this fundamental change, he had made commitments on previous walks that never needed to be evaluated again. Like walking out of Pineland and being able to brag about having been there and done that. For a man like him, every one of those steps had been taken before, under different circumstances and far different lighting, and now he felt as if he had been swallowed and his only chance was to stay up near the serpent's head and not tumble into its belly; everything from there on out was nothing but shit. He had to hang on, to cling to the sides of its gullet, and perhaps in time he could somehow or another choke it to death from the inside out.

He knew quite clearly what the serpent called itself and the rationale behind its conquest of the world, and he knew it was evil and would stop at nothing. He could not make mistakes. He thought about that a lot and found himself trying to refrain from saying, 'Amen,' at the end of the thought at times. Just a whispered

'Amen' in the wrong circles could mean the end of a well-made plan. He felt like he was having a headache, but it didn't hurt; God had come back into his brain.

Desch was anxious and started to feel as if he had done all those ears out there a favor by insinuating and demanding that they should be respectful. They may not know where they were, but he did. It was his turn to practice what he had been preaching, and he had a swimming sensation in his own reality, standing there at the entrance to his pew. He was instantly back to understanding that he didn't matter at all, nothing he did mattered, nothing he would ever do would matter, not in the long run. Not in the mind and the reality of that man on the cross. Even though he had never forgotten what he firmly believed, it had been a while since he had found himself in this exact position, and there were times in his nights when he wondered if he'd ever find this spot again. They were hard to come by, and all he had to do now was enter that pew.

Every eye in the room had just watched him get to that spot, every ear had heard everything he said, and out of respect he stood there a moment and looked up into the corner. From the back of the church, the entrance procession had watched him glide up the aisle, and when he got there, damned if he didn't genuflect perfectly to the right knee, rose and bowed his head while stepping into that first seat.

He sat like an uncomfortable log, wanting to kneel, but he managed to keep himself under control except for that brief and inexplicable failure of genuflecting before he entered, and it did not go unnoticed. Those old habits have a way of rearing their ugly ancient heads no matter how hard we fight them. He had actually genuflected in all his secretarial dignity. So what, he thought. They were all somewhat confused as it was, and it could be explained away as undoubtedly part of the charade, or so he would wink if anyone asked. He opened the rocket and started to read. The sergeant major saw him do it and was beginning to think that the entire unit was likely to end up being court-martialed together, and they would just have a mass execution after this mass of thanksgiving.

With the secretary firmly planted where he wanted to be, the colonel finished up a number of directives and had everyone lined up in the vestibule awaiting his direction for the cameras to roll.

He had been cautioned by his assistants that there were not enough candles glowing to guarantee their success, but the colonel told them all that he understood all that, but it was necessary for the effect. There would be plenty of light when they needed it, but the beginning would be somewhat dimly lit.

It was an absolutely insulting processional entrance. Four very imposing security guards followed the two priests, who followed the colonel, who followed four more guards. They were all very on-guard about something resembling a pig, and the cameras were rolling in the dim light from the candles. There were in fact enough.

They were one and all explicitly looking hard and fast for anything that resembled a large, bloodthirsty rabid pig that had been known to attack sleeping soldiers. Probably a massive forest boar, insane from the rabies, on a rampage in the house of God. Who could have possibly imagined that?

Father Hammer stumbled along in the middle, hanging on Basil's right arm and leaning on his cane with the other. Basil had managed to secure the entrance cross and held it high above his head with his left hand. Hammer found himself surrounded by younger men, tapping his cane loudly with every step, like the sounds of seconds on a grandfather clock, one after another, until he was in the absolute middle, dead center of his church.

The old man couldn't help himself and would never be able to explain his actions, and few people would be interested in it for long, but he might suggest that his cane had caught the corner of a pew. When they were all exactly half way up the center aisle, this somber little old man launched himself above his cane head as if he were a cat, thirty inches off the tiles, and screamed, "WHAT'S THAT?"

The colonel was a few strides farther up, and he too seemed to frantically propel himself into the air, spinning at the same time, pleats in palms, landing on the floor facing Hammer as he screamed back, "WHAT'S WHAT?"

No one could have possibly known what that simple question would inspire. Granted, it was a very loud question, considering how quiet things were at the time, and granted, the aerobatics might have been extreme, to say the least. Just the same, it had an instantaneous reverberation that prevented Hammer from answering the second question.

All of the guards instantly sprang into their version of a panicked guard, scouring the floor and the empty pews for the hog. Actually, the panicked part applied to everyone, and they were still in the first second. In the second second there was a great deal more screaming, and finally, after all that time had expired, the corner area by the north side door erupted in gunfire as four machine guns obliterated two shadows and a beautiful statue of an archangel who was praying at the foot of the Blessed Mother. They never had a chance. The shadows were gone, and the angel had simply gone back to heaven by the time the half-minute moment arrived.

Hammer and Basil were the only two persons left standing as the gunfire spread to the outside of the church and up and down the river bank. The sergeant major was lying flat on his back in the eighth pew on the north side, a spot his momma had always liked in a different lifetime, and was screaming "CEASE FIRE, CEASE FIRE," at the ceiling. He wasn't hard to hear at all if your ears still worked.

That command spread rapidly, and before long all of the soldiers were back to where they had been before the question, and things were regrouping back to the way they were a minute ago, except for the addition of the smoke from the eighty-bullet barrage. Fortunately, the wind was blowing some of it out the shattered windows behind the statue of Mary, and unfortunately, the double side-door and all of its framing assembly, including elaborate holy water troughs, were now fifteen feet out on the north side of the church. Much of the smoke was now trapped in the ceiling, and a fog of gunpowder smoke had thoroughly obscured everything above the head of Christ on his cross behind the altar.

"DID YOU GET HIM?"
"DID YOU GET HIM?"

There was no immediate answer, other than the muffled, "Locked! Locked, locked, locked," as the four 'grossfater' machine gunners chanted to each other and took their weapons offline. All four of their tumblers were empty, which was the way the Russian infantry generally operated during firefights, and just supposing for a moment that it was the pig they'd shot, it would be hard to find even a nibble of its bacon in the rubble. If it were rabid, the gunfire would have spread rabid pig guts out all over everything, and this entire place would have to be abandoned immediately, and just like with smallpox, be burned to the ground.

The colonel and all of his staff were now confronted with a serious new question, and none of the shooters seemed too interested in finding out if there was a dead pig in the rubble or not.

There was more gunfire outside, sporadic at first, then more intense as if dozens of rifles and machine guns were engaged with each other or something, and if that something was a pig, it didn't sound like he had much of a chance. Soldiers could be heard shouting at each other near every door to the place; it appeared something worth killing had been seen, and it had run off to the north.

For a while, the shouting and shooting had stopped, and then it started again on the far end of the abandoned town, down near the second well, not even north. Whatever happened down there included loud explosions, until finally that, too, stopped. Everyone was waiting for everyone else, asking each other what had happened and telling each other what they knew. It was pure bedlam.

The cameramen were regaining their composure, and every lens was on the colonel. He looked at his watch and discovered they had only lost a few minutes. This whole production was still a go. He was still in charge, and would have to do something about the smoke as soon as possible. He thought for a moment about executing the guards who'd fired first, but not until they were sure they hadn't killed the pig. He was daydreaming and imagining new scenarios as the minutes passed. Damned pigs, he thought.

The procession was about to begin again, and the colonel found himself right alongside Desch, up close to the altar. It was a brand new celebration. Everyone was still breathing fast and looking at the altar through a thick bank of gun smoke.

Up and down the side aisles, standing in a swarm on the back side steps of the altar and acting like sweepers, dozens of soldiers in the typical light brown uniform of the day had almost immediately managed to design a method for blowing the smoke out the doors and windows. Each man was holding two large slates that had a surface with five equal columns and rows, resembling a tic-tac-toe board, only bigger, and it was obvious to all the soldiers that the Catholics must have used them for some sort of church service. There were stacks and stacks of them in a closet, and a barrel full of tokens that fit in the slots so well some were still stuck from the last time they'd prayed, which must have been years ago.

As the junior officers were trying to get the air flowing, they created a technique whereby each soldier had a tablet in each hand, and four or five of them would act like a single squad. At the command of 'whoosh,' just that group would 'whoosh' the air in a favored direction. It caught on quick, and before long there were 'whooshes' all over the place. 'Whooshes' in groups of three was a favored technique. It was important for the soldiers in each cluster to be in harmony with each other, pushing the air to somewhere up above.

It was obvious what the Catholics had done with the tablets that proved to be perfect for what the soldiers needed. These Catholics were notorious for saying the same prayer over and over, the same Mass over and over; they did everything they did over and over, and these tablets proved it. Evidently everyone would get a tablet, a pail full of tokens, and like their rosary, they would say some sort of a monotonous prayer until the tablet was full. There was surely no secret here.

The 'whooshing drill' was based on a technique they were experimenting with throughout the military in an effort to get the mustard gas out of their bunkers, and that drill had a ten-second deadline. It was reported that some men could wave their arms so fast around their face when they tasted mustard gas that it appeared they were hovering for a time.

Even though he didn't possess two tablets, the colonel mimicked those who did and encouraged them to 'whoosh' harder, faster; time was short. He was glaring at Hammer with a cold steel gaze that insinuated he knew the old man was playing games.

"My old eyes must have been playing tricks on me," said the old man. "Rabid pigs are very nasty. I'm afraid of RABID pigs. They don't think right."

That was an understatement, and everyone already knew that, knew that the pigs were the most disgusting animals that roamed the back woods. They ate everything, ate dead people, dead dogs, dead anything. That's how they got rabies. And when they were rabid, they were absolutely terrifying.

Everyone relaxed when a soldier near the shootout area came into view and said there was no blood anywhere, and nothing had died that he could see. With that bold news, the entrance procession continued. It was somewhat reminiscent of ancient entrance rituals when the church celebrated the military. Not this one, of course; it was purely a state of mind and recollection for anyone thinking such thoughts. There was no telling how they would edit it, but Hammer was fairly sure the colonel's reaction would end up on that cutting floor the colonel always talked about, or at least parts of it would.

The colonel had finally found the hankie he was so desperately looking for, a pocket to hide it in, and he realized if he were ten feet tall he would need it for the smoke. He saw himself daintily holding the gentile white linen just under his nose, preventing him from inhaling the smoke. Then he thought about exactly why he had the hankie and why he had the smoke.

He was beginning to really dislike this priest, but he only had an hour more before this scene was over and a new one would begin. He could go back to his old form, his less gentile side; he had to keep the piss-stained hankie for later. He'd had worse things in his pockets in the past, and had decided it would be a lovely parting gift. He hoped to be able to remember to give it to Hammer when this opening scene was all over. Perhaps Hammer could use it to keep the smoke out of his mouth when scene two started.

The communion railing, which seemed to be their destination, was a work of art that ran completely across the front of the altar, with a passage through the middle. The guards turned left and right when they came to that first step up. The colonel took the step in stride, positioned himself directly in front of the altar itself and came to attention, his back to everyone. The lighting could have been better. There were cameras humming and running, but no lights other than a few candles. It was all part of his plan. Majestically, he turned to face his audience.

"We need light. We must have light." And he laid his arms out to the sides and then upwards. No one heard a word he said except the new guys, and there weren't many of them — mostly guards, and they didn't do candles.

The two priests were still standing at the communion rail, squinting at the image before them. From their point of view, some fifteen feet away, the colonel appeared to be the devil himself.

The devil looked down and told the young priest in a very calm and collected voice, "Light all these candles behind me and start your preparations."

The colonel had been playing Shakespeare, or at least the Russian version of some such playwright, and was on one of his own fantasy stages as they had marched in. Everyone on the crew knew the colonel had the propensity to almost instantly turn into Maurice Chivalavichia at the drop of a hat. So far, he had managed to be the center point figure in virtually every documentary the unit had made.

He looked at the main camera and over the head of the young priest, so that the camera would barely hear his command. The camera barely did, but Basil didn't at all, and would have gotten the award for the best deaf actor of the year if they had such a thing.

It was one of those moments when the colonel was the gifted director, and not the stern colonel of the Southern Army Film Detachment 12 to the Headquarters Regiment. In this scene that he had so masterfully directed with no rehearsal and no script other than the one in his head, with his simple commands, and him as the lead actor and director, the critics would surely recognize his talent. This scene would become a theatrical enlightenment as soon as the candles all around him started to glow. He hadn't looked down just yet from whatever it was he was looking at in the middle of the church roof, and for a humble moment, he felt this one introduction might make him a cinema legend all by itself. There would be fame in his future; his casual commanding demeanor was now on record. The setting — the backdrop of a truly magnificent church and altar. It would all be so perfect as the light became more intense.

With just the right touch, at just the right moment, he lowered his chin and opened his eyes to nothing. It was still dark. Basil hadn't moved, and yet the clock sure had. The scene was ruined.

"CUT, CUT, CUT, CUT. LIGHT THESE DAMN CANDLES!"

He was turning in a complete circle, holding his heels in place as he forced his toes in both boots to the right in chunky little jerks. Once again, he had hold of his rear area, and this pirouette he was spinning had ancient roots. Most of the cameras could be heard shutting down, except for the guy way in the back; he actually filmed the magnificent altar from a respectful distance, through no fault of his own, as two dozen candles resumed their death spiral.

Basil was a candle-lighting fool at times, and was done quickly. No one could believe how glorious the backdrop all became as all those thick wicks enhanced everything.

That was the way the altar and church were designed. An incredible stained-glass display adorned the entire eastern end of the holy place. At their highest points, some thirty feet up, the three completely separate fascia's merged into the one thought, that almighty image, while the ceiling in that area seemed to disappear into a cloud. It was truly one of a kind, masterful if not pure genius, while all the stories in the glass were simply awe-inspiring.

Anyone who found themselves there that morning knew there was a clock involved in the whole affair. You could already see a faint glow as the eastern mountain peaks started to show those very early signs and edges. The early morning was coming soon, or at least out the side windows it was.

The cloud of gun smoke was thick up high in the ceiling, but it was seeping out slowly somewhere and would probably be gone by show time. The colonel stood there, staring up into the rafters, wondering about the timing. He wished that a number of the windows up there in the distant corner could be opened to let the smoke out faster, but that wouldn't happen until later. He debated shooting them out, but was afraid of what might happen, once again with that memory of the last time still ringing in his ears.

CHAPTER 8

THE LAST MASS

For just about every area in the valley, sunrise was in and around 6:30 or so, depending on which mountain peak to the east was in the way. In the case of St. Francis and its particular location, Easter Peak itself, a spectacular pentacle-peaked mountain ten or so miles off to the east, was the highest obstacle preventing the sun rays from finally blasting through those church windows. When it finally did rise, it appeared that the sun came up off the tip of the highest peak, and in the old days it would be at that moment when the noise began. The people inside would be seeing the teardrop, and the people outside would be watching the sun rise; people a few miles away could hear it.

It didn't happen that way every year, mind you, but this season it worked out that way. It had to do with the fact the Easter season was actually more in tune with the cycles of the moon rather than the sun, incredibly complex, but evidently understood by the Communist Historical Site Community. You could see the Volga River from up there on top of Easter Peak, and if a raindrop fell on the other side of that mountain, it ended up in the Volga. If the raindrop landed on the Pfeiffer side, it ended up in the mighty Don River.

"Usually in the early sevenishes."

That's what Hammer used to call it in the old days. "Sevenish." It was all part of the plan, and on Easter Sunday morning the sun would peek above that mountaintop and shine in those windows, creating the momentary appearance of the Diamond Teardrop. The sun shone in those windows every morning as a matter of rotation, and the trick seemed to be the timing of the consecration. That was where the elegance came in, and Hammer used to love to try to coordinate everything so that when he held that sacred host high above his head on Easter Sunday mornings, in front of that anxious throng, as he did so, the sun would explode through the windows and there would be that optical illusion of the Diamond Teardrop. His congregation would begin to scream, sing, sign themselves and thank God in all forms of different traditions and postures. They pulled blades of grass, leaves off trees, small pebbles as reminders of the moment. The spontaneous praise would spread to those outside and wander down the roads for an hour.

He was an artist, a priest, a holy man, a magician, and he took advantage of everything the Lord provided. Someone else had designed it all, built it, planned and envisioned it all, leaving him as nothing more and nothing less than the current conductor, a title he had worn for quite some time. This would be his last performance, and as God seemed to wish, it would be filmed and hopefully survive all this chaos for the glory of God Almighty. Everything he did was for the glory of God, which ended up being a good thing.

One of the men who had been involved with all this from the very beginning, Secretary Xander Desch, promised there would be at least two copies made. The secretary gave it away that he was still very much a closet Catholic, thinking it needed to be confessed to Hammer, and laid it in between the lines of their brief conversations. His ancient confessor could see the need, heard the confession, kept all the secrets and forgave him his sins, also in between the lines.

They hadn't seen each other in over twenty years, with that last time being at the baptism of the secretary's son at this very altar. He left for Moscow not long later. Desch had come from one of the pioneer families of Pfeiffer and had been born into a clan that was as Catholic as Catholic could be. The leader of the 'Headhunters' had always been a Desch man. Hammer was their confessor and heard their admissions in great detail, forgave them, encouraged them, generation after generation, until there weren't any left, except for one.

After all these years, he could still see those headhunter lips, telling those stories through the screen in the confessional. Acts of retribution that redeemed the community's honor by eliminating a threat, or other actions that had to be done to protect the Church and her clergy far and wide. They were the community's secret private knights, highly mobile and heavily armed, the judges, juries and executioners when necessary, and when they were gone the Communists came in, took their place without the cross at their backs, and destroyed it all.

Hammer actually had no idea what was in store for himself, his assistant, or the rest of the world for that matter, but he did know that it appeared he would be allowed to perform the holy sacrifice of the Mass one last time in his beautiful church. That had always been his prime objective in life, to say Mass each and every day, and he had always understood that the people needed him to do what he loved to do. At least he hoped his Catholics did, and there weren't any of them left.

In this last case scenario, none of them would be in attendance, but he would pray for them when that time came in the Mass. If there was actually anyone in the audience paying attention the way Catholics do, he would pray for them, too, but he would do it in Latin. They wouldn't understand a word he said, no one ever did, which meant he could say anything he liked and they'd never know the difference. He smiled ear-to-ear inside his mind and resolved to say it the ancient way. In a month or so, someone in Moscow would be watching this, and if they knew anything about the Roman Catholic Mass, they would discover that the first two readings in Latin were not part of any Catholic liturgy, but a statement from an old priest who knew the truth and told them so to their faces. His young prodigy had learned the lesson from the get-go.

Colonel Sokolov was finally able to bring himself back from a disastrous first scene. He stood at the foot of the altar and realized it was now time for act two of scene one. He could cut out the bad parts of the first shots and continue from here.

"I would like for the two of … I WOULD LIKE FOR THE TWO OF YOU TO PROCEED WITH WHATEVER IT IS YOU NEED TO DO TO GET READY FOR YOUR MASS. DO IT NOW. I'LL WAIT FOR YOU TO SHOW YOURSELVES IN YOUR SEASONAL VESTMENTS. NOW!"

It was testing his patience to remain so gentile all this time.

That was the noise Hammer had been waiting to hear. That command to "Say Mass!"

He bowed to his master and hunched even farther towards the floor, leaning hard on his cane, and beckoned for his assistant to follow along. The two ramshackles headed across the altar to that doorway into their sacristy, still dripping a tad after all this time. Hammer considered changing the name of his destination from 'sacristy' to something more fitting, like 'refuge,' 'haven,' or any other name that barbarian out there might consider off limits. The backdoor to the sacristy leading outside was open yet he never thought of using it.

Both men were excited to be doing what they were doing, and no other men in the world except their kind could understand their joy. Barbarians were ordering them to praise their God the way their God told them to do it. The heathens were there to see and film an illusion, something the pastor knew in his heart had been designed for just this time, something that forced them to look up instead of down. There was really no such thing above ground, as diamonds are always found below. Barbarians are always living an illusion according to historians, and if you manage to live through a barbaric time, it's nice to know it was all an illusion, assuming you are not the barbarian. They were the illusion, and they didn't even know it.

Once inside their dressing room, the sacristy, the two men opened cabinets, drawers and closets they hadn't opened legally in a long, long time. Hammer had always considered them some sort of bait. He imagined them a trap; if tampered with they could tell a tale he couldn't repudiate. For that reason, he had never touched any of the garments all during his imprisonment. He used other vestments from another sacristy, performed the Mass almost every day at that altar out there and never left a trace of himself or Basil in that church over the past eight years.

This was the first time in a long time, and he relished the smell that came out of the drawers. Most everything the two men could have ever needed was now available, and that included brand spanking new, never-been-worn everyday work cassocks, new undergarments, and socks. Nestled into the corners of the second drawer were new ankle-high work shoes, with leather laces and thick soles. They stripped and dressed in only a few minutes.

They instantly went from poor priest to dignified priest with that first silken white cape they enveloped themselves in, tied in place with a sash they kissed before wrapping around their waist and drawing it tight.

For the priest, the Mass begins before he ever takes his stage, and there are many prayers from antiquity that can't be overlooked and rituals that date back to Christ himself. The Consecration of the Eucharist is really the entire backbone of Catholicism, and there isn't a priest in the pack who doesn't understand that token idea. Hammer knew, and so did Basil, that if they could get to that point in the Mass, for all intents and purposes, their lives would be complete. The barbarians had no idea how they had blessed these two men, no idea at all.

The two men talked about their apparent solitude and intuitively understood all sorts of detail about the upcoming hour without even discussing it. Hammer opened the cabinets and took out half a dozen altar necessaries and arranged them there on the table. There was the old chalice that hadn't much value, an item they would have never used at Easter, but would surely be good enough. After all, anything that could hold the blood of Christ would automatically be perfect for any wine-tasting event on the planet. In the farthest corner inside the sacristy vault, a tiny hourglass filled with gold dust waited to be turned over and for the time to begin.

When Basil took the lid off the ciborium, it was empty, and he looked up at the lead celebrant with a question in his eyes. The old man turned the unit over and exposed a false bottom. It came off just as it should have, and there was a three-inch in diameter unleavened host, ripe and ready for a consecration. All Basil could do was wag his head back and forth with that toothy grin of his, not one bit afraid of his imminent death.

They were getting close and could see out the door into the church, could see that high and mighty colonel standing near the altar and not even knowing he was vilifying a sacred spot. He stood out there with his knuckles pressed against his hips as if offended by the delay. He did, however, remember insisting that Hammer do this right and that Hammer had all of his confidence once the ceremony had begun.

The tables seemed to have turned, and the old priest walked out into the church and snapped his finger for the colonel to come over so they could speak at close quarters. The colonel was thinking, as he vacated the altar, that he couldn't remember the last time someone had snapped their fingers at him. He didn't even like it when his mother did it, and the echo of that action buckled his lips. He had not disliked anyone this long in quite some time, and he definitely disliked this old priest. Usually, he would have shot him by now.

"You seem to be deeply distraught, Mr. Colonel." Hammer paused and held his belly area. "It bothers me spiritually, deeply, down deep in my soul, hurts me… er… deeply that you maintain such an arrogant attitude out there, near this beautiful altar. It makes me very uncomfortable, and it distracts me from my assigned task. I must adore my God, your God, and our God at this Mass perfectly for there to be what you want there to be. No obstructions, no distractions — it's hard to explain, it's very much a part of this priesthood. We live by the law, by that I mean our Canon law, the law of this Church. It says, "If I'm not worthy, if I'm not honorable, if I'm not spiritually perfect, the Mass is invalid and everything that should happen doesn't happen, and it's just a wash-out, if you understand that sort of thing. Like you just wasted an hour. Do you understand that sort of thing? I might have said that too fast?"

Basil was by now looking and listening directly over Father Hammer's shoulder and squinting at all the soldiers and cameramen who were all also cuffing their ears and squinting at the three men standing in the doorway. For the benefit of all, he shouted, "WHAT DID YOU SAY?"

Everyone who wasn't completely deaf heard his outburst and were now focused.

Hammer looked at his partner, who was not quite twenty inches away, and returned the shout with, "DO YOU FULLY AND COMPLETELY UNDERSTAND THIS SORT OF THING?"

Basil gave it just the right touch and shouted back into his pastor's cheek, "WHAT DID HE SAY?"

"STOP! STOP! PLEASE STOP! I UNDERSTAND! I THINK I UNDERSTAND! WE NEED TO GET ON WITH IT, PLEASE. I UNDERSTAND!"

The colonel was now a step back from where he had been and fumbled with himself for a moment.

"I don't want to waste a lot of film on this and so I won't direct the cameras to come on until I see the two of you standing here in this doorway. I'll direct the cameras to begin, and you just pull those strings to these bells. It's all yours from there. Is that the sort of understanding you're talking about?" Hammer gave him the look they gave when they didn't hear it all, but guessed and gave an answer of sorts.

"I can only tell you, Mr. Colonel, that the moment when the teardrop falls is in a direct parallel to the consecration of the Eucharist itself, according to the Catholic Church, the teachings of the Vatican, the express wishes of the Holy Father and some other stuff. It's hard for me to tell you exactly when this should happen. Usually around that time, but not necessarily. It's just a feeling I feel at that time in the Mass, and I can feel it. I can feel it! It's a priest thing! You have to try to understand. You're going to waste at least an hour's worth of film this morning, and I hope you have enough. It may not happen until the very end of the Mass; only God knows for sure. Happened at the very beginning in 1883. It doesn't happen until it happens, hasn't always happened at the same time, and I'm still somewhat worried about that rabid pig. Pigs are not allowed in the Church during Mass. We once had a parishioner who had a seeing eye pig and it always pooped inside, so we made a rule against it."

Just like so many times before, when it was more or less just the colonel and Hammer talking, the colonel ended up nodding a lot and allowing the priest to be in charge. He really had no choice, and he understood that, and the Kremlin did too, whether they knew it or not. He immediately began to look into some of the darker recesses behind the altars and turned to yell at the guards to keep an eye out for the pig.

"DISPERSE YOURSELVES, BE VIGILANT, ESPECIALLY FOR WILD RABID PIGS!"

After which he winked at the old priest and relaxed just a little.

The old Capuchin priest stood there, seemingly taller than before, and outlasted the glare from the colonel.

"I'll be back." And he gazed up into the ceiling and seemed to be calculating something. "Ten minutes or so. Be ready. I'll be back."

From there he turned and walked straight into Basil's chest, who was standing inches behind his pastor and had heard the whole thing. His head was bobbing, and he was whispering loud enough for the colonel to hear, "That's right, that's right," leaving Sokolov wondering exactly what he had heard.

The sacristy was theirs, and both felt assured they could finish their preparations without that rock lizard bothering them for a little while. It would be the pure white and gold trim vestments for Easter, which were more flamboyant than all the other choices they might have had, almost gaudy in their style. To the Catholic world they appear quite normal for the occasion, but to the untrained eye, the Communist, the heathens of the planet, it would appear that the two celebrants were in some sort of a laughable costume. When the two men were ready, they walked up to the door that led out into the church, gave two shallow head nods to the colonel, and Basil reached up for the bell chime rope.

They resembled nothing the soldiers could relate to. Basil would concelebrate the Mass. He gently pulled on the entrance bells and that holy sound reverberated off every wall in the place and back again. The cameras were rolling, the candles were glowing, and more than half of the guards and most of the camera crew instinctively stood still where they were and focused on the celebrants. The other half of the audience belched out laughter and wolf-whistles, mumbling two-word epitaphs and looking like they were stunned.

Jumping up from that first pew on the south side, directly in front of the cameras, the colonel stood up and waved off the cat-calling with that look in his eyes, the look he used when he was directing one of his firing squads. Everyone became subdued, and they all seemed to realize that the look they all saw in the colonel's eyes applied to them and, one and all, they were now in, way over their heads. Some believed that there might be a slim chance this documentary would survive, but the honest men among them sort of knew it would be a genuine loser.

Directly across the center aisle from the colonel, Desch slowly rose from his seat and equally slowly turned his entire body until he had seen every man in the house. By the time he turned back, the priests were where they belonged to start their ceremony.

The church was now silent, except for the whirling of the cameras, as the two priests took their respective positions at the foot of the three-step altar. They removed their Berretta hats, folded them into the flat black stack and laid them down on the end of the first step. Tradition for Easter services could get extremely long at times, and that is precisely why God invented choirs. Steeped in tradition, the service demanded that the priest and his first acolyte recite a grueling and monotonous first prayer, lasting five minutes. Hammer began chanting a three note fifteen-word litany of Latin gibberish directly at the second step to the altar, with Basil kneeling on the painful marble floor and giving his reply. The same five Latin words, the same three notes, bent in half at the waist and talking to Hammer's shoes. For five minutes, straight down at Hammer's new boots, until most of the observers went crazy.

This formula for the opening prayer was mind-bogglingly difficult to observe, but it did manage to go on and on until it finally ended. The sergeant major would never be able to defend himself, but he belched out a "Thank God" when it was finally over.

The current audience was tiring, and Hammer realized that, back in the good old days, his magnificent choir would be winding up their opening songs and that alone was worth the price of a ticket. He had rattled off the long Latin prayer that was perfect for Easter, and as Basil read back the response, Hammer noticed that grisly little colonel was standing over on the south side of the altar, rocking his hands back and forth, hunching his shoulders up and down and asking with his big eyes, why? He opened his eyeballs as wide as he could and couldn't think of anything else to do besides yell at the old man to get it in gear. Hammer gave him the rocking two fingers crossways 'v' with his free hand, leaving the colonel with no information whatsoever. Having no idea what that meant, but knowing it meant something, he headed back to his pew. He made stern eye contact with Desch, the sergeant major, and two cameras.

Finally, they were both standing, and it appeared they were headed upwards to perhaps the second step, but no, they would need to do their incense routine, which was also traditional, and in those good old days, the choir would take off again and rattle the windows some more.

When all of that was said and done, they would have been finished with the incense burner and that smell of antiquity would be all over the place. Without the choir, without the commotion of the ushers and the collection, the incense scene became the only scene, and it, too, had a touch of monotony. It lost a lot of its mystique when it was the only show on stage, unless you were really into the sound of an incense burner hitting its hanging chain.

Desch never flinched and sat in his pew with perfect attention, while Sokolov had managed to turn every which way but loose.

Out of respect, tradition demanded that the incense burner be staged as far down and away from the main altar as possible, and tradition placed that location to be directly in front of Sokolov's personally selected pew and office area. He was going out of his mind with the first ten minutes of the Latin banter back and forth, and that was before Basil started the incense fire. It appeared to be dumber then bullshasheska to begin with, and the two priests spent the next few minutes passing this hanging apparatus back and forth several times, seemingly unaware that the more they swung it the more it smoked, until it was smoking like a rotten haystack fire.

Then they added more incense. They walked around and around and around the altar, intentionally flooding the smoke into the sides of the marble, then into each other, did the altar again, and then one more time for old times' sake. They made more smoke then the grossfaters had. Many of the attendees for that particular Easter sunrise service had no idea what those two priests were doing with their little smoke pot.

When they were done, Basil brought everything back to that incense stand the colonel had never noticed standing there ten feet in front of his first-pew office. Location, location, location. The colonel watched him hang the smoking cylinder right in front of his face and, just before he left, he put three heaping tablespoon-sized piles of incense on top of what he already had; he didn't want to have to relight it for the second go round, and there would be one. For the most part, it resembled a traditional military pork smoker, without the cooking fire underneath, and more the size of a squirrel smoker, something no one had thought of except for the Catholics. One thing for sure, it was definitely a smoker.

On his way back up to the altar, the priest untied a rope that opened a window high up in the top of the ceiling, just exactly where Sokolov had decided the best location for his vent holes would be, and it slowly sucked the smoke out. He turned and bowed to the colonel, and whispered across the aisle that he could close the hole if he got chilled. His pew was in the main air current line for that exhaust hole and every fragrance in the place passed by on its way up the wall. The entire army unit had enjoyed worked-to-death jackass and beans for breakfast, a rolled delicacy they called a "Hasstobean," but the serious downside was if the troops were confined indoors for some reason. Depending on how old the jackass was and how hungry they were, it could result in the soldiers not even being able to stand themselves, much less anyone around them.

First, Hammer kissed the relic embedded in the center of the marble altar, and he stepped aside to allow Basil to do likewise. They had begun. The old man raised his eyes up to the top of the stained glass windows and started the opening prayers in a loud and robust voice. Slowly and distinctly, he filled the chamber with the words. In that ancient language of the church, a language that only priests could understand, he called on God to come into their midst, which was probably a waste of time since this was God's house in the first place, and he had never left. Under any other circumstance, all of the attendees would have been kneeling, quiet and attentive, but this audience was sitting, legs crossed, or milling around and hardly attentive at all. The priests had lost their attention.

Latin had not been a conversation language in a thousand years, and not many people knew it, despite the fact that most other conjugated languages derived from it. People who understand it can make it flow and seem like the perfect conversation tool. Hammer and Basil were in that group, and no different from all their predecessors.

"Almighty God, Father of all mankind, your servants are here at your altar and everyone else in this church are serpents, barbarians and monsters, except for a few."

It was his own addition to those opening prayers, and Basil was astonished that the old man would say such a thing. He had no such devious thoughts, and it had taken him a few moments to grasp the fact that a few of the words were entirely foreign to the liturgy. After it had registered in his mind, his only response to what he had heard would be the usual, the recognizable, "AMEN!"

Both men waited to see if there was any reaction whatsoever from the crowd of armed infantry and officers sitting in those pews behind them. No response at all, nothing. Hammer continued once he realized that none of the intruders spoke Latin. They were his, and they had laid themselves at his feet. Only Basil and God himself could understand what he was going to tell the colonel, all of the members of that famous choir, and all those folks back in Moscow, and perhaps if history was on their side, the whole rest of the world someday. After all, these bastards were filming the whole thing, and Desch had made a promise.

Not having been outside the church in over a dozen hours now, the priests were studying the giant displays of stained glass windows and Hammer instinctively knew that there was something disturbing the glow he was accustomed to seeing at this hour in the morning. There never were any guarantees due to the fact that Mother Nature was always a realistic factor. With that realization, he began to consider the notion that there wouldn't be a sunrise after all. As if to underline the whole concept, God hurled a thunderbolt of lightning that must have stuck the ground a mile or less behind the church, with its typical explosion of bright light and especially loud thunder not all that far away. The building seemed to shake for a second, and anyone who had been drifting away from the situation was instantly back to the reality of what that noise was, and the consequences it might bring.

The colonel jumped from his seat, raced to the side door on the south side and pushed it open to see the conditions out there. He saw a crystal-clear early morning blue sky, no different than when he had arrived, only brighter. So did everyone else who had looked his way.

He disappeared outside and ran up to the far eastern corner of the church and saw to his horror that a single gigantic cloud formation was centered all over the top of the distant mountain range and appeared to be raining hard. The cloud bank was the only storm in the entire valley, had come out of nowhere, but was right in the way of the sunrise. Another bolt crashed to the surface and was followed again by the concussion.

He turned back to that doorway and staggered inside, frantically trying to find the closest cameraman. The priests were back to their service and had come to the point where they read the sacred readings for the day. The first reading, the second reading and the Gospel. Basil sat down on the bench next to the pulpit and Hammer climbed the three steps till he towered over the small congregation. Almost everyone became aware that the star of the show was about to speak. So far, everything that had come out of his mouth was foreign, and most were personally hoping that he was going to say something they might hear and understand. Wrong!

He studied the side of the Bible that was sitting there closed on the angled platform, and he fingered the colored page markers until he found the one he needed and opened the book to that reading. Normally the passages were there in the language of the people, but he decided to translate it and speak in Latin since he knew they weren't capable of understanding any of the words he would utter, no matter what the language. In fluid Latin, he began to read aloud.

"You bastards. You are monsters. You atheist pigs. The God of this house will strike you all down before this is all over. You may rule for a while, but God himself and his righteous men will end up ruling the day. You might think you've killed us all, and you might think the future will forgive you for that, but my God and your God may not. I cannot forgive you myself, and it hurts me so bad to say that. It goes against everything I've raised myself to be. I cannot forgive you for what you've done. You would have to ask me to forgive you, and I know you can't do that. Understanding that, your only option left is to kill me, kill him, and burn down this church. You can do all that today, and there's nothing I can do to stop you. So I pray at this Mass that you and all your kind burn in hell for all eternity. When you see the flames from this church devouring it, I hope you see your eternal resting place. Jesus Christ, remember me when you enter your paradise. Oh, one last thing, there is no rabid pig, you're all just stupid."

Basil loudly exclaimed "AMEN", and once again they both waited for any sort of response. Desch was looking down at his folded hands and repeated Basil's response, "Amen."

It was now time for Basil to do the second reading, and he, too, had some interesting thoughts for the deaf ears out there. The old man sat down, and the young man climbed the steps. He found a place in the big book and made sure the pages were flat as he scanned the faces scattered throughout his church. He saw Desch looking up at him with his hands folded on his lap. He saw the colonel last, before he locked onto the main camera and began.

"YOU BASTARDS. YOU MONSTERS. YOU ATHEIST PIGS. FUCK YOU!"

He wasn't sure, but he didn't think he had ever used some of those words before in his life. They were all looking at him, and he was pretty sure that the deafest one out there would have surely heard what he just said, and if any of them spoke Latin they would be deeply offended. He was prepared to be attacked, assaulted and beaten to death, but all they did was look up at him and show every sign they had no idea what he was saying to them, but it was evidently loud enough.

"FUCK YOU! FUCK YOU! FUCK YOU!"

He was trying to remember back at the seminary, Latin class, every day, and could see all those conjugations of Latin words in his study books. He couldn't recall ever seeing the word 'fuck', and the version he used here in his second reading could fall into the category of a brand new Latin word. That would be something. Those thoughts passed through his head as he prepared his next exclamation.

He had never been the sort of priest who appeared weak and reserved, except now. He had been so hungry for so long, but he was anything but that in his spirit. He had come from so far away that all of his exploits and conquests were unimportant, unknown and left deep inside his own consciousness. Nothing out of the ordinary, but he had managed to learn how to hate, and he hated these men.

"THIS HOLY OLD MAN DOES NOT DESERVE FOR YOU HEATHENS TO ENTER HIS CHURCH. NEITHER DO I, AND NEITHER DOES OUR GOD. I INSIST AND DEMAND THAT YOU LEAVE THIS HOUSE OF GOD, AND I PRAY THAT EACH AND EVERY ONE OF YOU SUFFERS A THOUSAND TIMES MORE THEN THE WORST SUFFERING YOU HAVE EVER CAUSED TO ONE OF GOD'S PRECIOUS CHILDREN. EACH AND EVERY ONE OF YOU WILL PAY SOMEDAY, AND, IF MY GOD ALLOWS IT, I MYSELF WILL MAKE YOU PAY. I WILL HELP YOU REMEMBER. JESUS CHRIST, REMEMBER ME WHEN YOU ENTER YOUR PARADISE."

It was Hammer's turn to add "AMEN," and once again a faint 'amen' came from the first pew. Basil came back down knowing that everything he had just said was on film, currently misunderstood by everyone except perhaps by Desch, but in time, if it survived, someone might see his protest. He would more than likely be dead in a little while, and for that reason he didn't have to worry too much about the future.

With that, the old man resumed his position at the top of the podium to read the gospel. He found his place, and this time he read it loud and in the native language for everyone to hear. He was certain that almost everyone had heard this story before, but he read it very loud and practically from memory. His eyes had widened and become round, and he concentrated on making eye contact with every man below who seemed to be looking at him. Often times in the past, when he'd had this opportunity, he hadn't appreciated the fact that there were millions out there who would never believe that such a thing had happened nineteen hundred years before. This time, perhaps the last time, he would proclaim the Easter Gospel as best he could, and if anyone was vulnerable to the message, they would never be able to hear it any better. For sure, they would never hear it that loud again; he made sure the deaf ones had a chance, one last chance. It was probably a wasted effort, but he gave it his best shot. When he was done, he paused and scoured his audience one last time. "GOD BLESS US ALL. PEACE!"

With that, he was down the steps, cane in hand, and instead of being slow and feeble, there was a spring in his step, with Basil right on his heels. The consecration of the Eucharist was about to begin. At all of the earlier Masses in his life, dating back to his very first one, he had refined the art of explaining the miracles or images or parables just about as well as any man could. People often told him after any such service that his homily had touched them. They all had a way of saying it their way; it was a personal thing between a woman or a man and their private priest. He knew them all and loved them all. Now they were all gone, and he knew who was to blame. He knew they were going to burn this church to the ground and kill him, and his assistant, probably before the day was over. There was nothing he could do about all that except perform this Mass with the grace and dignity with which Christ himself would do it.

"Do this in memory of me." Those six words had entered his ears and flowed off his tongue for the entire time he had existed, every day from his childhood to this exact time, and as he stood there uncovering the chalice he had no regrets at all. He wasn't scared. He reached over and laid his hand on top of Basil's, and gave it a slight tap. It was as comforting a feeling to both the giver and the taker, and the men dissolved into the occasion.

The colonel had been standing just inside the church doors and was trying to explain to the closest cameraman that he wanted him outside and he needed to film the entire eastern horizon, film a storm cloud that was preventing the sunrise. The cameraman was one of the most seriously affected from the night before and made it perfectly clear that not only could he barely see, he couldn't hear a thing. Sokolov grabbed him by the arm and literally dragged him through the doorway and out onto the side yard of the church, and forced him to point his camera at the distant horizon above the river. It was all the director could do, and would be proof that he tried, but this strange thundercloud seemed to have come out of nowhere, as the entire rest of the sky was crystal-clear and lighting up as the minutes passed. The cloud was a huge boiling mass of energy and seemed to be angry. The mountain peak was invisible as the storm engulfed it, and all of the neighboring peaks were standing visible both left and right. The highest peak of them all, Easter Peak, had always been a magnet for storms. It had attracted one right now and it was having a fit, none of which was the slightest bit unusual. She was even nicknamed by hunters and travelers "The Angry Bitch."

The film crew had to continue and allow the priests to finish their ritual, all the way to the very end, no matter what. Sokolov would have everything on film, and if they saw a teardrop, they would have it preserved. If not, he would be able to show there had actually been this unusual weather phenomenon that prevented their success. No one would be able to blame him for the failure, and he headed back inside to see where they were.

The cameraman had never heard a word he said and had no idea why he was supposed to film that distant riverbank, but if that was what the colonel needed, then he would comply. He continued to film the treetops and the river's edge. There wasn't much time left on his camera, but he followed his orders, and inside the church, so did the Mass.

CHAPTER 9

ONE LAST TIME

It's hard at times to appreciate a last time while it's happening. Usually in life all of our 'last times' happen, and we never know they have.

Hammer stood dead-center of the altar like he had never done before, definitely dead-center. He looked over at Basil, and when their eyes met, they both knew this would be the last time.

"This is it, never more, never more. It's going to rain, my friend."

For Hammer, the number of Masses he had said was incalculable. For Basil, not near so many, but he was getting the hang of it all. It's easy to say that a man is a priest, and by that accomplishment can consecrate the Eucharist. It's a whole different matter to be a priest and, in fact, do such a thing. The whole idea of changing bread and wine into body and blood is anything but a simple idea, and it takes time. Sometimes we get a lot of time in life and sometimes not; Hammer and Basil were proof of that truism.

First things first. The two men laid out their altar items and positioned the beautiful altar Bible and prayer book alongside that chalice and ciborium. They had their beakers of water and wine, and Hammer respectfully placed that host on a gold platter.

When it comes to pomp and circumstance, tradition, personal capabilities, everything before and then after the Consecration is sort of up in the air at times. This being the last time they would perform this ritual, it caused them to sit down in their minds at that last supper table as if they belonged there. Too bad there wasn't a church full of the faithful because these two men were preparing to do the commemoration exactly the way Christ wanted them to. Just one faithful person left, ready to say to the world that he was still faithful, and in so doing be saying he was ready to die for that faith. That's what it would take to be faithful.

They blocked out everything behind them and concentrated on everything in front and above. They were in a perfect state of mind for the occasion and would try to perform up to the level of sainthood. It would be as close to a perfect praise as possible. Hammer really didn't need the book any longer, and hadn't for a long time, but he still read it as if it were the first time, except he never stumbled with any of the words. He believed in an ancient teaching that it was disrespectful to treat chapter and verse without the book open.

Before long, Hammer found himself genuflecting, then holding that large host high above his head; there were the ringing sounds from the chimes at Basil's knees, "Ring, ring, ring." Every pagan eye in the place was fixated on the glass backdrop, but there was nothing unusual, nothing dramatic, nothing at all, for that matter. The moment had come where the sun should have shown through those magnificent windows, but it didn't. Instead, a thunderous bolt of lightning struck very nearby behind the church for the second time and reflected through the windows in a blinding flash of reds and blues and yellows. The noise convinced them all that it was a very good thing they were inside and not outside with the remaining army.

The men by the generator, those by the unit supply truck, and the cinematographer who filmed the bolt up close and personal would fervently say later that it had hit the hilltop near the Grotto. That particular piece of footage would show the world what it was like to be too close to that aspect of nature from that time on. There had been no 'teardrop' in anyone's view just yet, nothing different in any way on that stained glass except for that explosion from a lightning bolt. Unfortunately, for almost everyone concerned who had any vision left, this was what they had come for, and they were straining every eye muscle they had left squinting hard at those windows. No one had any intention of sleeping through this finale, and for those reasons, no one missed having their eyes wide open for the lightning bolt.

Hammer lowered his arms and set the precious item down where it belonged, and instantly picked up the sacred chalice and consecrated it in a similar fashion as the host. That, too, he lowered to the altar slab, and seemed to be finished as far as the colonel was concerned; he'd been to Mass many times in his youth and this much he knew, that was what everyone used to come to see.

"Er... er... er... Did you see it?"

"DID ANYONE SEE IT?"

"DO IT AGAIN! DO IT AGAIN!"

Hammer broke the host in two pieces and quickly handed half to Basil. They were both preparing to consume their portions when they turned and saw that Desch was kneeling at the communion rail and waiting for his Eucharist. Hammer quickly drank half the full chalice of wine and handed the remainder to his assistant, who did the same.

Basil took off down the steps with a large corner chunk of his piece and came up to Desch, raised it up a bit in front of his face and was about to set the entire piece on his tongue, when he saw the three blind soldiers in-between the two deaf ones headed for the communion rail. Each man got a tiny portion, and then they all went back to where they had come from.

Others had hesitated, took a step forward and then back, missing their chance to become a martyr. All of the body and all of the blood was now safely away from the heathens and inside the bodies of believers and future saints. Basil returned to his pastor's side and seemed to be in some sort of a daze. He had actually placed the body of Christ on the tongues of a half a dozen of the faithful, and that left him completely fulfilled.

Sokolov had completed his second pirouette, and that placed him about twenty feet off to the south side of the altar. Both priests looked over at him as he appeared to be having trouble with whatever it was he planned on saying next.

There seemed to be no doubt that a critical time had come and gone. The colonel was wide-eyed and breathless as he hurried up to the side of the long altar. From there, he could see Father Hammer's eyes; they could start a conversation when the old priest raised his left hand a little and said to the colonel, "Be patient. The hand of God is at work, and he may not be done with this painting. See up there how the glass is starting to get brighter? Anything could happen, be patient. We're not finished."

Sokolov stepped back, away, and seemed to be having some trouble with his vision. Everything was suddenly so white, so marble-like, and he had his orchestration finger circling around some concept just a little above him and up to the right. It must have had something to do with the cameras, as the sergeant major was physically commanding the cameraman to keep filming the altar and glass background. He had no choice, no one had any choice, and once again, the true conductor continued with finalizing his Mass.

Both men cleaned the chalice and ciborium quite meticulously, folded their napkins and placed different consecration items where they belonged, for ancient reasons, in an ancient order. They washed their fingertips one last time in a large bowl of water and then drank the whole thing. Pursuing the idea of doing it just like in the old days, they retrieved the incense burner and proceeded to dust every nook and cranny, down the main aisle and back, did the altar one last time and finally hung the contraption in its stand. Basil closed the lid, and the fire went out instantly.

Under normal circumstances, at the end of the Mass the priests always take a little break from the rigors of the altar and sit for a few minutes off to the side and say some final quiet prayers. When Hammer realized that the colonel was, in fact, being patient, both he and Basil did just that. They went off to the side of the altar and sat down on the bench just like they would have done any other time. To say they were testing the colonel's patience would have been an understatement, and they knew it.

Finally, they stood up, and the two priests re-centered themselves at the altar. Once again, they kissed the relic, only this time it was goodbye, and then turned to bless the congregation. Both men made extreme and somewhat exaggerated signs of the cross above and beyond all those heads. They were blessing the church itself, knowing full well that St. Francis of Assisi was doomed, and there was only one thing left to do.

They both turned back to the slab in front of them, Hammer picked up the Holy Pyramid with one hand and his cane with the other, Basil took the Bible, and they turned to face the monsters with their backs to the glass. As if God had simply waved his finger through that angry thunderhead, it fell over the top of that distant peak and down onto the Volga like a rock off a cliff, and then He let his sun shine in.

Everyone was still staring at the priests, and as they watched the blessing an incredible blinding blast of sunlight broke through the glass behind them from a sun that had actually risen completely. The storm was gone in an instant, and the altar became dazzlingly white. It was as if huge dark curtains had been covering the windows, and then had been suddenly pulled apart, hitting a sleeping face in the dark.

In this case, the men were not sleeping, but wide-awake and staring. All their senses were somewhat damaged from the lightning strike a few moments before, and suddenly now, without warning, blasted by a flash bulb that wouldn't stop, from a fully risen sun. A normal sunrise would have been a gradual sort of display — sunrise usually takes a while — but this Easter morning was proving to be anything but normal. The entire place had gone from excellent candle light to brilliantly reflected sunlight in only a few seconds. The big angry cloud had dissipated and was just a little fluff ball rolling farther east, over the side of Easter Peak. The cameraman outside missed that event, having run out of film, and still suffering from the effects of being the closest human being to that lightning bolt strike; his hair was still standing straight up on the ends of a million goose bumps that hadn't gone down. He simply added this new affliction to the list and didn't know what to do next.

The cameras were rolling, and the colonel was ignorantly excited, as were many of his subordinates. They were getting it on film for sure, and even though they could hardly see their hands in front of their faces, they tried and tried to block some of the reflections with this finger or that, both hands together, forming a tiny window in order to see that teardrop. All they could see were intense sun reflections until they had to look away.

Whether it had been part of the original plan for the church or not, Hammer wasn't sure, didn't know for a fact, but that was exactly why there was a two-hour period, a couple of hours after sunrise, when the light was too intense for Mass. In the wintertime and early spring, even on very cold days, that morning sunshine for those two hours always heated up the church very comfortably. The enormous marble altar foundation absorbed all that heat and then radiated it back into the church for most of the day. There had always been an early morning Mass in and around sunrise — usually before; they were farmers, after all, and that was convenient. If there would ever be a second Mass that day, it wouldn't be before nine.

Basil had the Bible up in front of his face, and Hammer had all the rest. Both men turned and walked to the bottom steps, where they genuflected, stood back up and bowed, walked off the altar and back towards that sacristy, and none of the soldiers saw them do it. It was over. They were finished, done, and they knew it. All they could do was wait for further instructions from Sokolov, so they both retreated into their own thoughts and prayers while the colonel worked his way out to where they had stood, bobbing and weaving, trying to see through the reflections and get a glimpse of anything that resembled a teardrop. It was impossible.

For all of the soldiers who had suffered from the night before, those black spots had been replaced with even larger white spots, and still they couldn't keep themselves from trying to see that image they could only imagine. When this morning was over, there would be many among them who would remember how their last clear vision in life seems to have been those two priests holding up a glass of wine. Most would stumble off into the day either partially blind or totally blind, either partially deaf or totally deaf, and that would be no way to enter the great worldwide depression that seemed to await everyone.

CHAPTER 10

BURN IT DOWN AROUND THEM

Easter morning, 1928, Pfeiffer, Russia, 50 miles north of Stalingrad. St. Francis Catholic Church, south side, looking down at the river.

There was little chance that Basil was going to live through the whole afternoon; he could feel it. These people were such barbarians, such hypocrites, and as he had noted, absolute monsters. Easter morning had been exceptionally beautiful after that incredible cloudburst at sunrise, at least weather-wise. 'Too bad, so sad,' there was not a sunrise. It was an old saying, 'Too bad, so sad.' There were no guarantees for anything when it came to the weather, and because the spring rains had already begun, often times the days never ended as they started. This particular Easter would have a mind all of her own, evidently, and there would be three seasons in one day, to the weather-reporting critics. It would very likely rain again in the afternoon and get flat-out ugly by sunset. He shivered at the thought of not ever seeing that again.

The two priests had been standing on the south side of the church ever since they had been beaten down the steps by the big ugly sergeant who was still standing in front of them and way too close. Other uglies were everywhere around them, while Colonel

Sokolov was consumed for the time being with other officers out in the parking lot or up on the steps in front of the church. The legend of the Diamond Teardrop had been the reason for this entire charade, and any honest onlooker would have to assume there was good reason to question any of the results one might conclude from the final product. The colonel knew there would be a few small treasures involved in the seizure of the church property — it was that way everywhere they had been so far — and besides all that, this church had been seized almost eight years before, and only an idiot would think he was the first looter after that long a time. There never seemed to be much left. The things that made St. Francis special were the facts that she was so huge, still there, and the legendary Easter sunrise service with the Diamond Teardrop in the windows.

The colonel, who stood there in the sacristy with the two priests after the fact, was not the same man who had allowed and insisted on it in the first place. The last solemn High Mass at this most special of all the Catholic churches in the valley. He had insisted that the final Mass be the Easter Sunrise Mass, knew the history of the place, knew the astronomical factors, and he, along with some of his staff, would respectfully attend. He acknowledged the well-known fact that, in the history of the area, "Easter sunrise at St. Francis of Assisi was exceptionally Catholic. Tradition, tradition, tradition!"

There was the fact that the Church had been specifically set and designed for that particular moment each year, and it seemed to Hammer and Basil that the colonel was actually honest in his desire to see the service at dawn on Sunday. He had explained in no uncertain terms that there would no longer be such holidays in the future, and they would be replaced with other holidays. Nothing he could do about that, and his orders were very specific. The Soviet State had seized all Church properties and possessions, in total, until further notice, and there would be no further services in any religion anywhere. Near the end of his programmed speech, the colonel mentioned that all of the clergy, absolutely and including these two clerics, would go through a re-education program at the state's expense, a protocol that would start the next day if not sooner.

That particular meeting had only been a few days before Easter, and both Hammer and Basil had been shaken to their core by all the information. They would not be seeing their bishop ever again, a man who had disappeared, and they weren't the slightest bit sure of where he was or if he was still alive. They were abandoned on the edge of the Ilava, had been ordered by the police to maintain the property, never leave the property, and always be at the beck and call of the Russian Red Army. Their instructions were to stay in the rectory or in the church and be prepared for that final Mass.

The colonel filled in a few blanks on his form and ended the meeting by telling Hammer that the ceremony should be exactly like all of the previous Easters with few exceptions, two of which were that there would be no need for a sermon and no need for the choir, of course. It was essential that they do everything to ensure the Diamond Teardrop exposed itself in those windows.

The colonel eventually followed the two priests into their sacristy after those final prayers. Father Hammer set the chalice down on the counter and turned to see the armed guards enter the room ahead of the colonel, who came in yelling for them both to take off their dresses and leave everything where it was.

"Follow the sergeant outside and stay by the steps out there."

There were procedures to follow, inventories to take, a treasure to box, and he might have a question or two. The chalice and other items for the liturgy were there on the vestments counter, along with the Bible and both sets of keys to the locked cabinet and the Holy Tabernacle. Both priests glanced away from the colonel's glare and then at the chalice, and then the beast snarled at them very abruptly, growling the question of whether or not they had heard what he had just said. It was not really a question, not spoken very loud, and then he realized they may have heard him. He may have been played a fool, and he knew it.

With that, the ugly sergeant slung the butt of his rifle into the left side of the old Father's rib cage with all his might, and then pushed him towards the door. It must have been as much a surprise as it was painful, and Hammer bounced off the wall and staggered into the doorway. His cane felt hot to the touch and glued itself to his grip. Basil followed almost on top of the old man, helped him with the steps, down to the ground level, and they hurried over to the southern sidewall by an old dead flowerbed. That's where they both stood for the next three hours, until Hammer collapsed in a heap. Their personal guard barely ever moved. He allowed the men to sit tight up against the building as the road through the small little hamlet was overwhelmed with the passing of the entire Southern Red Army. They were leaving the battlefields of the south as victors and were headed for the Polish border region a thousand miles north, and for more battles with dissidents.

As they huddled there against the wall, the old man pressed against the younger one until their faces were only inches apart. Split between their noses was a seam line crack in the foundation, a line with no cement between two large stones that made up the first row of foundation blocks. Basil could smell something coming out through the crack, and it smelled like roses. His eyes widened and he took a deep breath to confirm what he had smelled the first time. Hammer was breathing the air a little lower down on the block seam line and didn't seem one bit surprised that a foundation block would smell like this; after all, they were sitting in an ancient rose bed. It was now apparent that Hammer had pushed him into this spot and pushed his nose into that crack, and then seemed to pretend he hadn't done any of that at all. There they both sat all morning, past the noon hour and into the afternoon, watching the army coming up from the south, moving through the town, headed north.

Nothing of this magnitude had occurred on that street out in front of the church since the time the Commanding General of the Southern Red Army himself had come up that same road after winning a great battle over the White Army back in 1922, and managed to bring his entire army with him.

Sometimes there is no rhyme or reason to the average person as to why generals do some of the things they do. No reason to the common person why an entire army would come this way instead of that. All during the revolution, the huge port city of Tsaritsyn, a mere fifty miles south as the crow flies, managed to become the greatest prize for the Red Army, and a vicious campaign ensued against the White Army, in and around, up and down the rivers and coastlines, back and forth, for three years, until the war was everywhere. Both the Red and the White sides were plenty merciless.

Pfeiffer, Russia, had managed to sink its roots and create a lineage of family history only fifty miles from what most maps showed as bull's eye for the Russian Revolution. The bitterness and hatred spread far and wide, so did the fortunes of war as each side came and went a number of times, leaving their mark each time, until there was no one left to watch it anymore. Neither side wanted to lose, as unusual as that may sound, and that too was devastating to the common person. Throw in a terrible famine, a world war, a civil war, Communism, no religion whatsoever, and you have all the ingredients for living and dying in one pathetic place. There was no telling where the insanity ended, but nowhere near there. Pfeiffer simply died, except for the church. Hammer often mused over the idea that a man can never pick the place where he is born, his parents or his siblings. And if in the end he remembers any saving graces at all from all that time, then it was probably worth it. From his current vantage point on the side of the church, he couldn't see much saving grace anywhere. He felt as though he was well past halfway through his last day, and through the old eyes of a priest, he looked forward to seeing the eyes of his God.

The war in the region had lasted for almost three years when the news came up the river that sounded like the conflicts were over in that far distant port city, and the White Army had been defeated. For a small communal farming area like the deserted Pfeiffer, a place so far off the main road and train line, more than somewhat isolated, the question would have been, had there been anyone to ask, why did they come this way?

There was a way, a route, whether you were fleeing or pursuing, passing through this area from the southern port areas down where the Volga ran out into the Caspian, and the Don ran into the Azov Sea or coming down from the north. If a traveler was heading up into Ukraine or perhaps going all the way to Moscow, Poland or the North Pole for that matter, there was a route through the Pfeiffer region that did just that.

In the outback country regions, the land was flat and the roads were bad, and even though the army couldn't do anything about the lay of the land, they would turn the roads into mud bogs and destroy everything on both sides as if that were the whole purpose for coming through. Everything would be made much worse than before. It is widely understood that mobile armies have a way of transforming rural country roads into scars on the face of the land that can never be erased. Not only that, they have a tendency to treat the locals rather badly, according to a very long list of do's and don'ts that change dramatically, depending on who is writing the list. One thing was certain and without any doubt whatsoever, Father Karl Hammer and Father Edward Basil had certainly picked one of the wrong religions to be dedicated to in Soviet Russia, 1928.

CHAPTER 11

THE FIRST PASSING, 1922

1922, six years before the last Mass

Hammer could hardly remember the incident at all. It was 1922, springtime, something like that, and he was sitting all alone, watching through the side window of his rectory on the eastern end of a deserted Pfeiffer, Russia. His church and rectory were all that was left of the town, and when all the dust and commotion had cleared he was vaguely aware of what may or may not have happened.

He got a lot of his information from shouting soldiers and had a dozen vantage points the soldiers never knew about. Warning signs every so many paces were deeply rooted all around the entire church property, and forbid everything, from trespassing to merely looking, with the penalty being the end of breathing for the violator. He had a God-blessed sense of hearing that he treasured even more than his eyes, and his glasses were a highly protected possession. He had a wondrous cane he could lean on, like no other, and when he held it in front of his face with both hands, every sense he had was multiplied hand over fist.

Once he entered that rectory after his arrest, he very seldom ever spoke to anyone; four years now. No one ever came and told him much except for the police officers, and they never stayed long. Year in and year out, he had listened to anyone who would speak to him, which was very seldom, about anything they knew anything about. For the most part, the world became a mystery out there, after only fifty miles in any direction, and currently there didn't seem to be many folks left on the western side of the mountains, and even worse, for hundreds of miles north, into the distant outback. It was as if they had evaporated, just disappeared, were one and all completely gone. Hundreds of thousands, if not millions, had vanished, and that realization and the confusion caused by that knowledge pained the old man so badly at times that all he could do was kneel.

On the other side of the Ilava River, there were no people left. Nowhere in that valley that meandered twenty miles southwesterly were there any living Volga Catholics, no churches except for his, no parishes, no diocese, no faithful. Down where the Ilava merged with the Don River and along her opposite banks were two fishing communities with constant activity, but there was very little on the eastern side. There were fire lights at night on the other side of the Don, as compared to Hammer's side, where there were none.

From that intersection where the two rivers merged, he knew Rostov was bustling with Communists, and the revolution was in a full swinging sickle down there, three hundred miles as the boat floats. It was as if there was a continental divide that separated the Volga River from the mighty Don, and it turned it into a no man's land and had been for years. It hadn't always been that way, but any information a person might inherit would be so skewed and unreliable, you were forced to be skeptical of the traveler, of his newspaper, of everything about him. There always seemed to be something missing from the story, or too much added, to make it believable.

Beyond all that, it's hard to play dumb if you're not, and Hammer was anything but that. He could not hide his unbeliever look when he was being bullshashesked, knew that his forehead must have developed what he imagined being wrinkle veins that told the speaker the brain on the other side of the wrinkles considered that to be utter bullshasheska, unbelievable or just a flat-out lie. He was actually and in fact smarter than your average Russian bear and often times tried to rub his 'Bullshawrinkle' away with his fingertips before the bullshashisker ever saw it. It was nothing more than a nervous gesture and habit he had developed early on in his priestly career, a position he had found himself in so often for such long periods of time — sitting there in the center of his confessional, listening to his congregation telling him their sins, elbows on knee caps, rubbing his forehead. If ever there was a place on planet Earth where the bullshasheska got any deeper he didn't know where it was for sure, save for the barnyards on the other end of town. He wished, oh, how he wished for those days again.

They didn't come around often, but there was a police officer who managed to come to the rectory a couple of times a year and would practically beat down the front door as his introduction. Before opening it, Hammer would sneeze as loud a sneeze as he could squeeze, right up against the door seam, where he knew the officer's ear was. He was a big angry man and seemed to be the most in charge of the small group of unimportant local officials who circumnavigated the entire valley, evidently twice a year, making sure things were in order. He was arrogant, as usual, and didn't like talking to Hammer for long. His purpose was to leave some food and wine, see a face, get a signature and mark the box on his form. It was nothing more than a headcount and a rare situation, it seemed.

Hammer was under house arrest and had been for over four years. His arrest papers demanded that he never leave the premises, never conduct services of any sort or style and maintain the inside of the church. He was described in his own documents as the official custodian of a Soviet State historical treasure. That proclamation was plastered on every door, some of the windows, and on wooden warning signs here and there all along the property line and down around the corner. The church belonged to the State, and, even though the State was not exactly a well-defined entity just yet, there were plenty of new rules that applied. Civil wars, by their very nature, have a way of flowing back and forth long after the last shot is fired, so the rule of thumb in most situations like the one Hammer found himself in was that, if there is an army strolling through town, consider them in charge and consider them the winners. St. Francis of Assisi Roman Catholic Church fell into the category of 'Most Treasured,' seemed to be right in the way of the army, and was evidently very high on someone's list of things to preserve.

He knew what it was. He knew good and well what it was. It was the legend of the Diamond Teardrop. They would come and take it when they felt like it, but there were restrictions. It was an Easter sunrise phenomenon, and if they wanted to see it, they would have to wait till Easter.

No man in his right mind would tamper with the property, or ignore such a warning sign, and the property became an island at the end of a lonely road. It would be suicide disregarding those orders. Any time the bureaucratic puppet checked his papers, it wasn't hard to tell that he would have just as soon shot the priest himself right there and then, the very first time they met, except someone had told him not to do such a thing or he'd be shot. There was a lot of shooting going on as the society rearranged itself. As a matter of fact, he was to make sure the old priest was accounted for, deliver the wine, the food, and his garden seeds, and make sure he was still breathing on his own. Pure and simple, and just don't shoot him.

It was a very lonely life for an old man, and every time the policeman showed up, and Hammer, in fact, answered the door, the antagonism grew. One might wonder after a while why this old bag of bones was still alive. He appeared to be hanging from the cane somehow. Hammer never answered the door with his glasses on and never appeared to be in the best of health after he did. He coughed hard and usually managed to cover his mouth and look away just after the fact. If the timing is perfected perfectly, the only way out for the victim gets blocked by the porch pillar, and the cough seems to be "in one's face," so to speak. He had plenty of time to perfect everything he did and was working on being perfect. It can be a planned and scripted event if one considers the situation in advance.

Just about everything the old man had ever done in life was a planned and scripted event, usually for the show, and one of his talents was his timing. By the time the police sergeant realized that he had, in fact, been sprayed in the face with the spittle from what appeared to be a sick, old, practically blind janitor, it was too late. There was no warning, no ah, ahh, ahhh, just wham, big sneeze, noise, juices, sounds, followed by, "Oh God!" from the policeman.

Hammer would have finished with his signature by then, somewhat oblivious to where everything went, and would be handing back the paperwork and preparing to sneeze again.

This scenario had been played out before, and the policeman had been liquidly victimized for a second time. In his retreat, he appeared to understand that it had happened again, and once again he wasn't sure this might not be the one that would kill him. It had always been understood by everyone, everywhere, that sick and dirty people and dead bodies were something to fear and avoid. The only thing missing from this formula was that the priest wasn't quite dead.

Not long after the rumor about the end of the fighting had been confirmed, a large party of soldiers on horseback rode up from the south and camped for almost a week in front of the old main barn on the far side of town. There wasn't much left over there, but there were large open pastures for the horses. They were celebrating a great victory, and they were very loud about it. They were in the Red Army, and they were victorious, and he could hear them from a mile away. Two of the soldiers rode down the main street, late one afternoon, as if on patrol, until they came up to the church. Both were very curious about the reason why this church was still standing and was undamaged. One of them pushed his horse right up the front steps and dismounted in front of the four locked impressive front doors.

Plastered across the seam lines of those doors was that proclamation concerning the premises. They were the most official looking documents one could ever run across and notified the reader that this was Soviet State property. By order of the Commanding General of the Southern Red Army, anyone who tampered with the church would be summarily executed immediately.

All of the men in that army seemed to know their general's life history to one degree or another, and interestingly enough, he had once upon a time been in a Catholic seminary, which unfortunately hadn't worked out very well. Something about him not being able to pay his tuition, and he had to leave, quit and go find something else to do with himself. Rational, knowledgeable, more compassionate people might conclude all these years later that, if he had only had a scholarship or some form of financial assistance, perhaps some of the things that happened in the last couple of years could have been avoided.

The end of the revolution, the final battles, and the consequences of losing had become unimaginable, too horrible to even think about, to have to remember, and not even the most hardcore among them even wanted to talk about them. No one could possibly believe some of the things that had happened, probably not even God himself. These two horsemen knew all about the commanding general and summary executions. It was their job to do them for him. They knew him very well.

The older soldier calmly walked back to his horse, mounted and guided it quickly back down to the grass level with his partner. They turned away and trotted off under one of the giant shade trees just off the front steps, where they dismounted and tied their horses to the tree. They sat against the tree trunk twenty feet away from the side of the church and talked for an hour about everything they had recently lived through.

They were being monitored, and they didn't even know it, didn't have a clue. They smoked their pipes and celebrated the fact that they had lived through it so far. It must have been holy hell, thought Hammer as he discretely listened to every word. They were brothers, and realizing that no one could hear a word they were saying, or so they thought, they wondered out loud how their general could possibly be so cruel. How could he have made them do what they did, and would they ever forget? Could they ever be forgiven? The younger one cried out so loud his brother stood up and looked around to see if he should quiet him down. There was no one within sight, and he let his brother cry for the two of them. Perhaps because he was older, he knew in his heart that neither would ever forget, and neither could ever be forgiven. They had become savage death on horseback, but obviously hadn't died just yet on the outside. Maybe they couldn't die, shouldn't die, until they were punished.

None of that mattered, since they were headed for more battles and would probably die in one of those. More than likely, as there were odds out there that couldn't be denied. There were certain images they both had of a slaughter here or a slaughter there, a stream of blood coming from a building, flies, faces, pieces, all they ever saw was blood. If and when they did die, then they would be able to forget.

After a while, they climbed back up on their horses and took one long last look at the beautiful church. All they had really wanted to do was go inside and beg until they died, if possible. One had to be very careful about being a murdering barbarian monster, living in the midst of other murdering barbarian monsters, and being discovered to be not up to their standards. Brothers could manage moments like this one, together, where because of their blood they could go back to a previous time. Back home, back to momma. Strangers couldn't do that.

They headed back towards the center of town.

Hammer watched them and listened to them in secret and learned much. It sounded to the old confessor that they were ready to die, and they would render justice someday soon in a sense, for what they had done. They had a plan for redemption and rode away with a terribly sad conviction. After they had left, the rest of the mighty army started to come up the road from the south, led by small four-man cars, motorcycles with sidecars, and then big trucks full of soldiers. There were thousands of horse soldiers and infantry in what appeared to be a never-ending stream of the victors. Any of the large trucks were always pulling a trailer of some sort or another. It appeared the entire Southern Red Army was coming this way, had a long way to go and wasn't slowing down for any reason at all. There were thousands of soldiers and horses and commotion day after day. When they got to that hundred-yard long bottleneck where the warning signs paralleled the river, they finally slowed down and were able to catch their breath. Perhaps it was down there on purpose, to do just that.

Just before sundown on the fourth day of all this organized mayhem, three rifle shots rang out from what Hammer recognized as the old barn area. He had been watching and listening intently from different vantage points in the church and his rectory when the usual noise that afternoon was interrupted by the gunfire. There hadn't been a gunshot the entire time the army was passing through, and those three shots were so loud and unusual, he thought they might have been heard all the way around the world. That was a bit of an exaggeration, but they were unusually loud and final. It was one shot, a very brief pause and then two more, one on top of the other. There weren't near the quantity of the passing army any longer, not as many trucks as before, and the troops in the trucks seemed cleaner and more orderly.

Suddenly everything stopped out on the main roadway. They turned off their motors and stood around their vehicles, all their guns at the ready. Hours passed, and the sun went down. They were still waiting for something, and no one knew what that was. Hammer heard almost every word they said to each other out beyond the warning signs, and it seemed most unusual that something had not come down the line sooner than it did.

Very early the next morning, at the crack of dawn, the army started to wake up, and Hammer did, too. The big trucks that had all stopped after the gunshots were being started one after another, and all of the troops were back in their seats or standing on runner boards.

What they found out during the night through that magical military concept of 'spread the word' was that their general had been shot dead in his car seat by two of his own special cavalry guards. Two brothers, sitting side by side on their war-ravaged horses, high-powered rifles laid across their saddle horns at 'parade rest' — two of four hundred.

Their unit had been decimated for the most part, and had to its credit the story of having attacked and surrounded the last remnants of the White Army's tank battalions only a month before. The tanks had run out of fuel in their unorganized retreat and couldn't defend themselves against the relentless and highly mobile horse soldiers. Their infantry had been slaughtered, and without infantry, all they could do was retreat until their fuel gave out, which it all did in more or less the same river valley.

All of the crews surrendered and turned over their vehicles under white flags, and they all knew, they always knew. They would have been better off if they had fought to the death, and many did, but their six-shooters ran out of bullets early, and there wasn't one who wanted to burn to death. It was relatively easy to get them out of their tanks and headed in a certain direction, unarmed, until every tank team still alive were herded into a wide-open wheat field, where they were systematically run to death and trampled over and over, slashed with swords and then had their faces cut off and thrown in a huge pile. The tankers were dragged behind the horses, sometimes in pairs, side-by-side, still alive together, friends from the same tank, closer to where the pile was.

It appeared that many understood this tradition from the folklore of other tank battles against other organized horse soldiers, and perhaps the stories were true — that their fellow White Army horse soldiers had done the exact same thing to Red Army Tankers. It's a tanker thing. They were dragged just enough to stay off their feet and feel every bush and boulder. As they got closer to the center of the mayhem, if they were still conscious, they may have understood that they were about to become the center of attention.

A certain horror develops, knowing full well that was what they almost were, usually on their backs by their own choice, backwards, trying to hold their ravaged bodies up off the ground with their elbows. A gauntlet of horsemen, slashing swords at the passing bodies, and it wasn't long until their faces were removed. The chunks would be found and then stabbed by a sword tip and slung into the pile. The horsemen hardly slowed their light pace as they dragged the corpses away from their executioners, and sometimes a body indicated by a frantic hand gesture that it wasn't yet dead.

It would be virtually impossible for those men to ever forget what they had seen and done that day. Impossible! An organized frenzy of murder and savagery that went on for hours, until they couldn't stay in the saddle another minute.

Only days before this pending ceremony, there had been an incident in one of the small communities just north of the big city. The citizens were rounded up and interrogations began in earnest. The people didn't know much of what the interrogators wanted to know, and when the general found out he ordered that they be made an example for all the others. He wanted witnesses, people who could help explain to the peasants of nearby communes, survivors, what it meant to cooperate, and more importantly, what it meant to not cooperate.

The monster ordered that, since they couldn't find anyone who seemed to know anything, no one saw anything, and no one heard anything, they wouldn't need their eyes or their ears any longer. In a small little hamlet that had about five hundred souls, the barbarians filled a bushel basket full of their eyes and ears. They left a few of the children alone, tied them to trees and made them watch the horror of it all. After a few hours of this, they cut them loose and they wandered off to their homes, unable to even speak, stepping over and past all the people they had once known who had died and bled out not too far from where they had been butchered.

The butchers were covered in blood and had many wounds from where their victims had slashed back in terror. Few of the five hundred souls were even remotely cooperative, and the battle had lasted for hours. Most were shot first and then mutilated. They were lassoed with ropes and pulled out of the crowd, kicking and screaming, and their arms and legs were pulled out of their sockets by their loved ones who refused to let them go. Sometimes the lasso went around someone's neck, and they were hung on the ground and died long before their rescuers understood and finally let go.

The villagers had retreated into a right-angle corner of the courtyard and were fifty deep on the outer edges of the fan. The ropes kept coming in and were catching people far back in the crowd by a neck or a hand, sometimes their whole torso, and then they would be dragged to the front, across a ten-foot-wide no man's land, and into the fangs of the most vicious pack of savages imaginable. Even their horses were kicking at the closest villager, and that closest villager appeared to the horse much like a cornered wolf who was not about to be trampled lightly. They were dripping with blood, wide-eyed, and making noises that would frighten a wolf.

The cavalry had become insatiable killers and wouldn't stop until there was no one left to kill. Suddenly there wasn't anyone left, and the basket was full. A thousand eyeballs and a thousand ears in a puddle of blood the size of a truck. When there was no one left to gouge, that last cavalry man who was doing the gouging was the last one to know. He was in a horrible trance, where he would turn on the platform and gouge the eyes out of the face that his fellows were holding in place. On the previous platform, that same face had lost its ears, but once the eyes were gone, it was only a matter of time before that particular body would fall and start thrashing on the ground. He waited for a few moments, but that signal never came. He was done, and if possible, he planned to stand up and go find his horse that he had tied to a tree just back and around the corner. Sure enough, his horse was still there, and most of the soldiers were walking their horses away from the village and out to the fields they had decided to camp in. He stood there looking into the horse's ear and realized that the giant eye that was looking back at him didn't recognize him. It was his horse, and it was afraid of him. There was too much blood and the animal was obviously frightened, so he raised the leather sheath that held his war rifle until he could taste the steel of the barrel on his teeth, he unlatched the safety with his finger and pulled the trigger with his thumb.

The general's car had stopped in front of the unit's temporary flagpole, and the general had stepped out and hung another battle streamer atop the already cluttered mast assembly. Their battle colors were numerous, and there were many horses tied together in groups out in front of the main body with no men in their saddles. All of these horses were injured and had bandages all over their bodies. As soon as the ceremony was over, they would be led off to slaughter. They would have been shot long ago except they were still capable of walking, and would be led to their executions, closer to the mess tents.

They were a perpetually limping mess hall, and there were parts of them that were absolutely delicious.

It was a traditional ceremony, a necessary formality the general was obliged to perform, much like polishing a razor-sharp knife. He saluted the officers and their horses, and then all the horse soldiers lined up in ranks, after which he climbed back up into the sedan and sat down in the back seat. The car made a wide circle and went all the way around the top of the formation until it came back around and paralleled the noses of the front row of horses. Slowly, the car headed forward and the general stood up at attention, staring into the eyes of each and every man in the front row. At the precise moment, when the front bumper reached each horse, that soldier and the three men directly behind him would snap to attention, raise their weapons, and stand them on their butt end, dead center on their right thighs. At a mile an hour, the rhythm of the salute was almost like a military concert. It hadn't been rehearsed in quite some time, but, for the most part, all the horse soldiers had a reasonably good idea of what was expected. Horses, by their very nature, do not know what is expected, and the parade is further complicated by the fact that many of the animals and some of the men had shrapnel wounds and bullet holes here and there. As soon as it was over, the general would end up driving away, and the entire unit would deal with the horses.

The brothers Putinachov were there in that first row, numbers thirty-five and thirty-six. The general looked into the younger Putinachov's eyes and saw incredibly old man's eyes shedding tears on the young man's face, and the two pairs of eyes spoke to each other in vision talk for a split second. That was it! He raised his weapon and stood it where it belonged as the general moved his eyes to his brother's eyes. Like everyone before, he too snapped to attention and brought his weapon to his thigh as the general looked at number thirty-seven. Once again, there was a split second of recognition in time as Front Sergeant Putinachov lowered his rifle and shot the general right through the back of his neck. Another split second and both he and his brother fired in tune and removed the general's head. A fountain of blood geysered up and out of the ruptured neck where the demon's head had been.

Having succeeded with their hastily prepared assassination, they hurled their weapons to the ground in front of their horses and raised their arms high above their heads. A hundred rifles and pistols were instantly drawn and leveled at the two, but not a single weapon went off. They were dragged from their horses and arrested in seconds, still alive. The horses bolted when their reins were freed, and even though injured slightly like they were, they charged forward, directly over the brothers, without injuring either one, and plowed into all the symbolic horses tied together out beyond his motorcar. In a matter of only a half a minute, the entire ceremony had been completely disrupted as dozens of panicked and wounded horses stampeded in every direction with minds of their own and destinations far away from men and armies and tanks.

All of that aside, General Joseph Stalin would no longer be the commanding general of Red Army South due to the head trauma, and was replaced within hours by someone up to the task. They were difficult boots to fill, but there is, after all, the normal military procedure. Too bad, so sad!

Stalin had terrified many of his own troops, and he had proved to be merciless with his enemies. He had a very promising future with the party, and was eventually headed for Moscow, they said, for national acclaim for his heroics in the victory at Tsaritsyn. There was even talk that they would change the city's name in his honor.

The two brothers who killed him were part of their general's most vicious terror arm and were being awarded a unit citation at the time.

'General Joe' they called him, and he thought they all loved him. Many did, of course, but in this particular case there were two who didn't. Without being manhandled all that much, they were lead away into the inner reaches of the army and were allowed to indicate through a final shouted statement that they felt he had to die for what he had ordered. Every man on every horse and standing anywhere nearby heard that statement. It may have been somewhat garbled and unintelligible depending on whose ears we might be talking about, but it made perfect sense. Absolutely perfect sense. There was nothing to do but arrest them, and then it was decided they should be tried for their crime in Moscow instead of just shooting them there on the spot. They would shoot their horses instead if they could ever find them.

For some strange reason, those two particular horses seemed to have bonded, and as they were bouncing off all their fellow warhorses moments after the shooting, they managed to stay together and disappeared down into a ravine that was made for two horses to run side by side as fast as they could go. It's not often a conquering army loses one of its primary generals, and the murderers are captured alive. The Soviet State would probably want to have a run with this one.

In only a matter of days, it was all over, and they were gone, leaving almost everything much worse off than before the army had passed through. The roads, the riverbanks, and they even stole the bucket to the water well. Everything was worse off, except for the church, and besides the Putinachov brothers, not another pair of boots had crossed over that boundary line where the signs forbid it.

Hammer wasn't sure about anything for a long time after that. For months at a time no travelers ventured on this side of the river, not that there were many of them in the first place, and when the final troops had eventually disappeared, some of the last words that Hammer had heard in the ranks were that Lenin may have had a stroke and hadn't been seen in public in quite a while.

He lowered the handle to his hiding place and spoke to that distant trooper through telepathy, promising he would include a prayer for Mr. Lenin in his early morning Mass, if that was all right. He didn't expect to get a telepathic response.

He realized he was being somewhat 'unpriestly' when he thought about Lenin. He'd spent a lot of time analyzing himself, and when he wasn't thinking or acting right, he referred to it as 'unpriestly.' It wasn't that he didn't mind being that way, because he did; there was, however, a part of him that was very hateful. He never shared it with anybody, primarily because he was all alone, all the time, and it had been so long now that he was having trouble remembering what it was like to talk to someone, to have a friend, a confidant, a confessor. It was very hard being all alone.

As all people do when they're marooned in life and don't have someone to talk to, they usually invent something that understands exactly what they're saying and remembers everything. Hammer had a walking cane that had been carved to perfection, stained and polished, with an oversized knob on the end and the bust of Jesus Christ himself carved to perfection, front and back. That's not what he held onto; there was a grip just below the knob that gave him an amazing stability.

When he went on his frequent and sometimes nightly excursions into the lands around the church, for miles and miles, weather permitting, he always faced Christ's face in the direction they were heading. If he were going to sit for any length of time, he would set the cane so Jesus would be able to see him, and they could talk eye to eye. This image was so vibrant and beautiful, in three dimensions, and even if you weren't looking straight at Jesus, he was always looking straight at you. The old man told him everything and never lied.

They had been talking one day about Bolsheviks, Communists, and the fact that so many people seemed to have disappeared, and Hammer told him that in his opinion the world would have been a much better place if Jesus had not bothered with Mr. Lenin. They dropped the subject. After seventy-five years, more or less, he knew better than to try to tell Jesus how to do things. He did manage to drop hints now and then, knowing full well that anything he might have said or suggested was up for discussion, but it always seemed to be a one-way street.

The winters had been very difficult. He was an old man, didn't need much, read incessantly, and even wrote a novel. Then, one day in early December 1926, the police arrived. Two sedans came up the road from the south and pulled into the parking lot in front of the big church. Hammer had been sitting by the fireplace in his rectory cooking soup when the Holy Spirit or a sweeping rush of freezing wind invited him to get up and go peer out the window. He hadn't done that in months. There they all were on the front steps of the church, seven in total, distant but headed his way up the doorsteps of the rectory.

There were a few things that sprang to mind immediately, including hiding his glasses, working himself into the flu, and getting ready for a knock on the door. Perhaps just one last heaping spoonful of fish and noodle soup, since he hadn't finished. He could hear them coming, could hear the warning one of them gave to the group, and then they all chuckled. All except one. He heard six different chuckles, and he never did like people who laughed at their own jokes. It's not that he didn't like them, but then again, yes it was. He recognized the joker's voice, and the knock on the door was much more respectful than any of the previous encounters. He must have been standing back a bit.

The old man assumed his door-opening pose, something resembling his image of Igor in Frankenstein. He was now hunched at the mid-back, and when he opened the door, he squinted at his guests from the side of his face. He acted like the sun was offensive, which would be easy to understand even for a bureaucrat.

"Are you well, old man? We've brought you some food and wine. Sign here."

The old man was still inside his home, and they were all on the porch when the jokester insisted that the priest come out and meet someone they had brought with them. He signed the tablet and handed it back, and the policeman noticed that he had evidently drooled all over the top left corner and down over part of his checklist. It was disgusting. Whatever it was, it was thick and would probably require a stick or something to get it all off. He had no idea where it could have come from, and then he noticed the corners of the old priest's mouth. He must have vomited recently and had managed to get most of it cleaned off his beard. Not all of it; he probably hadn't planned on the company or was saving some for later. He was squinting at all of the men, and they were all taller than him, as he tried to get up close to see better. It appeared to them that he was either going to sneeze, cough or vomit, and when the one with the clipboard found his way down the steps to the twigs, the others were not far behind. All except for one, and there he stood. The two new acquaintances stared at each other up there on the porch, and all of the policemen were down on the front landing.

"We brought you an assistant; they say you need one. This man's name is Basil, and he's come a long way. He's just like you. They say you need him. First name, er... Edward. He is to be your assistant at the Easter Mass. They say you need one. Don't ask me who 'they' are; I haven't got a clue. You must have the church ready for Mass on any Easter Sunday morning, just like in the old times. If not this year, more than likely next. We will bring you provisions, if and when we can, but don't expect much and don't die. Your garden is your salvation; let's all hope it rains a little more often this year. Hey you, Basil, come with us and get the provisions, and you two can meet later." With that, they all turned and started to walk away, when the old priest hollered out to the policeman for him to stop.

"Wait! Wait! Mass? Assistant? I, I must tell you, stop, please, let me think."

All of the men stopped and turned as the old man nimbly sailed down the steps and straight up, face to face with the frightened policeman who had raised his clipboard up to his chest to protect himself. There was no telling how much damage the old man could muster, but better safe than sorry.

"Thank you, thank you, thank you. My assistant and I will always have it ready. Tell them that."

Suddenly the old priest was at least five foot ten, seemed to have lost the hump somewhere between the front door frame and the bottom step, and had the head policeman's face pinched between his hands. Primarily because he didn't seem to have any choice in the matter and the fact that the old goat was quick as a cat, he found himself captured by a thankful fanatic. Besides all that, he was still dealing with the filthy disgusting clipboard and hadn't had time to deal with anything except the board for the last few moments. He had enough to worry about, but now it was too late, and the old man had him ready for a good old-fashioned Russian manly kiss of gratitude. There was no threat here, and he just had to let it happen; he knew he had brought it on himself.

The priest seemed unusually strong for someone his age, and suddenly taller, which made that first kiss on the right cheek unavoidable, and hopefully it would all be over soon. Then the dirty old man quite intentionally dragged his tongue across the police officer's lips while changing cheeks. The second kiss, and the last one, for that matter, came with noise that no one could interpret to be anything but friendly. You could hear it ten feet away, which was verifiable.

The priest instantly released his grip. "Thank you, thank you. God bless you," he said as the officer stumbled backward trying to understand what had just happened. He was wiping his mouth as frantically as he could without losing his balance, but it was hopeless, especially after he discovered a large mushy relic of what appeared to be flesh with fish scales, there, between his fingers, at which time he simply lost it. He was instantly beside himself and did not think he liked himself much anymore as he tumbled backward and over one of his assistants.

"You're very welcome." Crash! "We must go. Now."

The officer was back on his feet and seemed to be having a bad moment; maybe it was just a human emotional confusion after being so positively thanked. Hammer found his hump, shrunk rather quickly, and was doing a little soft-shoe-shuffle while chanting "Thank you, thank you, thank you." The other officers were also surprised at the old priest's response, but not near as surprised as their senior supervisor had been. He was now moving quickly back towards the cars, with everyone else in hot pursuit. They were leaving fast.

The thank yous were disappearing with distance, and the first officer was hard to keep up with. As he led the hurried retreat, it suddenly occurred to him that what he really needed to do was go back and shoot that old priest right between the eyes, or at least somewhere in the face. He felt assaulted, invaded, damaged; there was so much wrong with the last five minutes, as his men caught up to him one at a time and patted him on the back to continue the thank yous. It seemed very appropriate, and confused him even more. He kept looking for more pieces of fish or whatever it was, in case any of it got stuck anywhere. Finally, it was Basil's turn to say something just as the group came up on the edge of the front steps to the church.

"This is so honorable and decent of you, and it looked to me like you positively made that old man's day." After which he set his hand on the police officer's left shoulder.

"DON'T TOUCH ME! Leave them the boxes right here by the rock. Four boxes of food and two crates of wine. Sign here." Basil took the pencil and started to write his name when the pencil tip hit a wet spot.

"I'm sorry, sir, but the place for my name has some sort of goop and—"

At which time the officer reached out and very deftly snatched both the board and the pencil directly out of Basil's grasp, who finished his previous thought with, "—it's all over the pencil, too."

"IT DOESN'T MATTER. THAT OLD MAN ALREADY SIGNED!"

A mild tremor seemed to ripple up the police officer's body as he realized he could now feel what the assistant was talking about.

Basil went on innocently, "If I had a hankie I could wipe that splotch from your lapel, just under your handsome beard. NO, don't look down."

Those were the last words spoken there in the parking lot that day, as both sedans filled up, backed out and left the area back down the south fork. Neither vehicle seemed worthy of a long trip, but that was surely not the case. They had a long way to go no matter where they were headed; Pfeiffer was not exactly 'just down the road' from anywhere.

There, by the rock, were the six crates, and Basil turned to see the old priest now standing on the distant porch with his glasses on. They looked at each other from a few hundred feet away and tried to come to the reality of the situation. After a few minutes, long minutes, the old man started down the steps and headed out to where the young man was standing. He had obviously lost the hump for good and was quick on his feet, had a walking stick, and

154

most of all he had a smile that was very contagious considering there was only the two of them. In half the time it had taken Basil and the boys to cover the same distance either time before, the pastor arrived in the lot, held out his hands and was literally shouting, "HELLO, HELLO, HELLOooo, MY YOUNG FRIEND, Father Basil. Hello!"

When he was right up on top of the young priest, he grabbed him by the face and gave him a huge kiss on each cheek. "My God loves me very much. Hallelujah, Hallelujah, Hallelujah."

"That he does, Amen." It was the only response, and Basil was astounded to see that the cane was perfectly balanced on its tip and should have fallen over a thousand times out of a thousand. It must have been some sort of a parlor trick for the man to stand it by his side while doing other things, and there it waited for him to reattach. It was the first of many times that Basil would be astounded by Father Hammer. And so began their introductions to each other, and they would go on for weeks.

Hammer would show him almost everything and tell him almost everything, but his plan was simple — not everything. Basil would never be able to tell about things he didn't know anything about, and it was necessary to hide so much. The monsters might come back and torture the young man to death and learn absolutely everything he ever knew, not tomorrow or the next day, but someday, maybe. During the interrogations, all they would have to do is ask, and he would tell them everything, not at the beginning, of course, but surely by the end. No man can withstand the pressure, and, unfortunately, the possibility existed. Things he didn't know could never be revealed, and he wondered why they hadn't already done that to him, but he knew they seemed to want the Teardrop more than anything else. They knew they needed Hammer, and he had to assume they knew he needed help. There was no other explanation for any of this.

CHAPTER 12

THE SECOND PASSING

Easter Sunday 1928

The two priests were crouched by the flowerbed all through the morning and could hear the commotion inside their church. Their guard was attentive and not too far away under a shade tree; they benefited from it, too. Off to their right was a side entrance to the front vestibule of the church, the favored loading dock from the past, and farther up and around the corner was where the front steps climbed up to the main entrance to the church. From their vantage point, they couldn't see everyone who went in or what came out. There were large covered trucks that rumbled into the front area, but they disappeared from view and stopped out of sight, were loaded and then they followed the army.

Every once in a while, there would come a tremendous crashing noise out the windows and doors of the sacristy. These were the most offensive noises; nothing close to those kinds of sounds should ever come from inside such a place. At least that was the way it had been in the old days. For all of its violence, there were voices inside that laughed out loud and continuously. Nothing could be that funny.

The south side of the church was visible from over a mile in either direction no matter if a traveler was coming up from down the river or from the big bend a mile north. It was a towering hilltop church and could be seen from either direction long before one came upon it. All day long there was a constant swirling dust cloud as the commotion of traffic out on the road stretched from horizon to horizon and the Army worked its way north through the bottleneck directly in front of their faces.

These were the victors of the Russian Revolution, and many were already tired of the way things had turned out. They hardly slowed their passage through the town, and no one approached the church or even got close. It must have been the signs, which didn't forbid them from looking. The entire army was witness to what was happening to the church and, even though most of those eyes out there only looked at it for a moment or two, they were witness and would probably talk about it later on. So they should, but they kept on moving, passed by and went on up the road.

All afternoon this spectacle of the infantry, the horse soldiers, long convoys of tanks and trucks, churned through the once quiet countryside, and what had once been a somewhat narrow country road was now twice as wide and completely pulverized. Hammer was remembering the past, the same army doing the same thing just like back in '22.

Just half a mile to the north, the road widened, and there was an intersection of sorts, where it branched into a side road that led off to the west and Romania, with the other branch going north into the wilderness, to the lands of the outback. The Ukrainian frontier was five hundred miles up to the northwest and had become a lifeless land. Pfeiffer's small tributary river, the Ilava, flowed out of the mountain range, down to the River Don, and had no allegiances to the Volga on the other side of the mountains. The army seemed to use both branches of the Y, and after that point they literally clogged their way into the never ending mud. It was along the banks of the river back through the town where the congestion seemed to cause the most confusion, and there was smoke in the air from fires on the other side of the river. The two priests could only sit and watch as thousands of Russian Red Army soldiers moved away from the river's edge, onto the road, and slowly out of sight, headed north, in a quagmire of mud never less than six inches deep.

The soldiers grouped up in long formations, four men across the front, and then long lines of the exact same image over and over. They were loud any time they were moving, with much chatter amongst the men. It was all their equipment that made most of the noise, frequently accompanied by someone shouting at the top of their lungs for everyone to hear. They were disciplined, and on few of the faces was there any sign of real life — just a face. It was astounding how much they all looked alike from that distance. Basil saw eyes look into his and frequently he felt as if they were saying goodbye somehow. Some were vicious, some were wet, scared or young, some very old, all kinds, and some were comforting. Not many. Nothing they could do about anything; but sorry nonetheless, if that was readable. More than a few looked at him as if they loathed his image and may have smiled a smirk knowing he was doomed. He looked away instantly. It's very hard to rationally interpret eye contact, but we all do it and we're probably wrong about what we see ninety percent of the time. He wanted to go back over to the rectory and sleep; that would be nice.

Hammer had started to choke and was obviously struggling with his breath. He appeared to be squinting hard at anything he looked at and was busily watching the entire goings-on out on the roadway. The man was hurt deep inside from the rifle butt shot. He was weak; there was blood coming out of his mouth, and what he needed was a drink of water, but the sergeant had screamed at them both to sit there and not move at all. At least they were sitting.

The colonel was with a captain there, in the sacristy, and they were collecting things from throughout the church. Many of the more historic and unique items were put in large wooden crates and stolen through the main entrance. Occasionally, the officers would walk out onto the top step and smoke. They were keeping exact records of it all and followed a checklist. From their vantage point, at the top of those steps, they could see the procession of troops out on the dusty roadway. The Red Army was unstoppable, had finally found Pfeiffer again, and they would rule the land from that time on.

There was one other thing for sure in the spring of 1928: The Red Army did not pray, and they did not believe in God. As a result, they had no use whatsoever for organized religion, towering churches and grubby old priests. In only ten years, everything had changed. Nothing was safe or sane, and seemingly overnight, a troubled society had disintegrated into oblivion. As far as Pfeiffer, Russia, was concerned, all that was left of it was dying inside the church, and that angry army on the road had its heathen representatives inside St. Francis, and they were collecting the taxes due.

Suddenly the walls of the church shuddered as machine-guns erupted inside its being. Bullets crashed through glass windows, everyone on the road looked in that direction, and the priests cowered closer to the building, hoping the foundation blocks were thick enough, and that they were for sure. The shooting stopped, and then a screaming voice directed the shooters to destroy the altar. Then came another volley of rapid-fire bursts, more shouting, more gunfire, then just a few isolated shots. Their guard came out from behind the tree and resumed his attention.

Around four in the afternoon, the colonel came out to the top of the steps and threw the Bible out into the grass as far as he could heave it, then another large book, and still another. All three ended up landing close by each other and at least fifty feet on the other side of the walkway.

"Won't be needing those anymore after tonight!" he shouted at the sergeant and then ordered the man to get the holy ones back inside the building. The colonel turned and walked inside the sacristy, leaving the guard with both priests. He stood there for a moment with his gun held across his chest and stared at both men leaning against the wall.

"You heard the man... Get back inside!"

He stepped back enough for the two to walk in front of him and then he took his first finger off the trigger and appeared to be wiping his lips. He never let go of the barrel guard, and the strap held the piece exactly where it belonged. As their eyes met, Basil watched as the soldier made a very tiny cross over his lips.

"Father, forgive me, for I know not what I do. I ask for your forgiveness," he admitted in fluent Latin.

The priests were climbing the steps when they both realized that they heard that confession in the ancient language. The soldier's eyes were sorrowful; he was asking for forgiveness, and both Hammer and Basil forgave him his sins with the blink of an eye and the blessing. Basil knew he might have been a good man once upon a time, in the past, but we all change, and now he was not much of that man anymore, but it was not his fault. It was a long story, and no one cared about the sergeant's problem. He was as much a victim as anyone else, and he too would regret that he lived during these times; almost everyone did.

All the people were gone, and no one knew where they were, where they went or how they got there. They just disappeared into a fog of insanity, whole communities up to the north, nothing left, nothing at all from them. They were all gone, murdered, massacred, enslaved. There was nothing but horrible news from Ukraine, and that was all anyone knew. Some of it seemed too unimaginable to be possibly real, and had to be exaggerations of war, but Basil had traveled through it to get here, and he knew it was all true. Every rumor, every story, every exaggeration was true. Time and distance and curfews all twisted the truth in a matter of a hundred miles no matter where one might call home in Russia.

When Basil got off the train in Kiev, he started the long walk, and after traveling a thousand miles with guides who always told stories, he ended up with a finely narrated guided tour of hell. Basil was sure the entire world had gone completely insane, and he wanted for Jesus Christ Himself to stop the madness. As he was guided into Russia, he wondered what Jesus was thinking about all this, and then he wondered if He was watching at all.

He often wondered on his journey, as in every day, if he really belonged wherever it was he was headed — this place called Pfeiffer. Did He know that they were there in the sacristy? Wasn't there anything God could do about all this? It wasn't the first time he had asked such questions, but it could very well be the last.

As he sat there against the wall, holding up the old priest, he was able to recall some of the questions he had asked himself on his journey to Pfeiffer, the ones about why. He was perfectly healthy except for the fact that he was slowly starving to death, hadn't been injured in any way, and could see everything perfectly clear. Hammer could hardly see his hand in front of his face, if you asked the guard, but he was seeing what he was seeing, and he confidently touched Basil on his shoulder many times. It was an amazing feeling, just out of nowhere; Hammer would lay his hand on his shoulder, and Basil would calm in a sense. If nothing else, they were both still alive, but getting closer and closer to their death beds with every passing step.

As ordered and supervised by their guard, they both clambered up the eight steps into and through that back door to the sacristy. Once inside, they could see that the entire room had been destroyed. All of the vestments were thrown in a pile there in the corner, and the empty closets intimidated both Hammer and Basil. Every closet and cabinet door was open, off its hinges in most cases, and empty. Up against a wall was a huge pile of all their vestments, belongings and items of worship all thrown together. It was a very brief moment of anguish. As they passed through, they both realized it was now over, and, even though both had wished and prayed that they'd never see this sight, it was what it was. It was the end and they were still in the sacristy.

In essence, the barbarians wanted that portion of the back windows that held the diamond teardrop panels. They just needed to know where it was. It was all they wanted, and they had to be sure. As the group stumbled across the broken altar area, Basil looked up and saw where all the side windows had been shattered, ending up both inside and out in piles of twisted lead edgings, with all the many pieces of colored glass scattered all over everything. The pillars that held up the altar slab had been blasted out from under it, and the slab crashed down and broke apart into many large chunks. The tabernacle was gone and not a part of the scene. It was hard, if not impossible, to tell that they had once upon a time been designed as treasure lockers. Many of the pews had been ripped out of the floorboards and piled up against that back window assembly, assisting the marauders in reaching high enough to get it all intact. The entire section was gone, and proved that someone somewhere wanted that teardrop for themselves. It was now on its way somewhere and Hammer was fairly confident they hadn't acquired the hourglass that made it all work. Sokolov had stopped the procession on the distant side of what was left of the altar and examined his work and final result for a long minute. While everyone waited, Basil was holding up Hammer and saw Sokolov in a bathtub, bathing in blood, just a fleeting image.

An enormous effort had been made to rip through the main walkway floor in search of something below, but the excavators ran into a thick base of rock and sand on top of rock and sand, and ended their dig after the shovels full of dirt, fell back into the hole every time they tried to throw it out. They finally stopped their dig at ten feet. It appeared to be a standard foundation, the old kind that lasted forever, without a basement.

The exit procession had to use the side aisle as they headed for the back of the church.

"We thought there might be a basement," the colonel motioned at the hole in the floor, "but, there isn't one, is there?" After staring at both men he said it again, "WE THOUGHT THERE MIGHT BE A BASEMENT!"

Basil was staring at the pit, as was Hammer, and neither priest managed to hear the first question, and in so doing passed the test. They were finally all standing near the same spot where Hammer had hidden his glasses, when the colonel stopped his current tirade about meaningless shit and started to pee all over the last pew. While he was occupied, the whole group milled about, and Hammer slid the glasses into his pocket. He too was relieved.

Sokolov was a very different man at this point in the afternoon. He was ruffled and dusty and obviously tired of the place and ready to be done with it. To celebrate the gathering, Hammer collapsed near that side door to the foyer.

"WHAT GOOD IS THIS OLD MAN'S CANE? HELP HIM UP AND FIND HIS CANE. Lean on your cane, old man, and listen to me for a few moments. Our film needs to be processed and studied, but we feel we may have succeeded in capturing the miracle of your windows. Thanks to the method of your performance, to the best of my own personal observation, it was a spectacular success, wouldn't you agree?"

Hammer and Basil were back to their deafness and squinting like never before.

When the colonel discovered that his planned performance to hopefully clarify whether or not the priests had seen the teardrop through that blinding sunlight had not been heard by either man, his eyes exploded and seemed to be bulging out of his face. He grabbed the back of his pant pleats and held on tight, rushed up to the old priest's face and screamed, "DID YOU SEE THE TEARDROP?"

The old priest had been cowering away from the lunatic and his two companions while he shouted the question and, during that epic moment, he straightened up from the cower and leaned into the colonel's space.

"Maybe next year." It was over, and all of the cards were out on the table.

"NEXT YEAR! NEXT YEAR? DID YOU SAY NEXT YEAR? I'LL SHOW YOU NEXT YEAR. Father, will you hear my confession? FATHER, WILL YOU HEAR MY CONFESSION?"

The colonel hurried toward the beautiful confessional and seemed to politely, insanely, open the center door for the old priest to enter his cubicle. There was no damage to the entire assembly; not a single bullet had ripped through it anywhere; it had been intentionally preserved for this performance. Hammer had no choice in the matter and stumbled into it with both hands clutching his cane. Without it, he couldn't have made those last few steps; he was very badly hurt. Sokolov was enraged; his eyes were huge as he pulled off his gloves and slammed them into the floor. On his third effort at a pocket, he finally found what he was searching for and pulled the white hankie out in a swirl. He held it directly in front of Hammer's nose and told him he could have it. A memento of the day they'd prayed together. The colonel closed the door, slowly, and tilted his head so both eyes could watch Hammer in those last few inches. The only thing the old man could do was give him the fingers.

Finally, the center confessor's door was closed tight, and Sokolov opened the right side confessional door and started to enter. He looked back at Basil and told the priest he might want to go inside the other door and also confess his sins to the pastor. Basil was still standing in the doorway as the colonel continued to slur how the confessional had always made him feel 'complete' back in his childhood days. He seemed to know all about it, and he still remembered the opening pleads. Basil was listening to every word, and when the man had finished, he brought both his fingers up to his ears and gave the colonel the look deaf people give vocal people in an effort to solve a problem. The colonel motioned with his finger for Basil to close the door, and after he did, he saw the tub again and saw Sokolov without a tongue. The colonel stepped out of his doorway, closed that door, too, and the forgiven guard wrapped a chain around all three door handles. The priests were now prisoners inside their confessional and could only stare at their doors in the very dim light allowed in through the ceiling slats.

"OH MY GOD, I'M SO HEARTILY SORRY FOR HAVING OFFENDED THEE, AND I DETEST ALL MY SINS BECAUSE OF THY JUST PUNISHMENT, BUT MOST OF ALL..."

The colonel was standing directly in between the two doors and screaming the first words to the contrition as loudly as possible, but abruptly stopped when things were just getting good. Those were the last words he said inside the church, and the priests could hear the heavy army boots pounding on the floor as they left. Each man stood alone inside his respective cubicle, staring at the door in perfect silence; time may have stopped.

All around the outside edge of the church, two soldiers sprayed the sides and footing with the end result from backpack flamethrowers. There was no need to apply any of this solution to the inside. They were instructed to start at the front, under the bell tower, and work their way to the back. There was no need for a rectory, no need for the empty convent or any of the sheds.

Within five minutes, every building at that intersection of the small hamlet was totally engulfed in raging fires. The two flamethrower artisans had to change their retreat and ended up climbing up onto the roadway hundreds of yards away upwind. It was in truth exactly where they needed to be, to be picked up by their truck driver. Many a 'flame thrower' operator in the history of such devices have misjudged the ferocity of their weapon and been incinerated in a matter of moments, depending on the retreat. The weapon has been known to leak, and that could turn a very aggressive situation into a giant fireball in an instant. They were both lucky and exhausted from the event.

There were a hundred or so soldiers left waiting for their trucks and troop wagons scattered back and away from the church. They congregated in small groups, and some sat down and dug around in their packs for something to eat. Some smoked, as the sides of the church started to disappear into the roaring fire. What had been a safe distance to start with wasn't nearly so safe anymore, and the fire forced the whole crowd back even farther. The noise from the fire was a common sound to most of them, and the occasion was, too. Most had seen this before, and it was no different in any way, shape or form from all those that had come before. Another church, another fire, another day.

The two priests in the confessional were only slightly aware of exactly what was going on outside the chained doors. They could both barely hear the inferno that was burning all around them. It was growling louder by the moment. The glow coming into their boxes from their ceilings kept increasing, and they could smell smoke, instantly, and were consequently terrified. Basil didn't know what to pray next, and kept falling back into his perpetual St. Jude Novena. Already that day he had prayed as much or more than any day before in his life, and that life was getting closer by the moment to being completely resolved. He looked at his hands for a moment and realized he was still very much alive. He started to see the smoke, which was very different from smelling it. "St Jude," he prayed, "patron of hopeless situations, this is just about as hopeless a situation as I could come up with. Pray for me."

CHAPTER 13

THE FIRE BEGINS

Hammer sat quietly on the bench inside his confessional and knew in his heart, or just a little below it, that the rifle butt to his side had damaged something quite severely. He considered his kidney, and that perhaps all of his ribs could have been broken — he didn't know, but it was now swollen far out from normal, and he could barely touch the region. He tasted his own blood constantly, and there was dried blood all around his lips. He needed water, it would help, and then he remembered his glasses. He looked at the sliding partition to the right side and softly and quickly slid it open. He knew Basil would be inches away, on the other side. They had been in this exact situation many times before, every two weeks or so, and just for the hell of it. Hammer heard Basil's confession, and Basil heard Hammer's, even though there was never anything to confess, and it ended up being the three Our Father, three Hail Mary, and three Glory Be penance.

Neither man had attempted to open his door; they both understood what that guard had been doing after they were inside, what that sound was, and what it meant. Both men could see those outside handles in their minds and what it would take to tie all three together, a concept that had never crossed their minds before this moment. Exactly the same handles as on the inside, and they were now chained on the outside. Neither man had said a word just yet, and were intently listening through the thick wooden closet doors, which were soundproof.

The confessional was this master centerpiece in the front vestibule to the magnificent church, ten feet tall, twenty feet long and six feet wide. The workmanship was exquisite, in dense wood with soft curves, perfect seams, cuts, and junctures. It was intended to be almost soundproof, and on very few occasions could either man ever remember someone raising his or her voice within the confines of such a place. Even after eighty-some years of constant use, the doors still opened and closed tightly, perfectly smooth every time. Neither priest had ever considered this particular fate, nor had the artisan who'd crafted the gliding apartment complex.

Basil had been standing the whole time facing the door, as he had no other choice except to kneel and face the window. As all petitioners can attest, there comes that moment when theoretically a saint is now walking out of the other unit, and the priest slides that window partition open and the dim light comes through. The concept of 'confession' is a very old and sacred part of most religions, but few compare to the Catholic version, and there are few moments in a Catholic's life that rival the Sacrament of Penance.

Basil knelt and looked through the cloth barrier that separated the two, and there was Hammer, three inches away, with his glasses on. They said nothing and just looked at each other through that film and screen, two silhouettes that were about to burn to death together.

Basil knew the end was near and was surprised to feel the calm in his pastor's gaze. The ceiling of the confessional appeared to be an intricate assembly of thin beams that overlapped each other, forming a checkerboard of light holes. Once one's eyes were adjusted, it was anything but dark, as the reflections of fire bounced off the ceiling and down through those slats. Hammer leaned forward and pressed his forehead against the screen.

"They've hurt me pretty bad, Father, and I'm afraid it's going to kill me."

Basil was as close to his fellow priest's face as he had ever been before, and in a hushed whisper he quietly added, "At least you have your glasses."

The old man pulled back from the screen and smiled his beautiful smile. It was hard to see, but Basil knew what it would have looked like.

"I don't want you to worry. I have a plan, and you have a destiny. Don't worry!"

Basil had not spent one moment the entire day not worrying; he'd still had not had a drop of anything to drink, except for the wine during the consecration and the water from the finger wash; nor had Hammer. As he waited for the old man to continue, it occurred to him that he could still taste that wine in his mouth. There was no doubt, and, in fact, he wasn't really all that hungry or thirsty. The subjugation of those two life-sustaining requirements might have been in response to the notion that he hadn't been this scared for this long a time in his whole life so far.

Now, here at the end, he found himself a prisoner, and with his beloved pastor, the two were being held captive in their own confessional, inside their ravaged church, with no explanation other than the fact that the barbarians evidently hated the idea of God so much there was nothing they weren't capable of. As he surveyed the four walls around him, he instantly realized he was inside his coffin and would be cremated. There was no way out unless they opened it from the outside.

Through the maze of slats above him he could see enough of the late afternoon light, the apparent reflections from fire on the inside of the church ceiling, and he knew they only had a little while left before the fire would incinerate them both. As nasty a scenario as it seemed to be, all the priests could do was wait for the fire to do what it does, or continue to hope their murderers might reconsider, come back and drag them both away, but that probably wasn't on anybody's things-to-do list.

Father Hammer opened the other side window cautiously and peeked through the curtain screen at the empty room; dead silence. Perfect quiet.

"Pssst, Pssst, PZZZZTTTT!"

Hammer changed windows and put his ear close to Basil's mouth.

"Yes, my son?"

"Father, I just wanted to let you know that I confess I think I may not have the worry part of all this under control, and I've always hoped I'd end up with a destiny of some sort or another. I don't believe I ever considered martyrdom, and I don't think anyone out there cares that we're here. Concerning what we talked about before, I was wondering if you had thought any more about the plan you mentioned."

"Just a moment."

Basil could see that the old priest had stood up and was fumbling around with the inside wall that separated the two, making noises, and when he did, he could smell the blood. In the next moment the entire window assembly, screen, sliding door, and decorative trim leaned into the center section, and the old priest set it on the floor in front of his feet.

"As I was saying, I have some good news and some bad news for the two of us. They're not coming back. That's the good news. In fact, my young priest, they haven't left yet. They're out there watching the fire. As far as the bad news is concerned, well, you know the bad news. About the plan, well, I suppose you could call it a plan."

"Very well, I will. I am one hundred percent ready to hear Father Karl Hammer's plan for him and his lowly assistant. Ready as can be."

The hole that had been made when Hammer lifted out the window assembly was a perfect square of some 24 inches or more. Basil was still kneeling, but now things were much more open, much better.

"I had no idea," he whispered.

Hammer began to explain that there would be more to come in the next few hours, and even though things might become very dire, Basil was to never give up, as his destiny was about to begin. Basil made a quick mental note that Hammer never spoke about putting out the fire.

First, Hammer explained how, for many years before Basil had arrived, there had been a constant flow of wagons carrying church treasures out of the Badlands away from the robbers and thieves, and they had been brought to St. Francis. The local priests for hundreds of miles in every direction had few options at times, and the only hope for much of their personal church treasures was to, somehow or another, get it somewhere safe. They would then claim that it had all been stolen by the militias, gypsy gangs, Arabs or who knows who. Anytime the marauding group confronted the priests about the lack of quality, they would always say that others had already looted the place and would be dead a little while later.

Most everything that was visible to the public and the congregations was in most cases a subdued version. The chalice the priests had used during the consecration earlier that morning somewhat lacked in quality when compared to the rest of the church. As did the candleholders, kneelers… just about everything was second-class, and that assumed one knew what first class was. There was no doubt that everything was a substitute. It was a short story, a historical story, and created as many questions for Basil as it answered, including the one that he politely suggested, "So what? I thought we were concerned about the fire!"

Next came a brief history of the site and all the things about its most unusual construction. It appeared to the keenest eye that the entire structure sat atop a rock formation. "Yes. Yes." "NO!" It actually straddles two formations and secretly hides a basement vault the likes of which the youngster wouldn't believe.

Finally, Hammer explained that the army was out there watching their final victory over this particular church. As far as anyone involved in starting the fire was concerned, the entire triple bell tower would eventually collapse directly on top of the confessional in an exploding mayhem of fire. He had to assume that they would wait until it cooled enough for them to take the bells, but that would be all that would be left worth anything. This magnificent wooden structure would be nothing more than a typical burned-out pile of black cinders where a truly spectacular Catholic church had once stood. A mini-cathedral on the edge of the plains, a wonderful idea, but truly in the wrong place, wrong time, wrong continent for that matter, but a beautiful try.

"You've seen the burned-down remnants of some of the neighboring churches; I've seen them, and that's our future."

The only news from that thirty-second revelation was something about a basement vault, which did nothing to quiet the noise from up above.

Their cubicles were now lighted from above, the ceiling far above had caught the flames.

Hammer talked about the architect, a man they only described as 'The Saint.' He noted that it had been The Saint who had carved the cane. It was he who had the construction plans for the church, the expertise, and a mission for life. He said it now appeared that this entire beautiful structure would end up covering the underground vault in the ashes of St. Francis of Assisi; it would take a massive fire to bring this church to her knees, and that's just what fires do.

The monsters stood off in the distance and watched it burn for a couple of hours after sunset. Even though the early evening rain was light at first, it steadily grew in intensity and put a solemn damper on the festivities. You just can't have a good church burning in the early evening rain no matter what you do, but the rain didn't seem to have any effect at all on the collapsing fireball. The last of the convoys had disappeared, and there were few remaining troops or trucks. The roads were nothing but mud ruts as the officers climbed into their jeeps and followed, almost last, after the army.

As Sokolov was driven away later that evening he was able to watch the fire in the driver's rear view mirror for just a little while longer, thinking to himself that he had taught them a lesson they would never forget. He knew to some degree what he had on film and hoped beyond hope that they had caught the very end, especially that Diamond Teardrop.

They had started the fire all along the base of the closed front doors heading down each side of the church, spraying the fuel all over the base and foundation. Filmed it like a sporting event. The entire front of the church burned much more intensely at the start than did the east end. The hundred-foot high bell tower started leaning into the chaos, and it fell over and not downward about thirty minutes into the inferno. Hopefully his cameramen caught the explosion when all that fresh timber hit the main body of the fire and almost instantly the fire doubled in size and evaporated the rain in a brilliant halo that completely surrounded the highest flames, two hundred feet off the ground. The moisture from the evaporated rain didn't know where to go and formed this incredible rolling white and gray halo just below the line where the smoke started running with the wind. Nighttime would erase the halo as the fire ate itself alive and began to die along with the rain.

The colonel was positive there would be nothing left the next day and wasn't sure there were any churches left to burn. He was satisfied with himself and anxious to get to the encampment. It was too bad that the truckloads of a theoretical treasure from the place left a lot to be desired, and he couldn't help that. As they searched every church before they lit the fire, as a general rule, they usually found nothing of any value. The priests and people always professed to be poor, but he knew better. Even though he knew better and tried his best to believe that, he also knew that someday they would find the mother load.

He sat back in his seat, satisfied with the work he was doing, and assumed he would never be back in Pfeiffer as long as he lived, not that there was anything to come back to or any reason why. In only a matter hours, the entire place was in ashes, the last remnant of a community, of people and a way of life. Sokolov was certain that when that fire went out that would be the absolute end of the German Volga Catholics. Everything they had ever built, everything they ever had was now gone. None of them were left, and if they had any valuables, they must have taken them with them. His right hand pinky drilled an itch away in his ear, drug his tongue back and forth on his teeth, and couldn't wait to get out of the rain.

Inside the confessional, Father Hammer stood up and leaned against the door. It wouldn't open much, but through an inch he could see the inside of the church was engulfed. It was time, and they didn't have much of that left. He turned around, reached out, and pulled the left side of his bench seat up and forward, revealing a staircase. It was a rather small opening, tight and steep, but it was an opening to somewhere. Basil peered through from his side and down into the darkness while Hammer explained how he was to crawl through backward and then straight down the steps to the bottom.

"Nice plan, Father. Praise God, praise Jesus, and praise our Mother Mary. Praise all the saints in heaven and those on earth. Praise God. Look at that hole! Where does it go?"

This revelation had come none too soon, as the roar of the fire, and the glow, increased through the ceiling boards. He followed the instructions and was able to get his feet through the window, and then his waist. It was very tight, and he squirmed backward while Hammer pulled on his legs. It was most tense all through his torso, and he was much concerned about his shoulders, but he popped through almost as if he were water and was now standing on the first step down into the darkness. The noise from falling ceiling tiles, crashing statues, windows exploding, fire, and all the other noises that fire makes when it's roaring, was now overpowering and terrifying.

With that sound in the background, he stood there, waist deep in the opening, and then down he went, through a long tube, a landing of sorts, and another dozen steps or more to the bottom floor, he lost count. There, on a small table next to the ladder, were matches and candles, and he hurriedly lit one.

Hammer was a ghostly figure far up the ladder and had worked himself into his descent. From underneath, he pulled the bench seat back towards where it had come from and seemingly shut out the mayhem above to a distant rumble. When he was slightly below the top of the ladder, he pulled another handle, and a steel plate slid out of a niche up there, completely sealing the cavity and blocking out all the noises. He limped down the ladder, one step at a time. His cane hit every step below, a bulls-eye, and he never touched the ladder with that hand until he finally reached the floor.

"We must hurry to the other end. The bell towers are going to fall, and the bells are very heavy. The whole church is on fire, and we'll be a lot safer on the other end. We need to go."

And they did.

CHAPTER 14

THE REAL DIAMOND TEARDROP

The two men stood there in the light of a single candle, and Basil could see that there was something terribly wrong with his pastor. He was trying to piece the past few minutes into some sort of order, trying to accept the idea that he was in the basement of the church, with the main problem being that he never even knew there was one. The candle gave him sight of some enormous vertical timbers that were holding up the ceiling, which was farther up than he thought, maybe fifteen feet, and there appeared to be more horizontal timbers similarly sized that formed the roof rafters. Everything was tight, massive and heavy-duty.

"Well, my son, here we are." A pause. "I have much to show you, but first I need to lie down for just a little while. I think they may have killed me. Do you understand where you are? I told you I had a plan."

Basil nodded, and the older priest motioned for him to light the tripod candle. They both now had their own light and the old man motioned with his for them to head up the pillared passageway directly under what Basil imagined being the central aisle walkway of the church above them. They were headed in the direction of the main altar; he could almost count the steps. He was amazed at the size of the pillars, the solid granite under his feet, everything about the vault so far, and that would prove to be just the beginning.

As they headed east, the long hallway finally entered a large cavernous room that he measured to be exactly the same size as the main altar area above him. He had noticed two or three doors that were closed on the left side of the walkway, and not much else as he followed the limping old man. The easternmost back wall was a sheer cliff of granite; smooth, clean and supporting some of the three foot in diameter ceiling timbers that fell into perfectly placed notches in the rock which had been created a few hundred million years before.

Right in the middle of this forty-foot-wide, fifteen-foot-high escarpment was one of the most amazing things he had ever seen. In the dim light from his three candles, it appeared to him that God had chiseled a magnificent human eye in black granite rock. Out of that area where our tears always come from, the rock poured out a stream of water, over the cheek and down to the floor. It flowed across the center of the room and was perfectly encased within the banks of a solid rock stream bed as wide as a man is tall and only an inch deep. On the other side of the room, some thirty feet away, it appeared as though the rock formation simply swallowed the stream by the back wall of vertical timbers. It just disappeared into the rock as if God had stabbed the granite with his saber, vanishing into a half a dozen long cracks in the floor. There were flat stepping stones in the stream, and it was easy to cross over it and into the other half of this enormous room. He could see more furniture, tables and chairs, couches, an easel with a bench stool, candle stands, and an elegant four-seat dining table.

"Father Basil, I would like to introduce you to the original Diamond Teardrop."

From this new vantage point, Basil now understood why they had constructed St. Francis where they did, and why Hammer had told him that brief history while they fretted in their fireplaces. His mind was racing with logistics and sizes, dimensions and square footage, quantities of timber and rock. All through the church's history, everyone had always marveled at the size of the trees in that whole area around the Grotto and the church itself. They didn't get any more surface water than all the other trees, but were taller and more beautiful to the casual observer, appearing healthier than even the trees down by the river. In the old times, many of the church gatherings, picnics, concerts, outdoor services had always been held outdoors, between the church and the statue of St. Francis inside his Grotto. It was a beautiful hilltop, and to the untrained eye it appeared the creators had built the church down below the Grotto on a rock-solid foundation.

Basil was awestruck at the size of the entire back wall of the room, solid rock, more or less straight up and down, that incredible eye, and the water pouring out of the tear duct, most of all. That was his initial introduction to something he would find enchanting and miraculous from that time on. He was already addicted after only five minutes.

Father Hammer set his candles down on a long table; it ran along the north wall that intersected with the rock formation. He lit a trio of thick wicks in front of a reflecting mirror, and the room lit up in all its glory. It was spectacular. The furniture was lavish and most assuredly must have once been the seating amenities in a much different environment, a long time ago. The granite floor was covered with a variety of carpet and wood, with only a light film of dust. Hammer sat down carefully in the big chair and yelped out a cough.

"They got me good. Father, I could sure use a tall glass of water, if you don't mind. There is a pitcher there by the waterfall, and all I've ever done is retrieved my water from there, whenever I've been down here. Everything a man could possibly need is down here."

Basil was practically falling all over himself until he set his candles down and found the pitcher exactly where Hammer said it would be. The water was crystal-clear, and his pitcher was full in a second or two, maybe less. He hurried across the room, trying not to splash it all out, handed the vessel towards Hammer, who raised a few fingers at Basil and politely declined.

"We have cups." He motioned towards another table in the corner.

Right there, nearby, were many cups, saucers, bowls, and they too were of a finer quality than he was used to in the rectory. Basil smiled at Hammer and found a matching pair of goblets, which he then sat side by side and filled to the halfway point. He picked one up and handed it carefully to his mentor.

"God bless you, Father."

They both sat there in silence, drinking the water, but could hear the distant sound — not so distant, they both knew, but it was buffered, muffled, and seemed distant.

"The church is burning down, isn't it? They've burned it down on top of us," Basil whispered.

"No need to whisper, my dear young friend, no need to whisper."

Hammer closed his eyes and started a prayer in his head, which is similar to a yawn among priests, and Basil did the same. After a few moments, he made the sign of the cross and bowed his head, then grimaced in obvious pain. Finally, he adjusted himself in his chair and leaned over on the right armrest.

"That's better."

Basil took a long drink of water and set his cup back down. He stared at the goblet and shook his head back and forth side to side. Pure water in this fairytale world, under the church... He was so confused, so relieved, and still worried.

Suddenly the entire structure began to creak, moan and wobble, those giant timbers were slightly shifting, and then an incredible thunder and concussion reverberated through the air and the walls. The two water goblets pinged against each other in the earthquake. From back up that hallway a blast of dust and noise billowed into the room, scaring them both as if someone had fired a cannon back there in the darkness. Instantly, it was over, except for the dust, and Basil's eyes were as big as pinecones.

"I would suspect that the bell tower just fell on top of us. That's what that was. Run down the hallway and see what's happened."

His last few words were at the back of Basil's head, which disappeared with his candles back to where they had come from. In no time at all, he was back, and informed the old man that there was no damage, just dust, no smoke and no fire, all the way back to the ladder.

"Just dust, Father. Nothing I can report. She took it very well."

With that, it was time to find out just how bad the injury was. Hammer lifted his shirt; the candles lighted his side, and they discovered a huge bruise, belt line to armpit. It was a dark, ugly goiter in the center of his ribcage, and covered the entire left side of his torso. There was not a lot of surface damage, but the imprint of a rifle butt was clearly evident on his bloated skin. The water had made him feel better almost instantly. Better — not a lot, but better.

"Father Basil, my friend, we won't burn to death down here. I know how this whole thing was made, and we will not burn. Trust me on that, okay?"

Basil had turned into a bobbing-head at times, whenever Hammer got his attention, and this was no exception.

"I don't know a lot about medicine, but I've seen enough to know that this is serious for me. I can't begin to explain what this is all about, but I do know that you, Father Edward Basil, will probably live through the next few days, at least, and what you discover down here is going to change your life forever. I think you've found that destiny we were talking about earlier."

He turned his lean a little and his lip trembled until his teeth chattered, and he sighed. Then he smiled a weak one.

"I cannot die until I've shown you all of the secrets encased inside these walls. Much as I would like to sleep, and I know you would, too, there are some paramount things that I must show you and tell you about, just in case my time is close. I buried a man once who had been kicked by a mule right here, just like me, and for the life of me I cannot seem to remember how long he lasted. We always seemed to be there at the very end, as you know, and often missed their journeys. I do not remember how long it took him to die, I only knew that he suffered, and then he died. We have seen a lot of death, Father, and I do believe you will end up watching me die. I consider that exquisite company. It won't be that bad, I promise."

As the two men rested, the volume of the tiny stream began increasing, making more noise, becoming more noticeable. In less than a day now, especially the last two hours — it was hard for Basil to tell — his entire life had been turned upside down. He wasn't dead, like he thought for sure he would be earlier that day, and he assumed it was early evening and dark outside. The fact of the matter was, he was still alive, in a gigantic basement. He kept glancing at the stream and then back to Hammer, who was also paying attention to the water. After a few long moments, Basil could not help but mention that there was a change in the volume. It was different from when they had first come close to it.

He had a mannerism that he loved to use in day-to-day life, where he turned his hands over, palms up, fingers splayed, anytime he was trying to make a point. It was as if you just had to agree with whatever it was he had just said. He looked back at Hammer and found the old man still hunched over the armrest, but wearing one of those magnificent Hammer smiles. It was as if the old pastor was seeing God himself, smiling ear to ear, showing every tooth left in his head, and had a glow in his eyes of almost euphoria. Big tears formed and began to stream down his cheeks. They had to be happy tears, for whatever reason.

"It's raining up there, really hard. Thank you, God! Thank God, thank you, Jesus. If it's raining, they'll leave and hopefully never come back." And his voice trailed off as Basil turned back to the stream. It was now twice the size of what it had been at the very beginning, and it stayed that way for the next few hours or so.

Hammer began to talk, and he had a story that was well-rehearsed. His words were precise and easy for Basil to listen to. From the time that very room was created until that conversation over a hundred years had come and gone. The history of the construction of St. Francis had been lost in time to all but him, the pastor of the church. It was now over; the church was gone, burned to its foundation, or so it now appeared, and it would be a monument for many years to come. Nothing but a pile of burned-down timber and pulverized marble, out on the edge of nowhere, surrounded by empty houses and barns, waiting for Mother Nature to overwhelm it all. Piles of debris like St. Francis were everywhere, from border to border, sea to sea, through a dozen time zones; a lesson to anyone who might object.

With everything that he now knew about the way things had turned out, the puzzle was complete. Hammer had always had the big questions inside himself as to why he was the caretaker, why him? Historically, all three of his predecessors had been able to pass on the keys, so to speak, at just the right time, to the next man. Hammer knew that history, and that knowledge had convinced him that he had been handed this fate, that he was simply a messenger, nothing more. He had been ordained to be the caretaker of St. Francis. That was exactly why he had been born.

He never was sure that it wasn't him, he himself, the man who would secure the treasure, save it, move it, do it justice, but now he knew. Basil was the man that God had chosen for that mission, and now all he had left to do was explain all of that to the young priest. And so he began. All the way back, at the very beginning.

They were both hungry, and besides, they had to change rooms for Hammer to continue; it was necessary. Basil would soon learn that many of the spaces between some of the vertical timbers were actually passageways that led to other rooms full of mystery and fortune. For the present time, they could begin in the kitchen area, and Hammer led the way, a candle in one hand, his cane in the other, over and across the stream, back to a corner wall and through a walkway. He lit a few candles in front of a series of mirrors that masterfully lit the new room so well they were all that was needed.

Everywhere Basil looked, there were pantries, cabinets, and closets. He had never seen so many jars in all his life. There were cans on top of cans, as deep as an arm could reach. Barrels on their sides in two rows, and more stacked one on top of the other. Some were corked, some had clamp-down lids, and there were large wooden boxes stacked in formations off in the distance.

Hammer had referred to it as the kitchen, but Basil thought there should be the word library attached in parentheses. On one wall, there was a splendid selection of well-bound books, a beautiful ten-shelf collection of books and scrolls, all shapes and sizes. There were two desks of the finest creation possible that must have been placed where they stood before they put the roof on. There were candles waiting to be relit, stacks of paper and fountain pens and pencils, other writing implements, including what appeared to be a solid gold yard-long ruler. So much for the young one to absorb as he glanced here and there.

He turned to the old priest and, without saying a word, he turned his palms up and waited.

"There would be cheese, crackers, bread sticks, and wine in the first cabinet, there, to your right. We could use some food before I go much further. Food might help us both. I might fall over and die after a few bites, but I doubt it. I hope not. Good luck, if I do." Any time he thought himself being funny, he chuckled a laugh he had nicknamed his 'duvalski' sound, and Basil could hear it while he headed to that mountain of cabinets.

Just like Hammer had said, when Basil found the right cabinet, it was full of everything he had mentioned plus a great deal more. His favorite jerky and even split peas, which he hadn't had in years. He gathered up a good selection and brought it all over to the couch where the old man had lain down, and he set it out before the pastor on a small table. They both began to nibble on the crackers, and Hammer was surprised that it didn't hurt to eat a little. He thought for sure it would, but it didn't. That was good. So was the wine. His cane was standing by his chair while Basil prepared cold-water compresses that he laid on the wound; they seemed to make all the difference.

"Have you ever thought about how you came to this assignment, Father Basil, my friend? This church was conceived, designed, constructed, and destined for today and tonight. It was built this way for this very purpose, and you, my young friend, are about to begin a journey that I could not possibly tell you where it might end. It is my belief that you have been chosen to write the last chapter of this church. Our beautiful church is now piled on top of us and is smoldering up there in the rain-soaked ashes of what it used to be. It has fallen, burned down, and is deep all over those old floorboards I've walked so many times through all the years. As with all the other churches they've burned, it must assume this new posture and will be left as it is until Mother Nature takes it all back. It's their sign to all the rest of humankind, and I've seen it many times. We were the last ones in this valley, and had been saved for later. Everyone knew that, but I am the only one who knows the whole truth. Eighty years from today, the only remnant will be the concrete steps that led up to the sacristy. A few concrete steps, tilted and half-buried in a barren field. I can see them in my dreams, and I have had that same dream repeatedly. All traces save for those steps will be erased. Too bad, so sad!

"There is a legend that I am going to tell you about here. It was all written down at the time and is told in great detail in that first book there on that second shelf. It seems to have taken almost fifty years from the time they started this basement until they actually began the construction of the church itself. A hundred years ago, there had been talk of a magical spring that poured out of the rocks and then disappeared back into the rocks, but it was more rumor and legend than provable fact at the time. The people who settled the land around where this church was being built had migrated from central Europe and knew full well what persecution was. It was what they had fled most, feared most, and would try their best to survive in this new place, just in case it ever happened again. The only way to survive, some felt, was to disappear and hide themselves, all their possessions, and leave all the rest to God. In this place and those times, they were so isolated they were, in fact, almost invisible, very secretive, and incredibly protective. They built this underground fortress before they ever started the foundation for the church directly on top of it. That survivalist mindset slowly evaporated over the years as they were succeeding in their dreamland and forgot to be afraid.

"The fledgling community, along with all the others from the same old world areas, same mindset, built a network of churches, and even though there seemed far more than necessary, some believed there simply couldn't be enough. Out of the north country, legend has it, this man they called The Saint arrived in the small village and met with the priest who would be its first pastor. He had the plans for St. Francis, and he had the plans for this basement foundation. He had many assistants and arrived with huge transport wagons that carried the altar marble and other strange containers. Wagons came and went for years, one load at a time. They came back with load after load of building materials or hauled in rock and gravel. They cut down the timbers and floated them down the river, positioned them one at a time, and were able to span the long distances with incredible strength and stability. They did it all in secrecy and guarded their creation against spying eyes. You will find that thick brown binder very interesting. It tells the story of the construction in detail and is well worth your time. Next to it is the volume of the ancient records, those early years, even before the death of Catherine. It tells about the early settlers, like my great-great grandfather and those trips across the Ukrainian badlands, who the families were, and when they were one and all baptized and, more importantly, died.

"As you and I sit here and contemplate those times, I can only conclude that to build everything you see all around us must have been an incredible undertaking, finished a dozen years before I was even born. Then they buried all these timbers under fifteen to twenty feet of rock, sand, and gravel. It appears from the drawings that they filled in a hundred-and-sixty-foot-wide, three-hundred-foot-long, solid rock ravine, and when they were done, it then appeared to anyone standing on the front steps of the finished church that it was built on leveled ground atop solid rock. It was a masterpiece of design, deception, and secrecy to the point that it was not long — a generation or two — before everyone who had ever had anything to do with the construction had forgotten or passed on. All except the pastor of the time. I am the most recent, have been for a long time, and you are the last. The Diamond Teardrop illusion up above appears to have saved the Diamond Teardrop below. Each one of those men kept his church record as exact as possible, and each man kept the secret until it was time to pass it on. I am passing it on tonight, and tomorrow, and however long I have left, or however long it takes."

CHAPTER 15

THREE DAYS OF REVELATION

And so, Hammer began.

"This enormous basement chamber you have now found yourself in is about the same square footage as the entire church above, and so, as you might have imagined, there is a lot more to it than what you've already seen. So much, I have to show you. We have to begin here in the kitchen where I need this break, and this is where we will come back to. People have lived down here for months at a time, back in the early nineties. There are many written stories, letters, and many diaries; you can read them later."

He carefully stood up, tested his balance and his pain threshold, discovering that his condition might not be as bad as he'd first thought; it was wishful thinking, and he knew it. He took his cane in both hands and rested his chin on the head of his Lord, and received the energy to go on. Basil was immediately standing there on his left side and trying to be of some assistance, candles in hand and awaiting any command.

Hammer continued, but stopped in the doorway and leaned over to Basil with a wish.

"Back in the room near the library wall is a push cart. If you could get that, I will have something else to lean on."

The cart proved to be perfect, and it rolled along with a little flutter on the left rear wheel. It even had a fold-out step that was perfect for sitting on. Between the cart and the cane, Hammer was unstoppable. Basil was ready, he thought, for whatever lay in store, but not exactly sure this was where he wanted to call home just yet. He knew for sure there were huge numbers of people on the roads above him who would kill him without a second thought if they caught him. For all intents and purposes, he was already dead; he had died a couple of hours before in a fire at St. Francis, a fact probably written down in someone's book. Yet he was not dead at all and was as ready as he would ever be for whatever it was that he was supposed to be ready for. He felt pretty good, considering Sokolov had undoubtedly marked him off as a cooked-in-the-closet Capuchin Friar.

After a dozen steps down the passageway, Hammer came to a doorway built between two huge vertical timbers that would have been directly under the sacristy, maybe the first pew on the right side looking at the altar. Basil needed a reference point and was about to ask Hammer if that would be a correct assumption when the old man turned the handle, and the heavy wooden door opened with ease. It was too late for the question as the two men passed into the darkness. Hammer transferred the fire from his candle to those on a tall holder just inside the room; three large thick wicks began to glow as the room became stunning. Basil was amazed at what he saw all around him. It took his breath away for a moment and he dashed out directly in front of Hammer and rolled his hands over, back and forth.

He turned back to the room and tried to count things for a moment, but gave up quickly. There were too many of everything and too many every-things. There were hundreds of candleholders, every imaginable design, and of the finest quality and workmanship. Dozens of ceremonial elevated entrance crucifixes that always preceded the processions up those center aisles in every church in the region, all treasured, all standing in one corner of the room firmly fixed in their base plates. A dozen chandeliers and a very well-organized display of a few dozen entrance bell chimes. They were, one and all, simply beautiful. There were golden baptismal stands and baptismal bowls that appeared to be remarkable. Each one was a masterpiece, a keepsake no matter where it had come from, and yet here, they were stacked with many others, which were just as finely crafted.

An unimaginable number of infant souls had been baptized over those bowls.

Too much, too much. He had to sit. Standing was over for the time being, and there was a chair fit for the bishop waiting empty right there, alongside Hammer. Across the floor and near the wall, a beetle was walking along the edge, and Basil considered stomping it out of existence, but Hammer told him, "Let it be, let it be."

Hammer was already sitting in a very flamboyant high-back chair that seemed to cozy up to what had to be an honest to goodness imperial side table, and he landed there with such ease and grace that Basil was sure he had sat there many times before. There were a half a dozen books on the lower shelf that were bound in beautiful leather with gold trim corners. He instinctively knew what they were — from the ancient world, all autographed classics by the original authors. There was no telling who the authors might be, but that tradition dated back to some of the earliest publications ever. Only the finest works by the most famous pens of the time were accorded such fame, and owning just one such book could make a man rich; there were six of them waiting for someone to open and read.

"So this is where you were? I've always wondered where you disappeared to and felt it was none of my concern, but I did wonder."

"I know you did and must have; who wouldn't? I decided early on that I had to protect you from knowing too much. I have always been afraid that they would come back and deal with us a little more harshly than normal. They know when you're hiding something, and they keep digging until there's a big hole in you somewhere."

Hammer began the story of where everything in this first room had come from.

"Starting back even before the church was finished above this basement, someone brought the first load, and the owners promised to come back someday to retrieve it, but they never did. Then there were more loads, as the churches were attacked in the outback, over and over again by many different enemies. You know all that. Nothing was ever the same again after the famine of 1891 and two and three, and it has taken a long time now for them to finally kill this last church. It very well may have died tonight if everything I have been told is true. We were the last church in this entire valley — at my best count, over a hundred Catholic churches alone, to say nothing of all the other denominations, all gone now, burned to the ground. They saved us for this day, simply to acquire those windowpanes and the fantasy of a Diamond Teardrop.

"Someone must have ordered that non-believer eyes witness the teardrop in the windows, and if it proves to be worthwhile, salvage it. They probably took it intact, thinking it had some magical powers, but the real teardrop is here in the basement. It now appears to me, in hindsight, that the designer created a diversion that took decades to develop and it forced them to look up instead of down. The miracle legend of the Diamond Teardrop on Easter Sunday morning, high up on that glass window of St. Francis, was known far and wide. Even Rome knew of the apparition and tried to diminish its significance, I was told, which only increased it, and the people seemed to always know the story, wherever one went.

"Perhaps the designers knew that the end would be by fire, and this last church would have something of interest to someone. It forced those pagans to sit and watch our last Mass. It forced them to hear our readings and they demanded that it be just like normal. If it were not, they thought that perhaps the miracle might not happen, and they needed to see the teardrop for themselves. If they did, they would know what to take, know what it looked like, and then they had to claim it for the state. It was all a creative optical illusion that the designers thought of a hundred years ago, long before they even built the church. Now it appears as a fitting memorial that they filmed the end and saved it for posterity's sake. I'll bet they filmed the fire.

"The original designers created this vast underground vault and disguised it under a magnificent church, along the banks of a small river, on the edge of nowhere. The foundation became invisible over time, and no one ever suspected there was any more to St. Francis than what you could see there on this hillside. In the old days, if you were lucky, you could get a seat inside the church on any Easter Sunday morning and see the teardrop. And this, my young friend is where they sent you.

"As I look back on those times before the famine, I remember most of all the Holy Week leading up to the Easter morning Mass of 1886. I was forty years old and had been the pastor of the flock for a few years already. Thousands of people were camping and sleeping all over the countryside, in barns and sheds and spare bedrooms. Every spot in every pew was reserved, with standing room only along the walk aisles and ushers at every corner. Common people, the local religious and government dignitaries from miles around would make the journey and would be patiently waiting for that sunrise. The weather was perfect that day, and all of the doors to the church were propped open. They were some of the most wonderful times for everyone, and nothing could have been any better in that Garden of Eden.

"Inside the church, everyone saw it, and the beautiful teardrop never failed to shine as long as it wasn't raining, but you had to be there. Only I knew how to open the vault door, turn over the hourglass in such a way as to set in motion the compass that gently altered the prisms high up the glass fascia in our Mother Mary's eyes. Now you know the secret and you can read about it in the big book. I've debated it all my life, being a fraud to some degree, but now, here at the end, I realize it was part of the divine plan. It was never intended to become what it did, or maybe it was. I'm still debating, I guess.

"Some of the people considered it their annual guaranteed miracle, and it was always well worth the trouble, helped them keep their faith. There was something about the place that always had people looking up or out over the vistas; the giant bell tower steeple on the west end and that magnificent altar up against three soaring stained glass windows thirty feet high. Up on the left side, the glass collage showed the face of the Virgin Mary, and at sunrise the teardrop miracle formed there, on her face, in her tear duct. A bright white diamond would suddenly appear, glisten and twinkle all throughout my choreographed consecration. It all had to do with that compass. That was easily enough to get the world's attention, I was told, as I've never been very far from here. No one ever looked down at the ground or the foundation of the building when they were anywhere near it; everyone has always looked up."

He drifted away for a moment, tired of talking, and closed his eyes. Then he came back and started again.

"That was the only reason they waited on us; all the other churches are gone, burned, and the people murdered. We are both now on that list, if they keep such records, and I'm sure they do. We are both dead men, incinerated in our confessional, back to dust. I wouldn't be surprised if those monsters aren't laughing about it as we sit here, blaming us for our own demise. I heard them say they had to burn it because of rabies and we had locked ourselves away in defiance and they didn't have time to dig us out. I'm angry because I'm dying, but I'm glad you're here. Maybe someday that Sokolov bastard could fall on a sharp stake. We can only hope."

He was gone again for a moment, and when he came back, he continued.

"The fire is probably struggling up there, if the rain was powerful enough, and since God himself has orchestrated everything so far, well... I'll pray that the holy remnants of St. Francis are enough of a disaster above us that most passersby ignore it forever. Nothing more than wartime rubble. In the morning, I will show you how to observe the views around the church from down here, and we'll know what's what. God sent the rain to keep the fire under control and stop the destruction at exactly the right time. I know he has.

"Perhaps we as a people should never have come here in the first place. For a hundred years now we have tried to make a living in this valley, and it seems it's always been ripe with danger and disaster, man-made and natural. When you and I died this evening, we might have been the last of the German Volga Catholics. There are others in similar places — in barns, in caves, up in the mountains, wherever — who will try to survive. I have to believe there are still some out there, somewhere. All we can do is try to survive, and not many of us will. Not just us Catholics either. There is little hope for the Jews and the Muslims, or the Mennonites. The Orthodox and the Lutherans will do no better... Unbelievable how it has all turned out. Too bad, so sad!

"Back to the history. Starting in the early 80s, a number of churches in the far north came under siege, and even though it was all over for them in a few days, three of the churches gathered their valuables together and brought them by wagon to St. Francis. There had been an arrangement between Bishop Andersoniski and myself that, if the items arrived at St. Francis, they would be cared for, hidden, as long as necessary and possible, if possible. It became one of the bishop's primary challenges, and kept a number of curriers and wagon masters busy from that time on.

"We understood there were no guarantees due to the immediate emergency of the situation, and when the wagons arrived with the bad news, they were unloaded into the main foyer of the church. There were two men, with two wagons; they unloaded them both and always did all the heavy work. In a matter of hours, they would unload the wagon as if the south-side steps of the church were actually a loading dock, and then easily slid the many containers through that side door and into the main lobby. Very few people ever saw this happen, and no one would have ever thought there was anything strange about it. The wagoners would stay inside the church for a day or two, sometimes all week, and then they would ride away.

"This happened many times over the last forty years, and I have personally unlocked that side door for the wagoners at least a hundred times, or so the records say. I've tried to keep track, but it became overwhelming and repetitive to the point where there was no point for an inventory. The man who drove the wagon was born and raised farther up the Ilava, even past the bridge works. I haven't seen him now in four years I think, and I miss him. His father was a very dear friend of mine, and I worry about his well-being. The father died from the fever in 1910 or thereabouts, and he and his son had worked for our bishop for twenty years off and on.

"The son is a massively powerful individual, a seaman by trade, the absolute gunslinger, and just one wonderful human being. He could lift boxes I was sure would take three men to handle, unloaded the wagons while I watched, and he brought all the contents down here into the basement. He moved it all around, made it presentable, as you can see, and then left. The last time his wagon pulled up was four years ago, and he stood there on the steps, a head taller than us, looking straight up the side of the steeple.

"Father, forgive me," he told me that day, "for having to tell you this, but… there are no more churches left. Your church here is the last one standing, and it's so beautiful. I hate knowing all this, and I hate telling you this. They burn them down to the ground, you know, and then walk away as if… I don't know what. I won't be back with any more loads; it's now all here. I have one last mission for our bishop, and it's very dangerous, only this time I go east to the sea. Give me your blessing, please, and keep me in your prayers. Perhaps you know what's in store, what you have to do? God be with you, Father. Good luck."

"He bowed his head while I blessed him. With that, he climbed out onto the seat of the wagon, let loose the brake and rattled away from the church grounds headed to his house ten miles away. He never looked back at me, never once, and I always wondered why. His name is Vincent Van Vedic, and he's a fisherman, and a freight hauler by trade. He's one of the most amazing men I have ever known, and I pray you meet him some day. If he's alive out there in the world, he'll come back, I know he will. That is my special prayer for you, that Van Vedic finds his way back. You be sure to tell him hello for me. I loved that man.

"We began to hear stories many years ago from survivors from that outback region who told stories that were virtually unimaginable. In some areas, there was not a single solitary survivor. There were now ghost lands for miles. Stories where whole communities were taken away with no warning, and then all that would be left would be this holy wreckage of a small community church, and everything would be burned, stolen, crushed, and everyone would be killed or drug away. Nothing was sacred to some of the marauders, but there were many holy relics, furnishings and church valuables. The people had their personal valuables, of course, and in some cases they included their treasures along with those from the church. Sometimes it was just way too late, and there was no defense.

"They were having gatherings in the stronger communities, weighing their options, discussing their chances or fates, and it was obvious they couldn't just leave. They had no choice, and the wagon that was leaving the church for who knew where might be a diamond's only chance. Envelopes, too full to seal with family heirlooms, and perhaps a note or two to a name or two. There was so little time to decide, and when the wagon left, doomed people watched it head down towards their particular river road and hopefully into a safe haven somewhere.

"Each parish priest was gently and politely offered a service provided by the bishop where this rescue wagon, with this most unique wagoner, would pick up a single load, and then safely transport it to a secret location where the contents would be protected, if possible. In those last days, in the chaos, and in the end, every single church decided in favor of the wagon stopping at their sacristy, and could only hope for the best, pray for the best, but the best was not to be, as you can see."

CHAPTER 16

ONE ROOM DOWN

"I don't know what to tell you, Father Basil, my friend. I've been looking at this room and all the others for many years and I can't imagine what might be going through your mind right now. I wasn't sure this day would ever come, or why it would when it did. Many of these artifacts in this room alone are now orphans. I don't know where they came from, how and why they're here, or if they were very special, just a little special or, for all I know, priceless. There is an unbelievable treasure in this basement that is quite possibly immeasurable, probably unmovable, and I wonder what is going to happen to it all. My friend, you have become the curator of this entire secret. I, for one, am absolutely thrilled to have you here and be telling you and showing you all of this. When we first met, I knew you were the one, it was then that I knew this day would be coming sooner rather than later, and now it's here. You are the chosen one. So, that's what I know."

Basil finally stood up and spent a few moments wandering about the room and into the distant corners, making notes in his mind of what he was seeing. Someone named Van Vedic, according to the good pastor, had traveled around this entire region for the last fifty years and picked up church treasures, bringing them all back to this basement and very neatly stacking them all with like objects. He had no reason whatsoever to doubt the holy man's word; somebody had to have done it. Hammer had told him that, as far he knew, this man, Van Vedic, and he were the only two people left in the entire world who knew this basement existed and how to get in and get out of it. He knew the bishop knew for sure, but he was probably dead, and he wasn't sure about Desch or two couriers from days gone by.

Basil was positieve those chandeliers had not been brought down the same staircase he had used earlier. Impossible! Some of these candelabras had to weigh hundreds of pounds, and even the furniture; it was all so big and heavy. It would be impossible to bring his chair down the confession ladder, and that was a given. He looked over towards Hammer and could only hold his hands out, one of his profound faces rolled off his cheeks and was followed by the smile of a very humble man, readily accepting his fate.

"There's so much more. Before I rest, I have to show you some more of what's down here. I sure wish I wasn't hurt so bad; it has never been part of my presentation, never crossed my mind that I would be."

The wounded old man rose to his feet and got both hands on his cart. His cane just stood there, waiting. He set his candle dead center of the cart and pretended to light it. He was smiling, and his pain was diminished, or at least that's the way it appeared for the time being.

They were back in the passage way, headed west, and quickly came up on the next room. It was a replay of the room before — the smooth opening door, the candles right near the front — and when the room lit up, Basil was once again overwhelmed by what he saw. There were rows and rows of cassocks, all of the vestments that were used in the Mass. Coats and cloaks, headgear and umbrellas, shoes and gloves. All along, he knew approximately where he was in relation to what used to be up above, what was probably still burning itself out. He figured they were directly below the usher station, just a few paces west of the south side entrance, where they had spent the afternoon. In front of him were the foundation pillars that supported the south side wall of the church.

They dwarfed a long row of beautiful solid wood cabinets with long thin drawers, and the ceiling for this room was another ten feet above the cabinets. Those drawers and closets he knew would be filled with the many different types of linen he would expect to find in any sacristy, the finest linen closets he had ever seen. He had never donned vestments in his rather brief career as a priest that even came close to the quality he had instantly recognized all throughout this wardrobe room. It was all handmade, and he was sure there were signatures and even dates sewn into the seams; it was all part of the tradition. He didn't know what to say, and when he turned, the old man was preparing to blow out the candles and leave the room.

He pulled the door closed behind him, and watched their shadows move along the pillars on a weird parallel path, in and out of the support columns, more closed doors off to his right side that Hammer suggested were full of more of the same, as they headed towards the back of the church.

Before he pressed on the handle, Hammer turned a little to his side and told Basil, "You're going to like this room a lot."

Basil was now directly behind his pastor and seemed to be willing to reach around and open the door himself, much like a little boy on Christmas Day. If Hammer would say such a thing before he opened the door, and the past few rooms were any indication of what was to come, time was a wasting. Hammer lowered the handle, and the door swung open.

As he lit the additional candles, like normal, Basil could see the piano directly in front and right in the middle of the room. It was a grand masterpiece the likes of which he hadn't seen in years. How in the world did it get down here and who had played it in the past? Pianists always ask themselves that question when they sit down to such a beautiful instrument. His passion in life besides the Eucharist was playing the piano, and he knew he was very good at it. Everyone told him so, but he knew deep inside his heart that he had much to learn, much to practice, and there had never been enough time, never.

The old man sat down in another chair of the usual quality, next to a beautiful table with a matching chair alongside, and merely smiled at Basil to do what he needed to do.

He nodded to the pastor and very softly and smoothly pulled out the bench, and stood there in respect. The old man had a very soft look on his face, and he knew he was about to be soothed.

Basil sat down, and his long-fingered hands spread out on the keys as he raised his eyes, looked up through the timbers, past the ashes and into heaven. It was still Easter Sunday, and he began to play the first song he had ever learned, the greatest Easter song of all.

Hammer closed his eyes and suffered there in silence, marveling at the music and relishing the fact that he was in the presence of a young master prodigy who might never play for the rest of the world. He had to appreciate it for its pure innocence.

Basil often made the organ there in the church sound as if they were back at the Vatican and St. Peter's; it was such a good memory... or was it a fantasy? The pastor would willingly wait for Basil to end his pre-Mass concerts. There were times when he would get so entranced at the organ that he would miss the starting time for the Mass by fifteen minutes, as if Hammer had a watch that he actually paid any attention to. After all, it could have been three in the morning, give or take, and no one seemed to mind.

Before long, his eyes closed; Basil was deep into complicated piano sounds that blended into the walls and ceiling as if he were in the concert hall in Budapest. They never invited him to play there, but he did get to listen one time. This music room was designed for a single piano, and no matter where you sat, the sound was perfect. There was only one door in, and this piano had not come through that door in one piece. He could look that one up later.

Besides the piano, there were instruments of every style and form. Violins that sat in their open cases tiered up a wall as if they were common. He was positive they were anything but cheap or casual. There was no telling where some of them may have come from. There were horns and flutes, trumpets, and all the other instruments that men and women loved to play. Huge piles of sheet music in stacks, too much of it, too tall, with spacers, and there were so many music stands... They appeared to be either bright gold or silver, and some had intricate designs with inlaid gems, tiles of gold, and all were elegant. While he was getting near the end of his third choice, he noticed the lights in the room were dimming. It was time to move on, and Hammer had left one candle burning as he pushed himself out the door. Basil hit a few last keys and sprang to his feet. Absolutely elated, he coasted back across the room and blew out that second to last candle. A very dim light from up the passage on Hammer's cart managed to light the way, and Basil said goodnight to his new friend as he closed the door and followed the dying man. More closed doors on the right as they walked by.

In a matter of twenty steps, Hammer was standing in front of another door and waited for Basil to scoot up and stop a pace or so behind and to his right. There was a smile on his face the pastor hadn't seen in quite some time. Basil could really turn into an all-gums-and-teeth sort of man if he were really happy, and there had been a few times in the last two years when Hammer had seen that smile, but not too often.

"This is what I call the main treasure room, and the other one is across the hall through that door down there."

Hammer lowered the handle and began to light the candles just like he had done so many times before. The light seemed to be igniting the room itself as Basil worked his way around the older man who was sitting down on a throne. Absolutely beautiful.

The west wall was a huge assortment of shelves and cabinets, with heavy gauge wooden tables sticking out into the room. The long southern wall was lined with tall vertical timbers and had four tables butted up to the cabinets. On every shelf, on every table, down on the floor and inside the cabinets were countless pieces of art. Chalices and monstrances, cups and saucers, all solid gold or silver, dozens of each and stacked together like they were mass produced. On one table were heavy wood blocks with dozens of two-foot long dowels embedded in the manicured wood. Hundreds and hundreds of rings were stacked on the dowels, with jewels and gems and diamonds imbedded in each one.

There were large wooden shoeboxes that were overflowing with necklaces made of pearls and only pearls. Other boxes the same size, buried, and Basil could only conclude they were all full. Everywhere he looked, he saw what appeared to his untrained eye as extremely valuable pieces of art, jewelry, and simple things that proved to be too exquisite to define. Small gold picture frames of faces, resting against a slightly larger gold-framed portrait, against a slightly larger one, until the back frame top was over five feet tall and the row was five feet out from the wall, row after row after row. There were small mountains of gold and silver eating utensils, plates and saucers, bowls and teapots. Stacks and stacks of wooden storage chests, full of matching dinner sets, family heirlooms, collected in those last hours before doomsday and thrown into the back of the wagon.

On some of the tables, there were pieces of jewelry in large, felt-lined boxes that had to have been someone's heirloom, someone's most valuable possession. One after another, side by side, precious and apparently priceless, bracelets and necklaces. Each and every item demanded more attention, but that would be impossible — there was just too much.

Finally, Basil finished his three-hundred-and-sixty-degree circle of amazement and faced the bent-over pastor who was staring at the floor in front of his feet.

"Father, there must be millions. Millions and millions."

He began his circle again but stopped right away when he noticed the six boxes in two stacks of three in the distant right hand corner. They were identical in size, perfect replicas of each other, and obviously the sort of containers that only kings would have in their closets. Even in this room full of look-alikes and exceptional beauty, they, for some reason or another, had garnished this unique location up against the interior sidewall. Basil almost knew better, but he turned to Hammer and rolled his hands back and forth with that never-ending question mark on his forehead.

"My son, that is the treasure that was lost in the great flood of 1796."

CHAPTER 17

THE GUIDED TOUR

Each room had been a step above the previous, and Basil was now staring into a fortune in gold, jewels, and plain old gunny sacks full of coin. On one shelf was an assortment of large storage pots, ten inches deep, with nothing but wedding rings, gold bands and other finger ornaments evidently not worthy of a dowel. The pots themselves were works of art. He saw a ruby as big as his thumbnail in a large, expensive hatbox that was filled to the top and overflowing with hundreds of other unattached jewels. Nestled on the front ledge of a spectacular glass cabinet were large glass storage jars with screw-on metal lids. They were filled to the top with what appeared to be diamonds; big ones, little ones, and everything in between. He had never owned a diamond in his whole life, never thought he would, nor did he even want one. According to Hammer, he was now in possession of thousands; he had no way to know.

He flashed back in time and saw the scene there in his childhood home when his mother discovered that the diamond was gone from her wedding ring. She never quit looking for it and cried off and on for days every time she even thought about it. Even back then, he felt like that was too much emotion over a shiny glass rock. Where could all of these diamonds have come from? How does one persuade someone else to put their diamonds in an envelope and give them to a wagoner? After a time, those individual diamonds end up in a one-quart jar that eventually gets stacked on a shelf with other jars full of diamonds.

As he stood there looking at the jars and trying to put it all into perspective, Basil mumbled to himself that it appeared he was looking at quarts of diamonds, a full gallon, maybe five pounds or so.

Most of all, his curiosity was consumed with the six individual crates up against the center wall. Through the generations, everyone had heard the story of a lost imperial treasure and the theories as to what had happened to create the legend. It had always seemed to be just one of those fairy tales that entertained the children. Old men told the story of what some people thought might have happened around late night bonfires, but only God and Hammer knew the real truth.

Like all things of that nature, time embellished the details of the treasure. The gifts from one emperor to another became immeasurable and too magnificent to imagine. The unknowns far outweighed the known, and over time no one could even remember the names of the folks who had disappeared other than the terms 'prince' and 'princess.' The legend told how Catherine the Great of Russia and Emperor Fredric William of Prussia both died on the same day in 1796, supposedly broken-hearted from grief over the loss of their children. Most of it, Basil had never paid much attention to, and never considered for a second that it would ever affect his life. Hammer told him the story one night, and in Hammer's version the treasure was recovered and hidden away in a secret vault. When the story was over, Basil felt like he had been told the story for another reason besides the pure entertainment of an old Russian legend. Hammer started the tale as if it were a fairy tale and ended it with a matter-of-fact guarantee.

"Open that top one, there," Hammer pointed and ordered as Basil put his hands on the corners of the lid.

He raised it open and stared at what was there as if he couldn't believe what he was looking at. It appeared to be the royal crowns, the royal necklaces, the royal rings and other bracelets. It was opulent and gaudy. These were two of the most precious crowns in both the Prussian and Russian monarchies, and even their carrying cases were adorned in jewels, including their golden hinges. The plaques declaring who these crowns belonged to and why were, as best he could tell, engraved in solid gold plates embedded in tanned and engraved leather binders the likes of which were not ever part of his world. The entire box was lined with fox fur, deep as his arm to the elbow, and longer than his outstretched arms, fingertip to fingertip. He could only wonder what lay below this top level of adornment. Without a doubt, there was more and more and more. Not only that; there were five more boxes, same size, same style, with only God knew what inside.

Basil had almost seen enough, but his curiosity was all but insatiable. There before his eyes in the top box alone was unimaginable wealth. Artistry in diamonds and silver and gold, steeped in antiquity. Forgotten, lost, and now right here in front of his face.

Hammer was sitting in his usual spot, in that beautiful chair, of course, next to that beautiful table, of course, with an empty chair just waiting for Basil's butt, of course. He turned to face the old priest, his jaw dropped, his hands out in front of his body, and all he could do was rock his head side to side.

"Father, I'm afraid... I... I..."

The old man invited him to sit.

"I have rehearsed this introduction no less than a hundred times, all by myself, in the strangest of times. I've pretended to be me, showing you, and you letting me do that. I've pretended to be you much more than I pretended to be me, and every time I was you, I didn't know what to say, to do, wagging my hands back and forth exactly like you do. You may find yourself that way someday, who knows? I didn't know at the time who you would be, but I realized as I played the different parts to this operetta that you would be destined to knock on my door. You would be the first tenor. You would be the maestro, you would be the conductor. You would, somehow... you would complement all of this, conclude all of this.

"Just like you, my friend, I am still confused by it all but I am so glad for this moment, so happy that you have just now discovered all this and are here as you are. So glad. I can die; I hate to say it for your sake and mine, but I think I have to die soon. I can't see very well, and I need to sleep. I hope I wake up, because there are a few more things we need to do... but I'm gone for now."

With that, he fell asleep, hunched over the right side of the chair. His knees drifted apart, and his hands fell limp. Basil couldn't remember the last time he had seen someone fall asleep, but he remembered how, as a child, they used to play a game late at night watching each other drift away. It was always so funny when the first one faded and didn't even know they had. So very, very funny, and a wonderful way to end the day — just one of the few childhood keepsake memories he still had up there.

When he realized how all alone he was, how very much alive he seemed to be, and the only man he knew was dying right before his eyes, a shudder overwhelmed him. When it ended, he thought for a moment how he might have possibly hurt his neck, and was surprised he hadn't fallen over in front of the boxes. Never had he ever shivered like that. He took a few steps forward and tried to rearrange the old man a bit so that he at least looked a little more comfortable and received no assistance or complaints whatsoever. He found a quilt and a pillow that padded and covered the pastor and he appeared to be in the perfect pose for sleeping in that chair. His cane stood straight up and down by his right knee, so Basil laid it onto Hammer's chest with only two fingers, with it rising and falling as the old man breathed.

Basil sat down in the empty chair and watched the old man's chest moving up and down. He was asleep; it was all he could do. Across the room, three walls looked back at him, stacked very neatly with all sorts of treasure, unimaginable wealth. There was a bottle of wine and another of water, two glasses, of course, and two hand-carved smoking pipes mounted to a carved log, with a snifter full of tobacco.

He filled his wine glass and packed a pipe, lit it and blew out a couple of candles, letting just one flicker in the background. It had a very long way to go. The ideas of conservation had always been a fundamental part of his nature; the sun wasn't coming up where he lived now. He instantaneously understood that it would always be dark down here, where he seemed trapped, unless he had a candle lit. For now, he needed to save candles for later.

And then a huge smile crossed his face. There had to be a million candles down here somewhere, and as long as he had just one left, he would look for them and find them. Somewhere, he recalled reading that when things were, get or are very dark, all one has to do is light a candle, and everything will be better. He toasted the old man and then blessed him, lit his pipe again and stared into the silence. He too needed to sleep, but he felt like he should stay on guard at least for a while. His pipe went out, and so did he.

CHAPTER 18

THE SECOND DAY OF REVELATION

The candle had burned till there was only an inch left when Basil opened his eyes, surveyed the chamber he was still sitting in and thought about pinching himself somewhere. For just a moment, he thought that the dream had been so stunning, vivid and weird that he almost thought it had actually happened. The day before had started rather poorly, but in the end had turned into this fantasy of survival, rescue, and now gold.

He remembered falling asleep, and that there was one candle burning back over his shoulder, and worst of all, his mentor was dying in the chair next to him. None of that could have been real, but in that split second where he woke up, he knew it was. That candle was still burning, all of that gold was still piled up in front of him, and that old man was still sitting in that chair next to him.

Basil jumped to his feet, stood directly over the old man, and he could instantly see that he was still alive. He wanted to do something, but doing nothing seemed to be the best plan. Leave him alone and let him sleep. Leave him be and pray that he was going to be okay. His best option was to sit back down and think.

He had slept long enough so he sat there and picked up his pipe. He was trying to quit the habit, but it had proven to be one of the vices he had no trouble violating, and he didn't even confess it. He and Hammer smoked all the time near the fireplace there in the rectory. Neither carried any smoke throughout the day, but when it was finally over they would meet there and light a pipe. He loved it. He would sit there and listen to Hammer tell the stories of way back when, as the century had turned, and all of the horrors that seemed to engulf the whole area. The valley had turned into nothing more than a rat hole on the edge of the world, and by the time the second famine arrived in '21 just about everyone was gone or dead. The survivors from the 1891 famine had learned a lot, and farming had a tendency to be at the mercy of the rains. All of those empty houses and farms out there hadn't always been that way. Hammer would often muse over how much work went into a field of wheat, a barn full of pigs and horses, six or eight children, and even the house itself. The complete insanity of the State taking all the seed for that next spring planting, and then the murder of the peasants for having hoarded it, murdering those who would plant it, nurture it, harvest it, and then discover that there's nothing to feed the army and the surviving people...

While Basil was listening to the stories, he knew it was all true. He had been too young, too lucky, too blessed perhaps to have understood the beginning of it all. He seemed to have missed it somehow, was ordained, and then assigned to St. Francis from the renowned Capuchin Seminary of St. Michael's in Czechoslovakia. At the time, he didn't even know where his assignment was, but he went there just the same. He was obedient, and that was a given.

The seminary where he had trained for seven years was nestled in the foothills of a far distant foreign country over a thousand miles away, and, back then, no one seemed too willing to talk about the way things were out there in the real world. The real world fought The Greatest War of all times for half a dozen years while he studied Roman Catholic Theology the whole time. He learned the piano like no other in the vaulted history of St. Michael's, learned advanced Mathematics, four languages, and most of all he became a Roman Catholic Priest. His family had disintegrated, his parents were gone, and his sister too. He was all that was left, and he had Jesus. He had the Mother of God, and he had convinced himself that everything was exactly how it should be for him. He had always understood the absolute and complete misery that befell most folks, up and down the line, who, through

CRAIG DOMME

no fault of their own, spend their whole lives living on the edge. The seminary protected him from the world for seven years until it was time for him to go, and they sent him to Pfeiffer. He was ready, eager, was mature, very well educated and headed off into an overwhelmingly crazy world. He had seen some of the insanity on his way to Pfeiffer, and then he heard the stories from a man who had watched it. He was here; could have been anywhere, but he was here.

His mind was drifting through the years, and he remembered things from the past that he hadn't thought of recently. One thought was of New Year's Eve. When the bell tower struck midnight his mother ended her day-long labor, and he took his first breath in those first seconds. The year was nineteen hundred. He'd remembered that night not too long ago, when he and Hammer were sitting there at the fireplace back in the rectory. He remembered telling the old priest the story of the night he was born according to his parents. Hammer had never heard that story before, even though he knew the young man was 28 years old. He appeared to be entranced by it all, and the young priest was flattered that the old man was so attentive. No one else had ever been. He remembered listening to his mother tell the story of his birth back when he was a little boy, and no one seemed to care too much about the nineteen hundred part or the midnight part.

"He may have been the first," she would always say. "He may have been the very first."

He remembered apologizing. "I don't know why I told you that, Father, but that's what she used to say. I do believe that I was born moments after midnight, 1900, well off for a baby by any standard, to a beautiful woman and her loving man, and that's all."

If there had always been one unique thing about their relationship so far, it was that each man would listen very intently to the other man's stories. People don't do that as a general rule, and Basil would stop sometimes in mid-sentence and have a bit of trouble with the idea that this wonderful, enlightened, undoubtedly holy and religious man wanted to know more detail about a semester of 'strict ethics' at his seminary there at St. Michael's.

Hammer seemed to enjoy hearing about those places back near the motherland, in the early nineteen hundreds, and even though he hadn't come from there, his forefathers had. Nothing could have been more unimportant in 1920 than his sophomore year at St. Michael's Seminary, nothing on the entire planet, yet Hammer wanted to know all the details. St. Michael's had always been a renowned institution for the Roman Catholic Church and had produced priests for years and years and years, who had traveled far and wide and written, converted millions, they said, and even been martyred. St. Michael's had a reputation among the living clergy, much like Oxford had on the other side.

Basil had been one of the 'common seminarians' while there, humble, quiet, unassuming, or so he said, and Hammer had a very detailed resume from the place, which contradicted that assumption. Basil didn't know it existed, even though he'd personally delivered the package, proving that young men have a tendency to underestimate themselves and older men who mentor them keep intricate records. The staff and faculty at St. Michael's were excellent at that and tried to keep the devils out of the system. That, too, they were very good at. It was as if they both had this complete sincere need to know all there was to know about each other. Basil was new to the idea that someone wanted to know what he thought about things. Hammer knew it was all part of being twenty-eight and just as much a part of being eighty-two.

There had not been an obvious church service there in St. Francis in a long, long time. Years. It was against the law, and the two priests had vegetated on the grounds by order of the local Soviet police. They always had the keys to the church, and there were times when not a single solitary soul came into view up or down the road from any direction for weeks at a time. Both men knew that someone knew they had been ordered to stay there, yet it was very seldom and terrifying whenever that police car came by to check. They had both spent enormous amounts of time simply working in their gardens, sitting on the porch of the rectory or out in the back looking at the desolation. Hammer loved the Grotto and went there every day, rain or shine, and had a favorite spot under a beautiful tree about twenty feet past the front kneelers. He would sit there for hours and meditate on his reading and his memories and sometimes he disappeared for hours and Basil never knew where he went.

All the streets were empty, all the houses, all the stores, everyone was gone. Both men were so ragged and thin, but both refused to give in and just die — never a part of the plan. They would spend their times apart reading and praying and then together performing every single ritual there was in the liturgy, over and over, in the church, and out by the Grotto to St. Francis. The church doors were shut and the music from the organ at three o'clock in the morning was hushed but perfect from Basil's fingertips, as Hammer performed the liturgy there at that candle-lighted altar. They were harmonious celebrators, maestros, and pure artists. They did it so many times.

This very old man and the young man would scamper the forty feet from the rectory steps to the side entrance of the fabled church, very secretively, especially in those early days of '26, at two or three o'clock in those early morning hours. That was until they both realized that it didn't appear anyone was paying attention to what they were doing at all, period, none, zero. Next thing they knew, two hours later, five a.m. or so, it would be the two of them standing at the back door to the church, looking left and right into the darkness and reluctantly getting ready to scamper back to the rectory. Could there possibly be someone out there prepared to shoot them both dead for what they had just done? They both believed there very well might be. They had performed the Mass and common liturgy, with music, candles, and faith. It would be close to dawn in the morning, sometimes cold as hell, and if there had been anyone lying in ambush, they too would have been cold as hell while waiting. It was all so absurd, but they paid attention just the same.

Eventually, by the spring of '27, they were having midmorning Sunday Masses and sometimes even propped open the front doors. They did that on both Easter Sundays, and Basil became a believer in the power of illusion, saw The Diamond Tear Drop through the eyes of a theological priest which is different from the way the laity saw it. Hammer told Basil that he was always feeling vibrations through his cane; it was guiding him, protecting them both, warning him and determining his speed. It gave him energy, stamina, and a host of other enhancements, being the one thing that had contributed most to his survival to this old age. The old man admitted that at times the face in the wood entranced him. He would sit in his chair, hold the cane between his thighs with both hands on the handle and stare into the countenance of Jesus that was carved into the top of the cane, discuss any subject that came to mind, contemplate his own existence, his isolation, anything.

It had been long enough now after they had been ordered and isolated, that perhaps they should have starved to death, died of fever, the plague, any of a number of common things that killed all the other people. That had been the fate for millions, millions, and more millions. Why not add two priests, who die in their church along the banks of a small river tributary that fed the Don River in the disaster region called the Fertile Volga Basin? Why not?

Basil had always been amazed how the old priest followed ancient maps to caches of food, buried and protected many years before by people who lived on the edges of the outback, and the excursions were usually well worth their trouble and actually a lot of fun. He found it difficult to keep up at times, gasping for breath after a long walk, and the old man who was only three times his age was acting a bit impatient. They moved like feral cats, dashing from one cover to another, from one forest to another, usually at night. The maps were often vague, sometimes written in haste by people who would be dead within hours, and these maps showed where they buried their treasures. Every family in every village had a map and a spot on their land that no one could find without help, and Hammer had thousands of those maps. Many times the stash would look bad and terribly aged, but the canned and jarred relics had plenty of shelf life left, and the hiding places were almost magical.

As a last resort, often times the people had to bury almost everything when they fled or were in imminent danger of being murdered, and they were very good at it. They would have planned it long in advance, and if they had the time, they did it right. Hammer took Basil everywhere, showed him all the other abandoned villages and taught him everything he knew about the valley. He showed him how to find the food, where the wild things grew, everything that Mother Nature automatically provided, and he came up with something for the two of them to eat, every day for almost two years. It was unbelievable. He became obsessed with the way the old man leaned on that cane, always rested it close to him and facing into the room, never went anywhere without it.

Basil went willingly with the old priest on every excursion, listened to every story about where they were, and on many occasions in their search for food in the neighboring communities, they found the mother loads. Without disturbing them, they marked the map for what it was and planned to save it for later. They became invisible, traveling at night, and he always learned much, watching and listening to his mentor with a passion.

Often times they found and trapped small game, rabbits and huge red-tailed tree squirrels, discovered wild gardens, overflowing fruit trees, wild potato fields, and pastures of melons, wild cabbage and miles of walnut orchards. In some places on the edge of the flatlands, huge wild sunflower plants had overtaken the land and all sorts of berry bushes were overwhelming the banks of some rivers, but there were never any people. Some of these places the old man had known about since his childhood. He had spent eighty years in the neighborhood and knew it well. His mission in life ended up being that he took his disciple, namely Father Edward Basil, and taught him everything he knew, about everything worth knowing anything about for over fifty miles deep into the outback. It was all abandoned and empty out there, unless you knew where to look, and Hammer knew every single place to harvest or hunt and what time of the year to make the treks. They spent their time from the spring of '26 to Easter in '28 preparing Basil.

They always found safe shelter, always stayed near wells and springs that were invisible in some cases. Hammer was a fisherman and gave all the credit for his success at the shoreline to his cane. He held that cane in very high regard and in fact admitted that it more or less led the way. They looked high and low in every building and shed they ever came to and usually found something well worth saving almost every time. The maps were almost flawless. After all, he knew the entire basin very well; he had been born there, as he reminded his student over and over again, telling fantastic stories at almost every corner and bend in the road. Stories about all those people who had built the basin, the families, and the generations, one after another, and he knew them by name. He knew the surnames for all the fallen houses, he knew the names of all the villages, the names of their churches and their pastors, the streets in some cases, and even the names of some of the side ditches to the main irrigation canal they had dug. The man was a walking atlas.

It had become a tradition, the idea of the family plot map. The only way to protect their most precious valuables was to find a spot on their land and bury it. Then they made a map, and in the end they gave it to their priest who put all these maps in saddlebags, and they ended up at St. Francis. Hammer never meant to lie, and in the truest sense of the word he didn't, but his explanation for where the maps had come from wasn't exactly the whole truth. He was always walking a fine line trying to protect the young fellow and never cause him to call the old man a liar. He was so sure the Communists would eventually tear their hearts out; he just didn't know when.

Whenever the two of them left the church grounds, they would leave no tracks, seldom used the same route twice as Hammer often joked to his companion that he pretended to be a very wary and now aged old fox and suggested to Basil that he should mimic one of the animals in the forest as an example on how to survive. It was food for thought and something to talk about, so Basil began to suggest different possibilities for his mascot, different from the fox idea. He suggested critters similar to the fox, like the wolf, different cats, and even the massive stag.

"You've been a fox all these years? Father Fox, is there anything that you particularly regret or appreciate most about having managed to become an old fox?"

The two men shadowed each other as the old man guided them to the edge of the river and one of their favorite fishing holes. The poles were already there; everything they might need was already there, hidden, safe, and highly effective. The old fox was very good at many things, but fishing and chess were his specialties. It was obvious that he had stayed healthy somehow, was still vibrant and even hard to keep up with. It didn't take long for Basil to realize that, without a doubt, the cane was a wooden miracle stick and enabled that eighty-year-old man to act at times as if he were forty instead.

"When it comes to being an old fox, I look back and appreciate how fast I was, and able to, as I called it at the time, 'out-clever my enemies.' I could easily maneuver myself with the help of my cane, my treasured cane, to where I could watch them from a distance, and I could always hear what they said without them knowing. I always knew they were coming long before they got here. There was a time when I had no idea exactly how fast I was, but there was surely nothing faster. That's what I appreciated most; I was very fast. I loved my ears, as they brought in sounds that were extremely distant, very specific if I needed that, and, of course, my nose was impeccable. In essence, my vision was almost always my last sensibility to encounter whatever it was I had heard or smelled first. It's a fox thing."

All of the trails and ditch banks had names; all the abandoned houses had family names, faces, babies, and death. He could go up and down each country road and tell Basil exactly who had once lived there and something about them. Hammer's abandoned Pfeiffer streets all had names. He'd baptized almost every child, married all the lovers and buried hundreds. He went to the cemetery often, actually more than often. He had said goodbye to all the hardy ones, the lucky ones, back in '91 and '92, the last ones to leave, Hamburg or bust, just before the famine and drought killed almost everyone who didn't leave. They wrote letters back and forth for years. Hammer was fascinated with the knowledge that there were places exactly like Pfeiffer, Russia, thousands of miles away on two different continents, where these former residents were now starting all over. Exactly, and so much so, that they actually named the new town in Kansas, Pfeiffer. He had pictures of the town in North America, and it looked fantastic. They had a church in the new Pfeiffer that rivaled St. Francis, but not quite, and a note on the picture said they still needed a bell, like the old one back home in Russia.

One of his favorite stories from back in the early nineties was when these two families in particular, who lived out in Oakland, the bad side of Pfeiffer, inherited for free four teams of horses and two power wagons, probably for no other reason than they were very good men and women and deserved it. Divine intervention, an act of God, a miracle, or just because they knew somebody. There were brand new babies involved, young children, and no money, when out of the blue, it seemed, they were saved at the very last minute of the very last day. They were the two Aloysius friends, the one Aloysius who gave up the horses and wagons, who really didn't need them, and the other Aloysius who left with his family, his friends and survived all the way to the new world. The generous Aloysius stayed behind, became a legend in that old Volga homeland, and so did his sons, the Van Vedics.

"Any regrets from the old fox?"

The old man was studying his fingers, watching his bobber at times, and out of nowhere, a very deep and lonely sigh came out of his mouth and nose at the same time.

"My dear Father Basil, I'm so very tired of all this. What these old eyes and this old mind have witnessed in this valley should have never been seen. It's all gone, except for you and me and the church. It's just gone. What was it all for and why? Perhaps this place was only a side note to an entire heritage that is hopefully thriving somewhere else. I wish you could have seen it like I did once upon a time. The babies just kept coming. I only wish you could have seen. It was so beautiful, holy, almost like a Garden of Eden. I don't know whom to blame for the drought, for that horrible famine, for all the hatred and jealousy, for that terrible war and the revolution. I ask our God all the time, every day, if he could enlighten me as to why it all turned out this way, and as of yet, he has left me in the dark. I have this mountain of anger inside my heart, and I've never retaliated, never drawn my sword, and that, I'm regretting at this old age. I regret that the Fox has little teeth and short claws."

There seemed to be no logic to the idea that there could possibly be anything left out in the wilderness, but there always was. The old man was every inch of eighty years old, and Basil would watch him scamper from one abandoned house to another, and he would in turn do it just like the old man had, until they disappeared into the fog or around a corner somewhere in the distance. That cane of his was always in hand and out front. They traveled together, and Basil would marvel at the route. Hammer had it down to a science, and the entire time he was like a sprinting fox that understood that the neighborhood had dangerous dogs everywhere, and the fox had better be very careful. He had never thought of the old man as a fox in the early days, but after their talk about mascots, he couldn't think of him any other way. A feral cat wouldn't have a chance against that fox. He was defenseless except for the cane and his knife, his knowledge of this town and all the other little towns, and the entire countryside for that matter.

He never moved without his cane, or without being cautious and deliberate, and taught Basil almost everything he knew, almost. There were two things he couldn't know too soon.

There had always been water, and Basil knew that water was here and there, and sometimes not, but there had always been water in the church, always. Basil knew that Hammer would have just as soon lived in the church as anywhere, a back pew would have been just fine, but the old cleric respected the fact that the liturgy forbid people from living inside the house of God. God lives inside the house of God and priests live in rectories if there were any, and there almost always were.

Basil would light a candle in the sacristy first thing after he entered, and Hammer would enter the room a moment or so later and don his vestments for the Mass of the day. Basil would hurry off towards the back of the church after lighting two candles on the altar. Once in the back, he would hurry up into the choir loft and fire up the organ he loved to play so much. There was a lever on the side that controlled the volume, and out of fear it could be heard outside, he always kept it low, but Hammer would signal from the altar that it was too low. When Basil played, Hammer would sit there on the solid marble seats off to the side of the altar and watch the two candles burn. Both men would complement each other throughout the Mass, taking much longer than any congregation would have ever tolerated or allowed for everything from the beginning entrance to the final prayers. Their Mass had evolved into a two-hour celebration. They tried to do it every day except when the winter was too much, and it wouldn't be long till their third Easter arrived. They both had big plans for that one, but so did someone else.

Hours passed, and the young custodian continued to monitor the old man's breathing. He would wander about the room and examine some of the contents while trying to estimate in his uneducated mind what any of it could have been worth. Coming from the world of 'poverty, chastity, and obedience,' there was no way he had ever concerned himself with diamonds, rubies, and pearls, other than to know there were such things and other folks often valued that sort of stuff far too much. He had not the slightest working knowledge as to what any of it was truly worth. One thing he did know was that there was sure a lot of it in this room alone, with there being at least one other across the hall.

High up along the edge of one of the giant ceiling support timbers he noticed there was a faint glow, a ray of daylight shining through his pipe smoke and striking the floor directly in front of the old man's feet. It was the most beautiful beam of light he had ever seen. He burst into a prayer of thanksgiving, humbled to tears as he realized that the sun hadn't died after all. It wasn't much, a thin stream of morning sunrise light, and he stood up out of his chair and let the beam hit him square on his face and chest. He actually felt the warmth on his eyelids and then he heard the old man behind him.

"You'd make a better door than a window."

"Welcome back, Father. How do you feel?"

The young priest was hoping beyond hope that he would get a good report as he turned and knelt down at the old man's feet and took both his hands in his own.

"Don't know just yet. How long has it been?"

"Many hours. I'd say eight for sure, ten maybe, but it's dawn up above."

He knew the old man well enough to know that he would play it down and only complain for a moment or two about his condition. He would automatically minimize his distress and be concerned about other things before he burdened his pain on someone else.

"Isn't that the most beautiful sight you've ever seen?" Hammer said as he waved a hand through the sunlight beam.

"Yes, it is... and so, how do you feel?"

The pastor sat up straight in the chair and grimaced at his side. "Let's have a look." He struggled to pull his shirt up and out of the way. Both men could see that his injury was gruesome. The whole side was now dark purple and bulging out and away.

"That doesn't look very good at all," the old man diagnosed himself.

"No, it doesn't."

It hurt him just to breathe, but it was bearable, and he asked his prodigy to help him to his feet.

"Have you seen enough in here to pique your curiosity? Let's leave and go back to the kitchen. We have all day to finish the tour."

Basil brought the book cart close, and Hammer allowed him to pull him up and out of the chair. With apparent discomfort, the old fellow worked his way towards the door and back out into the hallway. Instead of heading back the way they had come, he turned left and came upon another double door to what had to be the last room on the south side of the church. He opened the door and pushed himself inside, with Basil right on his heels. The room was twice the size of any of the others, and directly in the middle of the floor lay a huge contraption with chains and ropes attached to all the corners. Off to the side was a wheeled apparatus that looked much like the wheel in a fishing boat's cabin. It had handles sticking out in a perfect sequence around the circle, and the ropes hung down from the ceiling after passing through pulleys. It was all very elaborate and ingenious, and Basil instantly understood that this was the device that lowered everything down here from somewhere up above. There in the back of the church, somewhere between the end of the confessional and the side doors, had to be a secret opening he had never noticed nor had any knowledge of.

"I'll show you how this works a little later... we can't risk it now since we haven't seen what has happened up there just yet, but it's a marvelous elevator and has worked quite well for the longest time. I'm afraid that doorway way up there is covered with ashes and remnants of the bell tower." Basil was frozen in his place and could only marvel at this latest revelation. Dirty black water was trickling down the back wall and disappearing into a drain hole, and had been for a very long time.

CHAPTER 19

DEAD SILENCE

Even though the elevator room enthralled Basil, he knew there was more, and Hammer seemed to be urgently heading back to that kitchen, that distant corner, undoubtedly to show him something else. There was the distinct possibility he might find the coffee pot, some more of those split peas, and who knew what else. To follow the old man back up that hallway with the candlelight bouncing in and out of the massive vertical timbers was almost like walking in a forest at sunrise. He noticed all of the beautifully framed pictures of some saintly face decorating the highest sides of the pillars, statue pedestals nestled in the recesses and positioned on the pillars holding busts and statues of every saint ever known to a German or Russian Catholic. That was the left side of the hallway, and when he switched he could see that entire right sideline of the pillars was where the crucifixes went. Only the finest artisanship seemed to be the norm. There were huge ones, down to the more manageable size, and dozens of smaller ones. Every house, every barn, every church where those Catholics ever found shelter, had a crucifix near the doorway, and it appeared that someone had nailed the finest one hundred up and down this hallway.

They passed by the two treasure room doors and then the music room. Two more doors on the left that Hammer referred to as, "more of the same." At the end of the walkway was the linen room and finally they came upon the passage back to the kitchen. The old man was very tired and worn out, but his cane and cart had helped much, and he headed for a long couch that had two pillows and blankets. Beautiful end tables and two sitting chairs flanked it. Hammer positioned himself as he planned to fall onto the right side of the couch and could rest heavy against that end armrest. It worked perfectly, and his cane just stood there right alongside his left knee.

"Come and sit with me after you find us some more food and wine. Do not forget the pipes — I have so much more to show you and talk about. Before you go, hand me that tall book there on the shelf," and he pointed to one on the other side of the room. Basil quickly found the right one by picking the tallest and brought it back to his pastor.

"What else would you like? And while you're planning dinner, I would like to look at your side. Please?"

Hammer lifted his shirt again to find that things had not improved in the slightest, even though the lighting had. He was bleeding under the skin, and a giant dark black bubble seemed to lurk just under the surface, destined to burst. The old man had nothing to say and gently lowered the shirt.

"Does it hurt badly?"

"It hurts, but I would have to say it seems to look worse than it feels. A tall glass of wine might help." Within a second, it appeared he had been talking to an empty chair as Basil sailed off after the wine and goblets. Before long, he had the foods, cheese, nuts, and the pipes. He sat himself down in the chair closest to Hammer and started to pack the pipes. He was nowhere near comfortable; barely comprehended what he had been shown down the south side walkway and was only slightly familiar with the kitchen.

The one terrible wrong with everything was the fact he had seen the damage to the old man's body; it was a killer, and he knew it. It instantly became the bogeyman in the basement, and neither man could look away from or deny the fact that it would not be long and Hammer would die. There was nothing they could do to stop it — too bad, so sad.

"I want to say Mass one last time, and for that we have a chapel down the north side hallway. You will like that room too.

After we have talked a while and rested, we can go do that together. For now, I want to teach you about some of the finer points to our burrow. Behind us is a ladder that will take you to a walkway up above us that completely circumnavigates the foundation of the church. You will come to special viewing ports that look out over the valley from just above ground level through the foundation blocks, and in four of them you can actually crawl through and be outside. They all have very intricate locking and opening devices, and you will learn quickly how each one works and what you can see from standing there at that portal. As usual, you will find them stunning and exactly what I think you are going to need in the future. This particular book has the floor plans, and to some extent has the inventory, but I have never completed it fully, and it should not be considered the bottom line. When it comes to all the many secrets this place has to offer, this book tells the story, almost to the inch."

Basil followed the ladder with his eyes up to a square attic door that undoubtedly opened downward and would hang there when it did. He wanted to climb those stairs that very moment, but Hammer had just begun.

"Now for the big surprise that I'm positive will take your breath away. I want you to go over to the ladder and take hold of the right-hand rail, and then tap the second step with your toe. Not the first. You will hear a latch release and then just push on that handrail."

Basil stood up and walked around behind the furniture, studied the situation and turned back to Hammer.

"Now?"

"Now is good."

He raised his boot tip and tapped the step, heard the latch and pushed as instructed. It appeared that the ladder was attached to the wall as one might expect for an attic ladder, but in truth, the ladder was attached to a door whose side seams were invisible, for the most part. The hinges were on the other side, and as he pushed, he could see deep into a passageway that disappeared up and to his right and into the darkness. There was the smell of smoke and must, some cobwebs, but not many, and he thought he could hear the faint twitter of birds far up there in the darkness. He continued to push until the opening was complete, and his new-found door latched open, against the inside wall of the passageway.

When he slowly turned back to the candlelit kitchen, he could see that the old man was once again starting to acknowledge his pain and was making some effort to reposition himself without actually laying down.

"Come and talk with me. You can leave it open. When you want to close the door, tap on the step and pull it behind you. It opens from the other side with a bit more difficulty, because there isn't a ladder on that side, but you'll be the only one who knows there's a latch and you can find it without any trouble, simply because you know that. If you didn't know that, you might be there a while, and a word to the wise, the door will close on its own somehow or another. It always does. I have never been able to figure that one out."

The young man came around and asked if there was anything he could do for his mentor. Without thinking twice, he had the old man's pipe glowing, and then his own, he went over to the stream and filled a large bowl with water, found some fresh Turkish towels and made the compresses for the old man's side. They sipped on their wine and their pipes as Father Karl Hammer tried to stay alive. The light was going out of his eyes as he rested there on the couch, but they didn't close. He knew exactly what was happening to himself, approximately how much time he had left, and he was very thankful that the pain was not distracting him from understanding all that. He could still see, and he could still hear, and he knew there was a place that he needed to be. Not this room.

"I suppose you might be wondering about that passageway, just a little?"

"Now that you mention it I can only assume it heads all the way out to our Grotto. It does, doesn't it? It leads to the base of the Grotto, and then what? It must be the best way in and out of here. How insanely clever, and I never suspected anything. Never. When you went there to pray, I thought you knelt there, said your rosary, the office, our Capuchin meditations, and that's why I never bothered you. Not that I could even see you doing that. You did your prayers very close to the base of the grotto, the sun, the wind... I thought you were just out of sight. I can hardly wait."

"You'll have your chance, later today, but first I'd like to go say one last Mass. Help me up, please. I'm running out of time."

Basil carefully picked the old pastor to his feet and slid the cane under his armpit, which seemed to fit like a glove and turned the old man into a much lighter load, as in no load at all. Hammer hung on the cane with his right arm, and he hung on Basil with his left. Basil took that left arm, and they headed for the north side passageway again and those doors he vaguely recalled seeing. He now knew about the north walk and where it came from, had been flabbergasted by the south walk, both down and back, and was now ready for almost anything the north could throw at him. That was a sure sign he was a bit too confident in his abilities to quickly comprehend the finality of things.

The first time, he had been a few moments into not having just burned to death and was fairly excited about that, and the second time was to check and see if the church bells had crashed through the ceiling. It was fortunate that was not the case and, for the most part, he couldn't remember any further details on the passageway. It would all be brand new, but what more could there be? His eyes had welled up when he heard the old man talking about time, couldn't wipe away the tears, and had to let them fall where they did.

Once again, they crossed the stream in front of the Diamond Teardrop, and Basil noticed the stream was back the way it had been before the rains had started. It had widened for a while, reached the elevated banks on each side, but grew no further, and then receded. The water poured out that bottom corner of the eye, eye level to a man, and gently cascaded down the front cheek of granite. From there the water spread out an inch deep, a few feet wide, and gently flowed through the center of the room and through all the stepping stones. In essence, it was only a little deeper and wider than it had been at the start and had evidently never exceeded its boundaries, no matter how hard it rained. On the far western side of the room, between the two passageways, it disappeared into the floor. Simply vanished into a maze of cracks and crevices in the rock floor up against that distant wall of timbers.

They stopped on the northern bank, and Hammer turned back to the eye in the rock. She was crying, still, and he had only seen her cry like this a few times before. They sat down in the chairs nearby that ensured the best vantage point for watching the teardrop. She was mesmerizing and magnetic. Hammer had found it impossible to sit in his chair and watch the teardrop without eventually falling asleep and usually sleeping like a newborn baby near its mother. He had spent hundreds and hundreds of nights here in this very chair, and he was saying goodbye to the chair and the eye, one last time. This man, this rock, this eye, and this never-ending stream had been together for fifty-some-odd years now, and he had never gotten used to the sound. If ever there were a sound a man could never get tired of, it was the sound of the water coming out of the rock.

They rose and moved on. The giant pillars that lined the north wall supported a ceiling far higher than necessary. Some of the horizontal roof timbers were embedded in the granite rock face as if nature had planned it a million years before. Instead of there being just one door to the first room on his right, there were two.

Basil stationed Hammer against the left-side hinges and gently pushed on the doors, which opened together as if in a partnership, floating apart at the same speed, so quiet and smooth. They had felt light as a feather and the light from his candle splashed off an altar that suggested if God himself was looking for a platform, this might be it. To say it was the finest handcrafted small marble altar in the annals of altars might not do it justice, but that was basically just an incidental to the whole thing.

Basil lit the entrance candles and then returned to Hammer. There were twelve candles in all and as they took over, Hammer realized he had never lit that many for one of his services, much less that fast, and now that he saw the results, he thought that perhaps he should have. The damaged priest stood motionless, leaning on his cane, enjoying the way Basil was appreciating this magical and holy moment.

The assistant started to scan the altar area. He discovered the most magnificent private chapel in the history of the Catholic Church. There was limited seating, which was understandable, but there were, in fact, a number of kneelers and chairs that might have touched the knees and rear end of Catherine the Great herself. There appeared to be a small little sacristy off to the right side, built for one, and a curtain of gold lace could be pulled across a golden curtain rod to seal off that area for privacy. It evidently had never been closed. He could see a closet full of the primary vestments and, of course, there was a smaller cabinet with all the other necessities in its drawers.

On the small center table inside the sacristy stood all of the items they would need for the Mass as if some deacon had come along before this time and prepared everything in advance. Not only that, the chalice, the ciborium, the communion platter, the wine and water goblets and a small cup sat on a golden serving tray, just waiting. Never had Basil ever seen such quality, and that included the things he had seen in the treasure room. Someone had saved the best for here.

When he realized the old man was perfectly stable, he instinctively took off about his business. He lit the candles on the altar that all showed signs of having been burned before, but not much, and gradually the entire room began to glow with no shadows as if every candle holder, every ornament and every polished edge of marble was designed to reflect candle light. There was a spectacular Easter Candle, four inches thick, standing on its golden pedestal, just waiting for the Easter season every year. As the lone flame grew, the heat disturbed an elaborate hanging swirl of tiny silver and gold angelic figurines. They twisted and turned, pinged into each other, as this mini orchestra soothed the silence into something you would never get tired of hearing.

Basil scurried off to the sacristy, gathered up the vestments, and came out to the end of the altar steps and near where the lead celebrant was still leaning on his cane. He hadn't entered the room just yet and seemed buried in his thoughts so Basil stood there respectfully and waited for the old man to allow him to assist with the garments.

"Father Basil, we cannot put my Easter vestments on over these rags from yesterday. In my arrogance and lack of shame, I cannot allow it to happen. Even though everything I'm wearing is only one day old, they are tainted, smell like yesterday and I would like to wear new pants, new socks, new shoes, and a fresh shirt, and then I can don these holy vestments. I would like to die in fresh clothes, as strange as it sounds, and you can find everything I speak of in the small closet there in the sacristy."

As Basil headed off with his mental notes, he watched Hammer turn around in the doorway, leaving.

"When you find the clothes, I'll be in the next room. Our little corner of paradise comes equipped with quite possibly the finest lavatory and bath chamber this side of the Urals. I have a burning desire to take a Lenin."

Sometimes the old man's tenor and his demeanor led Basil to believe that something very profound and meaningful was about to be shared, sometimes not. It didn't seem strange at all that the old man wanted to die in clean clothes. Sure enough, when he found the closet, there was everything he would need, for not only the old man but also for himself. Two complete wardrobes, everything from boots and socks and underclothes to fresh cassocks and new collars. Hammer had used the humorous expression 'take a Lenin' routinely many times in the past and Basil had grown accustomed to the old man excusing himself for a time, for that purpose, and thought it was the perfect way to ask for a little time off. He would gather up the new clothes and prepare his vestments, and give Hammer some time to sit and contemplate the future or the past. Besides, everyone knew that Lenin was dead, and some other prick had taken his place; someone said his name was Stalin, but Hammer knew that couldn't be true, and whoever was in charge was a fake .

'Quite possibly the finest lavatory and bath chamber this side of the Urals' was an intriguing thought, and coming from that man's lips after seeing this chapel, the kitchen, the Diamond Teardrop, the piano, the treasure room, the passageway to the Grotto and everything else, Basil suddenly felt the twinge to take a Lenin himself. He couldn't wait to see the place, and there were at least two more doors past the lavatory. He could hear the old man moaning and groaning, struggling with the toilet, until he called out.

"Edward, I'm through, and Lenin is on the run. I feel like the king of the world, and I need my new clothes."

Basil had the garments hanging over the sides of his arms and had the new boots pinched tightly in front as he pushed the door and walked into the dimly lit chamber. The candles he held helped a great deal. Father Hammer was still on the toilet in the farthest corner, his cassock and underclothes were piled up near his feet, and he was bleeding out all over the floor. He was almost ready to tip over by the time Basil dropped all the clothes and rushed to his side. There was blood coming out of his mouth, and he was trying to apologize for something, but Basil wouldn't let any words come out. He forced Basil's hand from his lips and held his own hand against his cheek — a gesture that demanded Basil listen to these last words.

"Father Basil! Father Basil! Jesus!"

In a matter of only a few moments, Basil's Mass preparations had come to a halt as he raced into a what to do next panic in the basement lavatory of a burned-down church. This incredible man was bleeding out, dying, and Basil understood instantly why they were near the toilet and not on those altar steps in the other room. It wasn't his clothes that had prevented him from entering the chapel, it was his body and blood. Hammer knew he was about to explode, and there was absolutely no need to say his farewell inside such a holy room. He had considered everything, rationally and sanely, made it to the toilet on his own and disrobed himself in private. He balanced himself on the commode and held the cane out in front of his nose as he stared into the face of his Christ. He slowly defecated and then urinated until he was empty and thanked the Lord for allowing him to flush himself first. He kissed the forehead of Christ and gripped the handle hard with both hands and shouted out to his assistant as his side ruptured, tore a gash, and all of his life blood began to pour out of him. He could feel it flowing out, and as it was happening, he began to breathe a bit better, and that fear disappeared before it scared him too bad. Once he could breathe, he could speak again... and he was down to a hundred words or less.

"Father Basil, come and get my cane. Take care of me promptly; you'll be shown the way, I promise. The cane is now yours and, in time, an apostle, one of the twelve, a traveling pilgrim will need it. He'll come here to get it. Never forget about Desch or that Van Vedic will come back. You have to wait for him and continue the fight, never say die. Pray for me, bless me, forgive me my sins, Dear God, my Jesus, Mother Mary."

He closed his eyes for a moment and appeared to be gone, but then opened them and stared at his nurse.

"Perhaps we should question everything. We should have never been so blind, so trusting, we should have fought harder."

And they both began to cry.

Hammer insisted that Basil carry him to the edge of the bathtub, away from the toilet. By the time they got there his legs had turned blue and the look of life in his eyes just dimmed away. He kept breathing in, holding it in for a few more moments, staring hard into Basil's eyes. Without blinking or moving a single muscle on his entire naked body, he went from being alive to dead, and Basil saw that instant happen, deep inside the pupils of the old man's eyeballs. He saw the light go out. As he knelt there holding Hammer's shoulders, he watched as the old man's eyelids closed, and his color turned to white. The purple bubble had burst, and a huge amount of his blood had poured out his side by the toilet and all across the floor till there was one last puddle by the tub. It appeared to have been painless, and Basil didn't know what to do next. His mind was traveling a mile a minute, scanning this new room, thinking about the ones he knew about already, the ones just down this hall that he hadn't seen yet, all of the places in the center area. He was reliving yesterday, that last Mass the day before, and he wondered about Desch. He had never seen him again after the communion service, after that last image of the way he had received it and how much Basil had wanted to give it. He would never forget that tongue, those eyes, and that feeling of passing on such a treasure. A wish come true.

Hammer's last vision was looking past Basil and through the lavatory door out into the north passageway at a painting of the cosmic sky, without his glasses on.

For the longest time, Father Edward Basil sat there by the tub cradling the ancient old man. He, himself, was miraculously still alive, and this cold old man was gone. It was over for him; it was done, and he was through. His blood had flowed down from the toilet area, across the floor tiles, as if it were coated with wax, and merged with more of his blood near the tub. The entire red evidence of his life found a drain hole in the floor only inches out, past his fingertips. Time went by, and there was hardly any left on the floor by the time Basil stopped to think about it. Almost all of Hammer's blood had come out the hole in his side because of that position he had been held in, and all of that blood was already mingling with other life fluids deep inside these rocks.

Basil laid the old man out on the floor and uncoiled the shower hose from up on a wall. He couldn't imagine it having been any easier for him. He washed the left side of the old man until the gash was apparent for what had happened. It resembled an X mark, with a hyphen on the upper right leg of the X. His cold white skin and the tissue showed exactly where the butt of the rifle had slammed into his rib cage, and the hyphen was a broken rib fragment that had started the tear.

Basil disposed of the old clothes and did his best to prepare the old man's body for burial. He washed up clean and had a fine look to his face for a dead man. He dried quickly, and Basil dressed him in his new underwear, new cassock and boots, laid him flat on his back and interlaced his fingers on his belly.

Hammer had left his cane propped against the side wall an arm's length from the toilet as Basil had cradled him there and he uttered those last words. Neither he nor Basil had touched it again after they moved to the edge of the bathtub. Perhaps an hour had passed before Basil decided to stand and do all of the things he felt he should do. Now Hammer's cane was mysteriously but gently wedged into the notch between his right rib cage and the backside of his arm, and had gently nudged him back from a place we all find ourselves in every now and then. All he had been able to do was kneel there and weep, with both his hands folded atop the old man's hands. All he had to do now was reach up and wrap his fingers around the grip, and the cane would be his walking stick from that time on.

So he did just that. He felt energized.

Basil neutered every candle save for ones in the chapel and arranged his vestments near the sacristy, and even though he was grieving deep inside his soul, the thought of saying Mass in the very near future eased his pain immensely. He smiled at the Tabernacle.

He stood there, looking down at his friend and teacher, and turned the face on the cane into his. He could see life in those eyes, he could see it. The cane pressed away from his gaze and lay out along his forearm as he raised the point off the ground out behind him. He bent down, so his left hand and the top of the cane slid under Hammer's shoulders, and his right hand slid under the legs. He lifted the hundred-and-fifty-pound man with ease, and he knew it was the cane that gave him this unusual kind of strength. The pastor was almost as light as a pillow, and even though he wasn't quite sure what to do next, he knew his body didn't belong in the lavatory, and so he turned and headed for the door with the old man laid across his forearms.

He was a handsome old man in his new priest clothes, asleep in the arms of a rejuvenated young man. When they arrived at the door to the hallway, he reached down and picked up a candle; that caused the dead priest's feet to snag the corner of the doorframe, and the cane seemed to push them up the hallway and into the darkness.

"I've never been this way before."

Basil looked down into both stoic faces looking back at him, got no response at all, and so he continued on his way west. Slow steps, one after another, and when he came up on the next closed door, nothing nudged him to stop walking, so he didn't, walked by it and could see the end of the hallway now and the final doorway. He'd have to come back to this door later.

When he came to what he knew had to be the northwest corner, where the ladder went up to the confessionals, a beautiful couch was nestled against the wall and seemed to be the perfect place for Father Hammer, at least for the time being. He hadn't noticed any of this the first time through. There was a pillow for his head and another tubular pillow that was perfectly positioned for the crook in his legs. Basil laid him down and folded both his hands on his belly, then stepped back and away. He could only marvel at how peaceful the man looked, how calm, and how content with his new clothes.

He ended the dim light with two additional new ones and discovered his next task, as a priest, was to bless this body and give him the last rites. There it all was, a golden box sitting on that table with the candle and everything he needed to do it perfectly. The long chant book, all the traditional ancient words, the oil, the scarf, everything was there. Not that it had to be perfect, but when it was perfect, it made it a little better, a little easier, more acceptable to the chanters. It didn't take long, didn't change anything, of course, and there was no way he could extend it past the third page. Basil was done for now. He blew out the candle as he turned to the other side of the room, where he was being called.

There, he lit two soft candles that were waiting on the end tables and saw there was a single chair in the corner, with its own table, a three bottle display of wine and a single glass, a single pipe and tobacco, a golden lighter and a diamond rosary. Basil took his place. There was a spot on the floor where the tip of the cane belonged and had been before.

He would learn so much from the cane... That it could leave a mark in granite and not leave a mark in the sand... That this mark by the chair was the only mark in the room... It stood there on its tip and faced the dead priest.

After the quietest time in all the history of sound, an hour or more, Basil stood up with the rosary in hand and took the cane at the same time, walked back up to the pastor and wrapped the rosary around his hands. He rested the cane against the side of the couch so the carving could press on the lifeless body and went back to his seat. He filled his wine glass and toasted Hammer for a life well lived, drank the entire glass and filled it again before setting it down. Next, he packed an exquisite Russian Grandfather Pipe from a humidor filled with three different blends, choosing the middle one. The golden lighter was designed to light that particular pipe. They were a matching set, and they both worked perfectly. From five feet away, the old man looked quite content in his death, had his favorite prayer wrapped all throughout his fingers and had his trusty cane resting against his side.

Never having been this involved in death before, Basil let his guard down and began to cry. He was tugging on the skin on the back of his own hand, watching it lift and then spreading back out with no trace of the pinch, living skin, alive and yellow, and he wiped his eyes with the back of that hand. He sat there thinking about how completely all alone he was now that his beloved teacher was gone, how his soul was in paradise and his body had been left behind, and those closed eyes would never see what the Communists had done to his church. So far in his priesthood, he had had little to do with death, few funerals and hardly any consolation to the survivors, being as young as he was, and he discovered that there would be no consolation for him. He was angry, very angry, exhausted in his weeping, suffering in grief, the likes of which he'd never really known. All he wanted to do for now was sit with his mentor, be with his body and let his mind go anywhere it wanted. But then, after a while, the fog lifted and he came back to being himself, back to the logical Basil, only now he was the angry logical Basil.

Just off to his right, ten paces away at the most, was the last door, the fourth door on this side with this exceptional foyer out front. All he had to do was stand up and go open it, but it crossed his mind that there would be an order to everything he would do this day and opening that door right then and there might not be the thing to do first. He was finished crying, and wasn't ready just yet for Hammer's final adieu. He had a funeral Mass to say and a number of other priorities, with the only issue being some sort of logical order.

There was the fact that he had not opened the third door yet, and there was an obvious reason for that.

Perhaps he shouldn't get ahead of himself. He really needed to sit for a while, and had managed to land in the finest recliner he'd been in since early on in the tour, back on the other side of the basement. There were some really nice lazy-priest recliners by the tear drop, but this one would be just fine for an hour more. He had a fairly good image of what it looked like up there, and it was the number one priority. The passageway to the Grotto was all he could think about, and even though he'd seen burned-down churches before, seeing St. Francis that way would further break his heart, but it had to happen.

CHAPTER 20

FOREVER AND A DAY

There is silence in this world that can't be explained in normal words, we have to hear it, understand it and know it for what it is. Silence can be awesome, but to truly feel it, we have to be alone, secluded, still. Basil was now every bit of all that. He had prayed as best he could, but his mind kept wandering and his anger was all over the goose bumps on his arms. Wave after wave of pure anger, and his anger was building as the third glass of wine was disappearing, until he finally had to stand and pretend he was alive, remember he was a priest.

He held his new cane close to his face and then gently tapped it on the floor. Every sound he made, he heard. He needed to hear something else, and he knew where that was — in the chapel. With a formal bow to his predecessor, a light tap on the cold hands and a promise to be back, he headed back past the third door, past the lavatory, and he could hear the chimes from the Easter candle. That was the sound he wanted to hear. Standing in that doorway, he was dazzled by the altar, by everything in there. It was ready for his first celebration, but that too could wait. It was still the spirit of Easter and would be for weeks, so he let the big one burn.

There, behind him in the great room, were the eye and the waterfall, and that sound was as soothing to the troubled soul as any you might want to hear. Crystal clear and pure water falling and pouring out in just the right volume at just the right height, through a tear duct made of solid granite. Without a doubt, Mother Nature at her softest.

Almost begrudgingly, he stepped across the steps to the other side of the room, not wanting to miss any of the sounds from the teardrop. But he had to, he had to touch the step on the attic ladder, and he had to walk the walk, plus he had to do it now.

The door to the passageway was closed, just like Hammer said it would be; it had closed on its own. So he resumed that position again. "Now is good." It unlatched, and he pushed. The door opened all the way and latched again. The smell was the same, and he could hear the birds chirping as if he were outside, so he took his cane and his candle and walked the first few steps into the darkness without any fear. After having only used it for a short time, and only traveled a short distance, the cane seemed to be in the lead, pulling him, leading him on, and the last thing he wanted to do was let go.

The stagnant air from the basement pushed him and his candlewick while his cane leaned and pulled him forward. The passageway was easily wide enough for two people to walk side by side, and there was a constant right angle to it and an uphill slope for the first forty steps or so, until he came into a small chamber with a chair. There was water on the sides of the rock, and the passageway angled back to the left and through a very deceptive group of crevices into another mezzanine room.

Basil imagined he was getting close to the end of the tunnel. He crossed through a wide and long open area to its distant corner and his cane seemed to pull him to the not so obvious crevice that led farther up the cave, as there were many to choose from. He could see a light, dim, another thirty paces away, so he set his candle down and very cautiously hugged the wall until he came out behind St. Francis's right hip. He couldn't believe he was standing there. All the time he had been Father Hammer's assistant, all that time in the past two years praying at one of his favorite benches only twenty feet out and away, and not in his wildest imagination did he ever suspect there was an entire new world neatly tucked into St. Francis of Assisi's right rear pocket.

He stood in the shadow of the saint, hidden in the corner, diagnosing the way out — which was obvious — and the way back to where he had come from. As he huddled in the light, he tried to see over the huge pedestal the statue was standing on. It alone was five feet tall and only his right eye would have been visible to someone standing out there; all of the rest of him was concealed. There was no one out there.

Gradually, he worked his way around behind the pedestal until he was standing alongside the saint's left knee. He could see the mountaintop off to the east, and the rest of the beautiful hilltop garden. In that position, for the most part, he was still invisible but could now walk out in front of St. Francis and still have the five granite kneelers between him and the rest of the universe.

He picked the left side of the grotto first, cuddled up to the northern edge and peeked around to see what might be there.

St. Francis Church was magnificent by any standard but especially because it had been made out of wood, for the most part, and towered above the tree tops on the very edge of civilization. Coming up on forty-eight hours now, everything was gone except the foundation blocks. There was still a thick mingling of different-colored smoke rising into a blackish fog that was slowly dying. The smoke was drifting away from the hilltop, north, out into the long ravine, and then dissipating into the wind.

Fifty years ago there had been thousands and thousands of people out there in the outback, little communities of different religions, but primarily Catholics. Neighboring communities would have seen the smoke, tried to get there in time to help put it out — and might have; they were so close — but, of course, there was no one out there. All of their churches had already been burned down to their block foundations, and the scene ended up being the same, time after time. There was a standard rule throughout the Church, and it was fairly simple: make it last for five hundred years, a thousand if you can, and forever if you think you can get away with it. There were then three new rules after that. Location, foundation, creation.

Every church was different, unique, and built by the people who prayed there. They all had one thing in common: when they burned, they burned completely. As a general rule, the only people who were there at the end were usually the ones who had lit the place on fire, and were known to film it and rummage through the rubble when it cooled, looking for the bells and marble.

Basil was crying silent tears again and couldn't stop, the second time that day. He was pretty sure he knew what it was going to look like, but still it took his breath away and all he could do was kneel there in his peek-a-boo position and let the tears fall. He had plenty of those.

Basil could not see a single solitary person up or down the roads, anywhere along the river and over into the village. His silent tears turned into a crazy man's scream, and he made a noise that only a wild animal could make. Only one loud two-second wail, a veritable hair-raising roar, a deep-voiced scream that only he could make and only while holding the cane. He had never felt that before, and the sound made him feel good so he did it again, only longer, realizing that he was making a sound that would terrify anyone who heard it.

The priest changed on the spot, his eyes widened, and he instantly judged all he could see. He placed blame where it belonged, rendered a verdict, a sentence, and vowed to die for the cause if necessary. Vowed to protect and defend everything below the ashes, no matter the cost, for however long it took. He was so very angry, shivering and boiling inside, that he stood up and howled again.

He held the cane with both hands and closed his eyes with the wooden face only inches from his, soothing him, mellowing him while his anger diminished slightly and his curiosity took over.

He regained some composure. Now, he was on guard and certain that anyone within earshot had heard his anguished howl, every bit of which he was proud of, and was glad he'd been responsible for, but he wouldn't do that again without good reason. After waiting a while and scanning as much of the smoke-filled valley as he could, he suddenly discovered that when he was holding the cane with two hands and it was facing the way he was facing, he could see farther, clearer, and he could hear much, much better. That was why he had heard the birds, and now he could hear the fire still burning under the smoke, and the rapids in the river five hundred yards away.

Basil continued to edge around the giant grotto until he was standing in the middle of the walkway that meandered down to the back of the church a hundred yards away at least. From this vantage point, he could tell that the rectory and some back sheds were burned to their slabs, and those fires were now completely out, not even smoking; virtually nothing remained. The rock fireplace and its smoke stack, front steps, back steps, and this rectangular pile of ashes were all that was left of that beautiful little cabin and its front porch, to say nothing about all the furnishings and personal treasures that the two men had in their closets.

It was hard at first to comprehend what he was seeing or not seeing. Many times in the last two years he had been in this very spot looking at the back of the church, seeing the big trees close to the church on both the north and south sides, and only slivers of the abandoned Pfeiffer. He remembered doing that about a week before. This afternoon, he could see a lot more of the little brown village.

The entire church was now piled on top of itself, and the ten trees that bordered it and cornered it were also destroyed. The fire had been so intense that the trees were consumed and burned down to their stumps, and were still burning at their cores. Very little smoke, leaving twenty-foot wide white ash coal piles, and he knew from experience that stump hole would still be hot in a week. If he lived that long, he could test that theory.

Nearby trees that hadn't caught fire were wilted and damaged. All the grass and bushes were gone, and only the rock sidewalks and benches seemed unaffected by the heat. He was pulled farther down the walkway until he came up on the edge of where the heat had ended. All the grass had turned yellow and finally disappeared altogether in another ten steps. It was as if God had drawn a yellow halo around the entire smoldering bubble a hundred and fifty feet from the center.

It was still burning. He could feel the heat, the closer he got, until he was uncomfortable. Close enough for now. Once again, from previous experience, he knew it would burn for days unless it rained again, and it looked like it might.

St. Francis of Assisi Church had once stood a hundred feet tall on the west end with that spectacular bell tower, but it had been consumed, devoured and removed from the face of the earth completely. St. Francis was now just a mountain of white coals of what once was, and those ashes were burning out, still consuming themselves and the kneelers, pews, everything down deep, where there was still some wood left.

One of these nights, Basil decided, he would make sure all the signs were stood up straight and stable. He promised himself that he would never leave a footprint again and would check where he had already been and make sure they were invisible and erased.

For a basic starter, he seemed concerned about exactly where that bell had landed. He had to assume that Hammer had been right. The tower had fallen due east; the side walls had been pulled into the heart of the church, and the east end fell all over the altar.

His other area of concern was the confessional, and through the heat waves and billows of smoke he could barely tell there had ever been anything there to begin with. His coffin had been obliterated, and the two small bells from the tower were lying on their sides close to the rock foundation. They must have fallen straight down when their ropes burned through. The big one was nowhere to be seen.

Basil continued to pass by the southern edge of the smoldering mass of heat and smoke until he was even with the side steps that had gone up to the front doors. When he looked over to that area where he and Hammer had spent the day after the Mass, he could see the Bible still lying in the dirt where the colonel had thrown it. His Rocket, that Bible and 'The Teachings of St. Francis of Assisi,' all lay out there, hot and singed, but undamaged. That beautiful fifty-foot tall shade tree that adorned that sidewalk seemed to have melted where it stood and was now a twenty-foot in diameter smoldering mound of white coals and radiating heat.

Basil ran alongside the edge of the remnant and over to where the books were and scooped them up. He could feel the heat still trapped inside their binders. As they cooled, he headed back up to the grotto, held them tight to his chest and tried not to look back, but he did anyhow.

When he was back on the walkway and out of the singed area, he finally stopped at one of his all-time favorite spots, Station of the Cross — Number Two. It was so difficult to sit there on that bench and look down on that steaming mass of coals from a hundred yards away. Undoubtedly, he was the only human being for miles in any direction; he had decided that because of the way the cane felt in his hands. When he held it, the feeling at times was as if he was holding his father's hand, perhaps Jesus' himself, he didn't know, but it was very soothing. Sometimes he could feel it pulling him or stopping him in place. Touching the cane seemed to make him into something different than what he used to be, better in every way; every sense was enhanced, making him feel almost indestructible.

Knowing everything that he now knew, as he sat on that rock bench half way back to the grotto, he could see through the smoke once in a while, all the way to the center of Pfeiffer, a view that hadn't been seen in eighty years. Station number two had always been the most beautiful of them all, the best view of the valley, and commemorated Jesus being given his cross. Basil now seemed to have a new one himself, a cross that would have never crossed his mind, never.

Even from this angle, he still couldn't spot the big bell. He believed that it had in fact hit bull's-eye into the hole they had dug in the main isle, something he had barely paid any attention to on their way to the back of the church that afternoon. He remembered thinking what a total waste of time, digging through the center isle and looking for a basement, and him believing without a doubt that there wasn't one. Of all the things to happen, considering they took no measurements and dug it where they did, the bell fell into the hole, and the church burned down around it and buried it from the scavengers. In his mind, he had imagined it falling straight down, could see the bell sitting there in the rubble, cast iron and a trophy for any metal hunter. It would stand out like a sore thumb and, in all likelihood, it might end up being the only thing worth salvaging. Being in the hole as it was, perhaps the scavengers would just pass on by, thinking that the bones of St. Francis had already been picked clean. The mongrels could have the two little bells.

The books were sitting there by his side. Basil held the cane with his left hand and was blocking the sun with his right, trying to focus on the back right rear corner of this disaster. It was still one of the very hot areas; still had flames now and then and every so often the smoke would completely change color and get dark.

Underneath that corner of hell, down twenty feet or more, lay the body of the man who had been born in that village the same year the church had been started. His whole entire life had been dedicated to the Catholic Church and this church in particular. He died inside of it while it was dying, and now Basil had to bury the man somewhere fitting. He wasn't at all sure where that would be, and he hoped to get some inspiration before too long. He couldn't remember them ever having discussed that, except there at the very end, and he wasn't quite sure what he had heard. He had the time, perhaps lots of it.

As he sat there, Basil thought there was one thing that hadn't disappeared, and that was this anger he could feel throughout himself. With no flock except for himself, he felt even more anger. The only thing that repeatedly flashed before his eyes was Sokolov waving him into the confessional. They had filmed all this and probably cheered at times as the walls collapsed, and Sokolov would have watched and known that the 'two holy ones' were inside there, burning to death. Even though he had never seen a movie so far in his life, Basil fully understood what had been going on, and it was at that moment he remembered how Desch had promised him there would be two copies. There were hundreds of pictures of the church, and now a movie, but all Basil had left was his memories and this developing anger. He went for a walk down by the river, fished for a while and walked some more.

There's only so much a man can deal with at any given time, so Basil reverted to his favorite standby and began a long series of prayers that he had created in his mind. His mother had always prayed to Saint Jude, the apostle who became the patron saint of people who were lost, despaired, living in hopeless situations, and there came a point in the novena to ask for something in particular. She would pray out loud, and one of her particulars was that she would find her diamond someday, and even though she never did, at least her son had.

When he was finally finished, he decided that he had things to do that couldn't wait, and walked the short distance back up to the side of the grotto. The forty-foot high rock monolith would act as a black beacon for many years to come. What else was there? There was nothing left except for everything in the basement.

Peace enveloped Basil as he walked around the side back up to the kneelers and could see what St. Francis had always seen. The saint couldn't see the rubble behind him, never had, for that matter, and the look in the saint's face had not changed; he appeared to be at peace with nature. A few miles distant, the foothills climbed quickly into the forests, and that Easter Sunrise peak would always be where it was.

From up on top of that mountain pass one could see the Volga ten miles away and to the east flowing into the Caspian Sea. From up there, looking back west, the mighty Don River flowed towards Rostov and out into the Sea of Azov. Those rivers pinched a narrow strip of land that sent one river into a dead end and the other into the rest of the world. That's about all Basil knew about the land and the two great rivers. This had not been his country when he'd first arrived, but it was now; he had a new home and business to take care of.

Basil watched a beautiful red-tailed squirrel run across the rocks not too far away. Before he disappeared into the maze, he stood on his hind legs, screamed a warning and scoured the area before he vanished. Basil decided he might mimic the squirrel and be as cautious as that little animal appeared to be from that time on. He made one last inspection of the roads and the edge of the Ilava and vanished behind the statue.

Once in the passageway, he found he was blind, going from the sunlight into this pitch-black darkness, but in only a few blinks, his eyes adjusted, and he was quickly upon his still-burning candle. As he proceeded into the darkness, his curiosity was causing him to more closely examine the walls of his corridor, and he started to notice different ornaments and places to set a candle and meditate on a subject. Once he was past the last chamber, he could see up ahead and that the passageway door into the great room was still open, greeting him with the sounds from the Diamond Teardrop. It soothed him as he stepped into the room, calmed him and demanded his attention. His best option seemed to be to sit down in the chair by the waterfall and let his mind sort out some of the details.

He turned back in his chair, looking through the passageway into the kitchen, and was studying the open passageway door, thinking about where it had led and what he had seen when he got there, when suddenly the doorway unlatched itself and quietly closed without him ever touching it, sealing him in tight and secure, some form of mind over matter.

As he sat in the chair listening to this new sound, the tired and exhausted servant relaxed, and within only a few minutes, he was asleep. There was a small impression in the floor just inches to the side of the armrest; his cane had slid into it and then stood there straight, erect, waiting for him to wake up. That wouldn't happen until dawn the next morning, after more than a dozen hours of needed sleep, but he would open his eyes to that new day rested and ready to begin his destiny.

Basil's first day would involve him taking care of Father Hammer's body, most importantly. He wanted to bury him somewhere up on the hilltop looking out over the valley and would find the spot up there after he found some food.

There was still the issue of the funeral Mass, what was behind the third and fourth doors, that beautiful piano was calling his name, all the books and binders sat waiting, and he'd noticed a massive grandfather clock with the hands stuck on twelve. His pocket watch told him it was six a.m. almost. He set the big clock and wound the springs so that it came to life and would tell him the time, beautifully and accurately. He arranged the date dials for April eleventh, and then watched the second hand begin its perpetual journey. At least he would know what time it was from that time on.

On his second trip up the passageway, Basil was much more comfortable, and when he got to the statue he decided not to be a squirrel, but a ferret or a weasel perhaps. He wanted to be faster, smarter, and not near so loud. He had this new sound he could make and couldn't help but remember how Hammer had said his fox didn't have strong teeth.

As he stood by the statue and was thinking on the gravesite, he decided on his mascot, that he would mimic the Rosomarha, eat meat, and live angry. Father Hammer told a fireside story one night that was enthralling, a legend about an Alpha wolverine, Rosomarha, named Pocomaxa. The animal was so ferocious, so intimidating that it scared an army away. It roamed the countryside and left scattered remnants of its kills buried in pieces nearby, gave only glimpses of its shadow, and became a ghost. His noise in the night kept every living creature awake. The claws and the teeth of Pocomaxa frightened the bears, especially the old ones, drove the wolves away, caused horses to stampede, and he specialized in eating the old Alpha male wolves and sometimes the young ones when they got in the way. Basil had always asked Hammer to tell it again, the story of Pocomaxa.

He knew it would hurt him, hurt him again, so early in the day, but he had to measure the fire and see what it had done during the night. It was slowly dying, and the smoke was starting to fade. It would be out by this time tomorrow, and he could get closer then, but for now the ash pile was lower than it had been, and a faint ledge to the foundation was now visible. He scoured the landscape, and his cane led him out onto the hilltop where he found the perfect spot for the old man's body. He could see him standing there only a month before, gazing out into the snow-covered wasteland, with his memories of how it once was.

Basil needed a shovel and didn't know where it would be, but he had time to look for it and was certain there would be one in the basement somewhere. He'd seen enough, was growing into his new wolverine mind, and wondered what the old fox might think of his chosen mascot. With this new attitude, he felt aggressive and defensive, and for the first time in his life, he sensed this power wash over him, this aggressive-protective spirit. He felt very different as a wolverine almost instantly and started a debate with God as to what he should do and what kind of wolf man he should be. For all he knew, he was God's last warrior in the region, everyone else was dead and gone, and God wanted him to make a stand and fight to the end. It was the Communists who'd decided to declare war on God, and God's people hadn't been able to stop them, at least not in this valley. The Communists wouldn't be satisfied until every trace of God was removed, every soldier of Christ was dead, and every church was a pile of ashes. The soldiers of Christ had no choice in the matter, came poorly armed for the battle, lost, and he was simply one of them, perhaps the last. If the Communists came back and discovered his burrow some day in the future, this time they would find Pocomaxa. He gripped the cane with both hands, tilted his head back and screamed the war cry of the wolverine across the abandoned village rooftops and down to the barnyards. No matter what kind of breathing creature you might be, that noise would get your attention and keep it for quite a while.

The Lord only knows why we can do this, but Basil was nine years old again as he and his father were chasing a fox out of their hen house. The animal raced across the roadway and into a pen full of pig sows with all their little piglets. Without a doubt, this was quite possibly the worst escape route imaginable, but that was where the fox went, and all hell broke loose when the mama pigs objected. They became enraged and were trampling their own babies, lashing out at each other and the fox until the terrified little red critter vaulted into the air and bounced across the backs of the pigs until he cleared the fence and was gone. All his life now, Basil had carried that memory and had fantasized about what had been going on in that fox's mind, how he had managed to find the footing, and whether or not he ever knew how lucky he really was. For a brief moment in this old daydream, he wondered what it would have been like if it had been an alpha wolverine instead, and this time when he looked out at the roadways, his more than perfect vision had a brand new look in his eyes.

It was time to search for a shovel and finish the tour, so he left the light of day and headed for Hammer. The beautiful Easter candle was still burning and so were many others, and he felt no different than if he were inside the church or any other building, for that matter. The only difference was that the walls were a bit thicker, and the roof was a bit higher. The chapel was so beautiful, so private and personal, and he could see himself saying the Mass in the near future… but not right now. He turned and headed west into the northern hallway.

Door number three was up on his right, and he decided to open those two remaining doors before he started with Hammer. Pinched between two massive vertical timbers, the third door was wider than all the others, was two doors in one. Half of it opened inward, or the whole thing opened out into the hallway. In their haste to escape the fire and get to the great room, they had hustled by these doors, and in the panic and dim light of the moment, he hadn't even noticed they were there. It was a very clever illusion and not at all what he expected… which didn't mean a thing, and so he opened it.

The best description of what he saw was that it was almost the exact same situation as had existed at the rectory, only on a much finer level. The same hands that had built the rectory fireplace had built this fireplace. The living area out in front of it was exactly the same as what he had enjoyed so much at the rectory, back during those long winter days and nights, talking with Hammer and watching the fire. There was a side door that went into the bathing room and another on the other side that went into a bedchamber. Two large bookshelf arrangements created a new library with hundreds and hundreds of titles.

A lone chair stared at a chess set; that was centered on a platform table that spun the game around for whoever had been sitting there. At this point in the tour, it would be pointless to describe the chess pieces, the chairs, end tables, the bed, the carpet; pointless, pointless, pointless. He knew who that person had been and where that person was now.

Basil's anger was back but mellowed slightly by his environment at the moment, and he wanted to thank someone. He was a simple man, didn't need much, and it just wasn't necessary for it to be so lavish and perfect. There was nothing he could do about any of that, he had never wished for such things, but was grateful, very grateful. He stood there, studying the board in his humble chess-student way, an attitude that Hammer had instilled in him as his undefeated sponsor and tutor. Basil had been a respected chess player at St. Michael's, knew the math of the game, but his expertise was dwarfed by Master Karl's. He had to assume it was the black side's move out of check, and there were no less than three viable moves, most of which resulted in a reverse check. He could faintly see some of the consequences to at least half of the moves. Without touching a piece, Basil became so confused that he didn't know whether to 'shit or go blind' again. It was a private joke between the two of them from way back when, and now that memory was one of Basil's smiles. They were playing their usual games, when out of frustration, one evening, Basil stood up and shouted, "I DON'T KNOW WHETHER TO SHIT OR GO BLIND!"

The two were having a chess tournament, best of three with a two-minute hourglass, when Basil completely lost his composure as the third game ended. He had been checkmated after eight moves in the first game, ten moves in the second and seven in the third. The tournament had lasted just under an hour, and the loser had to go get more firewood. In this particular case, he would study the board until the right move showed itself, and not make a typical thoughtless exchange of pieces until he knew better. He would read about it, study it, and make the move that he knew Hammer would have made some day. Basil smiled at the thought of it all and decided his next move might include a Lenin.

As he backed out of the room and closed the door, he looked down at the floor and whispered out loud, "Why me, Lord, why me?"

He turned to face the end of the north walk and could see the top of the old man's head on the end of the couch. He touched his cane against the side of the old man's arm, left it resting there, and stepped back a few paces.

"Father, I found you a place on the hilltop, out past the end of the grotto, and it has a wonderful view of the valley. I think you'll like it there if such things matter… which I know they don't. I'll feel better knowing you're out there watching over everything, and you can see St. Francis from the spot I've picked. My only problem with all this is that I haven't found a shovel yet and was hoping for some inspiration. I hope it's not in the treasure room."

The tour was almost over. Off to his right was that fourth door. Basil walked up to it and put a hand on the handle, looked back at Hammer and asked out loud, "Now?"

He answered himself, "Now is good," lowered the handle and walked inside. His astonishment about everything was now complete and his inspiration was fulfilled. There were candles on either side of the entrance, and when all four were glowing he could barely comprehend what loomed in front of his face. A massive wall of marble and figureheads, symbols of life and death, intricately embedded throughout the fascia of a spectacular three-coffin crypt. The centerpiece of it all was a marble sarcophagus that was sealed with a cap plate that no man could handle alone. Carved into the front plate in Latin was a eulogy to a man with no name. Where his name should have been, it had the single word "Saint," and the date of his death, "1853". On either side of the "Saint's" repository lay two empty coffins inside their respective marble containers. The lids propped against the sides of the upper tomb were, in fact, unmanageable by one man; but then again, he had his cane. The cap stone was easily five hundred pounds and would shatter if just pushed over, but he saw himself lower it with the cane in hand and it would be no problem, no problem at all.

The casket itself was beautiful, a simple design in heavy wood, with a polished lid, and was of a finer quality than most bodies found these days. Basil raised the lid and propped it open. The smell of old wood poured out while he arranged the blanket that would eventually cover his friend. The blanket was a wonderful tradition that had its roots in the most primitive of times, and he could tell this blanket had been intended for someone else. It was ready, so he stepped away and considered everything he could see. He was back to seeing his own coffin again, and this one was far more acceptable than the first one he had been involved with. He wasn't quite sure how he would manage to end up in the thing, or who would lower the lid, but at least he knew where Hammer would lay for as long as Mother Earth allowed.

Hammer's entombment was no longer an issue. There were procedures and traditions that needed to be followed to some degree, and the most basic of all was that the patriarch of St. Francis have a Funeral Mass in his honor — no, make that a High Funeral Mass, light all the candles, play the music and sing.

Basil stood over the old man, picked away his cane and began his prayers.

Trying to find a place for his pastor at the service was one of his concerns. After thinking about that other room and what was available, he concluded that the couch the man was on was the perfect platform. Considering how light he had been when he carried him here in the first place, if the couch weren't too heavy he might be able to manage them both at the same time.

It was extremely awkward as he slid his hand and cane under the couch about midway and reached over his pastor's chest and took the top of the backrest with his right hand. When he tried to lift, he realized his load was back-heavy, and he had to slide his wrist even closer to the middle. That made all the difference, and when he raised the couch, it balanced on his forearm and the shaft of the cane. Once it was equalized, he headed east past the third door to the bedroom, past the lavatory, and finally up to the open doors into the chapel.

He gently pushed a kneeler off to the side with the end of the couch and was able to set it all down directly in the middle of the room, at the base of the first step. He rested the cane against the old man's arm again and began to light his candles. Two of the highest on each side of the candelabra were almost out of reach. While holding the candle lighter at arm's length he felt a pinch in his back that shocked him with pain. He had to be more careful, he thought, always be careful and not do irrational things that might get him hurt; wolverines surely didn't do that, even if they were mauling a bear. Somewhere nearby, there was undoubtedly a stool or a step that he should have been standing on.

Hammer was ready, silent, cold and waiting while Basil was in a wildly creative mood and decided to hold nothing back. He would display himself for the Mass in the finest vestments that the sacristy had to offer. He would burn incense and sing as much of the liturgy as was allowed. He would play the songs he knew the old man loved from the music room and, before the day was over, he would lay him to rest forever.

Once inside the sacristy, he found the beautiful vestments he needed and everything else, for that matter. In no time at all he rang the tiny bell and walked out in front of his God. After he placed all the altar items where they belonged, he returned to the bottom step and bowed, genuflected and headed out of the chapel across the giant room, over the steps and down the south hallway till he came to the music room.

He lit those candles that decorated the front shelf of the exquisite piece of art, raised the lid and propped it open, exposing the incredible workmanship inside the grand instrument, and inhaled the smell from that box as well. He carefully and respectfully pulled the bench back out for the second time and positioned himself between the two. He softly pushed the backside of his vestment out and over the bench, as if he were wearing a tuxedo, and sat down without touching the ivory. He thought about that first note and could hear it before he made it. He reached out and found the A, and in his appreciation for the perfect pitch, he knew it was faultlessly in tune.

Basil played a long rendition of the traditional Easter morning hymns, singing loudly in Russian, and when he was done he went back to the chapel and started the Mass. He recited all the prayers and answered in Latin. Left the altar again and played for an hour during the break before the preparation of the gifts. The sounds faded from the piano, and he returned to his altar and celebrated the Eucharist, with the memory of Father Karl Hammer as the purpose for it all. When everything was said and done, he returned to his recital and played for another hour, until he was sure that enough was enough.

One last time, he returned and gathered his chalice and other necessities, left the altar and returned all of the vestments to their closet. When he came out, he extinguished the candles on the altar one at a time until only the Easter Candle and the chimes above it were all that was left. All along, he knew there was only one thing left to do for Hammer. He found his spot on the side altar bench, a few feet from where the pastor lay, and concluded the final litany of prayers.

After some ending silent thoughts, Basil stood up and took his cane, reached under and lifted the couch and took the man back to the distant room. Without any further delay, he picked him off the couch and took him through the door into the crypt. He carefully laid him out in his casket, rearranged the rosary, and covered him with his blanket. When he was done, he laid the cane on top of the blanket and said a final prayer for the priest.

"Rest well, old man. Pray for me. Goodbye."

Basil took out the cane and stood it by his side, reached up and closed the lid to the coffin. It was over, and his cane fell against the side and rested there. In time, he gently reached out and took it by the handle, walked down to the end and reached up for the marble capstone. He pressed the cane against the upper corner and gracefully laid out the lid over the coffin. He lined up the corners and backed away. Inches at a time, he stepped backward and finally completely out of the room, pulled the door closed behind him and intentionally let the candles burn to their eventual bitter end.

CHAPTER 21

THIRTEEN YEARS

"Ninuneune! Ninuneune!"

From that Easter Sunday morning on April 8, 1928, through the Christmas winter of 1941, thirteen years, Basil managed to stay alive and quite a bit more. He became known to the man in the mirror as the wolverine, and he wondered as he wandered whether any people ever talked about the old times, The Turn, The Great War, The Revolution, The Famine, and why the land was abandoned. There probably wasn't much of that kind of chatter. He doubted that there were any people left still wondering — no one left who could remember such times and events — and he was fairly certain that he and his pastor, his mentor and friend, had been entirely forgotten by the years. Basil knew there were other hermits who lived in the mountains, were very seldom seen, would disappear into the woods, and could not be found. That was the way the land had become; the people were gone except for a few, and it would take time for the scars to go away. For miles and miles and miles back towards the north, there was nothing but rubble and ruin. Everything was empty, dead and falling down, everywhere. It had become a virtual ghost land. All of the people were dead and gone, and it didn't seem to matter one way or another — the world was dying out there. On the other side of the mountaintops, all along the Volga, the traffic was active out on the river, but on his side there was none. On the Don side, there was still very little.

The wolverine traveled at night, more quiet than a lynx wildcat, with his cane in hand leading the way on the darkest of nights, making his path sure as if the sun were shining bright. He stalked destinations like a famished wolverine tracking its next meal, and he managed to continually acquire everything he ever needed including a large collection of engraved revolvers. He owned the countryside for thirty miles in any direction and fancied himself a holy warrior, an avenger and a punisher. Thirteen years now, and his enemy had paid dearly for starting the war.

He had the most remarkable cane any man had ever leaned on, and it told him everything — where to go, when to stop, fast or slow or not at all. He was continually fascinated at how he managed to live through all the situations that could have, should have and would have killed him for sure but didn't, entirely because of the cane. There were so many incidents that he had become almost oblivious to the threat of death and the fear of it. He became bulletproof in his own mind, and gradually concluded that he had to have a mission in life besides being the curator of the basement, and that meant he had to figure out a way to get the buried church bell out of Pfeiffer, into a boat, and headed for Kansas, to the new Pfeiffer in America. The costs and price were no object at all, and in all those years he'd never actually considered that task at hand, but prayed that he would be shown the way when the time was right. It was all in the hands of God. The sanity of such an aspiration, to fulfill Hammer's dream, such a scheme, the logistics of transporting the bell from one Pfeiffer to the other might be clinically diagnosed as pure insanity and the result of having been in the basement too long all alone. Hammer had told him that one of the apostles was coming for the cane and a man named Van Vedic would return if he could, and all he had to do was wait.

Those were his missions in life, his goals: to protect the contents of the basement and put that bell on a boat and float it to Kansas. The bell lay hidden dead center of the burned-down church, under the rubble pile, and absolutely nothing had been disturbed from one corner of the ruins to the other after the fire, except for where Basil had made sure the bell was invisible, there, in its grave.

The tragedy of St. Francis of Assisi Catholic Church was now an island of Russian olive trees, nasty salt cedar bushes that were impenetrable, and beautiful rose gardens in their complete wildness, exactly where they had been planted twenty years before. The only things remaining were made out of rock, the massive blocks of the ancient foundation, steps up the side to nowhere, and remnants of a rock walkway, overwhelmed with vegetation, leading to the grotto. Grapes grew wild all along the ditch banks, along with wild melons and other plants the settlers had introduced so many years before. Mother Earth was starting to take it all back. She was working hard on the remnants of the town of Pfeiffer, hard on the fields and roadways those peasant people had nourished, formed, dug and plowed. It had taken the residents a hundred years to develop the valley, and Mother Nature less than forty years to erase those monuments. She was hiding it for future generations to uncover if sanity ever returned, assuming that this current and complete utter insanity of Communism that had seemingly sprung out of hell would leave anything in its wake. Mother Nature wouldn't leave much — she never does — but the lessons learned after the excavations would need a long epitaph.

The church steps would be the only tombstones left behind. Eighty years or more in the future, generations from now, a great-great-grandson of someone who once lived in the village would take a picture of the steps, knowing what they once where and where they went. That man would come all the way back from America, back to this spot, and put a boot tip on the church step and have thoughts of ancient feet, old relatives forgotten in time and who had once done the same thing when it was flat and level on their way inside the church.

Basil remembered how Hammer had said that he saw those steps that lead up into the sacristy in his mind, in his dreams, and that the steps were tilted and not normal. He told how it was vivid in his vision, clear, and it would take an earthquake to lift those step stones and move them the way he saw them off angle, tilted and slightly buried on one end.

The Russian Red Army appeared to be all that was left of humankind, and was all around him at different times, but then there were times when there was no one for many miles, for many months, and sometimes for a year or two, back in the early thirties. He could feel the traffic through the walls of the cellar and became invisible at night when he traveled. He felt so accustomed to living in the basement that he started to forget what it had once been like over at the rectory, or anywhere for that matter, when he had lived above ground. At the age of 41, now a full third of his life had been spent underground with him becoming a very comfortable and invisible wolverine.

He never quit being a priest and adored his God every day, if not twice on Sundays, seldom ever spoke words, and became one of the world's greatest pianists, but unfortunately, the world would never hear him play. He had to apologize to Amadeus for having made a few alterations and improvements to his *Réquiem,* and try as he may, he couldn't continue to play the piece without his additions. He ended his apology with the idea that surely Mr. Mozart would understand and approve, and if not, he could file a petition in heaven or wherever he went, but from that time on it would be played Basil's way. He couldn't help but believe he was not the first to make the changes he did, as they were so obvious, almost as if the author had been too sick to hear the flaw, or maybe he didn't write it all. Whatever, the changes were necessary, etched in stone, and it was a better piece because of his changes.

After only a short period of time in his hermitage, he discovered in his grief that it helped him to play the piano, and when he did, time disappeared into being something he didn't care about. He was always aware of day and night and where he was in those cycles, but in the piano room there was no such thing as time. It was measured by the candles or by his decision that what he had just played was almost perfect, and that was pretty much the reason he had been doing it in the first place, that was what he had been playing for. He was that way with the books as well, and paid very little attention to anything else, reading them from cover to cover in only a day or two, or however long it took, and almost always found himself anticipating the end of a book, because that meant it was the beginning of piano practice.

He couldn't do that with music — hurry through a piece — and no matter how hard he tried, he never did one perfectly, wasn't dismayed by that realization, and felt he was always improving and shouldn't quit now. For months and months at a time he wouldn't do much other than play the piano, say the Mass, and was perpetually planning his next excursion out into the wilderness. His cane would stand there by the bench seat, or there near his side in the chapel, and seemed to await the man, allowing him time to figure out in his head where he wanted to go next. The cane, in fact, would always lead him on their next adventure, show and guide the way, and there were times when the man held on for dear life and seemed to be simply running himself out of danger.

After one particularly violent encounter with a monstrous Russian Cavalry colonel, as he escaped the scene, he ended up trapped inside a nearby building and took refuge in a closet for four hours. Soldiers searched for him like bloodhounds, searched for him in every nook and cranny, but never looked in the closet. During all the commotion, the priest held onto the cane with both hands and never tired; he fell into a standing hibernation of sorts, and simply stood there and listened.

The search was based entirely on the notion that someone may have seen a ghost-like 'blur' leave the colonel's quarters just before he went into insane convulsions. After searching almost everywhere for the blur, finally the search parties left, as they were unable to find anything or anyone that matched that description. It would be beneficial for everyone concerned if there could be someone to blame for the condition of their colonel, but they came up with nothing. After far too many minutes of thrashing around in his quarters, the colonel had been physically rushed and then forcibly restrained by four of his own junior officers, then tied to a gurney and hauled away to a much more capable medical facility, where he would need everything they had to offer. The only thing missing from the inventory was his sidearm, including his engraved holster and shoulder harness. The colonel wore that revolver up until bedtime, hung it there on his bedpost, but it had vanished. The same old story.

Not a single one of the colonel's rescuers had ever seen anything like it. As they arrived on the scene, the only thing those young men knew was that he was flailing around inside the headquarters office tent, shrieking and bashing himself into tables and door frames, breaking his own arms, hands and feet. They had to stop him somehow, and so they rushed him and held him down.

They detained him in place and tied him to the stretcher, tied his head down with belts, wrapped him in layers of phone cable and ropes until he looked like a mummy. He had bit his tongue severely and was drowning at times, so they tilted the stretcher onto its side, and he kept mumbling a three-syllable word they couldn't interpret. Each of the men listened hard into the bloody mouth — "ninuneune, ninuneune" over and over — until they all decided it was the babble of a dying man. Before the dust settled as the ambulance headed away, Basil's cane sent an emotional shiver up the wooden shaft and into his hands. It was over, and he could leave; by dawn he was standing at the Grotto. There would be reports that had to be made, but in the end it was, once again, the same old story, another ice pick assassination in the forbidden zone, followed by the most frightening animal howl anyone had ever heard from the forest.

It was early December 1941, a beautiful day by any early winter standard. He listened and learned through the leafless grapevine — literally, the grapevine that covered the viewport near the bottom step on the southwest corner of the rubble. Travelers along the river road had this insatiable desire to sit under a group of trees, two hundred feet out from the corner of the church, near a wide intersection in the dirt road. From that intersection, the remains of the church foundation were now overwhelmed with vegetation and it hardly got a glance from the travelers. Basil could see them and hear them and now, after thirteen years, the foundation of St Francis had all but disappeared. There was nothing there worth wasting one's time over.

He learned that the Red Army was preparing for Nazi Germany to invade through this area, and they had the oil fields in Odessa, the Crimea, and the big port cities along the rivers in their sights. No one knew for sure, but the possibility existed that the Germans had stopped for the winter. But that rumor in the fertile Volga basin area had no validity; winter hadn't arrived. Some of the rumors suggested that the lunatic in Berlin had a wild hair up his ass to change the name of Stalingrad to Hitlerburg. Nothing could have been more absurd, and anyone who knew anything about the region and all the things that mattered knew that the oil was waiting in Odessa and should have been the primary objective. It was obviously a vicious rumor and part of the propaganda. They must have thought their soldiers to be complete idiots if they wanted them to believe that changing the name of a city was that important, which did not negate the utter terror Basil could hear in their voices. The Germans were only a few hundred miles west of the Don River and already on the shores of the Black Sea.

No matter what, everyone seemed to know the bastards were on their way, one route or another, for a wide variety of reasons. For the most part, the Russian Army was doing most of the defensive preparations down farther on the rivers and closer to the big cities, but there were so many soldiers out on the roads all the time that it was best he stay underground. Actually and in fact it was hunting season, and the hunting was good. The signs still warned any intruder that the commanding general, a man now dead almost twenty years, would have them shot if they even camped on the corner. The site was a historical landmark, now a pile of rubble, overwhelmed with thorny trees and bushes and protected by the state. Just a little reminder to anyone passing by that it was against the law to have a church, and society was now much better off without the hoodoo of religion. It would take a bit of imagination to visualize the church that once stood there, and the only eyes that did could not forget.

Basil kept the signs up nice and straight and spread them out a little more conveniently. He had also managed to disguise the water well on the end of the corner so that it appeared it didn't work. It fell into the category of 'a near occasion of sin' sort of affair. If the well worked, he surmised, the visitors might be inclined to stay, camp, hang around, and he felt they needed some encouragement to move on down the road and not be tempted. A wooden sign directed the thirsty to another well almost a mile away on the other end of the town, down near the abandoned barnyards, and he made sure that well always functioned properly. He made sure that it worked and always had a good rope for the bucket. He tried to make it theft proof, and in the end he used a steel wire cable that couldn't be cut.

Usually, the traffic stayed on the other side of the river as the army had built a much better road over there that did the same thing the road on the Pfeiffer side did. That road led to the Easter Peak Pass that no one wanted to do in the winter, and the old bridge ten miles farther up the valley was mainly used to get over the Ilava and onto that road. The only thing gained from having the road on the Pfeiffer side in the first place was that it made things much more difficult. That was precisely why those early settlers built it where they did. Those initial pioneers had never intended that tanks and huge bodies of cavalry and infantry would ever use their road. Nevertheless, ever more frequently, there were convoys and large bodies of infantry and the like headed south, but they never stayed long. The soldiers came and went in both directions and it appeared that the streams of refugees on the other side of the Ilava were always headed east, over and through the mountains, to where the Volga flowed south. From there they headed north. It was only twenty miles away up over the mountaintops, and down to the shores of Mother Russia's primary river. Fifty miles down that river was one of the greatest cities in all of Russia, a most strategic port and trophy, Stalingrad, named after the legendary general.

Basil had seen the Volga many times from some of his favorite vantage points high on the edges of Easter Peak, and even though it was only a dozen miles away down in the valley, he seldom ventured that far. Scattered throughout his side of the mountains, he had a number of listening posts he favored along the dirt country roads, and would sometimes travel for miles just to watch and listen at intersections. He was able to hurriedly get in front of refugees and then walk back into them as if he were a lone traveler limping along on his cane, simply someone going the other way, and he could talk to them for a while and learn much. Sometimes he would time it so as to have a meal and a smoke before he went his way, and they went theirs. They were always obvious for who and what they were, and the only thing he had to offer was where the water was up ahead, and so might be God if they cared to know — very gently; it was against the law, after all. It was seldom a difficult sale, and he became very good at it. All through the thirties, he perfected this ploy to the point that he managed to piece together a world out beyond the valley, and it appeared to be horrible and still as confused as it was before they'd burned his church to its foundation.

He listened to them talk about their situations, who they had lost and why, who was to blame, where they had come from and where they were going. It was one of the saddest and never ending stories of all times, and no one seemed to remember any good times; too long ago. There never was any real hope, and if there had ever been actual good times before these times, most people doubted that there ever would be again. The children, the young ones, had never known anything but the life of a refugee. Most of those people couldn't remember back that far, so he composed a symphony for refugees that he humbly confessed to himself was the most beautiful piece of music he knew, and gave all the credit to the cane. All during the creation of the symphony, he would set the cane between his legs in front of his bench, rest the shaft against his clavicle, and press his ear into the wood. His fingers found sounds that angels would be glad to hear.

Everyone was simply trying to stay alive, and no one knew what for. Sometimes he would sit and listen, and they would never know it. What he now knew about the world out there convinced him that he could stay in the basement forever, and there was no need to venture too far out into the mayhem. Something in the back of his mind was always reminding him that this situation couldn't possibly go on forever, but it had so far, and there was nothing in the outback country that suggested it wouldn't. People spoke of the depression, a Great Depression, and how it was everywhere, all over the world, which might or might not bring any consolation to anyone who was extremely depressed by it all. Worst of all, and once again, somehow or another the Germans were on another one of their rampages and presumably headed his way.

All during those early years, '30, '31, and '32, he learned all about being an extremely vengeful survivor and had declared war on the Russian Red Army. They had a motto, "All on one," they even sang about it, and when he found that out, he was left to make his own motto, "One on all," and made that the title of an overture. He and only he alone knew the truth as to why the army always entered the region on their highest alert. Coming or going, in the fertile Volga Basin they exercised intense security. Their highest levels of management were all positive that they still had a very aggressive enemy combatant in the area, and some believed it was a ghost, a blur. It had become known as the deadliest region in all of Russia for senior military officers, and it carried the nicknames

"Brigadiers beware" and "The colonels' last camp," but the joke in the ranks was that it could also be called "Stalin's Revenge."

The enlisted men and outer security guards would often talk about how anxious the higher-ranking officers where whenever the units were passing through this specific valley, that narrow neck of land between the Volga and the Don, perhaps just shy of a hundred miles long and fifty miles wide. Invariably, someone up the chain of command always seemed to end up disabled and in the worst imaginable physical condition a man could possibly find himself in. Someone would always find a way to terminate the residing colonel or general, always able to get through. It had been going on for a very long time, and the legends, rumors, and superstitions could never be ignored. In a secret report to the Premier, as of the last day of 1934, in a five-year period fifteen officers over the rank of colonel had been stabbed in the right ear with an ice pick and subsequently died from their own perpetual desire to break their own bodies.

It had all started with the assassination of the great General Stalin who was killed in the valley not long before Lenin died, murdered by two of his own men. From that time on, as the legend grew, there was a warrior's curse on the army, a curse on its officers, murdered by a blur that always stole their gun. Sometimes a piece of land becomes so deeply stained with the blood that is spilled there that it can never be erased, and the land becomes cursed, punctuated by that roar that always pierced the darkest night, hours after the latest victim was carried away. The Russian Red Army avoided it at all costs.

Some thought it to be an angry ghost that simply hated senior army officers and one navy admiral who had gone to his last dinner party in Litzi, just off the mighty Don River, up a neighboring tributary that paralleled the Ilava. He had arrived in a luxury yacht at an ancient mansion along that river. He only planned to stay a few days, fish and have some breakfasts, lunches, and dinners. The man was a fleet admiral after all, and he and his staff were entitled to that sort of distraction every once in a while.

On that particular outing, the admiral and two of his highest ranking captains all found themselves one morning with ice pick wounds in their right ears only. The tip of the pick ended up in a precise area of the brain that would, in fact, kill the men in due time, but at the moment of insertion and just after the twitch of the wrist, they found themselves totally incapacitated and would be so for the rest of their short lives. You could tell just by looking at them that they started praying for death almost immediately. For the first fifteen minutes after the insertion of the pick, the victim sat motionless from the shock, but that didn't last long. Their bodies erupted into these pulsating, gyrating, bouncing and flailing piles of flesh. They could no longer speak, but they all tried to communicate, tried through their gyrations and eye contact to make their caregivers understand something. It was impossible for any human being to comprehend anything the victims might have been saying, and it must have been very frustrating being a victim.

Because of the fact he had disabled so many, Basil had decided that he was on a road that few priests had ever walked. He was a disabler with a reputation, and they didn't even know his name. They had already burned him to death in 1928, and he had been radicalized on his birthday in 1929. He wasn't really sure where he was, in the whole scheme of things, but he knew he would die an avenger. It was he against the Russian Army, "One on All." He felt no regrets for anything he had done to them, committed no sin that he would need to confess. Someone had to fight back, and there wasn't anyone left except for him.

He could come out of his hole and travel for miles and miles, in absolute darkness, quickly, and could stay for days and nights out on the land. He only needed his cane, a pipe, and a bag full of split peas, dried fish, and bread. He knew where all the water was and had caches of food stashed here and there in every direction. He stored berries and nuts. The animals didn't bother them, and he usually left some for them, too. He loved the animals and never ate meat in front of them.

The birds were his friends. He fed them near the Grotto, and at times the different species had a hard time getting along in front of his feet. It undoubtedly had something to do with St. Francis, and he gave all the credit where it was deserved. There were about fifteen blue birds that seemed to turn black as they flew wherever they went, and they went wherever he went, were never a nuisance or demanded a single thing from him. He could see them far up in front of where he was headed and way over on his sides, sometimes just two or three little dashes above the horizon, sitting on branches as he walked by or soaring amongst the granite canyons all over Easter Peak. Whether he went into the mountains, out on the flatlands or deep into the outback, they were with him. Always out there, up early in the mornings and still active just after sundown.

The birds could be very noisy at times and would get his attention in a certain direction where danger was perceived, and that danger might not manifest itself at times for hours, but always did in the end. At other times, they were perfectly silent, as if taking hints from the way Basil was acting. They would sit on the ground and in far-distant trees, motionless, for as long as Basil hid, stationary, from a passing group of soldiers. They were his companions and his eyes in the sky. It took him awhile to learn who they were, and as time went on he began to understand their sounds, their warnings, their directions. He didn't need to feed them any more than he did, and they fed him, for that matter. They knew where the berries were, and the nuts, and the water. They knew everything including which way the wind was blowing, and he learned that they knew the weather much better than he and never seemed to be caught in it. They introduced him to the idea of being safe and out of the worst of it, long before it was too late.

He was now a fisherman, among many other things, and had learned how to cook fish and dry it. He ate it all the time. At times, it wasn't fair, because his birds always showed him where the fish were on any stream or creek he ever came upon. When he was first learning how, and they were too, it was exciting, and there were few things he enjoyed doing more. Once the birds associated the post activities with the fishing part, they took some of the sport out of it. They got the tails and the heads, all the bones and entrails, and any of the bottom feeders intact. It was an 'I smooth your feathers and you smooth mine' sort of relationship. When they realized that he was planning to fish, they would pack themselves along the bank and up in the closest tree to where the school was apparently fighting the current.

If Basil tied his line to the new pole he had just carved and began fishing in an area where there weren't any fish, the birds would start bouncing around on their branches and dropping out of the tree and onto the banks there, below. Before long, all fifteen would be cackling this bluebird cackle, fluttering around until a few would get so flustered they would dart across the banks of the river and fly right in front of his face. He would act like he hadn't seen them and they in turn became even more agitated. One of the older males would fly by first, and his brothers or cousins would follow. Once past his head they would arch themselves into a perfect climb, up to a hundred feet or so, and come back down without ever rolling over, right over the spot on the stream where the fish were waiting and shit in the water, cackled their noise and burst by his face again two arm lengths out. Only a blind man wouldn't be able to see their aerial maneuvers, and after only a few passes he would begrudgingly head their way. The birds would settle down on the near and distant branches as he captured the fish with little trouble until he had enough for all concerned. Bluebirds loved soft-sided stripers and speckled cold-water bandits almost as much as Basil did.

There was no one judging him except himself, and he was capable of traveling twenty miles in any direction, along any trail, beside any river or tributary, and his cane was ever aware. Sometimes his cane would walk him into a group of refugees, and he would cripple along with all of the rest of them and blend in as if he were at a reunion. Many times the refugees would be allowed to pass through the military encampments and quietly shuffle through the midst of thousands of soldiers until they got to the other side of where the danger was, out of the way, and it was times like that where he actually felt invisible and understood they simply couldn't see him. He was so totally harmless in his appearance that he instantly bored the average guard or sentry and they never paid him any mind, and then he might turn here or turn there, stop here or go over there, and eventually he was where he belonged.

His favorite point of attack was stepping out of a shadow from the backside. There was no defense in all cases, and all the disabled knew for sure was that someone had rammed a four-inch ice pick inside their unsuspecting and undefended right ear. Two quick flicks of his pick, find the gun and he would be gone.

Usually, when they found these colonels, they couldn't quite figure out what was wrong with them. They were very much alive, and there was usually a large amount of blood all over everything from the self-inflicted broken bones and gashes. In each and every case the colonel was now in need of a replacement and would never be back. He would flap around for the rest of his life unless they kept him tightly strapped down. That usually didn't last all that long, but just like with the flapping, all of their terrified wide-open eyes seemed to indicate they were completely aware of pain and what had happened to them. They all gurgled the same sounds, made the same facial gestures, and flailed their arms and legs into themselves and everything around themselves until they were broken a dozen times over. The military was quite capable of recording the death of each and every high-ranking officer that had ever served — how, where and when, and all the rest — and during the purges the ice pick had evidently been very popular with the assassination squads. It became an art form as the term assassination became better defined and the ideas of pain and suffering entered into the formula. In almost all the records concerning those horrible terminations, it became apparent that the injury caused every single victim to utter the same word over and over.

"NINUNEUNE,   NINUNEUNE,   NINUNEUNE, NINUNEUNE," which meant nothing to anyone who was ever there, checking the straps and broken bones in each victim's final days and hours, but in virtually every final report, on every colonel and general and the naval folks, there was mention and talk about the 'ninuneune chants.' At least fifteen times it had been recorded that the rescuers also heard a terrifying wolf scream — something was out there watching them — always howled some hours later for everyone to hear, and no one who heard it went to sleep.

Their autopsies always concluded that they had been stabbed in the ear and then a few very important parts of the inside of their brains were mulched and stirred a bit and sliced here and there by the edge of the ice pick. It didn't bleed much, and there was hardly a trace to the untrained eye, but in truth the pick was exactly the length it needed to be to do certain kinds of damage deep inside the brain. It was the same in all the autopsies, and the Soviet Army brass knew it had nothing to do with Moscow or internal terminations; this was an outsider. The ice picks the KGB used were twice as long as the one used in the fertile Volga Basin terminations.

As the years had worn on, Basil's clothes became rather ragged and worn, and even though he had a magnificent closet full of nice things, he was personally very comfortable looking like he needed much. Very few people ever saw his face, and if they did it was because he thought it would be okay — and his cane never lied, never once. Much of what he found and used to stay alive and camouflaged ended up making him look like a ragamuffin instead of the respected Catholic priest he had once been. He was handsomely bearded, strong, and in the prime of his life.

Basil started to remember the past. As he gently ran his beard through both hands, he flashed back to those long days and nights when he melted down the gold and poured it inside the bell hammer. The fire was so hot at times that he thought for sure someone had to see it, but they never did. He had been singed many times during those three months, and a beard would have cost him his face; it was such a hard thing to keep in line. All through the winter of 1933, in the dead of that winter, he worked every night on his project. He had decided that the clangor inside the bell would hold at least a hundred pounds of gold, and he had a hundred pounds of gold candle holders . Were it not for those fires, early in the mornings, Father Basil might have frozen to death. He became a goldsmith and melted the gold and arranged the gems inside the hollow 'hammer.' He wondered how some of those huge diamonds would handle the heat from molten gold and concluded they wouldn't mind a carrot. He never doubted the strength of a diamond, but he didn't know about all the other stones, most of which he was sure were precious.

He ended up nicknaming it "Hammer's Hammer." It was what they called a "double whammy" — an upside down cross, the tips of the arms hitting the inside of the bell — and because it was hollowed, the notes had an echo that softened the main impacts. A beautiful sound that would never bless the airways again. During that winter, after four very difficult years up to that point, he had decided the only thing that might make it out of this magnificent treasure trove would be the hammer for the bell; there was very little chance for the bell itself.

Basil was remembering Father Hammer, the quiet and thoughtful man. The man who only had one pair of glasses and guarded them with the utmost care until the day he died. He remembered how he saw the old man protect his glasses many times, and he would hide them, knowing full well the possibility existed that he would never be able to retrieve them.

Glasses often times failed during intensive interrogations, a fate he'd never experienced but had always thought was a distinct possibility. The priests were simply disappearing after the revolution began; one day they were there, where they should have been, and the next they were gone, never to be heard from again. The usual explanation for why such and such a priest had left so abruptly was that all of the clergy had to undergo an intense state-run re-education program. Without the priests, the state had no option other than to close the church, and that meant everyone — the Lutherans, the Mennonites, everyone.

There were stories of the laity, the knights, the nuns, the altar boys, the choir, and the old women, all trying to stop the Soviet Police at the steps of their churches. Everyone did it to one degree or another. It didn't matter the religion. There was this perpetual mob mentality by the police and the military towards the religious of all the faiths. It was against the law to be religious, to pray, to believe in God, against state policy, with the punishment being extremely severe. The Soviet State was atheist, and that was the plan. All those people, standing on their church steps, there by the dozens, trying to save their priest, their minister, their rabbi, their mullah — in many cases, that was where they all died.

The point was delivered to an unsuspecting audience with such ferocity and lawlessness that the society would not forget the incidents for decades. It was written that way somewhere, spoken by a tyrant, and the state didn't try to hide it in any way; rather, it left dozens of witnesses who would tell the stories of what they saw. It was very hard to be religious when Lenin was alive, but things got progressively worse when others took over the whole mess. Amazingly so. Destroying the Holy Russian Orthodox Religion seemed to be the highest goal for the Marxist-Leninists, and once they had murdered the entire lineage of the Romanoff Empire, they set their sights on everyone else who seemed to believe in the existence of an almighty being.

The German Volga Catholics had completely and totally worn out their welcome in Russia, a fact that was true everywhere in the Mother Land and had been true for quite some time. They arrogantly refused to speak the Russian language and held on tight to their German roots, their German Catholic religion, their German language and their German customs and holidays. Right in the middle of the heartland of Russia, somehow or another, an enormous colony of Germans had managed to take root and call the place their home. For the most part, they missed the subtle and not so subtle warnings of, 'When in Russia, do as the Russians do or else,' and every time true Russians tried to recover from some devastating apocalypse, in the end and with good reason, they always blamed the Germans.

The St. Francis of Assisi Roman Catholic Church on the banks of the Ilava River, fifty miles north of Stalingrad, ended up being the only church left in all the basin for an obvious reason, and had even been protected by a State Decree until they decided to burn it down.

Basil remembered how he was intently engaged with some refugees one day, just down the road from Pfeiffer, who were actually headed that way, and they told the oncoming traveler about the town he had just passed through, just in case he didn't know. They told him about the legend of the St. Francis of Assisi Church, and all they were planning to do was walk by it from a distance, and be able to tell their children that they had. They told him of a legend about two priests who had boarded themselves inside the place, refusing to leave while it burned, and had become martyrs.

The wolverine's eyes did it every time, every time he thought about how beautiful it had been, and what a wonderful old man Hammer had been. Every time they welled up, and a few big salty blues would trickle to the middle of his cheek. They itched too much and couldn't get any farther, and no one ever saw the tears, but it never failed. Those two years so long ago, when they were just two priests, just gardening and fishing janitors, services at three in the morning... and he remembered how they burned that beautiful church to the ground and tried to kill him.

CHAPTER 22

SOKOLOV, MY FRIEND

Dinner Is Served

Basil was standing in a right-angle corner of a miserable little mud-hut relic, most of which had fallen down throughout the years, step-by-step, block by block, timber by timber, leaving two mud tile walls and the small end room where he was hiding. He was virtually invisible, watching the elegant pedestrian meander up the main street, oblivious to almost everything. It was so hard to believe that this particular man would walk right by this particular shed, so close, of all the sheds and rubble piles on either side of the road, to be so close and yet so far, but that was precisely what he was doing. It was as if he had been guided, directed, you might think, to parade himself in this fashion, and only he knew what he was thinking, which was something he seldom explained to anyone — didn't have to; he was a general.

Basil had watched the man as he came up from an encampment that was on the far end of town, the far side of what used to be Pfeiffer, down where the original settlers would have called 'the barnyards.' The water well in that area of town had always been active and was dependable, and some of the passersby would marvel that the well itself was always so well maintained considering it was out in the middle of nowhere, and no one even lived on this side of the river these days; a little, abandoned village not unlike all the others, a square-mile relic from the ancient times, and yet the well still worked.

The pedestrian who was walking alone carried himself the way senior military officers always do, a swagger towards oblivious, a huffiness that is never or at last rarely present in the lower ranks, primarily because they usually don't have time for it and never practice such things.

It was late in the afternoon and Basil had spent the entire day listening and observing, figuring out who they were and how long they planned to stay. By mid-evening, he would retreat to the basement with all of his newly acquired information. He had worked his way through all the rubble of the little town just like a wolverine would, was angered by the fact there were so many soldiers and the fact they were so close to the entrance to his borough. He knew this area better than any other and could move and hide like a shadow.

In the early morning hours, he'd worked his way down from the north side of Pfeiffer until he was only a half a mile from the edge of their encampment. It was close enough, but not too close, and there was a zigzag route of escape that he could manage quickly. These soldiers were only passing through, resting and regrouping for a few days along the beautiful river, and looked forward to a forced equipment march, double time, headed south; no one knew why.

The shed he was in not only provided shelter to some degree, it actually discouraged most people from coming near or into it because it looked more like an accident waiting to collapse on itself and would not even make a good toilet. It was just one of many, but not even close to first on the list.

Originally, as the man was leaving the secure area, he told the guards where he was going and how long he intended to take. Basil heard every word he said. The general also instructed his privates not to be concerned for his safety. They were, after all, out on the edge of nowhere, so what possible danger could there be? He wanted to go for a walk, think and reminisce, and maybe take a few pictures of what was left of an old church, just down at the end of the main street, one of the last of the old Catholic Churches, a place he had watched burn down in twenty-eight. He told the guards he was only a colonel back then, and it would be interesting to see what seven years had done to the site. His revolver lay holstered over his left kidney.

They could see what seven years had done to him as the two red stars on each side lit up his lapels. He boldly assured the guards on both sides of the road that he was not in any danger; he was armed, and if they could find him some ass wipe paper he would be most grateful.

"General Sokolov, sir, by your own orders we are obliged to keep a guard on you."

"That you may do from this location. I will only be a few hundred yards up this road and need some quiet time to myself in this old worn-down village. I've been here before, and I know the place. When I'm through up there, I will immediately come back down here, through this checkpoint. No need to worry about me."

With that, he tapped on the butt of his gun, turned and walked up the road leaving the guards at a form of attention until they all relaxed and hardly gave him another thought for the time being.

Almost all of the wooden buildings were in shambles and mixed into the wild vegetation as if there was this burning desire by Mother Nature to engulf everything in these clusters of impenetrable olive bushes and other nasty and thorny entanglements, some of which included berries. Up and down the age-old streets were all the mud walls that had managed to stand the test of time to some degree, and the round rock handmade fireplaces were still standing in many cases. She would probably get it all back in time, and no one would ever know that Pfeiffer had once existed.

The general was quietly picking his way along the roadway, avoiding things in his way that might damage the shine on his boots, and he didn't appear to have any regrets or even the slightest worry in the world. He was just an old soldier, perpetually working on his own epitaph and memorial.

Off to the commander's left, sometimes slightly ahead, sometimes behind, one time as close as ten feet and at others almost a hundred, the wolverine was moving from one cluster to another, floating, stalking, literally panting and breathless, almost invisible. He was in a state of killing euphoria the likes of which he had never felt before. It was instantaneous; the cane was hot to the touch. It had everything to do with the rank, everything to do with the score, but especially to do with his memories. When he'd heard that name, Sokolov, and realized down deep in his guts what he had just discovered, he gripped the cane so tight with both hands that his feet came up off the ground. It was as if he was climbing a pole that was deeply embedded in the ground, to see over the cluster he was standing behind.

His heart was pounding with excitement, and from each new vantage point he watched the old lizard continue his walk. The guards were aware of the fact that the general was that figurine far up the street and appeared to be doing precisely what he told them he was going to do.

The wolverine was so familiar with the entire area, he felt as though he was watching himself from every angle, calculating and anticipating through many sets of his own eyes. He was very aware of what the guards could see or not see, what the general was probably seeing, and he was most of all trying to decide what the consequences to all this would be. His eyes were huge round balls compared to normal, and he shivered in anticipation as he watched the arrogant bastard high step around the vague remnants of St. Francis and take a few pictures of different angles he found himself in.

Basil held onto the cane most of the time with both hands as he stared at the cameraman from only fifty yards away, virtually obscured. He knew this euphoric feeling from the past, this power he controlled, the justice he would harvest, all being sensational, sexual, instantaneous. This time, he would relish the moment, take it personally, maybe even taste it, and watch the man for a time. He decided without any hesitation that the general needed to see his face, be sure who he was looking at, understand what he was seeing, and be reminded about the confessional and about Hammer; it would be a very difficult last thing for the general to do. Basil wanted to quote the general all the parts of 'The Act of Contrition' he forgot to say on his way out that afternoon, and he needed to be sure he whispered those words into the general's only good ear, and as fate would have it, he had Hammer's hankie in his pocket.

As the general was taking his pictures and thinking back to that fateful Easter memory, he reminisced on the filming of that

Mass, how all of those men ended up blind and deaf, and never, in fact, seeing that Diamond Teardrop on the big screen in the final product; unless, of course, blinding white light was it. He remembered when it came to light what the priests had said during their readings, the knowledge that there was no rabid pig and how disappointed the film crew was after they discovered that there was hardly any profit at all in their rampage of the church. They had been had, made to look like fools by the old priest and his assistant before they were burned alive. They'd hauled away truckloads of booty that didn't bring them all that much. The enlisted, blind and deaf, were told by Sokolov's assistants that there was no treasure in the magnificent structure after all, and almost all of the usual valuable items were mere lookalikes, substitutes, cheap and worthless.

Moscow was thrilled with the outcome when they had finished editing the production, made many propaganda films over the years and frequently had images of St. Francis — before, during and after — as proof of their cause. Pure Soviet propaganda, and the world never heard the readings. Sokolov himself was somewhat surprised and overwhelmed by the end product that had eventually established him as the Russian Mozart of war films. Usually, that memory caused him to smile inside himself because it was the cause of his promotion to one-star general, but not this time.

Suddenly, from out of nowhere, a goblin of dread engulfed his body, and he shivered for no reason, head to toe. He was standing on the uphill backside of the rubble, between that rock monolith and the prominent remaining edge of the foundation for the church, when he felt as if a blanket of cold blood had been poured all over his shoulders, and had to actually look to see if any of it was there. He exhaled until all of his breath had been pushed out of him, but the air wouldn't come back.

As he stared above the green islands of olive trees, he could feel the eyes of all his dead enemies looking down on him through that smoke he could still see in his memory rising above the inferno that evening. Remembering those moments when the church fell inside itself and on top of the confessionals, and the spectators cheered. He had often thought about those two confessors, thought he might have heard something screeching from inside the flaming mayhem, and frequently wondered what it must have been like.

Maybe he was standing too close to the rubble; maybe it was now a haunted ground. As everyone knew, there were such places almost everywhere. No need to be so close, no purpose in stirring up the dead and milking the past. He had done enough reminiscing at close range, so he moved down to the front steps of the church. Looking uphill he could now easily see that rock monolith, far back up the hillside, the one those priests had told him reminded them of their saint. It was nothing more than a piece of jagged rock sticking up out of the ground around it, nothing more.

For Basil, it would be hours before he returned back to normal, after the encounter, even though it had only taken a few seconds to turn into the wolverine, that beast that hid inside his belly. The wolverine did not play the piano. Going from one being into another in literally the blink of an eye, from a peaceful hermit into the most dangerous man in the world, hunting prey that was supposedly safe and nestled away from the edge, protected and heavily guarded, not that it did any good in the end. Eventually, he would pull out the bench, and it always intrigued him afterward how far away he could get with his Russian version of the famous campfire story, The Lapdog and the Werewolf.

One moment he had been observing some soldiers on the outskirts of his immediate home territory because their encampment was way too close, the next, out of nowhere, his own personal monster of all monsters suddenly appeared. That appearance would cost the demon his life. He now only had a matter of hours left to live.

Pocomaxa was now in a trance, on the hunt, and as patient and cunning as any that roamed the night; there were none better, bigger, stronger or more deadly. Later in the evening, as the entire camp faded into sleep and let its guard down, it would be easy for such a guided predator as he to enter the general's compound and then his quarters.

It would be later, much later, when Basil would eventually unwind and return to the reality of who and where he was. In this particular case, it wouldn't take him long to get to his victim and then back home. He imagined how aggressively they might search for the assailant. The army would know by sunrise that it had happened again. Was it a given that they would eventually find the Grotto, fumble around the edges of the old church and discover something, simply because Pocomaxa had found a victim too close to home out on the edge of nowhere? Like everywhere else, they would probably do some sort of investigation, but the army needed to be down the road no matter what, and the movement was to begin in the morning.

Sokolov had dust on his boots, which didn't bother him all that much as his day was almost over and he could look forward to an exceptional dinner the spoons had promised him before he went on his walk; that would be well worth the wait. They seldom promised such things, and when they did, usually the entire officer corps ate well and the food worked its way down into the ranks. His share was probably a healthy portion of a round rump roast from a recently captured wild milk cow. They would milk it dry and then slaughter the beast for the meat they needed the most. After dinner, he would be treated to a hot bath, and his tent and cot were waiting.

What he thought would be nothing more than a few moments of recollection of the past, where he had filmed that last day of the church and that supposed Diamond Teardrop, recalling the fire he had ordered and that last confession he confessed, had all turned out to be hardly worth the time. However, he was able to relive in fleeting memories that altar, the commotion caused by the pig lie, the late Secretary Desch, those two priests, and how high the flames had risen over the bell tower before it tumbled into the conflagration. It had been one of the last of many fires, and not much different from all those that had come before. The only thing that had made it unique was the fact that it had been filmed, and so close to the end of all the church fires. After all the editing and piecing together of film clips, the documentary had immortalized him in the annals of war films and led to assignments that furthered his career even more. He credited his promotion to general as a direct result of the acclaim he was awarded for that film. In Moscow, they showed it to everyone, free, at many of the new movie theaters, as his name and face had become very well known.

Done with his mental recant, he briskly walked across the driveway that he remembered encircled the front of the wreckage and back down to the main street of Pfeiffer. Finally, all those recollections were behind him. It was barely a path, a remnant, much less a right of way as it once was. He could see the guards a few hundred yards down the road and in front of him. He felt as if there was something in the air that was pushing him down, slowing him down, preventing him from stepping faster. He felt as though eyes were still staring at him, and he could see teeth, plus he could smell something indescribable, his own breath blowing back in his face, but not like any breath he had breathed out before.

The wolverine was very close, only meters away, and it, too, could smell that smell and feel that dread and cold. Very close. The general was now overly excited, and his age was starting to catch up to him as he shouted out to the far distant guards and waved his hand for their attention. They were still too far away to hear him. The sentries didn't hear the panicked shrill cry at the end of his call. He kept shouting out at them and putting one foot in front of the other, losing his balance and starting to faint, squealing out at the guards and flailing with both arms for them to see him.

He had suddenly turned into a panic. He lost his hat and managed to yelp out a, "HELP ME, HELP ME!" that was loud enough from the remaining hundred yards to get their attention. All six burst from their positions and raced to his assistance. As they encircled him and steadied his stance, each began to ask about his condition and what was happening, all of which were exactly the same since there was nothing obviously wrong with the man.

The general was somewhat pale and sweating, breathing hard and not one bit steady, completely without his pomp. He accepted their helping arms and they managed him all the way back to the first sergeant's tent deep inside the encampment. In no time at all, they decided he was simply dehydrated, and all of the rest of the evening's festivities were still on as the man regained his composure and healthy attitude. All he had needed was water, and he was once again promised a dinner he richly deserved. He was evidentially stressed out, worn down and needing the food, the bath, and a good night's rest. Two out of three wasn't bad.

A bugle not too far away sounded the end of the day; all the on-guard shifts were to be where they belonged, which would in fact not be very on-guard at all. The entire infantry encampment spread south along the river, away from the water well, with all of the cavalry and heavy vehicle units almost a mile that way. They were resting and had been scheduled to be subdued in nature and relaxed from strict attention to formality. Rest and relaxation for three days, and then they had to move — and that would be the next day.

There were, as of late and in reality, no enemies to speak of in the entire valley; most of them were dead, but not all, or so the legends had it. For the average soldier, the only consolation to the fact that they hadn't been paid in months was the promise that they would be, and usually they ended up with something, which was always better than nothing. Most people on the bottom side of things as far as the eye could see and the ear could hear existed on nothing.

Nothing, as a rule, now some fifteen years into the revolution, nothing threatened the Russian Army in nineteen hundred and thirty-five. It had evolved into the strongest and most effective arm of the United Soviet Socialist Republic and state of horror. It was huge and stupid, simple and deadly. The army enforced the rules and left the entire population so subservient that to describe the times as very bleak would be painting rainbows. There seemed to be no end to the misery, and now that there was no one to pray to, after everyone had quit hoping, the only thing left was the greatest depression possible. Everyone felt as if they alone were right in the middle of it all. Everyone suffered, everyone blamed someone else, and someone had to pay every time — that included dozens of millions of families.

By nine p.m. on that fateful day, which may or may not have been exact, Pocomaxa was three leather flap straps from the head of the general's sleeping cot, still unoccupied and waiting. His handsome dress uniform was perfectly aligned on the uniform stand and would be waiting for him in the morning, something he never worried about. High calf leather black boots, shined and polished, waited for his feet, fresh socks and clean underwear, every day, just because he was a general, and that was the way it was for generals, deep depression, great depression or not.

Generals' quarters have always been some notches above everyone else's in the history of armies camping out under the stars, dating back to the first time a group of Neanderthals went scavenging away from the home cave. There is a time-honored way to treat the generals, and the arrangement of the additional tents to his quarters is a specialty all unto itself. The assembly of six or sometimes eight extra tents created a reception entrance, then an office area, while another tent the same size created a seating, waiting and conference room, and on the far end of the assembly was the sleeping and private area.

In the case of General Sokolov's tent, it was simply a question of flap sections and support straps not tripping everyone. In between it all there were notches and overlaps of canvas and corners that got bundled and tied and then ignored — hiding places if you will. There would be no conferences in the conference tent before ten in the morning, and his sleeping tent would be occupied until at least eight a.m.

As for the present moment in time, the general was washing his head and complimenting the steward on the temperature of the water coming out of his shower, onto his head, and into the tub, as the whole affair didn't happen every day and wasn't always that successful. Everything was just about perfect, for a change, and that included the round rump roast and potatoes that were fermenting in his belly while he felt a belch bulging up inside his gut. He burped and jerked back from the atrocious invisible mist that floated there in the tub in front of his face. He felt so full, so clean, wet, and warm, and yet that smell told him something was awfully wrong inside his body. He didn't want to call it what he thought were the right words to describe it — he wouldn't let those words out of his mouth for fear they might smell like what he had just belched — and he didn't want to think it, but the knowledge was right there on the tip of his tongue. He concluded in an instant that he was dying and didn't know why, that it would happen soon, and instantly demoted himself to private and almost dead. Then he concluded he had no clue at all what he was breathing in or out or why. He was confused, clean, warm, wet and needed a towel.

The point of the ice pick went straight into the right ear hole half way through the brain, and when the wood stock blocked out the air to the eardrum, the hand twitched and wiggled half a dozen times. It was instantaneous, and the general froze in his fetal position, pressing his left shoulder against the tub wall while squeezing his legs and squirting the tub full of shit and piss. He bit the tip of his tongue off and watched through horrified eyes as blood gushed out of his mouth and all over his kneecaps. His eyes bulged out of their sockets as his arms trembled in their death clutch around his bent-up legs.

A hand pushed his entire locked and trembling body off the left shoulder and onto the right side, and he could feel the hot breath of something into his left ear and getting his attention. That would be hard to do, everything considered, but the voice asked if the face brought back any memories? The wolverine reached in, caneless for a moment, turned off the shower and took a firm hard grip all over the general's jaw and cheeks, with a few sharp shakes for emphasis.

"Remember me? I'm Basil, Father Basil, and I brought you this hankie, the same one you gave to my pastor. Remember Hammer, Karl Hammer, Father Karl Hammer? Sure you do. I can tell by your eyes, you remember me. I know you're surprised, and you just can't seem to get a good warm and fuzzy feeling about all this now, can you? Isn't it nice to rekindle old acquaintances? I know you remember me. You must have forgotten the rest of the prayer, the Act of Contrition, on your way out of our church that Easter Sunday evening. You remember, don't you? I remember it all. You remember the contrition, the prayer you were screaming through the doors at our God and us? Remember screaming the first few lines into our confessional? You don't have to tell me yes, I can see it in your eyes that you remember. You took pictures of it today, you remembered it all, and I watched you on the walkway, out around my church and back. I was only a few feet behind you out there today. Did you feel me? I came close to sticking this pick in your brain while you were out there, but then I could see you sitting in this tub and decided you could start off this evening's activities under water now and then; it's going to be very difficult for you. You'll get wildly frantic here in a short time, and it's not going to be fun, and all the while I want you to keep remembering everything you've done for the party. You were just following orders, I know.

It was at that moment where Pocomaxa remembered having seen the tub full of blood so long ago.

"I wonder if they will ever be able to conclude after their investigation that this hole in your right ear had anything to do with that walk today. I'll bet they end up writing you off, just like all the others. What do you want to bet? In case you were wondering, in case you were hoping that your favorite colonel, lover, and steward might be coming to your aid here really soon, I don't regret telling you that he also has a serious ear problem. For the time being, just like you for that matter, he's resting over there by the water heater. Paralyzed, exactly like you feel, but he can hear everything I'm saying in his good ear. It looks to me like he can't even feel that water heater torch on his feet, he's so in shock. He'll get over that within the next thirty minutes, and along with you, it should get pretty loud and crazy around here for the rest of the evening. I would imagine the two of you are going to wake up the entire camp here in the next thirty minutes or so when this initial shock and awe finally wears off.

"I know you can't speak very well, missing the end of your tongue and all, and never will be able to speak again, but you can at least try to think that contrition prayer all the way through while you drown in your own blood. Start at the beginning and say it right. 'Oh my God,' you know it, think about it here and it will all come back to you. Since you know the prayer, you can consider saying it perfectly, now that you're in your death tub, and as you may very well remember, there was a small little sub-clause in our Catholic teaching that goes something to the effect that... am I boring you? I know this sort of religious hogwash bores you, but if you say the Act of Contrition perfectly in your death tub, God will forgive you for everything you've ever done, he will accept you back, forgive you, and grant you entrance into paradise. You want that, don't you? You want to be with God when this thrashing and self-destruction thing is all over. You want that, don't you? You didn't believe that bullshasheska the party flushed out about there not being a God, did you? I can assure you that God, in fact, understands, and all you have to do is say the contrition all the way through, perfectly. Perfect being the critical word.

"While you're working on that, I wanted to let you know that I've been living in the basement of that church you so ferociously burned down seven years ago this past Easter Sunday. I had no idea what had become of you. I missed you; we never got to say goodbye. Hammer and I escaped into the basement through a secret escape hatch in the confessionals, believe it or not, thanks to you for putting us there. I'd say there's a billion rubles' worth of gold and diamonds and all sorts of other treasure methodically collected from all over the ancient region and stored down there. Remember that hole you dug in the center walkway? Remember? Ten more feet and you'd have found it all, maybe twelve. It's without a doubt one of the greatest treasures ever accumulated in a basement anywhere in the world, and it could have been yours; only ten more feet. I'll bet you never thought about something like that. Would you believe the lost ancient treasure from the Kysar of Prussia to Catherine the Great is down there? Believe it!

"It's time for me to go, but before I do, I want to let you know what's going to happen to you. The same thing that happened to all those other Russian pigs you know about. I'm sure you know, those many colonels and generals that have disappeared from the ranks in a cloud of horror. You've read the reports, and you know what they ended up doing to themselves. In your particular case, naked in this tub, if you haven't drowned by the time help gets inside this tent, I promise you that both your arms will be broken when they pull you from the water. They'll eventually get you tied down, but your hands and feet will be broken and bloody and you will not like the bondage at all. From some earlier experiences, I've noticed, when there are two or more with the ear problem, the help seems to get overwhelmed rather quickly, and you'll be able to hear all that through your good ear. You'll hear their confusion and panic that in fact they really won't know what to do for you and him, except tie you both up and watch. You'll be fairly well aware of the pain and the confusion, soon now, but, of course, you'll never be able to tell anyone with any degree of accuracy or clarity. No telling how long it goes on, as I've never been there at the end. Last of all, I would like to end our visit with my sincere gratitude to you for taking that walk today. I never thought I'd ever see you again, and I'll bet you are just as surprised as me at our fortuitous reunion. Now I want you to work on the contrition thing until you think you've said it perfectly. Perhaps we'll meet someday again, and you can surprise me. Thanks for the revolver and have a nice bumpy ride in the lead ambulance."

CHAPTER 23

VINCENT VAN VEDIC FINDS PFEIFFER

Christmas 1941

Basil was standing on the north side of the Grotto, and his cane was watching out over the valley, showing him that there was a man on horseback headed his way. Out on the muddy snow-covered flatland a full mile away, the small dark figurine of horse and rider was working its way to Pfeiffer. Not many visitors ever came from that direction, as in none in forever. Moscow was five hundred miles away just shy of due north, and there was very little in between.

He cautiously disappeared behind the granite, except for his eyes and his cane, as he watched the figure until the horse and the man were only half a mile away down the hill, where they finally stopped. Basil was prepared to vanish into the Grotto and head down into the basement, but he continued to watch from his vantage point knowing that only the top four inches of his body were visible, or so he thought, feeling vibrations in the cane he had never felt.

To his absolute complete astonishment, he watched as the man on the horse raised his arm and waved directly at him. There was no doubt in the priest's mind that the horseman had seen him, had waved at him, and had not moved since while apparently waiting for a wave back. His cane suggested to him that he should stand up and fearlessly do just that. The cane would never have let this happen if it weren't safe, and so he did.

The winter-worn mountain of a man rode up the hill to the Grotto. Basil couldn't remember having ever seen anyone even walk up from that side before. He was coming out of the Badlands, wasn't using the roads, and his horse was as big a beast as Basil had ever seen a man saddle, eighteen hands tall. Its hooves were feathered in thick hair, and so was its face. His snout was a full hand span wide, and he carried two saddlebags, two large saddle packs, and a bedroll.

The horseman rode up through a group of trees and onto the sidewalk. The steel shoes thudded the silence with every step.

Basil had stepped out in front of the giant statue and was looking at his new guest, who had dismounted and then took a knee and made the sign of the cross. He stood back up and towered over the gentle mid-sized man, reached out his hand and said, "I'm Vincent Van Vedic. This is my horse, Brutus, and I don't believe we've ever met."

Basil was astounded. He had dreamt of this moment. The man standing in front of him was much bigger than the man Hammer had talked about. As their hands met, Basil took it and wrapped his other hand all over the two, and popped it up and down a half dozen times before any words came out his mouth.

"Vincent Van Vedic! If that doesn't beat all! Praise God. My name is Edward Basil, Father Edward Basil, and I was here with Father Hammer when he died. That was a very long time ago, and he told me, he hoped for me, he prayed about this moment, that you would come back someday. Praise God."

"Father, would you by any chance know what day it is?"

"I think the Solstice was about a week ago, Christmas was a few days ago, and my birthday is just around the corner. Without being at my desk, I couldn't say for sure; I usually don't care."

"When is you birthday, Father?"

"I was born on New Year's Day, nineteen hundred, just a moment or two after midnight, and the last time I celebrated my birthday was with Father Hammer in 1928. Long time, very long time ago."

The enormous human walked over to the edge of the Grotto and peered down at the remnants of St. Francis. "Last time I was here was '23-'24 — I don't remember exactly — and I told Hammer way back then that this was what they had done to all the other churches, deep in the outback, and his was the only one left. I told him that, but I think he already knew. He was a wonderful man."

"Mr. Van Vedic, are you hungry, thirsty, in need of a good night's sleep and a warm bed? I'm sure you had a favorite spot down there, and it's all still here. Everything is waiting, and I don't know about you, but I must go to my chapel and tell my Jesus how thankful I am that you've stopped by."

"Father, I'll join you in that Thanksgiving, but I want you to know I'm not a deeply religious man. I confess nothing and honor my Lord my way, not yours, but I honor our Lord. I'm worried about the tracks in the snow, hadn't worried about that the way I should have. I probably shouldn't have made such a direct route."

Basil walked over to the corner of the Grotto and faced north, leaned on his cane in such a way that the horseman thought sure he would fall over forward, but he didn't; it just looked that way. Undoubtedly, some sort of parlor trick; Hammer had one just like it.

"Not to worry, my new friend, there's no one out there and the tracks will be gone in the rain. My trusty weather cane, nose and previous meteorological experiences have confirmed that forecast. I can't very well refer to you as 'my son' now, can I, and so I won't. I have not been a confessor in so long I may have forgotten how, and besides, they burned down the confessional, as you can see. I'm not sure I'd want to hear yours, and probably wouldn't be able to forgive you if I did. I still do the Mass every day and I'm not one bit worthy to do such a thing, but I do it anyhow. What are we going to do with Brutus?"

"Well, he's not sleeping with me; he has terrible farts. I could leave all my stuff here at the top of the walk, take off his saddle and just let him roam around. He's good at that. And when I need him, all I have to do is whistle. Brutus likes the cold, and it's really not all that cold. He'll be fine. We need to go have coffee and a smoke, and I was wondering, Father, have you drank all the vodka?"

He unstrapped the saddle and the head gear, released his horse after talking into its ear for a few moments, and pulled in a fist full of hair just under its left front leg pit. The horse reared up on its hind legs, two thousand pounds of fury, and screamed at the human demon, landed back down a few yards distant and tried to lick the spot where the hair had been pulled. It was a game they played, and as the horse was calming down, giving his master an evil eye in between licks, Van Vedic was bent over laughing, pointing at the animal and telling Basil, "Look at that fool!" He continued to chuckle under his breath as he picked up the saddle, two of the bags, and allowed Basil to get all the rest. Brutus galloped east.

They headed into the Grotto and down the walkway, past the first bend, and the daylight dimmed into nothing as they came up on the open passageway into the kitchen. The candles were already lit from earlier, and Basil even had his favorite fish and noodle soup already cooking in a pot near the fireplace. The big man set his things down and took off his hat, which may have accounted for eight to ten inches of his height and established him at well under six foot ten. He took off his coat, which brought his weight down to around three hundred and fifty, and finally unstrapped his gun belt, which might have rounded him out at three-forty. Those were impressive guns, notched on both grip ends, on both sides of the grip, showing little room left for any more notches.

"I never go anywhere without them, and I'm one of the best there is with them. Don't mean to brag, but I am. Good Father, I can't wait much longer for that vodka, and I want you to tell me everything there is to tell. I must say, I am overwhelmed that you are alive, and this place is still as it was. A few miles from here, as I was getting close, I remembered back to the old days, when my father and I would have seen the top of the church three or four miles out, the rectory, the barn... and when there was nothing there, I thought maybe I was mistaken as to where I was; but I wasn't. I could see the side of the Grotto, and there was no mistaking what it was, and before you saw me, I saw you, and then you backed down. As Brutus got me closer and closer, I prayed that whoever you were, I wouldn't have to kill you and everyone you were with. I'm very tired of all this, and I'm tired of having to kill people who think they can take other people's belongings and treasures. I just kill them, Father — not a confession, just a fact. I have a rather conservative set of rules when it comes to the bad guys."

Without really starting his confession the proper way, it appeared he had confessed to murder, and from the look in his eyes he wanted Basil to know about the killing part before they went too far. The priest had found the vodka in no time, held two glasses close together with his fingers and filled them both to the top. He sat the bottle down on the table and handed Van Vedic a glass. They toasted each other with a smile and drank those first glasses without taking a breath. Van Vedic was pounding his right thigh and hissing in the air as if he couldn't breathe. The priest held his eyes shut by pressing his right wrist hard into his face and also made a whooshing noise.

"Damned if that isn't the finest vodka I have ever tasted. The finest. I should have brought some olives. Where in the land of Mother Russia did you get it and can I have another glassful, please."

The priest walked over to a cabinet and returned with a jar full of one-inch pale green Russian olives. They were beautiful. He reached down along his pant leg and pulled the thick-handled ice pick out of his sock and rolled it out on the table. It tinkered as it rolled into the pile of pistols, and Van Vedic could see that it really wasn't an ice pick in the truest sense of the words, and it too was heavily notched all over its handle.

"As far as the vodka is concerned and where it came from, you would be the man who would have the answer to that. You brought it here some twenty or thirty years ago. As far as killing the bad ones is concerned, sometimes, that is all we have left."

"Oh My God! The Ice Pick Assassin?"

Who is Vincent Van Vedic?

Van Vedic had always been a part of the local fishing community. He and his wife Vanessa had a beautiful little home with its own pier. They lived ten miles, as the crow flies, northeast of Pfeiffer and the big bend on the Ilava, maybe twenty-five river miles and thirty hairpin switchbacks one after another. He owned his own land and used it for grazing, though some said it was wasted.

Van Vedic never did like farming. He liked hauling the fruits of their labor. His father's father had been one of the original settlers who had come from the Hamburg area of old Germany. He had always spoken German. Russian was his second language, and he knew enough of other languages in the area to be considered an accomplished trader. In his very early days, he had always found work at the shipping ports there on the Don and had traveled down into the Black Sea many times. He had brought Vanessa home to the Pfeiffer area from Istanbul, parked his fishing boat out in front of their cottage, and that was where they tried to live.

When he was twenty years old, in 1908, he earned a position on a fishing trawler, a three-hundred-foot-long fishing machine that operated out of the Kharkov ports. It was the job of a lifetime for the giant young gunslinger, and he was able to work on the boat for years when all of his brothers, cousins, and friends were working in the fields. He spent his winters in the fertile Volga Basin hauling freight.

He lived on the trawler for months at a time and was paid handsomely for his work. Once the giant multi-net trawler left the river and entered the Azov Sea, the boat fished twenty-four hours a day at times. Nets were filled, retrieved and reset with clockwork precision. It was scientific, the way the steamers prowled off the coast, as if there were precise areas, at precise times of the year — and the catch would be astounding.

The three big boats usually stayed within sight of each other but not exactly close. They each had two smaller thirty-eight footers that stretched the lines and monitored the distant sides of the sweep. The trio of boats was a team, and the competition was fierce while all three trawlers tried to be the first one full and headed back to the docks in Rostov, where the Don flowed into the Azov.

There would always be a sizable bonus for the crews of the winning trawler. The price of the fish would be higher for the first boat in, and sometimes they took the shipments to foreign ports in Turkey and Romania. He had always loved the Romanians; they seemed to be the most sensible in the whole region.

The next ten years of his life turned him into a seasoned seaman, and he managed to save enough to buy his own deep-water boat in 1918. The entire world had gone completely insane during that time, but at least he had his boat, he loved his wife, his Church, and ended up dedicating all of his time to his bishop. From that time on his time was absorbed with his freight business and he kept his boat at the dock most of the time.

Early in the spring season of 1910 the fleet was contracted to fish through the Black Sea and sell the loads in Istanbul. As soon as they were unloaded and re-iced, the ships crossed through the straights of Istanbul, the Bosporus, into the Sea of Marmara, through the Dardanelles and finally into the Aegean Sea. By the time they had traveled through the Dardanelles on their way to Athens, they were full again with a bountiful load. It was never-ending, the result of being so seasoned and efficient, and seldom making mistakes. Vincent passionately wrote down just about everything he ever learned, wrote about the most insignificant of things and did it every day.

In less than three months, they started fishing again across a bay just east of Athens and headed for Izmir, Turkey, where the people were said to be starving. The Izmir folks were every bit of starving. He had seen it before in his younger life, knew all about starvation, and the trawler had to unload their cargo under military protection. From what the crew could see from their decks, there were tens of thousands of starving people in a small port city. As big as their haul had been, it wouldn't be near enough. The load was paid for in solid gold pieces, and that was how the crew were paid.

The people on the beach were in fear for their lives, their city was burning behind them, and they were starving and dying by the hundreds. Men like Van Vedic did their jobs and unloaded a sizable catch and were witness to the horror of it all.

They were safely towed out of the harbor and promised to return with more fish, but that was a lie. The fleets set the nets just northwest of Izmir and were once again full of the catch that they sold again in Troy. They fished the Sea of Marmara and arrived back in Istanbul with another full load. The crews were rested for almost a month while the ships were cleaned and washed by the Turks. It was a much-deserved leave for all concerned; the season was almost over. They would fish the Turkish side of the Black Sea and be back in Rostov by September.

Van Vedic was a hulk of a young man. He enjoyed being physical and was always trying to overpower the nets and drag lines. His workday was hard to match, and he passionately studied in the pilothouse. This would be the trip when he learned Cajun English from the two black men who had lived in America; he loved to hear them talk and sing in English. He was a journeyman merchant marine, and many of his fellow mariners were from all over the world. They were respectfully patient and tactful with the Volga German and worked the brashness out of his voice as he wrestled with the English. They told him stories about America, showed him pictures, but neither had any intention of ever going back; it was a very hard place for a black man, and they didn't miss it at all. Van Vedic found little use for the day room on the ship, as it was foul in every regard. Often times at night he would plot and design on the control table or write in his journal while all the other men on the bridge were asleep. He practiced his English and earned the high regards of the Fleet Master and both his assistants.

Istanbul had always been a city of intrigue and danger, huge by any standard, crowded and very Arabic. They had exceptionally strict social laws, and there were few places where a traveler might feel safe and comfortable. Van Vedic was made aware of all this on his first visit a couple of months before but had heard of a restaurant not too far from the boarding house where he was staying. It was there that a young lady named Vanessa stole his heart away.

It had been the day of all days, he thought when he walked into the dinner. The boarding house had a reputation for taking tired, unshaven, unclean and exhausted seamen to a cleanliness level many would never forget.

The procedure started with a fee; he couldn't remember exactly how much, other than it was a pittance to a sailor on shore leave. He remembered paying his money and walking around the counter and down a hall. He came into an immaculate white tiled room and was invited to sit down and undress. The ladies took his dirty clothes and assured him they would be cleaned and returned. He had bought a new pair of boots, socks, and a new shirt for his night on the town and he had a new pair of hand-made khakis, all wrapped in newspaper, fresh from the market. The ladies searched for words that he might know, continually smiled, and fed him little treats on top of crackers. It was all very good.

He stood naked under a warm shower in the corner of the bathing area. Their sponges were like nothing he had ever felt before. The soap was billowing with suds, and at first the white tiles at his feet showed visible dirt and grime pouring off, but it cleared up as those grimy months at sea were washed away. There was a solid white marble bench next to a marble table which held a tray of drinks in tiny glasses that resembled Turkish headdresses. Bowls of nuts and raisins surrounded a three-foot tall, two-straw hookah. In silver bowls were different fragrances of tobacco, hashish and two blends of cannabis.

The young masseuse poured a spoonful of the hashish into the burner, and the older lady lit the pot with a flaming wick from the candle. The women smoked after him, and he smoked it again and again. She put the lid on it after the third and smiled, explaining in a universal language that three would be plenty. She was absolutely right.

There he learned what a Turkish bath was, what a Turkish shower was, and how two women could pamper a man. They had strong liquor and even had ice. The two ladies cut his hair and shaved his beard without cutting his skin. Their tools were ancient but extremely sharp. Cleaned his hands and his feet and washed his privates with vigor. They cleaned his ears, his teeth, and his tongue, and then dried him on a table with the softest linen he had ever known. After two grueling hours, they dressed him in his new clothes and he walked out, promising to return tomorrow and the next day and the next. It had been a long time, him being alone as he was. He felt so clean and fresh but hoped the perfumes would wear off before he went back to the boat at the end of the month. It was time for that dinner he had been told about.

The head waiter put Van Vedic at a table from where he could see much of the restaurant but also the street out in front. It was a busy street with a market on the corner. He was interested in all of it, but that feeling was erased when Vanessa walked up to the table. For some unfathomable reason, he jumped to his feet and dusted himself off; he wiped the corners of his mouth with his fingers and smelled his own breath (it was fine).

She was the most magnificent creature he had ever laid eyes on. "Thank you, God, for this restaurant and my waitress!" He tried to shake hands with her, as she blushed with her hands full of his water and utensils. She motioned for him to sit back down, and set her collection down on his table having experienced this reaction before. The menu was in Turkish with French subtitles, neither of which he knew very well at the time. He could hardly take his eyes off hers as he glanced back and forth from her emerald green eyes to the menu, back and forth, with his look telling her he couldn't read it. His dinner confidant had suggested that he just order number five and that he would not be disappointed. He sat back in his chair and rose out all of the fingers on his left hand.

It was their first contact of understanding, and she lit up like she instantly and completely understood everything about him. It was easy from there on out. She opened the menu and pointed at what was obviously #5 since a five is a five just about everywhere. It's the arrangement of the letters that makes it difficult, and besides, the Turkish alphabet didn't have any. Her eyes were brilliant, and her smile was irresistible. She seemed to be radiant, and he instantly realized that she had been hand-crafted by God himself, not that Van Vedic would ever criticize the quality of God's work in any way. Someone had once counseled him in regards to women, and it was quite simple. When a good Christian man sees what he thinks is a beautiful woman, he should instantly pray, "Thank you, God!"

Next, she brought wine and liquor, and two little snacks. He memorized her every move. She seemed to glide around the tables and mesmerized many of the men in the place. She brought a salad with vinegar and pepper, and tiny onions with red and green peppers that had been raised in hell. Just their touch to the skin burns and, unfortunately, he had innocently bitten one in half and swallowed it before he realized its true nature. Someone had inadvertently forgotten to warn him that the peppers were mainly used to stir rice and the like on the end of a fork. They were dangerous peppers and perhaps they thought he knew; those creatures even look dangerous. Ninety-nine percent of the citizens of Turkey know that, and that tiny fraction which doesn't are either tourists or under the age of four.

The fire engulfed his lower lip and the very roof of his mouth. He instantly couldn't breathe, couldn't move for that matter, and there was panic in his eyes. When she walked up, after seeing his frantic gestures for help, saw the tears in his eyes and his desperate need for more water, she realized she might have killed him.

She filled his glass with water, and he drank the whole thing in a dither. She refilled it, and he seemed to be blurballing his lips and tongue in the glass. It didn't cause him any emotional discomfort or embarrassment, standing in front of all those strangers, making those noises and rapidly dunking his fingers into the now half-full glass and then dabbing his lips, back and forth, really fast. He was practically running in place and up high on his toes, which put him at seven-foot-one. He did everything really fast, big and loud.

Another waiter finally brought him a rolled-up towel filled with ice. He crashed back into his chair with his legs out in front, and the towel firmly pressed against his mouth.

He felt exhausted, run over, his new haircut was a mess, and he was pretty certain he would never eat another pepper in his whole life, no matter what. Never again, not big ones or red ones or green ones, long or short ones, smooth ones, crinkled, it would never matter, with a holding stem or not. He wouldn't even stir rice with them out on the end of a fork at arm's length. What if a small piece fell off in the soup and you didn't know it? Never again, assuming he lived through this encounter. He wasn't sure he was breathing exactly right and was considering whether or not he might have welded his lips together. He could feel his lips with his fingers but couldn't feel his lips with his lips. For all he knew, his tongue had exploded, and he was drowning in his own blood and didn't know it. He imagined his tongue looking much like a severely burned thumb. Gradually, the other tables went back to their dining, and he tried to put himself back together.

The head waiter and perhaps owner walked up and began to apologize in a most heartfelt manner, and even offered to look at Van Vedic's lips to see if they were okay. He seemed to be scolding Vanessa, who was just behind him a step. He wobbled his finger up and down and then turned to glance at her as if all that gibberish had been intended for her ears especially. As he walked away, he said one last thing to her and Van Vedic heard little wisps of laughter from the nearby tables.

She ever so softly and humbly came up closer to his table and purred out her sorrow in Turkish. She held her perfect fingers to her lips, and looking into those eyes was like looking into heaven. He reached out and almost touched her hand, but she pulled back with a frightened look in her eyes. He didn't know that rule either, but motioned to her that it was over, that his face was fine, and then brought the towel quickly back up to his lips.

She nodded that it would be fine. Then she smiled and began to bring him the rest of Dinner #5. He would eat his meals there for the next three weeks and when the fleet was ready to leave, he wrote Vanessa a rambling love letter promising her he would return and take her for his wife, an elaborate effort that took a year. Her life was so miserable that she agreed to wait, secretively, and when he saw it in her eyes, those unbelievable eyes, he promised her on a bended knee, something she had never seen a man do, that he would be back. His mission in life by the age of twenty-two was to return to Istanbul, find, rescue, and marry Vanessa and take her home. She would be his everything for as long as she lived, and he carried her over the threshold into the house his father had built, transporting her into a brand new world where they planned to live happily ever after.

CHAPTER 24

THE VANESSA

Winter 1941, the Grotto

Much later that afternoon, Van Vedic and Basil sat there together on the south side of the rubble pile, exactly where Hammer and Basil had spent that afternoon so many years before, waiting for the Russian pigs to be done with them. That was then, thirteen years before, and Van Vedic had missed it all, but Basil's story was exact to the inch, and together they relived that fateful day. The last time he left his load on that now crumbling main entrance platform just off to their right, he and Hammer had wished the best for each other knowing full well that the best would be hard to come by, being such a sad time in 1924. His Vanessa had died the year before from a cancer, long before her old age, and her body had been prepared for later entombment at the time. She rested in her coffin in the back shed of his homestead, a decision he'd had to make in haste. His instincts at the time told him not to bury her in God's little acre as he couldn't quit thinking about leaving his homeland and planned to take her with him when he returned some day. He would put her in his boat and they would float away on the Ilava. Unfortunately, he had one last immediate mission for the bishop, and it took his mind off his grief. It had originally been timed to take four years to complete, was now over and had taken four times that long. The strangest of life-altering changes in direction, one after another, and affecting his destiny had brought him back to these church grounds. His life seemed ruled by unseen forces, and even though he tried to have a plan for himself, this mysterious hand of fate always interrupted him, always changed his path, and now headed him to Pfeiffer, and then back home to his hidden ranch. There were many a time in the last so many years that he was positive he'd never see either again.

Back in the early twenties there was absolutely no doubt about terrible trouble boiling all around them, and Van Vedic told Hammer that day the only way out of their predicament at the time was to float in a boat, down into the Don, down through Rostov and out into the Black Sea and beyond. He told the old priest they could simply float down the river, into the world of water, and eventually be a thousand miles away from the Communists. It was his belief that there was no hope in being a Russian Catholic anymore, and worst of all, this was the last Catholic church there was. He told Hammer that the time for escaping may have already passed, just like everything else, but that if there were a viable way out, it was via the river to the sea. Hammer told him he couldn't leave the church behind, that there was a reason for everything, and in due time God would have his way with things. That was 1924, the church burned in '28, and here they were, watching the beginning of sunset on the first of January 1942.

The two new friends talked about everything, even the missions for the bishop. Talked about the past, the hundreds of wagon loads of treasure, and bragged to each other the stories concerning all the notches on their killing tools. Van Vedic talked about Vanessa, how she changed him, took care of their home, and what it was like when she died. He told the priest she couldn't have children because of what her father had done to her when she was a child and believed in her heart and soul some of the strangest ideas about where God existed that had nothing to do with Islam or Catholicism. She believed that she was basically just a tiny living piece of the world and appreciated the idea that it would be best if her piece ended up near where it started, or else in the sea, something she spoke about after a funeral there in God's little acre. She didn't like the place at all. The priest was hearing stories about what it had once been like in the valley from the layman's point of view, from a man who saw it all at its best and at its worst and hadn't forgotten a thing.

"Vincent, you were saying that you would take her body back to her mother in Turkey, that you would take her to Istanbul? Why? Why would you do such a thing?"

"She spoke of it often and talked about a blessing that comes to all people if they are buried near where they were born. It might be just Turkish bullshasheska, but she did seem to believe it, even after she converted our way. Besides, I'm a sailor and a seaman, I truly love the sea, and there's really nothing keeping me down on our farm. Now that she's been gone so long, the revolution and all, everything has changed, and if my home is still there, it's worthless. I honestly don't think I'd stop in Istanbul, to tell you the truth, but keep her with me on my boat and travel all over the world. She was a keeper, as you now know. I've always believed I could get the necessary papers to do that, transport her body back to her childhood home, and even though it sounds crazy, I could easily convince them that I am, too. Besides, you can't be a Catholic in these lands anymore. Maybe you can, but the rest of us can't. So…"

"I now know, like you say, she must have been unique. I'm glad you found her when you did and were together as long as you were, and my next question to you, my gunslinger friend, is why don't you do that?"

"The basic problem is my boat. I've had it for many years, it was old to start with when I bought it, and it needs to stay in safe harbor, assuming my place is still there. She's always been a two-man job, and even though she's only a ten-meter, it always took two. So am I. I'm old and tired, and I think my race is just about over. Those waterways out there are now full of warships and very dangerous people; the war is all around us, Father, everywhere, and we just don't feel it yet. To be honest, I couldn't believe that the river isn't frozen solid when I saw it yesterday. That's amazing! New Year's Eve and it's still flowing? One man in a boat would be difficult to manage. It would take two. You ready to go? All I can add to my reason is that it would be wonderful to end my life boating, fishing, and floating. Just dreaming, Father, just a dream."

Basil stood up from his broken and tilted concrete remnant and went over to the steps that leaned in the direction of where that side entrance had once been. He glanced at the center of the rubble pile and thought of how the bell had ended up buried in a hole dead center of the main walkway. It was still there and really needed to be gone. The only thing keeping it there was the fact that he had never had a way to get it anywhere else, and so he systematically buried it level with all the rest of the debris, and Mother Nature disguised its grave so that no one ever paid any mind to the middle of the rubble. His only option had always been to hide it from the marauders and perhaps, someday, set it on a boat and take it to Kansas like Hammer had talked about, that place where Domme and Desch went.

When Basil had finally started to come up from down below on a daily basis, one of the first things he discovered was that they had sunk the old community boat just out in the Ilava, a hundred feet from the pier. The pier was still a pier, but the old community boat was a sunken wreck. Besides that, he needed a captain who knew what he was doing, and they all seemed to be gone as well. Everyone was gone. Where had they all disappeared to, and were any of them still alive out there? It's a hermit thing.

He knew in his heart and soul that he would never leave the basement as long as there were treasurers in it to guard. Besides, he wouldn't know where to go, and he could never lie about what he was. He was a Catholic priest, and that was that and admitting that usually got you killed.

In one of his stories to Basil, Hammer recalled the neighborhood dogs, and how some of them hung around their old home sites, even though the humans were long gone. The dogs didn't know that and didn't know where else to go, and now Basil didn't know where to go either. Most of all, and probably most importantly, the main reason for his success and survival was his cane and the way it had guided him for the last thirteen years. He wouldn't know how to approach the day without it and wouldn't be able to sleep unless it was propped there by his bedpost, but something told him he was about to learn how. It would be impossible to leave the Grotto, his underground altar, or his piano, impossible to leave those sunrises and sunsets and especially the quiet.

Basil was now forty-two but looked older. Most of the time during that long hermitage in the basement he would lose track of the days and even the months at times; the winters were worst of all, but not just for him, something he deeply appreciated. Hammer had hoped and prayed about it, especially in those last hours, that the man who had put all this treasure in the basement would someday return and help Basil or whoever with all the issues of what to do with it next. Suddenly, he had that man in front of him, and Basil realized that it was all part of some grand plan, preordained to happen and designed to succeed, and he knew that in his soul.

"Captain Van Vedic, you are fully aware of what lies below this old church floor, but did you know that the old church bell is embedded in it, dead center of the main walkway, and has waited all this time to be rescued? Hammer wanted it taken to Kansas and given to those Pfeiffer residents as a memorial to all the people who were left behind. More importantly, he hoped the bell would enable them to honor all of those who came before and built the fertile Volga basin, something from here for there. Armies have ridden by, come and gone, and are being consumed just down the roads and over the hills, and they never saw the bell. They passed by and couldn't see it."

He lifted his glass from the edge of his broken footing table and took a slow full drink of the freezing vodka. It was harsh and absolutely the best quality. The priest stood there staring at the captain.

"Are you as good and solid a man as I pray you are?"

"Yes, Father, I think I am. Therefore, I know I am. Yes, I am."

The priest began to recant a number of the things the captain had said earlier about the dream and asked him if that had been a doable dream or just make-believe.

"Very doable, Father."

He asked the captain if he could really leave like he said he wanted to do or was that just some fantasy, to which the captain said, "Oh no, Father. I could leave and, like I said, I'm literally astounded that the river isn't frozen, because if it were, we wouldn't be having this conversation. As you very well know, when it freezes, that's the start of winter and not until. Truly amazing that the winter is going like this... all the rain, all the time… it's such a mud hole out there, and I must predict that it probably won't last. I remember in the past there were winters that ended up being almost this mild, but never this warm. Maybe it's only in this area. Very strange! I'd need to go home, if it's still there, pack a few things and gather up my Vanessa. I suppose I could do that. You know, I may have distant relatives who live in that Kansas land. I know people in Brazil, and I even read an article that tells how they're planning to build a great dam out in a desert, in a place called New Mexico, where they plan to irrigate a million acres. Those Americans are always doing things like that, and I was intrigued by it all. It's just a little ways west of Kansas. Unfortunately, I doubt I'll ever get out of here; it's so late in life for things like that. It's just the way it is, though, and I'm stuck here with you in this valley. Besides, I'm somewhat fearful of the world out there."

"Me too," said the priest, "me too. Mr. Van Vedic, I would like to make you a proposal and I want you to reserve your answer until I am totally finished with my plan for us. I'll probably need another hour of your time tonight."

Van Vedic sat up and told Basil he could have as much as he needed. He was so curious about this wonderful priest and anything else he had to say, plus he was thrilled with the vodka.

Basil asked him if he thought there was anything unusual about the way faith and fate had brought him back to the village of Pfeiffer, and the widower suddenly fell back into his thoughts of Vanessa and all that had come to pass, where he had been for so long, and how he and Brutus could have gone another way but were pushed this way instead. Sitting there as he was, drinking like he was, and bringing all the pieces of the puzzle into their groves, knowing the past like he did, he had to agree that there was some sort of predestination involved.

"The whole thing seems to be part of a plan, out of my control, almost like a dream for me, Father. Yes, it's all been very unusual!"

"Do you believe in destiny? Make that pre-destiny."

"As a matter of fact, I do. I thought that was not part of our teaching, our beliefs, not that I have much of that, but I've seen it in life, and it has always amazed me how people seem to have it, and they live it and you can only see it in hindsight. You know what I mean?"

The priest began to fumble for his words and said he wanted to modify the question. He asked Van Vedic if he thought, if he believed, that God worked in mysterious ways and was basically always trying to help men make the right decisions.

"Sometimes I believe that, but sometimes I wonder if God is really paying any attention at all. You know, Father, there are terrible things going on out there, and have been for quite some time, we both know they're true, unimaginable horror and we both know we are completely surrounded by crazy, ruthless and barbaric people. I used to ask God to look down and intervene in things, but he never did and so I quit asking. You're a very lucky man to still be alive and so am I. Then I look at myself, where I'm at, how I got here, and the only thing I can conclude is that God has his finger on my nose, pulling on the back of my neck."

"Well, I as a priest believe that God is firmly in charge and us mortal men cannot ever know his mind or his calendar or his watch. I believe he has orchestrated all this, for these exact moments, for you and me." He paused, went away in his thoughts, and returned in a moment.

"Let me ask you some other questions about boating, being a captain, sailing around the world, those sorts of things." There was another long pause. "Could a boat travel the seas from here to Kansas?"

"Well, no. Kansas is in the heart of the United States and the closest I think I could get to it would be down in the Texas coastline country."

"How big of a boat would you need? If the one you have is too small and dilapidated, what could you buy in this region next week that could make the trip to America, wherever, before the river freezes?"

"Next week, you say? In this region, before the river freezes? That's a load, Father! You didn't miss the German invasion idea, did you?"

"Forget the weather for a moment, as my trusty wooden thermometer here tells me not to worry about that. Forget about those blind and ignorant Germans; they're stuck in the mud. How big a boat would suit your fancy, and... oh, by the way, I have an excellent hand in mind to carry half the load. Something tells me he'll be here soon."

Basil had no idea where that thought had come from, but he knew it wasn't a lie or a dream. Someone was coming, and he could feel it. All he had to do was wait; it was almost that hour in their destiny.

"You do? Well, in that case, I'd want something at least 45 feet, and, it just so happens that I know of such a boat in this region."

"You know of such a boat?"

"Yes, there's a rather expensive refurbished fishing boat, not even fifty miles from here on horseback. It belongs to a family over on the next tributary to the Ilava, and rumors suggest they have decided to sell it. There had been a fire on the boat, there was damage, and the engine was destroyed. Everything, they say, has been repaired, but it's very expensive and no one will ever be able to pay the price she wants, even though it's undoubtedly fair. It's unlikely that the Germans didn't hit that area hard. There's probably nothing left. It's hard to say from here, but a few months ago that was the deal."

Basil took another drink and handed the bottle over to Van Vedic, whose glass was always at least half empty.

"I tell you what, my dear friend. I'll buy you that boat, but you have to take our church bell to Kansas. Once you get it there, you can keep the boat. You have to take that hand I was talking about — he will need a ride somewhere — and then live the rest of your life wherever you want. I am not that hand, by the way, and I promise you, you'll like him. I understand he needs a ride out of here. Don't ask me how I know, but I know. I also know the boat will be there, it has to be."

Now he was making promises about the character of someone he had never met, never seen, and as of yet didn't even exist, along with guaranteeing the existence of a floating rumor. It was the cane talking; he knew that. Someone was on the horizon, out of the chaos, and would be the reason for all this. All both of them had to do was believe in some sort of pre-ordained destiny, orchestrated by God himself.

The hulk of a human was quickly devouring this new bit of information; it was so exciting that the vodka wore off, and he needed another drink already. He began to develop a plan in his mind that flowed from his lips as if he was reading it from his journal. Father Basil was suddenly all ears and was feeling some sort of euphoria as the captain began his needs list. He felt as if he had read these plans before in one of the books he had read so fast. Everything was fluid, made perfect sense and was in perfect order.

The plan started with Van Vedic standing up and looking for Brutus; it was that quick. Together, they would race up the Ilava bank road to his house twenty and one-half miles northeast and load up his trusty old boat with his wife's coffined body and some of their possessions, but not many. His main problem was that he would only have a small amount of useable fuel when he was finished filtering what he had. When Basil heard about the problem, he told Van Vedic not to worry. He had stolen eighteen five-gallon containers of diesel from the Red Army not long ago, spent all night doing it, and the fuel dump was hidden alongside the Ilava a few miles upstream, half way between the edge of Pfeiffer and the big bridge. He could pick up a container on his way and load up all the rest on his way back down, completely solving the fuel problem. He could float back down the Ilava River, past Pfeiffer again, in only a day, with Brutus following along as patiently as possible until his upcoming release date, but they would need him up until the very end. The huge animal was like a sixth sense to Van Vedic, and he wasn't sure how it would feel out there in the world without him sitting in that saddle someday soon. He'd been in it all the way to Tunguska and back.

Basil could have him, and could ride around in the region instead of always walking. Brutus had been hand-made by God, and intentionally just for Van Vedic, much the same way that Van Vedic had been made just for this moment in the whole scheme of things. He needed to go back to his home and get Vanessa's body, all of his papers and journals, a few other keepsakes, and say goodbye to his birthplace. He now understood that it had to have survived, it would still be there waiting, remote as it was.

His great-great grandfather had decided to settle there at least a hundred years before, and there were many gravesites that he needed to go stand by, whisper to, and say goodbye to; it was the tradition. He became overwhelmed with the idea that this plan of his had started way back then, and he was now the last of his kind alive. All the rest were gone, and each of them had had a plan, back when it was all once upon a time.

Vanessa wouldn't be buried there, be one of them, and he was glad about that. He would find her a more fitting spot, having learned after her death that he didn't want to be buried in that cemetery, and he didn't want his wife there either. It was a strange, unusual end for her body at the time, but now it, too, fell into the category of being part of some other plan, and she had more life to live and another place to rest. This land was cursed, and the curse of all curses, The Third Reich, was very close, and waging war on Mother Russia. Once upon a time the land had been valuable, worth fighting for, building on and being buried in, but no one could have ever imagined how their fortunes would turn, all because of a language and a belief. Too bad, so sad.

"Father, I hope that the boat is still for sale and still afloat. There's absolutely no way of knowing unless I go up there and ask, and now you say not to worry. I can only assume that it is still there because we need it so badly. I agree, it's all part of the plan. I'll go buy it and bring it back, and we can load the bell. I can meet that new hand you promised me, and we can be out of here before that river freezes over. How's that for a plan?"

"Works for me."

"I'll leave tonight for my home and be back here in Pfeiffer at midday with my boat. I could be in Litzi by sunset tomorrow and be back here the next day with the new boat. I'll leave my old one there. My only concern right now is that the bell is so deep in that hole not even Brutus could pull it out. Let's go study it for a while and see where we're at."

The bell was not near as huge as one might suspect, ten feet down and tilted on its side like it was. One could barely make out the ring if Basil was pointing directly at it from five feet away. Basil was trying to describe how it looked before all the debris and foliage had buried and hid the ancient relic, intentionally, you could be sure. He said he could prepare and clean up the site while Van Vedic was gone, and they would see it better, soon. It was all part of the plan. This was the part he had seen before, in his dreams — clearing out the disguise he had purposefully set in place; it had surely deterred the thieves from looking for a third bell.

He had watched four men come up the road from the south a few years after the fire. They camped hundreds of yards from the church, but early the next morning they hand-carried the two smaller bells to their wagon and went back to where they came from. Even though they saw the signs, it didn't seem to matter and didn't take long. That was more a blessing than anything because they left the big bell down in the hole and took away the only reasons left for someone to bother the site. They never saw the big bell or even suspected it existed.

"Thank you, Colonel Sokolov. Hope you're having a wonderful day."

The priest seemed to be talking to himself, visiting with that colonel he had told Van Vedic about.

"Can you believe they dug the hole right here? The bell should have fallen straight down but ended up here in this hole as if Sokolov had some sort of premonition or a drawing or a plan. Why east and not west? Why here and not over there? And all the while, my friend, I keep hearing Hammer talk about seeing it in a church bell tower in Kansas. If it hadn't landed here, it would have already been melted down and destroyed. I will have it ready and assume the whole time that all we have in the way of muscle at the present time is you, Brutus and I. Don't worry, we can do it."

The men left the church site and walked up the pathway to the Grotto. Brutus was down in a field a half a mile away and therefore only needed a half whistle to bring him back. Seeing him run straight on, no rider on his back, that fast, was a bit intimidating. The priest was hoping he would be able to stop in time, which, of course, he did, right in front of Van Vedic, and they nosed up to each other, and looked each other in the eyes. It lasted a little longer than normal, and the man reached over the neck and pulled the horse's head down till they were ear to ear. While he patted the animal on a big vein there on his neck, Brutus stared at the priest and said hello.

By sunset, Van Vedic was ready to leave and had the mighty Brutus primed for a long, fast, and hard ride. They knew the route from memory, and the giant animal, with the proportionally large human on his back, glided away from the Grotto and down to the road that headed north. The night was cold for most men, but Van Vedic liked the cold and so did Brutus. On this side of the river, he was almost positive he'd be alone, but there were two small bridges on the way that seemed to invite people to stop and camp nearby, at least in the old days. He'd deal with that when he got there, and if unimpeded, Brutus would have him on his doorstep in four hours; it would take him at least that long again to get his old boat ready to float to Pfeiffer, and he would have to do all that in the dark. He had to retrieve Vanessa's coffin from the back shed, all of his journals, extra ammo and pack a long-range duffle bag full of his favorite and necessary clothes, but not too much.

While he rode through the night, he couldn't help but remember the times when he and his father had made this very trip, back up to their home after a delivery to the church in Pfeiffer. Dozens of deliveries, as he recalled, and they were all so similar — same weights, same containers, same reason for the trip, and there was always that ride back home, to his wife and this ranch. If there was one thing he had plenty of, it was the memories, and with the wind in his face, cold and wide awake, he knew it was time for him to start a new life, say goodbye to the past, and start all over somewhere else, because it appeared he was a part of a pre-ordained group-destiny of sorts. He didn't know why, but he felt compelled to follow through with all the fury he could still muster and follow the leads to wherever they led.

A sliver of moon topped the trees at nine that night as he came up on the cemetery where all of the ancients were buried, and he dismounted and allowed the brute to wonder a few paces away and catch his breath. There was some disrepair to a few of the crosses, but most were still erect, and their name stones told who was buried beneath. He sat down between his mother and father and spoke out loud about where he had been lately and what he was planning to do, stood back up and said his goodbyes. A snap of his fingers brought Brutus from thirty yards away, and the animal walked up through the cemetery as if it understood what was under the ground. The man slowly walked ahead of the horse and out to the pathway that led up to the house as his checklist already had a mark by a task.

In no time at all he was done with his packing, poured in a five-gallon container of diesel fuel and started the boat's engine. She purred back to life, waiting to leave.

Vanessa had been a bit awkward, but that was all. When he finally got the casket onto the deck, he was glad he hadn't put her in the ground already, and the fact that she had been prepared for burial in the future made her and her coffin well within his lifting range. He had trouble with the tears a few times, and that also happened when he pulled their bedroom door closed for the last time. He took her favorite picture album, a few little keepsakes, and ended up with a small bag full of those types of things. A thick suitcase held all of his journals and the diary, a fist full of letters and the deed to his land. He left all the rest. There was a time when he thought for sure those journals were history.

Exactly the amount of time he thought it would take, it did. Everything he needed was packed, and he could feel it in the air that this was the start of the change in his life.

He was convinced that God had to be involved, for the weather to be like this. He knew that God was involved with the treasure, with Basil, with the Grotto and the way things had turned out in Pfeiffer. That dream that Hammer had had, the simple plan, might very well be the plan that God had determined, decided, and, in fact, was orchestrating. As this concoction of ideas was unfolding in his mind, he became profoundly humbled, because these weren't his ideas, and these weren't his plans, but they were now his assignments, and the courier this time seemed to be the Holy Ghost. Who was he to question who was responsible for what he could so plainly see?

It had been a long day already, and he could sleep for a while after he prepared the grounds for his final goodbye. He would leave at the crack of dawn. The river was too narrow and had far too many bends to attempt it in the dark. S-bends, one after another, sand bars, dead trees, and quite possibly Germans, Russians, or some other kind of mongrel, only God knew who. Then he thought, 'Oh yes, God is in charge, and that means there probably won't be too much to worry about. I'll leave at dawn and do it right.'

It took an hour for him to arrange the catalysts, old cans of lantern oil, sour diesel and bundles of dried horse hay. Then he stacked the kitchen furniture into a center piece, same with the dining room, and made a trail of cloth covering saturated fuses of straw. He laid out the entire maze of lines from the delayed timers that would lead to the extermination of the entire Van Vedic family home and barns, a place that he and his forefathers had built, and as they did, they had designed it so that it could be destroyed if necessary. And that's exactly what it was, necessary. He had begrudgingly decided that he wouldn't leave the commie bastards, or Nazis if they won, his beautiful little estate. He was sure they wouldn't appreciate it if he did, and he blamed God for having protected the place for all those years.

Vincent was finally able to lay down on the couch, there in their living room, and watch one last fire in the fireplace till he closed his eyes and slept for six hours. When he awoke, it was difficult to rise up off that couch because he knew it was time, and he had to set the timers. While he fiddled with the fluids that would eventually expand to the point of ignition and activate the fire and the fuses, he hoped this would be his last teary moment. Once he screwed the caps on the jars it would take about an hour till the fires started back over his shoulder. There was a very good chance that no one would even notice this far up the river as he was, but he didn't want to watch it and was sure that he had enough igniters to do the job. He sure wasn't saving them for later or as backups. His home was going to burn in a very short while, and there would be nothing left to ever come back to. He had barely found his way back this time.

There were two igniters in the main barn, one in the canopied walkway between the barn and the house and two inside the house itself — and that was the order in which he walked away from his old life. He screwed on the lids and set the fuses, carefully and one at a time, knowing full well that, the way he did things, two would have been plenty. He stepped onto his boat and untied the lines, turned on her engine and puttered out into the river with all of her obstacles, turns, bends and switchbacks. Nothing he hadn't ever seen before, and all he had to do was stay safe, slow and steady.

Brutus meandered along the shoreline, usually ahead, and seemed to understand what S-bends in a river meant. At first it was slow going, still somewhat dark, very quiet and cold except for the putter out the smoke stack. At the thirty-minute mark, he could see the arches of that first old bridge, and even though no one ever used that old road anymore, the bridge was still there. The same held true for the one after that, with a dozen switchbacks between the two and much better lighting.

He was picking up speed and would be near Pfeiffer in six hours or more, depending, when the general silence was broken by a very faint and distant thunder from back where he had just come. He knew if he made the effort to look back he wouldn't be able to see anything for all the trees, and that concussion was all he really needed to verify his work was complete. That proved it was all over back there. He notched the throttle a little faster.

What the horse had managed to do in a little over three hours and not even close to the way a crow flies took six hours for the boat, but the closer he got to Pfeiffer the better the river became. He pulled into Pfeiffer's little boat dock just before noon and tied up to the cleats.

Basil had been digging out all the bushes and debris that protected the bell all that morning and wasn't expecting Van Vedic to be back so fast, but his cane had warned him and he was standing there waiting, with Brutus by his side. The priest had never seen a boat tied up there at that dock in all the years he had looked down on it, but sure enough, that giant of a man was back and probably wanted a glass of vodka.

"Welcome back, my friend. That didn't take long. Could I offer you some lunch and liquid refreshment?"

"That you can, good Father, but I'm only here for an hour. I could be in Litzi by sunset if my calculations are correct, and I could be back here by sunset tomorrow if everything continues to go well. So far everything has. I was able to walk away from the old home and must admit a tall stinger would be right up my stern."

The priest bowed away and headed for the Grotto while Van Vedic walked with Brutus down to a spring by the edge of the river. After a while, Basil came down the hill carrying a beautiful ancient picnic basket. It had everything the sailor would need for his trip, including napkins, utensils, and plenty of nibbles. There was his favorite pipe, favorite tobacco, and a full bottle of that vintage stuff from Poland, plus another bottle of champagne.

The captain opened the basket and examined the contents. He crinkled his bridge when he saw the champagne and asked the priest what it was for.

"Pop the cap and celebrate with the people who sell you the new boat. I saw you in my dreams last night. I saw an old woman and I saw you coming back and I saw someone else on the boat with you — maybe my Jesus watching over you, maybe his mother. I don't know who that was. But most of all I saw the boat. I saw you safe and coming for the bell."

"That's wonderful news, Father, and I'll do just that if it's the right thing to do when the time comes. As far as my passengers are concerned, I'm pretty sure He was with me when I left my house this morning. It was either him or the patron saint of narrow little rivers and almost hopeless causes. Those were some mighty tight and narrow passageways."

Vincent found some jars of sauerkraut and crackers in the basket, and drank a tall glass of the vodka, then looked out down the river towards the Don and where he was headed.

"Time to go. I'll be back tomorrow or the next day. We're out of time, Father. If this river freezes like it already should be, we're not going anywhere. I am so utterly amazed that it's not frozen yet. Unbelievable. That's why I have to go. Every hour counts. Keep an eye on Brutus; we'll need him to get that bell out of that hole. Give me your blessing, and I'm outta here."

After the blessing, he started the engine again and headed down the Ilava towards the Don. He would be there in an hour or so. From there, he would plow up the starboard coastline till he came to the river that flowed past Litzi. Up that river for twenty-six miles — that was where Ms. Sophia would be.

EPILOGUE

Lady Sophia of Litzi

Van Vedic had been invited to tour the boat by the legal liaison of the Lady Sophia of Litzi. The liaison, a lawyer by trade, handed Van Vedic the keys and apologized for not knowing much about the boat or how it worked. Vincent said it was OK because he did.

The liaison stepped onto the boat the way a lawyer would and held out his hand to Van Vedic. He was officially in the way. The seaman waved off the offer and took hold of the rail, which had always sufficed. Handrails are very important in the psyche of seamen. Besides that, he simply had a hard time chumming up to lawyers. He hadn't known many, but there seemed to be a common thread, and he had been privy to seaman logic all his life — and they had a universal opinion of the profession. He judged every man he could, as best he could, fairly, and often times took the man to some distant shore of his own life.

How would this attorney handle himself on some of the backstreets of Istanbul, for example? Probably not too well. It could easily lead to his death.

They stood there in the remodeled cabin.

"The wheelhouse," the lawyer read from his list of amenities, "has a tuck-and-roll leather bench with reinforced storm windows and typhoon shutters."

The words got his attention; he hadn't really thought about those types of things lately. Van Vedic scanned the room for what was there and nodded his approval at everything he saw. It was pleasant, but whoever did it and designed it hadn't been professionally fishing ever in their life. He sat down on the tuck-and-roll bench in front of the wheel and turned the three-foot in diameter disk half a turn to port and then back to center. Over to starboard and then back to center again. The lawyer was observing his wheel movements as if interested when Vincent asked, "Where are the safety belts?"

The lawyer fumbled with the answer by asking the obvious, to which Van Vedic explained how he always wore leg straps and a waist belt harness when he was in waves over ten feet tall. "All sailors have a hard time forgetting the biggest wave they've ever seen off their bow..." he joked.

Nothing. Nothing at all in response from her liaison. He was still trapped in the part about the leg straps and the waist belt.

Both men were done with the cabin inspection; it had passed. Van Vedic motioned with his head and shoulder that he seemed anxious to be down in the engine room.

Just as the lawyer had escorted him onto the boat and into the cabin, he continued that pattern by suggesting they both descend into that place down there where the engine was. At first, he considered the fact that the handrails were filthy, and he apologized for that. He said he'd make a note for the maintenance man, but Van Vedic told him not to worry about such things because that was the way it was supposed to be.

"Get a good grip, hang on tight and always expect it to be greasy."

He smiled, and the man headed down into the one-light abyss. Once the lawyer was out of the way, Van Vedic used only the top step as a guide and landed flat on the floor a few inches from the ladder and only a foot from the lawyer, who hadn't moved far enough. While holding onto the hand rail, he surveyed all the areas behind the steel ladder and slowly turned to his right until he was facing chest to chin with the legal counsel. There is not a lot of room to begin with, and if one doesn't know what one's doing in an engine room, one shouldn't be in an engine room.

The liaison had worn an exceptionally nice suit for the occasion and had never in his wildest imagination anticipated that he would find himself in such close quarters. Much less that it would occur in the engine room of a small fishing boat.

The lawyer blurted out that this was the engine room, and that was a brand new engine. When he was finished with his list, instead of turning around completely and walking up the ladder like normal, he ended up sideways, searching for a handhold on the ceiling until he was finally up and out of the chamber without touching anything. Nothing could have been more awkward, as he was not very good at negotiating that greasy ladder. He eventually stood there looking down the steps into the lightly lit, grease-covered metal place, not knowing that Van Vedic was looking for the on/off switch.

He screamed out a panicked, "Wazzat?" when the engine started instantly from down below. Van Vedic scrambled up the stairs in half the steps and touched a few controls near the wheel there in the cabin, pulled out a throttle, just a little, then fed it back in slowly. The engine began to calm and came to an idle. He politely told the lawyer not to go anywhere.

"I'll be back," he said and jumped back into the dark hole with no intention of needing the staircase.

Vincent gave the engine area a quick inspection while the lawyer leaned over the edge, and then he shouted over the engine that he was coming up. It was a seaman's trick, to be able to grab the handrail of an eight-foot ladder inside the bowels of a big boat and with the muscles of his arms and a high step propel a strong man to a higher deck level in an instant. It was poetry in motion, it was ballet, and it was necessary at times to be, if nothing else, out of the way.

The engine seemed to calm down and began to purr. The lawyer had backed away from the engine compartment door when, almost like something magical, Van Vedic seemed to pull and jump at the same time from down below and was suddenly standing alongside him there in the cabin.

"Used to be a lot faster than that but I'm getting old." The lawyer nodded. "Let's go sell me a boat." The agent nodded again.

He motioned towards the dock and seemed to be confused. He turned around, looking for a way off that was different from the way he got on. There wasn't. There were two handrails involved, and he managed to use them both appropriately and when they were most needed. No big deal, and soon he was back, safe, on the dry earth where he was very good at being a lawyer.

Van Vedic stood there for a while in what he knew was going to be his new wheelhouse for the rest of his life, he hoped. It was a spiritual moment the likes of which he couldn't remember. The boat was the right size, had the right engine, didn't leak, and even had a tuck-and-roll seat that could easily be replaced.

It was incredible that he was actually standing there and feeling this feeling. If Vanessa hadn't died the way she did, when she did, and especially where she did, none of this would have ever happened. To Van Vedic, it seemed to border on the miraculous. Almost unequivocal predestination; words he knew but seldom used.

Why did he already know the way to Kansas in his mind without much hesitation? It was almost as if those earlier fishing times had been preliminary runs for the beginning of this journey. For just an instant, he thought he saw the clouds out over the Mediterranean in his daydream. He knew how to get there, and he'd been about that far before. Now, all of sudden, he very well might do it again. Only this time in his own boat, in real life, real time, and hopefully have this 'special hand' that Basil had promised, as his new boat would take two men at least.

In his journal, which was now a rather cumbersome piece of his luggage, there were many stories of other men and women who had acquired his attention, and he wrote about them all. He had a tiny penmanship for such huge hands, but it was very legible and neat, for the most part. He seemed to write on and on and favored many of the exotic tobaccos and especially the vodka while he composed. His penmanship failed and the vulgarities came out proportionally to the vodka. It would be obvious to the reader that something was affecting his attitude during that particular entry. He could defend the faith with his pen, and often found himself rereading one of those entries and wondering if he really believed it all. Unfortunately, not a single person besides Vanessa had read any of it to any degree.

It was a very guarded stack of binders and tablets that had rested quietly in his bedroom there with Vanessa for all those years. He told her they were open for her to read if she wanted to, but she told him to read it to her if he thought she would be interested. He would sit by the fireplace and read the stories to her, and she listened to each and every one as if she had nothing better to do. Sometimes he would finish an entry of a few thousand words and turn to see what she thought. After an uncomfortable moment, she looked at him and said, "Okay, go on!" but there wasn't anymore, and he had to tell her that instead.

She was his biggest and only fan there at the end. She told him she loved the way he wrote and still had all of the love letters he had written her. She told him not to let anyone ever throw them away, and she was pointing straight across the room at the vanity closet he had made just for her so many years before. All those letters were in there somewhere, and he knew that she had kept them all. He had been sitting on the side of her bed for what must have been hours, waiting for her to fall asleep and maybe, just maybe, have a good night's rest. He turned from her face and stared for a brief time at the closet she was pointing at, and he heard her take a deep breath. Before he could turn back, she was gone, and she had tricked him into looking away at that last moment.

He'd spent hours saying goodbye and marveled at how peaceful she looked as she turned into a white angel.

The old woman, Sophia, was a widowed matriarch, and she had a large family that doted over her and her every whim. For the most part, they were all quietly terrified of the future, and horrified by the last six months. Three members of the family were too sick to move, two were virtually invalids, and they were tied to their nest. Two entire armies had barely missed their valley homes, a large family of people who appeared wealthy by poor standards, inhabited the main house and had quarters behind for the help and her own grown children who hadn't gotten too far from her front door; five houses in all.

They were wonderful people with the most excellent manners and had invited Van Vedic to dinner when they realized he was serious and able to buy their family boat. He brought his best manners to the table that night and they were duly impressed and put at ease by his demeanor, including the fact that he needed the piano bench to sit on. He was Catholic by admission, and so were they; they said the same prayers. They all spoke German and Russian, but the German was a watered-down version, different in almost every way from the homeland version. Not near as much shouting and none of the white eyeball part.

He had puttered up their river late in the afternoon in that old boat of his, from down where all the chaos was, unharmed, unafraid, and wanting to buy their boat. Even though they'd had a premonition that such a man was coming, or at least one of them did, when Van Vedic showed up, they were jaw-dropped from one end of the homestead to the other. Everyone except for Ms. Sophia, that was, who now occupied a completely different level from the rest of them when it came to premonitions and predictions regarding the future.

Following a long-standing tradition people in that area had, and all over the world for that matter, there would be a toast and prayers after dinner, after the business transaction had taken place, and, in this case, there was a bottle of champagne.

They finished the dinner and the children and their mothers all left, leaving Van Vedic, Ms. Sophia, two of her sons and the lawyer sitting around the table, consumed for an hour with the business of the boat sale, which was anything but a slight formality. Each party had a dozen papers to sign, forms to read and sign that made it all legal. The lawyer for Ms. Sophia was this very tightly wound little bureaucratic sort of fellow named Detwiller, and he seemed to have absolutely every single document that any government could have possibly insisted on as part of the transaction. It was all there, prepared in advance, sitting on a counter top and just waiting. It was as if they'd known he was coming and had been waiting all along.

Everything Van Vedic had debated in his captain-of-a-boat mind — the documentation, the permits, the bill of sale, all the things he might worry about, were he ever to be confronted by the police or a toll gate attendant or anyone for that matter — all of that documentation sat there on the table and confronted him back. The only thing that was lacking was his signature and theirs and a few exaggerated official stamps, including puddles of wax and plywood holding tubes for the whole mess. Not too long ago, twenty-five years or so, and at least a number of years before the

Communists took over, it could have been done with a handshake and small pile of the current money.

Detwiller explained that these documents secured everyone's safety and used the words, 'legitimized this transaction anywhere in the world.'

Now that the Germans seemed to control the land and the Russians were gone, the only thing that had saved them so far was their last name and the argument Mr. Detwiller had made to the Gestapo. In a dramatic do or die defense of Ms. Sophia's family, he provided the logic and the reason for them staying alive only a month before. They were all on the verge of being escorted outside and shot when Detwiller yelled out at the German gunners, "WE ARE ROMULANS!" To which one SS Captain looked at the other and sarcastically asked, "What the fuck is a Romulan?"

Detwiller claimed in a loud and proud voice at the time that these people were descendants of some of the most renowned current members of the Third Reich in Berlin, and he showed the vultures a letter from Ms. Sophia's cousin who was the current field marshal of the German campaign in North Africa. When the two Gestapo agents read the letter and saw the signature, they both arrived at the same conclusion almost simultaneously. They snapped to attention while slinging their right arms up into the corner of the room and shouting "Heil Hitler" in perfect tandem, including two heal clicks, and holding the pose long enough for a picture even though there was no camera.

Detwiller went on to explain how her family was proud of their ancestry, proud of their tree, and proud of their efforts to colonize the German blood into the heartland of Russia — heroically, he would add. They were in fact only a small humble family, an example of some of the ethnic Germans that Hitler had planned and vowed to save; much more distant than the ones in Czechoslovakia, but well worth saving just the same. Just after they fully comprehended what a 'Romulan' was, and before the two SS robots found the front door, Detwiller interrupted their retreat and asked for a favor.

"Gentlemen, Ms. Sophia asked me to beseech you if there was the slightest chance that you gentlemen could assist her with getting a letter to her cousin. One of their dearest mutual cousins, someone who had been an inspiration to them both, has recently passed away at the hands of the miserable and bloody Russian Red Army, and she didn't know where Erwin was or how to get him a message. She knows he would want to know."

Neither man knew quite what to say, as both recalled how, in the last ten minutes, neither had turned into the complete blithering horses' asses that they were quite capable of turning into, before they'd discovered this family tree growing down on the edge of the Don, here in the Volga Basin. They'd both also experienced what was sometimes referred to as a self-awarded battlefield promotion on the spot, plus back pay for two years and each one stuck out that 'heil hand' which had only moments before been converted into mail clerks' hands.

Detwiller hurried back over to the desk and found what appeared to be an already written letter, an envelope, and brought a fountain pen for Ms. Sophia to personally write the address in her own pen to her cousin. She politely read the letter in private and wiped away some tears, wrote a brief note at the bottom, dated it and signed her name. It happened to be a letter she had written to her newborn grandson and was destined to be read in twenty years by the young baby, something she would be able to easily duplicate since she had already done it seven times. She folded the papers into thirds and tucked the letter into the envelope, ran the glue bottle over the flap and sealed it tight. She dropped the wax drops on the seam line and gently put her initial stamp in the puddles. On the back side, she wrote, "Dear Erwin, hope you are well. Come and see us again someday; it's been so long. Love, Sophia." She turned it over and wrote his name, 'To My Dear Cousin, Erwin Rommel.'

The vultures flew away and left the Rommel family alone with a written guarantee, and went on down the road looking for someone else to kill. They took the letter, read the writing on the front and back and looked at each other understanding in a crystal clear vision what, "come and see us again someday," actually meant to a German soldier, field marshal or not. It meant the Eastern Front, and so far that had not been a welcome assignment.

The Germans had discovered that the Russians fought hard, died hard, tried not to give an inch, and there didn't seem to be any end to them. These two soldiers knew what lay behind them just getting this close to the Volga, they knew there were millions and millions of Russian corpses, left to rot where they had fallen, slaughtered in a carnage of unimaginable horror which absolutely had to be erased; they knew what they had done. If these Russians ever had the chance to retaliate for what had happened back there, the Third Reich would be in for a truly tragic payback.

The Rommels knew they had been extremely lucky to have been spared, and it was their ability to speak German, show historical family crests, say just the right thing, not too much and not too little, at just the right time that had saved them. Detwiller had performed his argument with such bravado and cunning that he managed to save nineteen lives along with his own, and that in turn saved their fishing boat newly named The Vanessa. All in all, the entire clan knelt around one night and prayed an hour-long 'thank you rosary' to the Mother Mary, and one of them interjected that the entire sequence of events had to have been planned by God himself.

That was the kind of lawyer that Detwiller was, and he had a similar story for the Russian vultures, which rallied around the idea that the family also had ties to Nikita Khrushchev. He had a gut instinct that only lawyers can digest that suggested the Russians would surely be back and would want to discuss how the locals had behaved when the Germans manned the fort. It might not be so easy the next time, and from different vantage points along the banks of the mighty Don River everything seemed to indicate that the Germans were already in some sort of a defensive mode, stepping back at least for the winter.

The civilians could only assume that the monster machine the Germans called the Sixth Army had accomplished their task and might be going home. It was wishful thinking. The first month of nineteen forty-two in the land they called the Fertile Volga Basin suggested that the world was totally insane and anyone who was somehow or another still alive in all this was in fact very close to being dead. The German Army had destroyed virtually everyone and everything in its path so far, save for a family named Rommel, and there was no way in the world to stop them. It appeared that the Germans were controlling the weather, the air, the water, and if it drank, breathed or grew, they killed it. When this winter ended, the Germans would only have a few hundred miles left to go and Stalingrad would be theirs.

Ms. Sophia was quietly sitting there, endorsing different pages of the closing documents and watching as Mr. Detwiller shuffled the piles of papers back and forth to her and her sons and Van Vedic. She excused herself and started to speak directly to Van Vedic as she laid out her thoughts on the whole matter. She was intrigued by the fact that he had never once quibbled over the price and was stunned when he had handed his bag of gold coins and a small jar of diamonds to Detwiller one minute after they told him the price. He had never been anything short of serious about his quest and had not complained about anything, and that included the greasy handrails into the engine room during his inspection. He had noted that he needed as much fuel as they could spare and all of the spare parts they had.

Once again, Ms. Sophia began to talk, and she asked Van Vedic if he planned to fish the local waters and what some of his plans might be if they were not too personal. She reminded him that there seemed to be a war going on everywhere, and he thought to himself how he had reminded Basil of that very fact the night before.

He started by saying that he only fished enough these days to feed himself and anyone close by, and their price of 34,600 rubles was almost exactly what a boat like that was worth in other ports down the river and out into the seas. He said he knew that from all of his travels throughout his life, and he was fairly certain she had done an investigation herself and set her price accordingly, with the council of the other three gentlemen there. She was flattered by his compliment. He said it was as if she had secretly been reading his mind, and once again she smiled. She had rebuilt the boat just for him and she knew it, he knew it, and now so did all the others.

He told her how he had lost Vanessa and that he was going to change the name on the boat as soon as he could find a can of emerald green paint. When he'd lost her, he'd lost every reason he might have had to stay in the area, and planned to sail around the world. He told them about the bell back in Pfeiffer and how he would attempt to load it on the boat and then take it to America. He explained that he had rid himself of everything he owned, his land and his business, and would have enough money left after the sale to stock his boat and sail away. That was enough of a story for now, and perhaps their curiosity had been satisfied.

Finally, Van Vedic told them how he and Vanessa had ended up together, and she had wanted him to take her body back to Istanbul. He could do that now with this new boat and could continue to grieve at sea because her death had been a very sad and solemn time, and he knew he wasn't through.

On one of those long nights out under the moon, the two had sat together and gazed up at the heavens and discussed the conditions of life and death. It was during one of those talks that she confessed to the seaman that she simply wanted to go back where she had come from, where her mother was, back near her birthplace, and she wanted to reenter the system naturally. This land she was dying in was not worth being buried in for all time. She said she could feel the earth already, and believed no one could be buried deep enough to not be violated by what was coming for the region. At the time she was just wishing in her anguish, she knew it would never happen that way, hoped and prayed that it might... and then just went ahead and died.

Van Vedic told the old lady how so many of the people from his region had frantically left long ago, one way or another, from over in the Pfeiffer area and north of that. Those early explorers traveled half-way around the world and built a little community out on the plains of Kansas, in the heartland of America. Letters seemed to indicate that, for the most part, the settlers were making the best of it, and there was all kinds of promise.

None of that was news to her, as the same story could be told about almost everywhere, including the villages near Litzi, and all of those people were gone as well. She told him that she and her family had decided to stay and live their lives as best they could exactly where they were because their spirits told them to do that; they couldn't leave. Van Vedic looked at the people around the room, leaned forward in his chair and said that he too was governed by the Holy Spirit, had somehow or another been groomed his entire life for that exact moment in time, the voyage was his destiny, and he knew the way. The way he said it convinced them all.

He had decided to purchase the lady's boat a moment or two after he pegged the throttle the first time on that first test run, not that he actually had a choice in the matter. A brand spanking new Benz diesel motor nestled in her belly, far more than necessary to lift her up in the water, and she could do twenty-five knots on a silk river. Very few subject areas top the engine on a boat when it comes to the purchase, and little else mattered except for the issue of whether or not it leaked.

Ms. Sophia was one of the sweetest old ladies left alive, and he knew it wouldn't leak; there was no way her boat could leak. Her price was regionally correct, and there were not a lot of fisherman at the time that could afford or even want the beautiful craft. It was not a cheap fishing boat, and the work on the cabin and engine room had been of the finest quality available after the fire. She had mentioned to her son that she didn't want a prospective buyer walking away because the work seemed shoddy or expedient. The boat was better than before, for sure, and it had been built by artisans in the first place, atop an ancient keel they had come across with the word 'Gildas,' carved into its side. It was unlike any keel they had ever touched before, had predetermined holes and the craftsmen spent six years building it into the Vanessa.

Van Vedic was somewhat interested in the story about the previous owner, his disappearance and untimely demise, but most of all everything they knew about the construction. The man in question had bought the boat with Ms. Sophia financing the whole arrangement and then had not been heard from for the longest time. The boat was found bobbing in a washed-out cove down where the Ilava merged with the Don. The old engine had caught fire and was destroyed, while most of the damage was confined to the engine room and that spot in the cabin where the staircase came up. Someone had left a lot of blood on the bow, and the river police had towed the smoldering wreck back to the tiny port of Litzi, where they knew the original owner lived and was about to become the new owner again.

When Sophia was reunited with her boat and confronted with the task of fixing the vessel or having the State claim it as unsalvageable, she reluctantly allowed her son to assign all the works and to buy two new diesel engines, one for the big schooner they owned, and one for the fishing boat. There was no point in owning either if neither motor worked — and neither motor did. Besides, the money they used to pay for the motors was almost worthless by then, according to Detwiller, and they would be better off with motors than worthless paper. Diesel motors are hard to declare worthless by any government. The motor on the Vanessa was designed and built for long-term use, state of the art at the time, but Van Vedic succumbed to an old sailor's belief that it was always better to have two of those things that matter most, especially motors.

The next morning, at just past dawn, Van Vedic had already motorized his new craft up and down the narrow river for an hour and even out-rigged the small sail just to get a feel for what it could do, which was basically nothing. He found her to be steady, incredibly powerful, and highly maneuverable for her size. He had consulted with her banker, lawyer and previous owner the night before — her being the boat. He had slept with her for the first time last night and had discovered that he already loved her very much. He had renamed her Vanessa, and in the break of dawn he found a large can of emerald green paint sitting on the side rail, a new paint brush and a tall glass full of grape juice; everything was done except for goodbye.

Basil had suggested in the most general of terms that the success of the mission was all that mattered, and the cost was of absolutely no concern. Van Vedic found that hard to accept, as he had never thought that way before in his life, but knew it was entirely correct. He could buy anything he wanted, and so when he discovered the spare engine, he bought it just because it was brand new, still on the crate, and surely didn't belong in the boat shed.

Ms. Sophia and her family made it perfectly clear that they would never need it now that the other boat had been sunk and, unfortunately, that mess in the water down by the bend was their schooner. There was very little debate in his mind at the time, and he told them he'd take it, too.

Why would he not buy it? He could always sell it in any harbor anywhere for at least what he paid Lady Sophia. He could trade it, barter with it, and it belonged on his deck. Even though he didn't know why, he just knew that it did. He paid for the boat that night, bought the extra motor and filled all his fuel tanks paying three times the normal amount. They took his gold pieces and gems and gladly loaded the motor for him and helped him transfer Vanessa's coffin from the bow of his old boat to the bow of the new boat.

Right before he was ready to leave, he allowed two of her sons to tie up the craft, and while they did Van Vedic threw a set of saddlebags over his shoulder, picked up the glass and headed up the walkway to Ms. Sophia's back porch, where she had been watching and enjoying her morning coffee. He sat down on a two-person swing, leaving little room for anyone else and turning it into a one-person swing, with the saddlebag taking up that extra space.

"I'm sorry for the way things are all around us, Ms. Sophia. It's just terrible what they've done to us. But I'm pleased that we could make our deal, and I'm thrilled and thank God that you and your family are still alive. I know you know how difficult things might become, and I'm also glad that you have Detwiller, but that's only going to get you so far. You need to survive, and I've brought you these two bags to help in that cause. It's mine to give away, and I give it to you, and I thank you for being such a beautiful part of all this, for repairing my Vanessa the way you did, and I thank you for the green paint. A few nights ago, Father Basil and I were discussing the bell on the bow of a boat, and I remembered hearing about your boat. Now she's my boat, and I must leave. Tell them all goodbye for me, and I hope you can use my gift without getting yourselves killed because of it. No one saw me bring it here. Please, be careful. Goodbye, dear lady."

He stood up, shook her dainty hand with two of his fingers and realized she might not be able to move the bags if he left. She instantly knew what he was thinking and stood up out of her chair. She walked up to the giant man and pulled on his vest till his cheek came down to her level. She pressed her tiny lips against his beard line, kissed his face and then whispered into his ear, "Goodbye. God bless."

There by her coffee table was a brand new coffee table cover that she was planning to use later after everyone was finished spilling his or her coffee on the current one. By the time the captain was at the bottom step, she had covered the saddlebags with it and was standing there, watching him leave.

He walked down to the little pier and climbed onto his old boat and gave it a one last fingertip touch. She had served him well, and she had many years left if one were gentle. Sophia's grandsons were back to their early morning fishing and could

319

hardly take their eyes off the giant captain; he was the biggest friendly man that they had ever seen.

Vincent dug down in his coat pocket and pulled out the key that hung from a long leather strap. "She's old and worn, boys, but she's yours if you want her." They were ecstatic and definitely did. He stood there and invited them on board and handed the oldest one the key.

He hop-stepped up onto his Vanessa, and without a great deal of fanfare, he glided out of Ms. Sophia's personal corner of paradise, just alongside and past her sunken schooner, and never turned to wave a final farewell. One goodbye was his rule, and he never looked back, whether he was in a boat or guiding a team of horses pulling a wagon. He and his father had never looked back; it was always too painful.

Vanessa hugged the shoreline until the river widened. After only an hour or so downriver from Ms. Sophia, he came to a bend in the river and an aggressive current forced him to change banks and then change back still a few miles out from the Don. It was a never-ending maneuver on these switchback rivers, following the current until it carried him out into the big river.

Standing there on the west shoreline, way far up ahead, a lone figure was balanced on a rock point, so far down river that he couldn't decide much as to who it might be, but he knew the person was staring straight at him as he came around the bend and into view. When the man on the rock point was still a few hundred yards out, Van Vedic heard the man whisper into his ear that he 'needed a ride to Pfeiffer.' What else could he do but pull over and let the man on board?

As the huge fishing boat graced the edge of the rock, the hitchhiker tossed his backpack and suitcase onto the deck, floated through the air and landed on the bow like a seasoned deckhand, took to a knee and blessed himself, bowed his head and touched his hands flat out onto the deck. Van Vedic watched him from the pilothouse as he blessed the coffin there on the bow and then turned and gave the captain a blessing.

In another ten miles or so the Vanessa would come up on the point where the Ilava merged into the mighty Don, green water to brown, very cold and almost frozen. He would turn to his port at that point and start the long trip up her never-ending bends and reversals. Ten more miles of hairpins and river crossings before he would see the Grotto off on a distant hilltop, and then another mile to the secret cove that was waiting and ready. In those next twenty miles, he would meet Father Jude, and the captain's life would never be the same again. Jude would tell him the story of Theresienstadt, about where he had come from and where he was going, and everything fell into place, everything was now clear. He was introduced to the idea that doomsday was four years away. Van Vedic in turn told his story, and they both would know each other fairly well by the time that day ended.

Basil was waiting on the dock, cane in hand as the Vanessa came into view, the sunset as her backdrop. He knew this man Jude from a previous life; they had known each other at St. Michael's. It was a miracle. His cane instantly and gently allowed him to understand who the pilgrim was and that it was time. He'd be able to let go, but not just now. Tomorrow or the next day, but not now. Now, knowing what he knew, the story Jude told, the gift, and the journeys of everyone combined, he knew this was the man; this was the man who the Saint had carved the cane for. He would be able to live without it, and Jude would surely need it. The pilgrim would be able to find those ears now, find that face, and tell the story of Theresienstadt to the man out there who would make a difference and save the world.

The End.

Please support the author by leaving a review from your favorite online store.

ABOUT THE AUTHOR

Craig Domme: Worked at 1st Special Forces Group. Studied at Pineland University. Lives in Farmington, New Mexico.

CONTACT

Facebook: https://www.facebook.com/craig.domme
Email: craigdomme@gmail.com

Your online review would be great appreciated. Craig.

Book 2 coming soon.

Made in the USA
San Bernardino, CA
20 November 2016